DRAGON'S CHOICE

It was said it took a lot of physical and mental toughness to bargain with the energy dragons and manipulate the earth forces. It was even whispered among the candidates that a Dragoneye slowly gave up his own life force to a dragon in return for the ability to work the energies, and that the pact aged him beyond his years. My master had been the Tiger Dragoneye during the last cycle and, by my reckoning, would only be a few years over forty. Yet he had the looks and bearing of an old man. Perhaps it was true—a Dragoneye did give up his own life force—or perhaps my master had aged under the strain of poverty and ill luck. He was risking everything for the chance of my success.

I stopped walking and reached out further with my mind toward the Rat Dragon, trying to touch the energy of the great beast. I felt his power spark through my body. *Talk to me*, I begged. *Talk to me. Choose me tomorrow. Please, choose me tomorrow.*

There was no response.

FIREBIRD
WHERE FANTASY TAKES FLIGHT™

The Blue Sword	Robin McKinley
The Coyote Road: Trickster Tales	Ellen Datlow and Terri Windling, eds.
Dragonhaven	Robin McKinley
Eona	Alison Goodman
Firebirds Soaring: An Anthology of Original Speculative Fiction	Sharyn November, ed.
The Hero and the Crown	Robin McKinley
The Magic and the Healing	Nick O'Donohoe
The Neverending Story	Michael Ende
The Seven Towers	Patricia C. Wrede
Singing the Dogstar Blues	Alison Goodman
The Tough Guide to Fantasyland	Diana Wynne Jones
Water: Tales of Elemental Spirits	Robin McKinley and Peter Dickinson

EON

DRAGONEYE
REBORN

ALISON
GOODMAN

FIREBIRD

AN IMPRINT OF PENGUIN GROUP (USA) INC.

FIREBIRD
Published by the Penguin Group
Penguin Group (USA) Inc., 345 Hudson Street, New York, New York 10014, U.S.A.
Penguin Group (Canada), 90 Eglinton Avenue East, Suite 700, Toronto, Ontario, Canada M4P 2Y3
(a division of Pearson Penguin Canada Inc.)
Penguin Books Ltd, 80 Strand, London WC2R 0RL, England
Penguin Ireland, 25 St Stephen's Green, Dublin 2, Ireland (a division of Penguin Books Ltd)
Penguin Group (Australia), 250 Camberwell Road, Camberwell, Victoria 3124, Australia
(a division of Pearson Australia Group Pty Ltd)
Penguin Books India Pvt Ltd, 11 Community Centre, Panchsheel Park, New Delhi - 110 017, India
Penguin Group (NZ), 67 Apollo Drive, Rosedale, Auckland 0632, New Zealand
(a division of Pearson New Zealand Ltd)
Penguin Books (South Africa) (Pty) Ltd, 24 Sturdee Avenue,
Rosebank, Johannesburg 2196, South Africa

Penguin Books Ltd, Registered Offices: 80 Strand, London WC2R 0RL, England

Australian Government

Australia | Council for the Arts

ARTS VICTORIA

The Place To Be

This project has been assisted by the Australian Government through the Australia Council,
its arts funding and advisory body.

First published in the United States of America by Viking,
a member of Penguin Group (USA) Inc., 2008
Published by Firebird, an imprint of Penguin Group (USA) Inc., 2010

9 10

Copyright © Alison Goodman, 2008
All rights reserved

LIBRARY OF CONGRESS CATALOGING-IN-PUBLICATION DATA IS AVAILABLE

ISBN 978-0-14-241711-9

Printed in the United States of America

Set in Goudy Oldstyle
Book design by Jim Hoover

For my dear friend Karen McKenzie

EON
DRAGONEYE
REBORN

Ox Dragon
N

Tiger Dragon
NNE

Rat Dragon
NNW

Rabbit Dragon
ENE

Pig Dragon
WNW

Dragon Dragon
(Mirror Dragon)
E

Dog Dragon
W

Snake Dragon
ESE

Rooster Dragon
WSW

Horse Dragon
SSE

Monkey Dragon
SSW

Goat Dragon
S

Ox Dragon
Compass: NORTH
Color: Purple
Dragoneye: Lord Tyron
Keeper of Determination

Tiger Dragon
Compass: NORTH-NORTHEAST
Color: Green
Dragoneye: Lord Elgon
Keeper of Courage

Rabbit Dragon
Compass: EAST-NORTHEAST
Color: Pink
Dragoneye: Lord Silvo
Keeper of Peace

Dragon Dragon
(Mirror Dragon)
Compass: EAST
Color: Red
Dragoneye: None—the mirror
Dragon has been missing for over
500 years.
Keeper of Truth

Snake Dragon
Compass: EAST-SOUTHEAST
Color: Copper
Dragoneye: Lord Chion
Keeper of Insight

Horse Dragon
Compass: SOUTH-SOUTHEAST
Color: Orange
Dragoneye: Lord Dram
Keeper of Passion

Goat Dragon
Compass: SOUTH
Color: Silver
Dragoneye: Lord Tiro
Keeper of Kindness

Monkey Dragon
Compass: SOUTH-SOUTHWEST
Color: Ebony
Dragoneye: Lord Jessam
Keeper of Resourcefulness

Rooster Dragon
Compass: WEST-SOUTHWEST
Color: Brown
Dragoneye: Lord Bano
Keeper of Confidence

Dog Dragon
Compass: WEST
Color: Ivory
Dragoneye: Lord Garon
Keeper of Honesty

Pig Dragon
Compass: WEST-NORTHWEST
Color: Dove Gray
Dragoneye: Lord Meram
Keeper of Generosity

Rat Dragon
Compass: NORTH-NORTHWEST
Color: Blue
Dragoneye: Lord Ido
Keeper of Ambition

MAP OF THE IMPERIAL PALACE

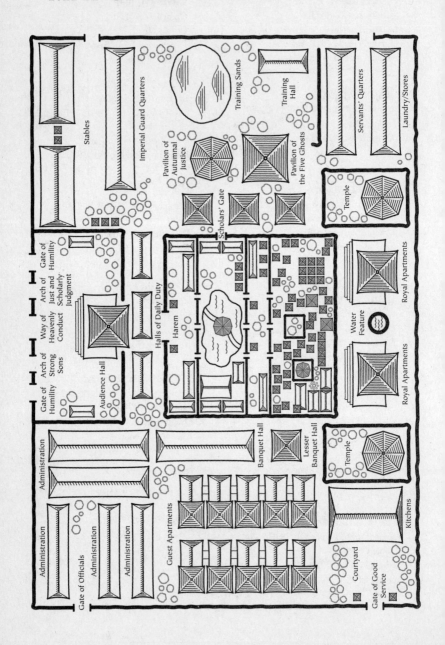

From the Primer Scrolls of Jion Tzu

NO ONE KNOWS how the first Dragoneyes made their dangerous bargain with the twelve energy dragons of good fortune. The few scrolls and poems that have survived the centuries start the story well after the deal was struck between man and spirit-beast to protect our land. It is rumored, however, that a black folio still exists that tells of the violent beginning and predicts a catastrophic end to the ancient alliance.

The dragons are elemental beings, able to manipulate *Hua*—the natural energy that exists in all things. Each dragon is aligned with one of the heavenly animals in the twelve-year cycle of power that has run in the same sequence since the beginning of time: Rat, Ox, Tiger, Rabbit, Dragon, Snake, Horse, Goat, Monkey, Rooster, Dog, and Pig. Each dragon is also the guardian of one of the twelve celestial directions, and a keeper of one of the Greater Virtues.

Every New Year's Day the cycle turns, the next animal year begins, and its dragon becomes ascendant, his power doubling for that twelve months. The ascending dragon also unites with a new apprentice to be trained in the dragon magic, and as this boy steps up to his new life, the prior apprentice is promoted to Dragoneye and into his full power. He replaces his master, the old Dragoneye, who retires exhausted and fatally debilitated by his twenty-four-year union with the dragon. It is a brutal bargain that gives a Dragoneye enormous power—enough to move monsoons, redirect rivers, and stop earthshakes. In return for such control over nature, the Dragoneye slowly gives up his *Hua* to his dragon.

Only those boys who can see an energy dragon can hope to be a Dragoneye candidate. It is a rare gift to be able to see the dragon of your birth year, and even rarer to be able to see any of the other energy dragons. Every New Year, twelve boys, born twelve years before, face the ascending dragon and pray that their gift is enough for the beast. One of them is chosen and in that moment of union—and only for that moment—all men can see the dragon in all his glory.

Women have no place in the world of the dragon magic. It is said they bring corruption to the art and do not have the physical strength or depth of character needed to commune with an energy dragon. It is also thought that the female eye, too practiced in gazing at itself, cannot see the truth of the energy world.

CHAPTER ONE

I LET THE TIPS of both my swords dig into the sandy arena floor. It was the wrong move, but the dragging pain in my gut was pulling me into a crouch. I watched Swordmaster Ranne's bare feet shuffle forward, rebalancing his weight for a sweep cut. Training with him always made my innards cramp with fear, but this was different. This was the bleeding pain. Had I miscounted the moon days?

"What are you doing, boy?" he said.

I looked up. Ranne was standing poised, both of his swords ready for the elegant cross cut that could have taken my head. His hands tightened around the hilts. I knew he wanted to follow through and rid the school of the cripple. But he didn't dare.

"Are you spent already?" he demanded. "That third form was even worse than usual."

I shook my head, gritting my teeth against another clamping pain.

"It is nothing, Swordmaster." I carefully straightened, keeping my swords down.

Ranne relaxed his stance and stepped back. "You're not ready for the ceremony tomorrow," he said. "You'll never be ready. You can't even finish the approach sequence."

He turned in a circle, glaring at the other candidates kneeling around the edge of the practice sand. "This sequence must be flawless if you are to approach the mirrors. Do you understand?"

"Yes, Swordmaster," eleven voices yelled.

"Please, if you allow, I'll try again," I said. Another cramp twisted through my body but I didn't move.

"No, Eon-*jah*. Get back in the circle."

I saw a riffle of unease run through the other eleven candidates. Ranne had added *jah*, the old ward against evil, to my name. I bowed and crossed my swords in salute, imagining the feel of driving both blades through his chest. Behind Ranne, the huge opaque form of the Tiger Dragon uncoiled and stared at me. He always seemed to rouse with my anger. I concentrated on the Rabbit Dragon, bringing him into shimmering outline, hoping the Keeper of Peace would help calm my rage.

In the candidate circle, Dillon shifted and looked around the arena. Had he sensed the dragons? He was more aware than the others, but even he couldn't see an energy dragon without meditating for hours. I was the only candidate who could see all of the dragons at will, not counting the Mirror Dragon, of course, who had been lost long ago. It took all my focus to see the spirit beasts and left me weary, but it was the only thing that had made the last two years of hard training bearable. It was also the only reason why a cripple like me was allowed to stand as a candidate—full dragon sight was rare, although, as Swordmaster Ranne liked to remind me, no guarantee of success.

"Get back in the circle. Now!" Ranne yelled.

I tensed and stepped back. Too fast. The sand shifted under my bad leg, wrenching it to the right. I hit the ground, hard. One heartbeat of numbed shock, then the pain came. Shoulder, hip, knee. My hip! Had I done more harm to my hip? I reached across my body, digging my fingers through skin and muscle to feel the malformed hip bone. No, there was no pain. It was whole. And the other aches were already fading.

Dillon shuffled forward on his knees, spraying sand into the air, his eyes wide with concern. Little fool—he would only make things worse.

"Eon, are you . . . ?"

"Don't break formation," Ranne snapped. He kicked at me. "Get up, Eon-*jah*. You're an insult to the Dragoneye profession. Get up."

I struggled to my hands and knees, ready to roll if he kicked again. There was no blow. I grabbed my swords and pushed myself upright, another cramp catching me as I straightened. It wouldn't be long now; I had to get back to my master, before the blood showed. Ever since my body had first betrayed us six months ago, my master had kept a supply of soft cloths and sea sponges locked away in his library, away from prying eyes.

The half-hour bell had just rung—if Ranne gave me leave, I could get to the house and back again by the full hour.

"Swordmaster, may I withdraw from practice until the next bell?" I asked. My head was respectfully bowed, but I kept my eyes on Ranne's blunt, stubborn features. He was probably born in an Ox year. Or maybe he was a Goat.

Ranne shrugged. "Return your swords to armory, Eon-*jah*, and don't bother coming back. Another few hours of practice won't improve your chances tomorrow." He turned his back, calling his favorite, Baret, to take my place on the sand. I was dismissed.

Dillon looked over at me, his face worried. We were the weakest candidates. He was of age—twelve, like all the boys in the circle—but as small as an eight-year-old, and I was lame. In the past, we wouldn't even have been considered as Dragoneye candidates. Neither of us was expected to be chosen by the Rat Dragon in the ceremony tomorrow. All the gambling rings had Dillon at a 30:1 chance. I was at 1000:1. The odds might be against us, but even the council did not know how a dragon made its choice. I pretended to yawn at Ranne's back, waiting for Dillon to smile. His mouth twitched up, but the lines of tension did not ease.

Another cramp dragged at my innards. I held my breath through it, then turned and walked carefully toward the small armory building, my bad leg scattering the fine sand. Dillon was right to be worried. Candidates no longer fought for the honor of approaching the mirrors, but we still had to prove our strength and stamina in the ceremonial sword sequences. At least Dillon could complete the approach sequence, even if it was poorly done. I had never once managed the intricate moves of the Mirror Dragon Third.

It was said it took a lot of physical and mental toughness to bargain with the energy dragons and manipulate the earth forces. It was even whispered among the candidates that a Dragoneye slowly gave up his own life force to a dragon in return for the ability to work the energies, and that the pact aged him beyond his years. My master had been the Tiger Dragoneye during the last cycle and, by my reckoning, would only be a few years over forty. Yet he had the looks and bearing of an old man. Perhaps it was true—a Dragoneye did give up his own life force—or perhaps my master had aged under the strain of poverty and ill luck. He was risking everything for the chance of my success.

I looked over my shoulder. Ranne was watching Baret go through the first form. With all of the strong, able-bodied boys vying to serve him, would the Rat Dragon really choose me? He was the Keeper of Ambition, so perhaps he would not be influenced by physical prowess. I turned to the north-northwest and narrowed my mind until I saw the Rat Dragon shimmer on the sand like a heat mirage. As though he was aware of my focus, the dragon arched his neck and shook out his thick mane.

If he did choose me, then I would hold status for twenty-four years; first working as apprentice to the existing Dragoneye and then, when he retired, working the energies myself. I would earn a mountain of riches, even with the 20 percent tithe to my master. No one would dare spit at me or make the ward-evil sign or turn their face away in disgust.

If he did not choose me, I would be lucky if my master kept me as a servant in his house. I would be like Chart, the slops boy, whose body was permanently twisted into a grim parody of itself. Fourteen years ago, Chart was born to Rilla, one of the unmarried maids, and although my master was sickened by the infant's deformity, he allowed it to live within his household. Chart had never been beyond the confines of the servants' quarters, and he lived on a mat near the cooking stoves. If I failed tomorrow, I could only hope my master would show me similar mercy. Before he found me four years ago, I had labored on a salt farm. I would rather share Chart's mat by the stoves than be returned to such misery.

I stopped walking and reached out further with my mind toward the Rat Dragon, trying to touch the energy of the great beast. I felt his power spark through my body. *Talk to me*, I begged. *Talk to me. Choose me tomorrow. Please, choose me tomorrow.*

There was no response.

A dull pain in my temple sharpened into white agony. The effort to hold him in my sight was too great. The dragon slid beyond my mind's eye, dragging my energy with it. I dug a sword into the sand to stop myself from falling and gasped for air. Fool! Would I never learn? A dragon only ever communicated with his Dragoneye and apprentice. I sucked in a deep breath and pulled the sword out of the ground. Why, then, could I see all eleven dragons? As far back as I could remember, I had been able to shift my mind into the energy world and see their huge translucent forms. Why was I given such a gift in such an ill-favored body?

It was a relief to step off the sand onto the paving of the armory courtyard. The sharp cramps in my gut had finally settled into a dragging ache. Hian, the old master armsman, was sitting on a box beside the armory door polishing the furnace black off a small dagger.

"You been thrown out again?" he asked as I passed him.

I stopped. Hian had never spoken to me before.

"Yes, Armsmaster," I said, tucking my chin into a bow to wait out his scorn.

He held the dagger up in front of him and inspected the blade. "Seems to me you were doing all right."

I looked up and met his eyes, the whites yellowed against his forge-reddened skin.

"With that leg, you're never going to get the Mirror Dragon Third sequence right," he said. "Try a Reverse Horse Dragon Second. There's a precedent for it. Ranne should have told you."

I kept my face expressionless but couldn't help the skip of hope that caught in my throat. Was it true? But why was he telling me this? Maybe it was just a joke on the cripple.

He stood up, holding on to the doorjamb to help him straighten. "I don't blame your mistrust, boy. But you ask your master. He's one of the best history keepers around. He'll tell you I'm right."

"Yes, Armsmaster. Thank you."

A loud yell made us both turn toward the candidates on the sand. Baret was on his knees in front of Ranne.

"Swordmaster Louan was considered one of the best approach ceremony instructors. It's a pity he retired," Hian said flatly. "You've got practice swords at home?"

I nodded.

"Then practice the Reverse Second tonight. Before your cleansing ritual starts." He walked stiffly down the two steps, then looked back at me. "And tell your master that old Hian sends his regards."

I watched him walk slowly to the gateway that led down to the forge, the distant clang of hammer on anvil drumming his progress. If he was right and I could replace the Mirror Dragon Third with a Reverse Horse Dragon Second, then I would have no difficulty finishing the approach sequence.

I stepped into the cool, dim armory and waited for my eyes to adjust. I was not as convinced as the armsmaster that the council would allow a change to the ceremony, particularly to the Mirror Dragon sequence. The Dragon Dragon was, after all, the symbol of the Emperor, and the legends said that the Imperial Family was descended from dragons and still had dragon blood in its veins.

Then again, the Mirror Dragon had been gone for over five hundred years. No one really knew why or how he had disappeared. One story said that a long-ago Emperor offended the dragon, and another told of a terrible battle between the spirit beasts that destroyed the Mirror Dragon. My master said that all the stories were just hearthside imaginings, and that the truth, along with all the records, had been lost to time and the fire that took the Mirror Dragon Hall. And he would know; as the armsmaster had said, my master was a great history keeper. If there was an old variation to the approach sequence, then he would find it.

But first I had to tell him, a day before the ceremony, that I could not complete the Mirror Dragon form. I shivered, remembering the welts and bruises of his past displeasure. I knew it was desperation that provoked his hand—in the last ten years, my master had trained six candidates and all of them had failed—but I did not look forward to his anger. I gripped the hilts of the swords more tightly. I had to know if the Reverse Horse Dragon Second was allowed. It was my best chance.

My master was not a fool; he would not beat me too hard before the ceremony. Too much rode upon it. And if his history scrolls agreed with Hian, I'd have at least four hours before the cleansing ritual to practice the new form and its bridges. It was not long, but it should be enough. I raised the swords in the overhead cut that started the Reverse Second and sliced the left sword down shallowly, conscious of the limited space.

"Oi, don't fling those around in here," the duty armsman snapped.

I pulled up, lowering the points of the swords.

"My apologies, Armsman," I said quickly. It was the skinny,

sallow one who liked giving lectures. I held out the two hilts to him, angling the blades down. I saw his hand clench briefly into the ward-evil sign before he took them.

"Any damage?" he asked, holding one out flat to check the steel.

"No, Armsman."

"These are expensive tools, you know, not playthings. You have to treat them with respect. Not hack away with them indoors. If everyone—"

"Thank you, Armsman," I said, backing toward the door before he could go into a full tirade. He was still talking as I cleared the steps.

The easiest way out of the school was back across the arena and through the main gate, but I didn't want to walk over the sand again, or draw the attention of Ranne. Instead, I took the steep path down to the school's southern gate. My left hip ached from the strain of the practice session and the cramping in my gut made me breathless. By the time I reached the south gate and was passed through by the bored guard, I was sweating from the effort of not crying out.

A dozen or so house-shops lined the road behind the school, forming the outer edge of the food market. The smell of roasting pork fat and crispy-skinned duck oiled the air. I leaned against the wall of the school, letting the stone cool my back, and watched a girl in the blue gown of a kitchen maid weave through the tight knots of gossiping marketers and pause at the hatch of the pork seller. She was about sixteen—my true age—

and her dark hair was scraped back into the looped braid of "unmarried girl." I touched the end of my short queue of black hair, the candidate length. If I was chosen tomorrow, I would begin to grow it to my waist until I could bind it into the double-looped queue of the Dragoneye.

The girl, keeping her eyes down, pointed at a cured haunch on display. The young apprentice wrapped the meat in a cloth and placed it on the bench. The girl waited until he had stepped back before laying the coin beside it and picking up the package. No conversation, no eye contact, no touching; it was all very proper. Yet I sensed something between them.

Although part of me knew it was not honorable, I narrowed my eyes and focused on them as I did with the dragons. At first there was nothing. Then I felt a strange shift in my mind's eye, as though I was stepping closer, and a surge of orange energy flared between the girl and boy, swirling around their bodies like a small monsoon. Something soured in my gut and spirit. I dropped my gaze to the ground, feeling like an intruder, and blinked away my mind-sight. When I looked back, the girl was already turning to leave. There was no sign of the energy around them. No sign of the pulsing brightness that had left a searing afterimage in my mind. Why could I suddenly see such intimate human energy? Neither my master nor any of my instructors had ever spoken of it; emotion was not the province of the dragon magic. Another difference to keep hidden from the world. I pushed away from the wall, needing to work the backwash of power and shame out of my muscles.

My master's house was three roads away, all uphill. The pain in my hip had changed from the familiar ache of overuse to a sharper warning. I needed to get to a hot bath if I wanted any chance of practicing the approach sequence. The alley beside the pork seller was a good shortcut. If it was empty. I shaded my eyes and studied the narrow walkway. It seemed safe; no dock boys sharing a quick pipe or waiting for a limping diversion to chase. I took a step out but hesitated as a familiar wave of motion moved through the crowd; people scrambled to the edges of the road and dropped to their knees, their chatter suddenly silenced.

"Make way for the Lady Jila. Make way for the Lady Jila."

The voice was high but masculine. An elaborately carved palanquin was moving down the road carried on the shoulders of eight sweating men, the passenger concealed behind draped purple silks. Twelve guards, dressed in purple tunics and carrying curved swords, formed a protective square around it—the Shadow Men, the soldier eunuchs of the imperial court. They were always quick to beat down those who did not clear the way or bow fast enough. I dropped onto my good knee and dragged my bad leg beneath me. The Lady Jila? She must be one of the emperor's favorites if she was allowed out of the Inner Precinct. I lowered into the "court noble" bow.

Beside me, a stocky man in the leggings and oiled wrap of the seafarer sat back on his heels, watching the approaching procession. If he did not bow down, he would attract the attention of the guards. And they were not careful about whom they struck.

"It is a court lady, sir," I whispered urgently. "You must bow. Like this." I held my body at the proper angle.

He glanced at me. "Do you think she deserves our bows?" he asked.

I frowned. "What do you mean? She's a court lady, it doesn't matter what she deserves. If you don't bow, you will be beaten."

The seafarer laughed. "A very pragmatic approach to life," he said. "I'll take your advice." He lowered his shoulders, still smiling.

I held my breath as the palanquin passed, squinting as the dust raised, then settled. Beyond us, I heard the crack of a sword laid flat against flesh: a merchant, too slow in his movements, knocked to the ground by the lead guard. The palanquin turned the far corner and a collective easing of muscle and breath rippled through the crowd. A few soft remarks grew in volume as people stood, brushing at their clothes. I dropped my hands to the ground and swung my leg out, preparing to stand. Suddenly, I felt a large hand under each armpit, pulling me upward.

"There you go, boy."

"Don't touch me!" I jumped back, my arms across my chest.

"It's all right," he said, holding up his hands. "I just wanted to return the favor. You saved me from a sword across my back."

He smelled of fish oil and old sweat and seaweed. A memory flashed through me: holding up a heavy string of black pearl kelp, and my mother, nodding and smiling and coiling it into the basket strapped across her slight body. Then the image was gone. Too quick to hold, like all the others I had of my family.

"I'm sorry, sir, you took me by surprise," I said, tightening my arms around my chest. "Thank you for the assistance." Bowing politely, I stepped away from him. The shock of his grip was still on my skin.

The alley opposite was no longer empty; a group of dock boys had congregated near the far end, squatting around a game of dice. I'd have to take the long way around. As if in protest, the pain in my hip sharpened.

The seafarer stopped beside me again. "Perhaps you will help me once more," he said. "Can you tell me the way to the Gate of Officials?"

There was no suspicion or puzzlement on his face, just polite inquiry. I looked at the dock boys again, then back at the seafarer. He was not overly tall, but his chest and shoulders were powerful and his face was tanned into stern lines. I glanced to see if he was armed; a knife was slung through his belt. It would do.

"I'm going that way myself, sir," I said, beckoning him across the road toward the alley. It was not strictly in the direction he wanted to go, but it would still be quicker than the main streets.

"I am Tozay, master fisher of Kan Po," he said, pausing at the mouth of the alley. He clasped his hands together and nodded—adult to child.

From my ley line studies, I knew that Kan Po was on the

coast. It had one of the most fortunate harbors in the realm, shaped like a money pouch and ringed by seven hills that trapped good luck. It was also the port access to the islands and beyond.

"I am Eon, Dragoneye candidate." I bowed again.

He stared down at me. "Eon? The lame candidate?"

"Yes," I said, keeping my face impassive.

"Well now, isn't that something." He dipped into an "honored acquaintance" bow.

I nodded awkwardly, unprepared for the sudden change in status.

"We've heard all about you from the news-walker," Master Tozay said. "He came through our town a few months back. Told us the council had decided to let you approach the mirrors. Did my son a lot of good to hear that. He's a year younger than you, just turned eleven. By rights, he should be fishing with me, learning his craft, but he lost an arm in a net accident last winter." Master Tozay's broad face tightened with grief.

"That must be hard for him," I said.

I looked down at my twisted leg—at least it was still intact. I didn't remember much about the accident that had crushed my left hip, but I did remember the physician holding a rusted saw over me, deciding where to cut. He was going to take my whole leg off, but my master stopped him and called for the bonesetter. Sometimes I could still smell the old blood and decaying flesh on the jagged teeth of the saw blade.

We started walking again. I sneaked another look at the end

of the alley—the dock boys had already shifted into a watchful line. Beside me, Master Tozay stiffened as he noted the lounging gang.

"It is hard on him. On the family, too," he said, brushing his fingers across the hilt of his knife. "Wait, I have a stone in my shoe," he said loudly and stopped.

I turned and watched as he bent and dug a finger down the side of his worn boot.

"You're a shrewd one, aren't you," he said, his voice low. "Well, then, if you want a bodyguard, you'd better move to my other side." The look in his eyes made the soft words a command, but he didn't seem angry. I nodded and shifted to his left.

"I just hope you're not taking me too far out of my way," he said as he straightened, keeping his eyes on the boys.

"It *is* a shortcut," I said.

He glanced across at me. "More for you than for me, hey?"

"For both of us. But perhaps a little bit more for me."

He grunted in amusement and placed his hand on my shoulder. "Keep close."

We walked toward the group, Master Tozay shortening his stride to match my slower pace. The largest boy, thickset, with the darker skin and bull-necked strength of the island people, casually kicked a cobblestone into our path. It skipped and bounced, narrowly missing my foot. His three friends laughed. They were city boys, thin and sharp, with the aimless bravado that was always in need of a leader. The island boy picked up a large stone, rubbing his thumb across its surface.

"Afternoon, boys," Master Tozay said.

The islander spat out a wad of tannin leaf, the fibrous mess landing in front of us. His movement made a pendant swing out on a thin leather cord from his clothing; a pale shell carving in the shape of bamboo branches enclosed in a circle. Master Tozay saw it too and stopped, checking me with a hand on my arm. He pushed me behind him, then turned and faced the islander. The other boys nudged each other closer, keen for a show.

"You're from the south, aren't you?" Master Tozay said. "From the far islands?"

The boy's shoulders stiffened. "I'm from Trang Dein," he said, lifting his chin.

I leaned to my right to get a better look at him. A year ago, the emperor had ordered raids on the Trang Dein people as punishment for their bold independence. It was whispered in the city taverns that all the male Trang prisoners had been viciously gelded, like animals, and forced to serve on the imperial ships. This boy was only about fifteen but big enough to pass as a man. Was he one of the Trang cattle-men? My eyes dropped, but he wore the loose tunic and trousers of the dock laborer. I couldn't tell by just looking.

Or could I? A cattle-man's energy would be different from a whole man's energy, wouldn't it? Maybe my new mind-sight would work on him as it had with the kitchen girl and apprentice. The memory of watching their bright monsoon union made my skin prickle with shame, but I still narrowed my mind into the energy world. There was the same strange sensation of stepping forward, and then light, so bright that tears came to my eyes. I couldn't separate anyone's energy; it was a roiling blurred mass of red and yellow and blue. Then, like a flickering cloud shadow, another presence. And pain, deep and low in the belly. Ten times worse than the monthly pain, as though barbs were being dragged through my innards. Only a power born of evil spirits could have such agony ride with it. My mind-sight buckled. I drew in a shuddering breath as the alley twisted back into view. The pain vanished.

Never again would I intrude upon such savage energies.

Beside me, I heard Master Tozay say, "I fish the Kan Po coast. Hired a few of your people as hands on my boats. That was before the raid, of course. They were all good workers."

The island boy nodded warily.

"The islands are quiet now," Tozay said softly. "Not so many soldiers in Ryoka. Some of the missing are making their way home."

The boy let the stone drop to the ground, his hand groping for the shell carving. Holding it like a talisman, he glanced back at his friends, then faced Master Tozay and hunched his shoulders as though to separate himself from his companions.

"Are you hiring now?" he asked, stumbling over the words.

"I may have a place," Master Tozay said. "If you're looking for honest work, then meet me at the Gray Marlin dock tomorrow. I'll wait until the noon bell."

Master Tozay turned, herding me with his body. As we walked out of the alley and into the busy Sweet Sellers Road, I looked back at the island boy. He was staring at us, oblivious to his friends, his hand clenched around the pendant.

"What is that thing he wears around his neck?" I asked Master Tozay as we crossed the road. "A good luck symbol?" But I knew the pendant had to be more than that.

Master Tozay snorted. "No, I wouldn't say it was good luck." He looked closely at me. "You have a politician's face, Eon. I'd wager you know a lot more than you show the world. So what have you noted about the change in our land?"

More beggars, more raids, more arrests, more hard words against the imperial court. I had also overheard my master in low conversation with others of his rank: *The emperor is ill, the heir too callow, the court split in its loyalties.*

"What I have noted is that it is safer to have a politician's face and a mute's tongue," I said wryly.

Master Tozay laughed. "Prudently said." He looked around, then pulled me over to the narrow space between two shops. "That boy's pendant is an islander totem, to bring longevity and courage," he said, bending close to my ear, his voice low. "It's also a symbol of resistance."

"To the emperor?" I whispered, knowing the danger of such words.

"No, child. To the real power in the Empire of the Celestial Dragons. High Lord Sethon."

The emperor's brother. The son of a concubine. According to the old ways, when the emperor came to his throne, he should have ordered his brother Sethon killed, along with all the other male children born to his father's concubines. But our emperor was an enlightened man, an educated man. He let his eight younger brothers live. He made them his generals, and Sethon, the eldest of the eight, he made his commander in chief. Our emperor was also a trusting man.

"But High Lord Sethon commands the armies. What can islanders do against such might?" I asked.

Master Tozay shrugged. "Not much. But there are others, more powerful, who remain loyal to the emperor and his son." He paused as an old woman stopped at the shop-hatch next to us to poke through a display of yeast cakes. "Come, this is not the talk for such an open place," he said softly. "Or indeed for any place." He straightened. "I fancy a sweet bun. How about you?"

I longed to ask him who opposed High Lord Sethon, but the subject was clearly at an end. And I had not had a sweet bun in a very long time—there was no money for such excesses in my master's household.

"I should not dawdle. . . ." I said.

"Come, it will not take long. We'll get them as we walk. Can you recommend a seller?"

I nodded. One bun would not take long. I spotted a break in the slow-moving crowd and led Master Tozay through it to the corner of the White Cloud Market. It was busier than usual, the afternoon sun driving people under the shade of the broad white silk sails that had been stretched between carved poles. We passed Ari the Foreigner serving some merchants in his coffee stall, the heavy perfume of the strange black drink thick in the air. Ari had once given me a bowl of his coffee, and I had liked the rich bitterness and the slight buzzing it left in my head. I touched Master Tozay's arm and pointed at the pastry stall to our left, its counter blocked by customers.

"The red bean ones are said to be good here," I said, standing on my toes to see the trays of buns arranged in neat lines.

The nutty smell of bean paste and sweet dough radiated in a wave of heat. A sharp roil of hunger joined the ache in my gut. Master Tozay nodded and, bowing politely, managed to neatly insert himself ahead of a woman hesitating over her choice. As I watched his broad back and sunburned neck, I felt another flicker of memory; of being carried on a big man's back and the salty warmth of sun-leathered skin against my cheek. But, once again, I couldn't make the image stay. Was it a memory of my father? I no longer had any clear idea of what he looked like. A moment later Master Tozay turned, holding a bun in each hand, wrapped in a twist of red paper.

"Here you go," he said. "Be careful. The seller said they're just out of the steamer."

"Thank you, sir." The heat from the bun stung my palm through the thin wrapping. I slid the paper down, fashioning a handle. It would be best to wait until it had cooled, but the smell was too tantalizing; I bit into it, juggling the steaming pastry around with my tongue.

"Tasty," Master Tozay said, fanning his mouth with his hand.

I nodded, unable to speak as the hot, dense filling made my jaw seize and ache with its sudden sweetness.

He motioned forward with his bun. "Is this the way to the Gate?"

I swallowed and sucked in a breath of cooling air. "Yes, you follow the white sails until they end," I said, pointing at the silk roof, "and then turn right. Just keep walking and you'll come to the Gate of Officials."

Master Tozay smiled. "Good boy. Now, if ever you make the journey down the coast to Kan Po, you must look for me. You can be always sure of a welcome." He hesitated, then put his hand on my shoulder. "If that dragon has any sense tomorrow, he'll choose you," he said, giving me a gentle shake.

I smiled. "Thank you, sir. And travel well."

He nodded and raised his pastry in salute, then joined the flow of people in the center of the walkway. As his solid form merged into the shapes and colors of the crowd, I felt as though he was taking my mother and father with him. Two half memories that were already fading, leaving only an imprint of a smile like mine and the smell of sun-warmed skin.

CHAPTER TWO

THE FULL-HOUR BELL was ringing as I finally lifted the latch of the gate that led to the kitchen of my master's house. Irsa, one of the bondmaids, was standing at the delivery door with the miller's man. I watched as she laughed, her hands spread on her hips to show their generous shape, as the young man hoisted a large sack onto his shoulder. Then she saw me and quickly stepped back into the shelter of the doorway. Her coy giggles dropped into the hissing undertones of gossip. The miller's man swung around and stared at me, his fingers curling into a ward-evil sign. I looked away and made a show of shutting the gate. Better to wait until he followed Irsa into the storage rooms.

When the courtyard was clear, I walked slowly up the path toward the kitchen. Lon, the gardener, was on his knees repairing the low bamboo fence that enclosed the Sun Garden.

I nodded as I passed, and he waved a dirt-crusted hand. Lon mainly kept to himself, but he always greeted me with gentle courtesy and even had a smile for Chart, the slops boy. But his kindness was not copied by many of my master's other staff. Our small household was very much divided: those who believed a cripple could be a Dragoneye, and those who did not. All who served my master knew that his wealth had nearly run dry; there would be no funds to train another candidate. If I did not secure the apprentice bonus and the 20 percent tithe tomorrow, my master was ruined.

The kitchen doorway was open and I stepped over the raised threshold that kept evil spirits from entering the house. Immediately, the heat from the large cooking stoves pressed against my skin and I smelled the sharp tang of sour plum sauce and salt-baked fish: my master's evening meal. Kuno, the cook, glanced up from the white-root he was slicing.

"You, is it?" He turned his attention back to the vegetable. "Master has already ordered the gruel," he said, tilting his shaved head at a small pot hanging over the spit fire. "Don't blame me when you eat it. It was according to his instructions."

My evening meal. As part of the cleansing ritual, I was allowed only one bowl of millet gruel before praying throughout the night to my ancestors for guidance and help. A few months ago, I had asked my master whether it mattered that I had no knowledge of my ancestors. He stared at me for a moment, then turned away before saying, "It matters very much." My master was being very careful; he said we must do everything according to Dragoneye tradition to avoid attracting council scrutiny. I could only hope that old Hian's precedent for the Reverse Horse Dragon Second was in the history scrolls. And that my master could find it in time.

A rasping noise rose from behind the large wooden preparation table that stood in the center of the room: Chart, calling me from his mat beside the stoves.

"He's been waiting for you," Kuno said. "Been getting under my feet all day." He sliced off the end of the white-root with an extra heavy chop. "You tell him I'm not blind, I know he's been at the cheese." Although they had worked in the same kitchen for eleven years, Kuno still refused to speak to Chart or even look at him. Too much bad luck.

I skirted around the end of the table and used its worn edge for balance as I sat on the stone floor beside Chart. He tapped my knee with a clawed finger, his lolling mouth slowly forming a smile.

"Did you really get some cheese?" I asked softly, shifting my weight off my aching left hip.

He nodded vigorously and opened his hand to show me a piece of dirty cheese rind. The muscles in his throat contorted as he struggled to speak. I listened for his words in the strained, elongated sounds.

"For . . . the . . . rat." He pushed the rind into my hand.

"Thank you," I said, slipping the cheese into my pocket. Chart was always giving me food he had found. Or stolen. He was convinced that if I fed the big gray rat that lived behind the storeroom where I slept, the Rat Dragon would repay the kindness by choosing me as his apprentice. I wasn't so sure an energy dragon would take note of such a thing, but I still gave the scraps to the rat.

From beneath his body, Chart pulled out a thick slice of fine bread covered in dust. The master's bread. I glanced at Kuno; he was still bent over the white-root. I moved to my right until I hid Chart and the bread from view.

"How'd you get that? Kuno will whip you," I whispered.

"For you . . . only gruel tonight . . . you be hungry tomorrow." He dropped the bread into my lap.

I ducked my head in thanks and stuffed it into my pocket with the cheese. "I think that's the whole idea. They want us to be hungry," I said.

Chart twisted his mouth into a puzzled grimace.

I shrugged. "We're supposed to prove our natural stamina by doing the approach ceremony hungry and tired."

Chart rolled his head back and forward across the mat. "Stu . . . pid," he said. He took a deep breath and steadied his head against the side of the firewood box, fixing his eyes on mine. "Tomorrow morning you come . . . say good-bye?" His fingers closed around my wrist. "Come say . . . good-bye . . . before the ceremony? Promise?"

Chart knew that if I was chosen, I would not come back. A new apprentice was taken straight to his Dragon Hall after the ceremony. A new home. A new life. My scalp prickled from a sudden wave of heat and sweat; tomorrow I could be a Dragoneye apprentice.

"Promise?" Chart said.

I nodded, unable to talk through the squeeze of panic in my throat.

He let go of my wrist, his hand suspended in the air. "Tell me . . . what the . . . Rat Dragon Hall . . . is like . . . again."

I'd only seen the hall once. A few months ago during training, Ranne had marched us around the Dragon Circle, the avenue of halls that ringed the outer precinct of the Imperial Palace. Each hall had been carefully built at the compass position of the dragon it honored and was the home and workplace of the Dragoneye and apprentice. The Rat Dragon Hall was in the north-northwest of the circle, and although it wasn't the biggest or the grandest, it was easily three times the size of my master's house. We were not permitted inside any of the halls, but Ranne allowed us five minutes' rest in the garden that marked the position of the Mirror Dragon Hall. Five hundred years ago it burned down; only the stone outline of the building remained embedded in the grass. Dillon and I had walked its perimeter and were amazed at the number of rooms.

Beside me, Chart closed his eyes, preparing for my words.

"Two gray stone statues of the Rat Dragon guard the gate," I said, closing my own eyes to remember my brief glimpse of the hall. "They stand bigger than me and twice as wide. The one on the right holds the Dragoneye compass in its claws, the other cradles the three sacred scrolls. As you walk past them, their stone eyes follow you. Inside the gate, a courtyard made of matched dark cobbles leads to the—"

"I don't know why you bother," I heard Irsa say. I opened my eyes. She was in the doorway, briskly brushing down her skirt. "The freak doesn't understand your words." She smoothed the looped braid of her hair.

Chart and I exchanged glances. No doubt the miller's man was going home happy.

"Sl . . . u . . . t," Chart said loudly.

Irsa pulled her face into a mockery of Chart's and mimicked his elongated sounds, unaware of the word within them. Chart rolled his eyes at me, his body thrashing against the floor in laughter. I grinned as Irsa backed away.

"Freak," she said, her fingers making the ward-evil sign at Chart. She turned her attention to me. "Master said you were to go to him as soon as you returned," she said, then added snidely, "although he wasn't expecting you until the end of training time."

"Where is he now?" I asked.

"Moon Garden. On the main viewing platform." She smiled slyly. Irsa knew I was not allowed in the Moon Garden—my master had forbidden it. "He said *as soon* as you return."

I grabbed the edge of the table and pulled myself upright. Should I obey my master's ban on the Moon Garden, or obey his command to attend him immediately? He would not be pleased that I was home so early. Let alone the other news I had for him.

"Irsa, do your work," Kuno said. "Stop wasting time or you'll feel the back of my hand."

Irsa gave me one last gloating look, then hurried into the dark passageway that connected the kitchen to the main house.

There was a saying in one of the earthier Dragoneye texts: A man on the horns of a dilemma ends up with his arse pricked. My master would find fault whether I went into the garden or I waited. Since there was no avoiding his displeasure, I would go to him. At least I would finally see the garden that had won him such fame.

"Tomorrow," I said to Chart. He gave his slow smile.

I stepped over the threshold into the courtyard. To my left was the gray stone fence of the Moon Garden, its low metal gate etched with the shape of a leaping tiger. I headed over to it, the promise of my master's anger dragging at my feet. There were many ways to tell the truth—I just needed to find one that would satisfy him. All that was visible over the gateway was a black pebble path leading to an impressive stacked slate wall. Along its face, a waterfall cascaded down a carefully haphazard run of ledges, pooling into a white marble bowl.

My master had designed the garden to symbolize female energy, and it was said that during a full moon, the garden was so beautiful it could rob a man of his essence. When I heard that, I wondered what would happen to a man robbed of his essence—would he become a woman, or would he become something else? Something like the Shadow Men of the court? Or something like me?

There was no latch on the gate. I traced the strong lines of the tiger on the metal for luck—or maybe for protection—then pushed against it until the gate swung open.

The black path was made of pebbles and seemed to move in front of me like a slow ripple of water. As I stepped onto it, I realized why; the stones had been laid in a subtle graduation of matte to polished that caught the sunlight. On either side, a flat expanse of sand had been raked into swirling patterns. I pushed the gate shut behind me and followed the path to the waterfall wall, my uneven steps sounding like the chink of coins in a pouch. The path diverged around the wall. I paused for a moment, listening. Underneath the sound of the waterfall splashing into the bowl was the muted hiss of more flowing water. No other sounds of physical movement. But deeper, in my mind, I felt the soft thrum of carefully contained power. I chose the left path and walked around the wall into the main garden.

It was a severe landscape: clusters of rocks on flat sand, swirling paths of black and white pebbles, and an intricate weaving of waterfalls, streams, and pools directing the thrumming energy to the wooden viewing platform. My master was kneeling in its center, as spare and severe as his surroundings. I lowered into a bow, watching for acknowledgment. He didn't move. There were no signs of anger in the lean lines of his body. A shadow above made me flinch. I looked up, but there was nothing. No bird. No cloud. But the cramps and the pain in my hip had eased.

My master's body stiffened. "What are you doing here?"

"I was told you wished to see me, Master," I said, crouching lower. There was still no pain.

"Why are you back so early?"

"Swordmaster Ranne said I need not train any more," I said carefully.

"You should not be in here. Especially not now. The energies are too strong." He stood up in a single practiced movement, the frayed silver embroideries on his tunic flaring in the sun. "Come, we must leave now."

He held out his hand. I hurried forward and extended my arm, bracing myself as he leaned on me and stepped off the platform.

He paused, still holding my arm. "Do you feel them?" he asked.

I looked up into his gaunt face, the prominent bones made even starker by his shaved skull. "Feel them?"

"The energies." Irritation edged his voice.

I bowed my head. "I can feel the flow of water energy to the viewing platform," I said.

He flicked his fingers. "A novice could feel that. Is there nothing else?"

"No, Master." It was not the truth, but how could I explain the heat of an imagined shadow? Or the soft unraveling that was the absence of pain.

He grunted. "Then perhaps we have succeeded."

He turned and walked quickly toward the house. I followed two paces behind, concentrating on keeping my footing on the shifting pebbles. For once, each step did not jar with pain. We passed a simple moon altar—a smooth concave stone resting on two smaller rocks—surrounded by a shallow amphitheater of cut marble. Ahead, the pebble path widened in front of another viewing platform that also served as a step up to the house. Two carved doors stood open, allowing a view of floor-to-ceiling scroll boxes, a cabinet, and a dark wood desk. My master's library—another area forbidden to me. Until now. I paused, staring at the shelves of scrolls. My master had drilled me in my letters, and I'd read all of the classics and Dragoneye texts, but I longed to read about other things.

"Don't just stand there gaping like a fool," my master said, holding out his hand.

I helped him onto the platform as Rilla, Chart's mother and my master's body servant, stepped out of the library and knelt at the doorway. For the first time I noticed the swirls of gray hair in the neat loop of her "unmarried" braid. It was meant to be her disgrace, but she wore it with quiet dignity. My master extended his foot and she slid off his scuffed silk slipper, then the other, placing them neatly on a small woven mat.

"We are not to be disturbed," my master ordered. He held out his hand and I helped him over the lip of the threshold.

Rilla looked up at me and raised her eyebrows. I twitched my shoulder into a shrug, then hurriedly pulled off my woven straw sandals, grabbing the doorframe for balance. Black dirt striped my feet around the pattern of the straps. I licked my fingers and rubbed the top of each foot, but the dirt just smeared into streaks.

"Stay still," Rilla said softly. She took a cloth out of her pocket and wiped my left ankle.

"You don't need to do that," I said, trying to pull my foot away. No one had touched my bad leg since the splints had come off three years ago.

She held my foot still. "A Dragoneye has servants," she said. "Best get used to it." She scrubbed my other foot clean. "Now give me your sandals and go in."

Four years ago, when I came to my master's house—a half-starved drudge willing to become a boy for food and warmth—Rilla was the only person who showed me any care. At first I thought it was because I was a cripple, like her son, but later I realized she desperately needed my master to have a successful candidate. "No one else will have us in their house," she once told me, stroking Chart's dusty hair. "I've seen a lot of boys come through here, Eon, but you're our best chance. You're special." At the time I thought she had guessed the secret, but she hadn't. And even if she did know, she would never say anything. Rilla was bound too tightly to my master, his tolerance of Chart a hundred times more compelling than any bond of indenture.

I handed her the sandals, smiling my thanks. She shooed me into the library.

"Close the doors, Eon," my master said. He was standing at the cabinet sorting through the keys he wore around his neck on a length of red silk.

I pulled shut the doors and waited for further instruction. He looked up and nodded at the visitor's chair in front of the desk.

"Sit down," he said, shaking a key free.

Sit down? In a chair? I watched him insert the key into the lock. Had I heard correctly? I crossed the soft, thick carpet and gingerly laid my hand on the back of the chair, waiting for a reprimand. Nothing. I glanced across at my master. He had a leather pouch and a small black ceramic jar in his hands.

"I said sit down," he ordered, closing the cabinet doors.

I perched on the very edge of the leather seat, my hands tight around the carved armrests. I had always imagined a chair would be comfortable, but it was hard against my rump bones and made my hip ache again. I shifted around, trying to recapture the warm ease I'd felt in the garden, but it was gone. I looked at the closed double doors, imagining the stark landscape outside. Did the garden take my pain? Did its moon energies call to my hidden self? I shivered. My master was right; I could not afford to enter it again. Not so close to the ceremony.

On the desk in front of me were two small black-lacquered death plaques. I tried to read the names carved into the wood, but I could not make sense of the upside-down characters. I quickly looked away from them as my master sat in the chair opposite me. He placed the leather pouch and jar next to the two memorials.

"So it is tomorrow," he said.

I nodded, keeping my eyes fixed on the desk.

"You are prepared." It was a statement, not a question, but I nodded again. An image of old Armsmaster Hian flashed through my mind. Now was the time to ask my master about the Reverse Horse Dragon Second.

"I went to a ghost maker today," my master said softly.

I was so startled I looked up and met his eyes. A ghost maker dealt in herbs and potions and, it was said, in the spirits of the unborn.

"She gave me this." He pushed the pouch toward me. "If it is taken as a tea every morning, it will stop the moon energy. But it can only be taken for three months. Then it becomes poison to the body."

I hunched down in the chair.

"Your moon cycle must be stopped for these ceremonies," he continued. "And if you succeed tomorrow, then—"

"I am about to bleed," I whispered.

"What?"

"I have all the signs." I ducked my head lower. "It's early. I don't know why."

I saw my master's hands clench the edge of the table. It was as though his anger weighted the air between us.

"Have you started?"

"No, but I have the—"

He held up his hand. "Quiet." I watched his long fingers tap the wood. "If it has not started, then all is not lost. She said it was to be taken before your next cycle starts." He picked up the pouch. "You must take a cup now."

He leaned back and pulled on the bell cord hanging behind the desk. Almost immediately, the far door opened. Rilla stepped in and bowed.

"Tea," he said. Rilla bowed again and stepped out, closing the door.

"I'm sorry, Master," I said.

"It would be most unfortunate if the whims of your body undid four years of planning." He steepled his fingers. "I don't know why you have the gift of full dragon-sight, Eon. It must be some plan of the gods. How else can I explain my impulse to test a girl on my candidate search? It goes against all that is natural." He shook his head.

I knew he was right; a woman could not have power. Or if she did, it was from the shapeliness of her body. Not from her spirit. And certainly not from her mind.

"But you have more raw power than all of the Dragoneyes combined," he continued. "And tomorrow that power will attract the Rat Dragon."

I looked away, trying to hide a sudden rising of doubt. What if my master was wrong?

He leaned closer. "When he chooses you, there is a bargain that must be made. There is no advice I can give you—the bargain is different between every dragon and his new apprentice. However, I can tell you that the dragon will seek an energy in you that he wants, and when he takes it, you will be united."

"What kind of energy, Master?"

"As I said, it is different for everyone. But it will be linked to one of the seven points of power in the body."

My master had taught me about the points of power: seven balls of invisible energy positioned in a line from the base of the spine to the crown of the head. They regulated the flow of *Hua*, the life force, through the physical and emotional body.

It seemed that the whispers around the candidate school were true—a Dragoneye did give up some of his life force. No wonder they aged so fast.

"When I was chosen by the Tiger Dragon," my master continued, "the bargain I made was the energy that no man gives up lightly." His gaze met mine, then slid away. "So be prepared—it will not be easy. You cannot gain the dragon's power without giving something valuable in return."

I nodded, although I did not truly understand.

"And then when your bargain is made and you are the Rat Dragoneye apprentice, we must be even more careful. You cannot place a foot wrong, Eon, or we will both die."

There was fear and hope in his eyes, and I knew he saw the same in mine. The far door opened again. My master sat back as Rilla entered, carrying a black-lacquered tray laid with tea implements. She placed the tray on the desk.

"Only Eon will be taking a bowl," my master said.

Rilla bowed, unrolled a round gold mat, and arranged it in front of me. It was a representation of the Dragoneye compass, intricately painted with the twenty-four circles of energy manipulation. As a candidate, I had been drilled in the first and second circles of the compass—the cardinal points and the dragon animal signs—but only apprentices studied how to use the other circles. I leaned closer and touched the painted Rat near the top of the second circle, sending out another silent plea to the Rat Dragon: *choose me.* Then, to complete my private petition, I swept my fingers around the twelve painted animals in the direction of their yearly rising. Rat, Ox, Tiger, Rabbit, Dragon . . .

Rat turns, Dragon learns, Empire burns—

The harsh words echoed through my mind, twisting into my gut. I gasped and jerked back my hand as Rilla set a red drinking bowl in the center of the mat. Her eyes flicked to mine, wide with concern.

"What are you doing, Eon?" my master snapped.

"Nothing, Master." I ducked my head in apology, pressing my hand against my belly. That rhyme must have been something I'd read in one of the Dragoneye texts; they were full of strange sayings and bad verse.

"Well, sit still."

"Yes, Master." I took a careful breath. Only an echo of the stabbing pain remained. These cramps were the worst I'd ever had—maybe the ghost maker's tea would ease them. Rilla lifted a small brazier of hot coals from the tray and placed it on the desk, setting a pot of steaming water over the heat.

"I will prepare the tea," my master said.

A shivering unease twitched across my back. Rilla nodded and positioned a larger mixing bowl with a small bamboo whisk in front of him. He waved his hand toward the door. "You may go."

She bowed and backed out of the room.

My master waited until the door shut, then picked up the pouch and untied the leather fastening.

"You must use only one pinch," he said. He dropped a gray-green powder into the mixing bowl. "And do not use boiling water or you will destroy the power of the herb." He lifted the pot off the brazier and poured a small amount of water into the bowl. With a few flicks of the bamboo whisk, the tea was mixed.

"Give me your bowl."

I passed it over. He deftly transferred the murky liquid and passed it back.

"The ghost maker said it was best taken in one swallow."

I eyed the dark surface of the tea, watching my reflection slide and settle.

"Take it."

The bowl smelled of damp leaves and decay. No wonder it was best taken in one swallow. The oily bitterness washed through my mouth. I closed my eyes, fighting the urge to spit.

My master gave a nod. "Good."

I put the empty bowl back onto the gold mat. My master tightened the leather cord around the pouch and passed it across the table.

"Keep it hidden."

I slipped it into my pocket, next to the cheese and bread.

"I have also prepared your way with the council," my master said. "Do you know what this is?" He tapped the sealed top of the black ceramic jar.

"No, Master."

He turned it around slowly and the white painted characters of my name twisted into view.

"It is a vessel of proof," he said. "On the records of the council, you are now a Moon Shadow."

I stared at him. Somehow, my master had registered me as a Moon eunuch; a boy castrated before puberty for family advancement and opportunity. Such boys were never touched by manhood, forever retaining the physical form of their youth. I leaned closer to the eunuch jar. I had never seen one before, but I knew that sealed inside was the mummified proof of the operation. Without it, a Shadow Man could not gain employment or promotion. If he was not buried with it at death, he would have no chance of returning to wholeness in the next world. What Shadow Man would give up such a precious thing? There was only one answer: one who was already dead.

"Master," I whispered, "surely this will bring bad luck."

He frowned. "It will ensure that your size and voice will not be remarked upon," he said firmly. "And any evil spirits have been well placated with coin." He picked up the jar, motioning to a new layer of wax around the lid. "According to the records, you have already been examined and pronounced a true Shadow. When you are chosen tomorrow and move into the Rat Dragon Hall, you will no longer be under my protection. You must use this Shadow status and your deformity to ensure no one sees you unclothed."

I bowed my head. It was bad luck to bathe or sleep in the same quarters as a cripple. And a crippled eunuch would bring even worse fortune. My master had thought of everything. But there was still one problem.

"Master?"

"Yes?" He put the jar back onto the desk.

"I spoke to Armsmaster Hian today. He wished to be re-membered to you." I clenched my hands together in my lap.

He nodded. "I hope you thanked him for his courtesy."

"Yes, Master." I swallowed, a sudden dryness in my throat grabbing at my voice. "He . . ."

My master pushed the two death plaques across the desk. "Your ancestors," he said abruptly. "For your prayers, tonight. They are only women, but they are better than nothing."

It took me a moment to realize what he had said. "My an-cestors?"

One plaque was inscribed with the name Charra, the other, Kinra. I lifted my hand to touch them, but stopped, glancing at my master for permission.

"Yes, they are yours," he said, nodding. "I retrieved them from your previous master. When he bought your bond from your parents, your mother insisted the memorials stay with you."

I stroked the smooth surface of the Charra plaque, the name and a plain border the only adornment. My mother had given these to me. I blinked rapidly, clenching my teeth against the threat of tears. The Kinra plaque was old and worn, with a faint sinuous outline of an animal under the name. Who were these women? My grandmother? My great-grandmother?

When I looked up, my master was watching me intently.

"Pray hard tonight, Eon," he said softly. "We cannot afford

to fail." He gestured to the plaques. "Go, set up your altar and prepare for the cleansing ritual. You may ask Rilla for what you need."

I was dismissed, but for the first time in four years I did not obey. I kept my eyes fixed on the chiseled name of my ancestor, Kinra, and tried to push my need into words.

"I said you may go, Eon."

I did not move.

My master brought the heel of his hand down on the table, the crash making me jump.

I grabbed the armrests, glad of their solidity. "Master," I said hoarsely. I risked a look; he was scowling. "Armsmaster Hian told me the Mirror Dragon Third sequence could be replaced with a Reverse Horse Dragon Second. Is that true, Master?"

"Why?"

I heard his voice sharpen ominously, but I had to know.

"I can't complete the Mirror Dragon Third, Master. My leg. I can't do it. If I could do the—"

I saw him move, but I was caught between the armrests. The back of his hand cracked across my ear, slamming me into the edge of the carved wood.

"You wait until *now* to tell me?"

My head burned from ear to jaw. I hunched around the jabbing ache in my ribs, trying to move away from his hand. The punches hammered into my thigh, shoulder, back; jarring through my whole body.

"You have killed us," he hissed.

"Armsmaster Hian said you would know if it was true." I gasped. "Please . . ."

Through a blur of tears, I saw him lift his hand again. I shut my eyes and ducked my head. My body waited for the blow; my whole existence narrowed to the fall of his fist.

No blow.

No pain.

I opened my eyes.

He was not there. I scanned the room, holding my breath. He was at the far wall, reaching up to a shelf, his fingers feverishly flicking across the scroll boxes. I carefully uncurled and ran my fingers down my ribs, flinching as they hit the swollen heart of a bruise.

He pulled a box out of the stack. "The Chronicle of Detra. That should describe it."

He shook the roll of priceless paper from the wooden container. The box clattered onto the floor. In a few strides he was at the desk, the whole scroll unfurled across its length. In front of me was row upon row of cramped calligraphy.

"What did Hian say, exactly?" he demanded.

"He said there was a precedent for replacing the Mirror Dragon Third with the Reverse Horse Dragon Second and that Ranne was wrong to have kept it from me."

My master's face darkened at the shift of blame.

"He also said you were one of the best history keepers and would know if it was so," I added hurriedly.

He eyed me for a moment, then turned his attention back

to the scroll. His index finger hovered above the words as he read. I stayed as still as I could, searching his pale, drawn face for the flame of discovery.

"The alternative form was in practice five hundred years ago, before we lost the Mirror Dragon," he finally said. "It has not been used since."

"Does that mean I cannot use it, Master?" I whispered.

He held up his hand. "Quiet." He studied the scroll again. "I cannot see any prohibition on its use." He shook his head. "No, there is no reversal of its standing. It has just not been used for five hundred years." He looked across at me, a fierce light in his eyes. "This is a good omen. It must be a good omen."

I straightened in the chair, the new bruises aching as they stretched. "I can already do the Horse Dragon Second, Master. All I need to do is practice the bridging forms," I said.

"The way must be smoothed," he muttered, rolling up the scroll. He pulled the bell cord. The door opened and Rilla appeared.

"Order a rickshaw—I must go to the council," he said to her.

He turned back to me. "Go and practice. You know what is at stake."

I crouched out of the chair into a low bow, unable to contain the smile on my face. The Reverse Horse Dragon Second was allowed. I still had a chance.

CHAPTER THREE

A TOUCH ON MY arm awoke me. I was sitting slumped against the wall next to my altar, my face pressed against the cold stone. I focused on the slim figure squatting beside me in the dim light.

Rilla.

"The master will rise soon," she said softly.

A spike of apprehension cleared my head. The red prayer candle in front of the death plaques had burned to a stump of wax, and the small offering bowl of fish and rice smelled of the hours gone by. I pushed myself upright, smoothing a crease in the sleeve of my ceremonial tunic.

"I shouldn't have slept."

Rilla touched my tightly clubbed hair. "Don't worry. No one saw you." She stood, stifling a yawn. "The dawn bell will ring soon. Be quick if you wish to say good-bye to Chart."

I nodded, massaging the chill from my face and neck. My master had made the smallest of the stone storerooms at the back of the house into a dormitory for his candidates. In these summer months it was a sanctuary of cool air, but it was a bitter cell in winter. I looked around the cramped room that had been home for four years: my bed, still in its roll against the wall; an old clothespress; the writing rest where I had knelt for such long hours and studied; and a squat earthenware brazier topped by a pot I'd found on the rubbish pile. Such luxury compared to the salt farm. Was this the last time I would see it all? Or would I be back?

"I'll send one of the girls to tell you when the master is dressed," Rilla said, pushing open the shutters that covered the narrow window.

"Thank you, Rilla."

She paused at the door. "Chart and I have been praying for your success, Eon. But know also, we will miss you."

For a moment, her eyes met mine and I saw fear and worry in the sharpened lines of her face. Then she smiled and left. If I failed today, would my master sell Rilla and Chart? Their service bonds were not even half paid; Chart had shown me Rilla's reckoning stick hidden behind a loose brick in the kitchen.

I crossed over to the brazier, my movement releasing the rich smell of the cleansing herbs on my skin. And me? If I failed, would I be returned to the salt farm? The memory of working in the choking dust made me cough and gag. I pressed my hands against my chest, feeling for the flow of *Hua*, the life force. All I could feel was the fine silk of the ceremonial tunic and the unyielding flatness of my tight breast band. My master had taught me the basics of tracing my *Hua* through the seven points of power, but it was a technique that took a lifetime to control. I turned my mind's eye inward, groping along the meridians. Finally, I located the blockage: in the base of my spine, the seat of fear. I breathed slowly until the rigid knot softened.

I knelt on the stone floor and cleaned the ashes out of the body of the brazier. Something was stirring within me. A familiar flicker of awareness. It was during my moon days that my shadow-self—Eona—darkened into strange thoughts and uneasy feelings. It seemed that while the ghost maker's tea had eased yesterday's cramps and prevented the bleeding, it had not yet washed the shadows away. I could not afford to let Eona come forward and bring her troubling desires into my mind. I pushed her away, concentrating on stacking twigs and small slivers of charcoal in the brazier. A strike of the inch-stick, and the tinder sparked into life. I blew on the wavering flame until it caught and held, then angled the pot to check the water level. There was just enough to make the tea. Perhaps this dose would chase her away.

If I failed, my master would not need me as a boy.

I tried to shake off the unwelcome thought.

Then offer him a girl's body. It was in his eyes during the cleansing ritual.

No, that was not true! There had been nothing in my master's eyes during the ritual. He'd said the words, poured the fragrant water over my head, then left me to wash and oil myself. I had seen nothing in his eyes. I leaned over the pot, urging it to heat faster.

A pinch of tea in my cup, then the near-boiled water, all mixed with a twig. I drank it in one swallow, the sting of the heat and the foul taste driving out Eona's unsettling thoughts.

The sky through the window was brightening. I fastened the tea pouch inside my trouser waistband and brushed specks of ash off the ceremonial tunic. I had worn the rich garments during my vigil to honor my newfound ancestors. It was the softest material I had ever worn, a close silk weave in the vibrant red of the candidate. Twelve gold embroidered dragons were worked around the hemline of the tunic, and the sash ends were edged with gold tassels. The cloth was like oiled water against my skin and, when it moved, the sound was the wind's whisper. No wonder the nobles acted like gods; they'd captured the very elements in their robes. I pulled on the matching red leather slippers, flexing my feet at the unfamiliar confinement. They were edged in gold thread and had the same dragon design painted on the toes. What had all this finery cost my master? I stood and practiced a few steps of the first sequence, feeling for the difference in toe grip as I spun from the Rat Dragon First into the second form. The leather soles had greater slip than my old sandals; it could be treacherous on the hard-packed sand of the Dragon Arena. I spun again and again, adjusting my weight into the floor, enjoying the swirl of the silk tunic as it flared and settled around my body.

The clang of the oven lid in the kitchens brought me to a halt. Kuno, banking the fires. It was close to dawn break and there was still much to do. I hurried over to the clothespress, digging under my folded work tunic for the scroll. After three months of snatched moments, I had finally finished it: a black ink painting of the roads and landscape around my master's house. It was made up of scraps of mulberry paper from the paper maker near the school; he'd allowed me to have the edges of the clean cuts and I'd stitched them together to make the roll. The painting was in the style of the great Master Quidan—a long, thin rendering that was meant to be opened in small sections for meditation upon the landscape. Would Chart like it? I knew my artistry was poor, but perhaps it would help him imagine the world outside the kitchen. I fingered the plain wooden sticks fixed to the ends. I would miss describing our neighborhood to him and laughing at his wicked comments.

The small inner courtyard was quiet. I tucked the scroll into my sleeve and stood for a moment in the doorway, the soft morning air and stillness moving through me like a meditation. Should I chance calling the Rat Dragon? One last look before the ceremony? Maybe this time he would acknowledge me. I took a deep breath, narrowing my mind's eye to the north-northwest. A shimmering outline of the dragon formed, a hint of the huge horselike head and snake-shaped body. Then the edges of the vision began to fray.

My legs buckled as a hollowing drain dragged at my consciousness. I snatched all of my self back, falling painfully onto my knees. I had never felt anything like it before. Panting, I leaned against the doorframe and turned my attention inward, clumsily tracing the flow of my *Hua*. There didn't seem to be any damage, and my strength was already returning. Maybe it had happened because the Rat Dragon was ascending today. I took a few deep breaths, then pulled myself upright and headed slowly toward the kitchen. At least the strange mind-sight that had brought me to this day was still within me. Whether that meant anything to the Rat Dragon would soon be made clear.

At the kitchen door, I slipped off my shoes, then stepped inside. Kuno was standing over the stoves, stirring my master's morning soup. The smell of the rich broth and steaming buns made my stomach pinch. I licked my lips, remembering the piece of bread hidden in my room.

"Eon?" Chart peered around the leg of the preparation table. He rolled his eyes at my finery. "Little . . . Lord."

Kuno sniffed at me as I brushed past him to squat painfully beside Chart.

"There'll be hell to pay if he dirties those new robes of yours," Kuno said. He stamped across the kitchen and disappeared into the dry-goods pantry.

Chart twisted closer to me. He touched the bottom of the tunic. "So soft . . . like a girl's bottom."

"How would you know?" I scoffed.

"Know more . . . than you." He waggled his eyebrows. "Maids think . . . poor Chart . . . doesn't know what he's doing."

I shook my head at his cheerful lewdness. "I have something

for you," I said, pulling out the scroll and placing it on his mat.

He touched it, his eyes wide. "Real paper?" He looked up at me quizzically. "You know . . . don't read."

"It's not words," I said. "Open it."

He hoisted himself onto an elbow and slowly pulled apart the wooden handles. I watched his puzzlement smooth into understanding. Then his face tightened.

"I know it's not very good," I said quickly. "But see, that is the crossroad at the bottom of the laneway." I pointed to the place on the scroll. "And that's old Rehon's pig. See, I've drawn it in the middle of Kellon the Moneylender's vegetable garden. . . ." I stopped. Chart had turned his face away.

"I know it's not very good," I said again.

Chart shook his head, pushing his face into his shoulder.

Was he crying? I sat back. Chart did not cry.

He touched my hand, a clumsy press of fingers against mine, and took a deep, trembling breath.

"I have . . . something . . . for you, too," he said. He glanced at the pantry doorway. "Quick . . . before Kuno comes."

I held out my hand, expecting more bread or cheese. Instead, something heavy hit my palm. A coin, covered in grime. I ran my thumb over it and saw a flash of gold—a Tiger coin, more than three months' wages for a freeman. And a certain flogging if discovered.

"Where'd you get it?" I whispered.

"I . . . not stuck . . . to this mat," he said, grinning slyly.

"Did you steal it from the master?"

He pulled himself closer, his hand batting the question away.

"Heard Kuno . . . and Irsa talking . . . last night," he whispered, his shoulders and throat tense with the strain of lowering his voice. I bent my head until I felt his warm breath against my ear. "Master . . . sell you . . . to salt farm . . . if you not Dragoneye. Sell you . . . like the boys before." I flinched back, but Chart raised his body to follow me, frowning with the effort. "If you not chosen . . . you must run away. To . . . the islands." Panting, he dropped back against his mat.

Run away? But I was in bond—I had always belonged to a master. I tightened my grip on the coin. That was not quite true. There had been a time when there was a family and no master.

"What about you?" I said.

Chart snorted. "Run?"

I held out the coin. "You should keep it," I said. "You and Rilla might need it."

Chart caught hold of my hand. The muscles in his neck twitched and bulged as he struggled to hold his head still. "Mother knows. She said . . . give it to you."

I stared at him. Rilla thought I should run away, too?

"You still here?" Kuno said, swinging a sack of beans onto the table. Chart and I jerked apart. "You'd better get moving or you'll keep the master waiting."

Chart closed my fingers around the coin. "Good-bye, Eon. . . . Go with . . . good fortune."

I stood up and bowed, low and deep—a bow for an honored

friend. As I straightened, he turned his face away, his narrow jaw set.

"Thank you," I whispered.

He didn't look up, but I saw his hand clutch the scroll closer to his chest.

Outside, I stood for a moment in the half light, steadying my own breath. Could I really run away if I was not chosen? The idea was almost as frightening as being sold back to the salt farm.

It was only a few minutes to dawn. I still had to pack my belongings. And hide the coin. The warm weight of it pulsed in my hand. Where would it be safe? I pushed my feet back into the leather shoes and ran across the courtyard. Perhaps in my brush-and-ink box? I paused in the doorway, my eyes adjusting to the gloom. Just inside was a straw travel basket, already packed. Rilla must have done it for me. If I was chosen, my master would have it delivered to me at the Rat Dragon Hall. I opened my hand and studied the coin. It wasn't big—maybe I could press it into the soft back of my ink block.

What was I thinking? If I failed and had to run away, I could not come back for my things. The coin had to stay with me. I looked down at my costly silk tunic. Would it fit in the tea pouch? But Chart always said you should never hide two forbidden things together. The hem? I turned the tunic over and studied the fine stitching. If I unpicked a section covered by the embroidered tail of a dragon, I could slide the coin inside and no one would see its outline.

I found my eating knife and slit a stitch, carefully pulling out a section to save the thread. Nearby, the dawn bell rang. It was nearly time. With shaking hands, I worked the coin into the hem. Would it show? I smoothed the tunic back in place and tried to gauge the effect. It dragged at the cloth, but not enough to be noticed. I lifted the shelf in the clothespress and pulled my needle tube out of the hole I had carved in the wood. Dolana, my only friend at the salt farm, had given it to me before she died of the coughing—a precious gift. My fingers were clumsy as I tried to thread the fine silk into a needle. Finally it slipped through the eye. The hem closed with a few large stitches. Just as I tied off and cut the strand, Irsa appeared at the doorway.

"What are you doing?" she demanded.

I let the tunic drop. "Loose thread." I closed my fist around the needle, hiding it from view. "Is the master ready?"

Irsa eyed the tunic suspiciously. "He says you are to go to the front courtyard."

I ostentatiously tossed my knife back into the travel basket. "Thank you."

She didn't move.

"I know where the front courtyard is, Irsa."

She crossed her arms. "You're a sorry creature for the master to pin his hopes on, Eon. But I hope for your sake, and ours, that you succeed."

She sniffed and left. I waited for a moment, listening to her retreat, then slid the needle back into its case and pushed it back into the hole. It would be hard to leave it behind, but I could not risk packing a woman's tool. Irsa or one of the other maids would no doubt go through the basket as soon as I left.

The importance of the day weighed down on me. There was no time to eat Chart's bread, but it didn't matter; I was no longer hungry. Perhaps the rat would find it; another offering to the Rat Dragon.

I scanned the room one last time. And suddenly I knew that it *was* the last time; if I failed, I would run away. The knowledge swept over me like a monsoon rain. I turned and stepped into the courtyard, the life-changing decision marked only by the twitching ear of the kitchen cat.

My master was already waiting in the front courtyard. The wood and wicker palanquin he used for official journeys was resting on the lift stones. A hired team of four bearers was standing patiently between the carrying shafts—two at the front, two at the rear—their broad shoulders padded with thick leather. I caught their curious glances as I hurried past. They were not the only ones; the whole household had gathered in the doorways and windows of the house to watch our departure. I searched for a friendly face; Chart was not there—too far for him to crawl—but Lon raised a hand in salute, and Kuno, to my surprise, ducked his head in a quick bow. Then I saw Rilla standing behind my master, her eyes properly lowered. She glanced up as I approached, her quick smile giving me courage.

I bowed to my master. He was wearing his court robes: a long midnight-blue tunic with silver embroidery, girdled by a red sash of intricately pleated silk. His colorless face was framed by a high fluted collar, the graceful curve making his gaunt hollows even more pronounced. He looked old, and he looked ill.

"Turn," he said, motioning with an elegant blackwood staff.

I obeyed, the swirl of the tunic making the coin hit the back of my thigh. It was hard not to look down to check the strength of my stitching.

"Good," he said. He turned to Rilla. "My cap?"

She carefully placed the red skullcap on his shaved head. He glanced around the silent courtyard, then held out his hand, leaning on Rilla's outstretched arm to step up into the palanquin.

"The tribute?" he said, settling himself down on the silk-cushioned seat.

Rilla held up a small wooden casket, highly polished and inlaid with sea pearl. He placed it on his knee, then beckoned to me.

I gingerly climbed into the palanquin, smoothing my tunic before sitting next to him on the cushions. The wicker walls seemed very flimsy. I pushed against the side next to me. It creaked.

My master studied me for a moment from under hooded eyelids. "I can assure you, Eon, it is quite safe."

"Yes, Master."

He tapped his staff on the shoulder of the bearer in front of him. "We shall depart," he ordered.

As one, the bearers bent and lifted the palanquin. I braced my feet against the floor and grabbed the canopy post as they hoisted us onto their shoulders. So high. Rilla was looking up at me, mouthing the words "good luck." I tried to smile, but the ground was too far away and the strange lurching motion made me dizzy. I closed my eyes. When I finally opened them, we were already passing the stone lions at the front gate.

I looked back. Only Rilla was still in the courtyard, her hand raised. Before I could wave, we turned into the side road and she disappeared from view. Did she know I would miss her?

I faced the front again, warily watching the two lead bearers. They seemed to know what they were doing; perhaps we would not fall to our deaths. My master bent his head down to me.

"Has the tea been effective?" he asked quietly.

"Yes, Master."

He grunted his satisfaction. "And you have perfected the bridging forms?"

I nodded.

He stared ahead, the skin around his eyes tight with strain. "The council has grudgingly accepted the Reverse Horse Dragon Second variation," he said. "They did so only because they do not consider you a viable candidate. Ascendant Ido, in particular, was dismissive."

There was loathing in my master's voice. He had long distrusted the current Rat Dragoneye. Lord Ido had come to full

Dragoneye status early, due to the sudden death of his master. Too early, according to some. Now that today started the Year of the Rat, Ido was the ascendant Dragoneye. For one year his powers would be doubled and he would lead the Dragoneye Council in its task of manipulating the earth energies for the good of the empire. He would not have made it easy for my master to plead my case.

"When you are chosen, be very careful of Lord Ido."

"Yes, master," I said, then cast a silent apology to the gods for my master's arrogance.

He rubbed at his eyes. "Ido will persecute you for the very fact that you were *my* candidate. You will, of course, have to attend him for training in the Dragon Arts, but avoid him when you can. He is"—my master paused, searching for the right words—"treacherous and unpredictable. You will also be spending a good deal of time with Master Tellon, learning the Staminata. He is a good man, but keep your wits about you—he is a keen observer."

"The Staminata?"

A smile touched my master's bloodless lips. "The council would strip me of my Heuris status if they knew I'd spoken to you about the Staminata." He looked sideways at me. "Although such an indiscretion pales in comparison to what else I have done." He bent closer. "The Staminata is the mental and physical training required to become a full Dragoneye. It is intended to help the apprentice bear the energy drains required to commune with the dragon he serves."

"Is it difficult, Master? The communing?" I asked, sensing that he was, for once, in an expansive mood.

He stared down at the casket on his lap. "Difficult?" Again, he smiled humorlessly. "Is it difficult to take the land's life force and twist it to your bidding? To clear energy blocks built of ancient dreads and narrow thinking? To untangle the past, present, and future and knit it into another possibility?" He sighed. "Yes, Eon, it is difficult and painful and exhilarating. And it will kill you." He looked over at me, his eyes dark. "As it has killed me."

It was said almost as a challenge, but I did not look away.

"Better to die in such service," I said, tightening my grip on the post, "than to die laboring in a salt farm."

He blinked at my vehemence. "There are worse ways to die than choking on salt," he said softly.

I had to look away then; away from the strange softening of his eyes.

"And the Staminata, Master?" I asked quickly. "Will I be able to do it?"

"It is not like the Approach Sequence," he said. "There will be no swordmaster drilling you endlessly. The Staminata does not rely upon brute strength or agility—it is a mixture of meditation and movement. Once you have learned the basic form, it is up to you to develop your mastery and thus your mental and physical stamina."

"It's what you do in the Moon Garden, isn't it?" I said.

He tilted his head to the side. "And how would you know that, Eon?"

I shook my head, unwilling to answer with the truth. Nor would my master want to hear that I *knew* by intuition—the "irrational" knowledge only claimed by women.

"Yes, it is what I practice in the Moon Garden," he said. "For all the good it does me." He looked out ahead with a bitter smile. "Until recently, I did not regret my calling. Now, I find that I resent not having a future." When he turned back to me, I saw the fierce light in his eyes that I had seen during the cleansing ritual. He reached toward me, as though to stroke my cheek. I flinched, and he dropped his hand, his face once more a mask of cool irony.

"That bargain was made a long time ago," he said, almost to himself.

I drew back into the corner of the seat and brushed my hand over the coin. Would it be enough to buy my way to the islands? My master's gaze was pressing against me. I turned away and pretended to be absorbed by the passing view. We had turned into the main thoroughfare that led to the Dragon Arena. It was just past dawn, but the street was lined with curious onlookers, the house-shop shutters already open and the vendors hawking for business. A man noticed our palanquin and yelled, his call rippling along the street until we became the focus of attention. Faces turned up to watch us pass by: excited, skeptical, searching, disdainful. Then a murmur started, the soft words shifting through the crowd like leaves shivering in a breeze: *It's the cripple.*

I straightened in the seat, my hands in tight fists, and kept my eyes fixed on the banners that billowed above the entrance to the arena. Every so often, out of the corner of my eye, I saw the familiar jab of a ward-evil gesture.

"Does your leg pain you?" my master suddenly asked. In the four years I'd been in his service, he had never asked me about my leg.

"Not a lot," I said, stumbling over the lie.

He gave a curt nod, his face even more unreadable. "But it has proved useful."

The lead bearer called to his team, and we stopped outside the gated entrance of the arena. A huge gilded carving of the Mirror Dragon—the emperor's symbol—swirled across the lintel. On either side, the heavy supporting pillars were decorated with two ferocious door gods, their carved swordhands rubbed flat by years of people seeking protection. I peered through the crisscrossed slats of the heavy gate but only saw a dim corridor and the bright flare of sand.

The lead bearer looked to my master for instructions.

"Follow the wall until we come to the Portal of the Twelve Heavenly Animals," my master said, pointing to the left.

We moved slowly around the periphery of the arena, passing the bright jade and gold Emperor's Gate, through which the Eternal Son of Heaven would make his entrance. The grand boulevard that spanned the distance from the gate to the outer precinct of the Imperial Palace was already lined with people, most holding handmade red flags for the new Ascendant and apprentice. Last Ascension Day I stood in that crowd and watched as Amon, the new Pig Dragon apprentice, was show-ered with flags of good fortune on his way to the Dragon Halls. Would I be walking behind the emperor's horse in a few hours, a rain of red paper falling on my head?

"Sit still, Eon," my master ordered.

I leaned back into the seat, turning away from the crowd. Ahead, an open palanquin was waiting outside the Portal of the Twelve Heavenly Animals. We stopped a little way behind it and I recognized the delicate shape of Dillon's head and the fat, neckless form of Heuris Bellid. Their bearer team slowly lowered the palanquin onto two large lift stones. Dillon climbed out, turning to help his master down to the ground. In braver mo-ments, when we were alone, Dillon called him "Master Belly." I stifled a smile as Bellid adjusted the red pleated sash over his huge gut, then waved the palanquin away.

Two gate officials stepped out from the small guardhouse. They were both of similar height and stiff bearing, but one wore the white robes of mourning to symbolize the waning year, while the other was dressed in shimmering green for the New Year.

"The man in the New Year robes is one of Ido's supporters," my master said softly. "He will be a good gauge of how things stand in the council."

The officials bowed to Bellid and Dillon, who returned the courtesy. Then Bellid gave a carved box to New Year. I glanced down at the casket on my master's knee. Inside was the tradi-tional tribute for the retiring Dragoneye. Each Heuris paid for the honor of presenting his candidate, softening the blow of lost earnings for the departing lord. But this time there was no old Dragoneye—he had died many years ago, leaving his then-young apprentice, Ido, to serve the Rat Dragon. Presumably Lord Ido would get the tributes. No wonder my master looked pained.

New Year opened Bellid's offering and studied the contents. They must have been adequate, for the box was closed and taken away by a guard. Bowing again, the two officials stepped back. Heuris Bellid and Dillon walked through the circular gateway to muted cheers from the crowd.

"Forward," my master ordered.

We moved into position in front of the Portal of the Twelve Heavenly Animals. I had always thought it was the most beautiful gate in the city—even more graceful than the huge Gate of Supreme Benevolence, the entrance to the Imperial Palace. The portal was a complete circle, the twelve dragon animals carved around it in order of the cycle of ascension: Rat, Ox, Tiger, Rabbit, Dragon, Snake, Horse, Goat, Monkey, Rooster, Dog and Pig. The imperial engineers had set the huge carved circle on a system of pulleys and locks so that on the first day of the New Year, Ascension Day, it could be rotated one position, moving the new Dragon of Ascension to the top of the gateway. The Pig Dragon was still in supremacy, but as soon as the Rat Dragon chose its new apprentice, the two gate officials would turn the circle to indicate the beginning of the New Year, and the start of a new twelve-year cycle. A most auspicious day. Nearby, one of the hawker stalls was already baking cinnamon mooncakes for the First Day celebrations, the smell creating the phantom taste of buttery spice on my tongue. My stomach tightened. I should have eaten the bread.

The bearers lowered our palanquin smoothly onto the lift stones. I quickly climbed out of the cabin, glad to be on the ground again, and handed my master down.

"Wait for my summons after the ceremony," he said, dismissing the team.

Old Year and New Year bowed to us in perfect unison.

"Do you bring one of the twelve who seek to serve the Rat Dragon?" New Year said. His eyes flicked over to me with hostility. Behind us, the murmuring crowd quieted. I felt as though a thousand disapproving eyes were upon me. A Dragoneye was their only way to buy themselves some good fortune; why was a boy of such obvious ill fortune offering himself as a candidate?

My master and I bowed.

"I, Heuris Brannon, bring one who seeks to serve the Rat Dragon," my master said.

"Then present your tribute to the Dragoneye who has served, who now makes way for the new Dragoneye and the new apprentice," Old Year said. At least his gaze was neutral.

My master opened the lid of the inlaid box. A heavy gold amulet, worked in the shape of a coiled dragon, lay on smooth black velvet. I sucked in a breath. It had to be worth a fortune; enough to keep the household for months. How did my master manage such a gift? He stared at it for a moment, then straightened his shoulders.

"I present this tribute to the Dragoneye who makes way for the new; may his strength be restored and his life be long."

He passed the box to New Year, who shot a strange, challenging look at his colleague. Old Year frowned and shook his head slightly.

New Year snapped the box shut. "It is acceptable," he said curtly, passing it to the guard. "Go through."

The two officials bowed and stepped back.

"Thank you," my master said dryly.

We walked slowly through the gate and into a long, dim passageway. Behind us, a huge cheer erupted. For me? I looked back, my heart lifting with the sound. But the gate officials were greeting Heuris Kane and Baret, the crowd favorite. No cheers, then, for the cripple.

"Another of Ido's minions," my master said, following my gaze to Kane. "But do not fret, Eon. Ido may be able to bully and buy a following, but even he cannot influence a dragon. And it would seem that his supporters are not inclined to stand against the council. At least for now. We shall see what happens when he ascends."

Although I wore thin silk, sweat was collecting under my arms and around the waistband of my trousers. My heat had raised the smell of the cleansing herbs again and I longed to scrub off the relentless perfume. Ahead, a half circle of light flickered with passing figures.

We walked out of the cool tunnel into a long chamber lit by lamps fixed along the walls. The smell of sweat and burning sesame oil cloyed the air, and a tense silence amplified the shuffling footsteps of gray-robed officials as they crossed the stone floor. At the far end of the room, the other candidates were kneeling in meditation, their ceremonial swords laid out in front of them, tip to hilt. Three gaps had been left in the row, spaces for Dillon, Baret, and me. In the ballot to determine order of appearance, Swordmaster Ranne had drawn me fourth position—an ill number and probably not drawn by chance. All of the kneeling candidates had their eyes closed, the yellowish light making their faces look like death masks. I shivered, turning to the comfort of the natural light that filtered down a wide ramp in front of me. The way to the bright sands of the arena.

A thin young man, wearing a red feather pinned to his gray robes, stepped up to us. He swept a curious glance over me before bowing low.

"Heuris Brannon, Candidate Eon. I am Van, sixth-level official to the council," he said softly. "I am here to assist you today. Please come this way to collect your ceremonial swords."

I swallowed, trying to dredge up some wet in my mouth. I did not want to hold those swords again. A week ago, Ranne had taken us all to the huge armory of the council's treasury to be fitted with the precious weapons kept just for ceremonial use. I was the last to be measured and the old armsman, a scar puckering one side of his face from mouth to jowl, took a long time to find the right swords for me. He had stolidly ignored the sighs and shiftings of Ranne and the other candidates, making me hold pair after pair of extravagantly jeweled swords, tip-down, judging their length and weight against my lopsided body. Finally, he frowned into the dim depths of the armory, then disappeared for a few minutes, bringing back a plainer pair of swords. The two hand guards were decorated by a simple ring of alternating moonstones and jade, each translucent gem set in a silver moon crescent.

"Powerful luck bringers," he said, brushing a thick thumb over the stones. "These two haven't been used for a long time— too short and light for most. But they'll do you fine."

He held them out and I closed my hands around the leather-bound grips. A roiling anger burned through me, blinding me with bursting lights, flooding my mouth with a sour metallic taste. It was a vicious rage, powerful, cold, and at its center, very, very frightened. Or was that me? Startled, I let go. The swords clattered onto the marble floor.

"Idiot!" Ranne roared, starting toward me with his fist raised.

Calmly, the armsman stepped in between us. "No harm done, Swordmaster. No harm done," he said, scooping up the swords. He turned a thoughtful gaze on me as he deftly racked them in a large wooden stand. "They must have very old energy," he said cryptically.

I opened my mouth to say I didn't want them, but he had already bowed and retreated into the shadows of his domain.

Afterward, on the walk back to the school, I wondered who could have put such violent feeling into the steel. It was part of the Dragoneye art to imbue physical items with the capacity to absorb or deflect energy. Some items absorbed the good energy that surrounds us—the *Lin Hua*—and some deflect the bad energy—the *Gan Hua*—so that the flow of good fortune could be enhanced and directed. But I had never heard of rage being woven into the fabric of a thing. However it had happened, I was reluctant to touch the swords again.

I followed my master and Van to an arched doorway set near the ramp. The squat figure of Heuris Bellid blocked the threshold for a moment, then moved awkwardly into the main chamber. Dillon trailed behind him, holding two large swords. Bluish circles ringed his eyes, and his face was stark with the pallor of hunger. Did I look as strained? I certainly felt as though a touch would snap me like a winter-dead branch.

"Is it true? You're not doing the Mirror Dragon Third?" he asked as we passed each other.

I nodded and saw something flicker across his face.

Relief.

I stared after him, a dry ache closing my throat. The relief was not for me, it was for himself. I was no longer a real rival for the Rat Dragon's attentions.

I could not blame him. Fear made misers of us all.

The arena armory was a small cavelike room dominated by a wooden stand built for twenty-four swords, the rests cushioned with fine leather. Only two pairs were still racked—mine and Baret's. The old armsman standing beside it was the one who had fitted me. He promptly slid out my swords and held the hilts up to me.

"Go on then, boy," he said, his familiarity prompting a disapproving huff from Van.

I gritted my teeth as my hands closed around the grips again. A faint taste of metal, but no rage. Instead, there was another kind of power, lying in wait like that expectant stillness between breaths.

"Not so bad this time, hey?" the armsman asked.

"How did you know?" I whispered.

He smiled, his skin stretching white around the scar. "A good sword is an extension of its master."

"Armsman, return to your post," Van said, bristling at the breach of protocol. "Candidate Eon, please come this way."

I wanted to ask the old man who had used the swords before me, but Van was herding me out of the small chamber. I tucked the blades, blunt edge up, under my arms and followed my master.

Outside, Heuris Kane and Baret were waiting to enter. Baret was leaning against the wall, his athletic body and smooth patrician face a study in arrogance. My master bowed, intent on passing, but was stopped by Kane's hand on his arm.

"Brannon," Kane said, his voice low, "I would like to speak with you." He flicked his fingers at Van, who quickly moved away.

"Yes, Heuris Kane?" my master said, his dislike plain in his stiff formality.

Baret smirked at me with his arms crossed, each half-hidden hand curled into a ward-evil sign.

"I have heard Eon will be using an ancient variation of the sequence today," Kane said, staring down at me until I shifted under his gaze. He blinked too often and in a strange pattern of three.

My master inclined his head. "You have heard correctly. It is a variation from the fourth Chronicle of Detra."

A sly smile pursed Kane's thin lips. "I am sure your records are impeccable on the matter." His small eyes blinked rapidly, his gaze darting down to my bad leg. "Of course, one wonders how changing the sequence that honors both the emperor and the Lost Dragon will be received."

"The council has verified the precedent," my master said quickly.

Kane waved a dismissive hand. "So I have heard. But then, it is not the Council who has the final say in this matter, is it?" He bowed. "I wish you and Eon good fortune." He continued into the armory.

As Baret passed me, I heard him whisper, "You don't have a chance, Eon-*jah*. You are as weak as a girl."

He was inside the armory before I made sense of his words. There was no true knowledge in the jeer, but it hit home, splitting my tight kernel of control.

Van came hurrying toward us. He said something, but I heard no meaning in the sounds. I stared over at the row of kneeling boys. They were the real candidates; I was a girl, a cripple, an abomination. What was I doing? What madness was in my master? How could he think we would succeed? He was wrong—I could not do it. We had to stop. We had to get away. Before we were discovered. Before we were killed.

I grasped at his robes, my sword tips tangling in the silk.

"Master, we must—"

His hand closed on my shoulder. Bone and sinew ground together, radiating agony.

"I will say good-bye now, Eon," my master said, his voice an order. His thumb dug into the soft hollow of my shoulder, squeezing away breath and movement. "Our fortunes lie with you now." He shook me slightly, his eyes locked on mine. "Do you understand?"

I nodded. The edges of the room faded into a gray haze.

"Get in line."

He pushed me away, the sudden release making me stagger. There was no choice. No going back.

I made my way around the row of kneeling candidates, all of them with their eyes closed, praying to serve the Rat Dragon. I would pray for something different: a chance to escape. I placed my swords on the stone floor in front of my position. Number four: the number of death. Clumsily, I settled onto my knees. The hard edge of the hidden coin dug into the back of my thigh, the pain joining the hot pulsing in my hip and shoulder. I felt my master's gaze still on me, but I did not look up. There was nothing in his face that I wanted to see.

CHAPTER FOUR

WE KNELT ON the floor for two hours. For the first hour, I carefully tensed and relaxed my muscles from toes to scalp, a method my master had taught me to keep my body warm and flexible. By the second hour, the cold was overcoming my efforts, locking my joints. I made tight fists and released them, welcoming the sting of warmer blood.

To my right, Quon was shifting against his haunches, his face twisted into a grimace. On the other side, Lanell was working his hands like creeping caterpillars up and down the front of his thighs, bunching the silk.

Suddenly, at the top of the ramp, a ball of excited voices unraveled into a single, harsh shout.

"Get out of my way."

A group of officials burst out of the rampway and clustered into a gray barricade, halting the progress of a tall, solidly built man. An older official stepped forward, his large ruby pin of rank catching the light. He bowed low.

"Lord Ido, no further! Please."

What was Lord Ido doing here? It was against tradition for the ascending Dragoneye to have contact with the candidates. I had only ever seen him from afar playing his part in official ceremonies, his features smudged by distance. Now he was just lengths away. Along the row, the other candidates stirred at the disturbance.

I squinted, trying to distinguish more detail against the bright glare of the ramp opening. He wore his oiled black hair in the double queue of the Dragoneye, looped high into a knot at the crown of his head. I caught the planes of his face as he moved, broad strokes painted by light and shadow: a high scholar's brow, a long nose like the foreign devils the emperor had allowed into the city, and a jutting dark beard. But it was the menacing power in his body that made the officials scatter before him. Lord Ido did not move like a Dragoneye. He moved like a warrior.

He swept through the officials, using his forearm to knock the slighter men aside. Every move was decisive, with none of the careful conservation of energy that marked the other Dragoneyes. Although he wore the traditional robes of the Ascendant, they did not obscure the line of his body: the cutaway coat of deep blue silk—the costly fabric barely discernible beneath heavy gold embroidery—showed the breadth of his shoulder and chest, and the pale blue trousers cross-bound from ankle to knee accentuated the muscular shape of his legs. I dropped my gaze to the ground.

"Move," he ordered. "I will see the candidates."

I straightened and knew that, all along the row, every candidate filled his chest and lengthened his spine as Lord Ido approached.

The old official scurried ahead of him. "Lord Ido," he announced to us, trying to wrest back some protocol.

Beside me, Quon hurriedly dropped into a deep bow. I followed, holding myself a finger's length above my swords, wide eyes reflected in one polished blade, bloodless lips in the other.

"Greetings, Lord Ido," we chanted.

"Sit back," he said. "Show me your faces."

Obediently, we all rose from our bows, eyes properly lowered.

His feet, in gold-painted shoes, passed by me. I chanced a quick look up at him, expecting to see his back. Instead, our gazes met, and I saw the strange pale amber of his eyes.

"Who are you, boy?"

"Eon, Lord."

He studied me for a moment. It was like being staked out, naked and helpless, under the burn of the sun.

"Brannon's cripple," he finally said. "Be ashamed. You rob an able-bodied boy of his chance."

I heard the intake of breath along the line of candidates, but my own air was gone—knocked out of me like a blow to the stomach. Even if I was to win the attention of the Rat Dragon,

Lord Ido would never accept me as his apprentice. I shrank back, curling into a smaller target, but he was done with me. Slowly, he paced along the row until he stopped in front of Baret, in tenth position.

"You are Kane's candidate?" he demanded.

"Yes, Lord," Baret said.

A yelp of outrage and the sound of scuffling snapped us out of our stiff obedience. Quon shuffled forward to peer down the line. I hesitated, but then rose onto my knees, craning above Lanell.

The old official was pulling at Lord Ido's arm, trying to release the Dragoneye's hands cupped around Baret's head.

"Lord Ido, you go too far!" he cried.

"Away, fool." Lord Ido shook off the old man's grip. "You answer to me now."

"No. The council is still Lord Meram's." The official ducked back and grabbed at Lord Ido's arm. "You shall not influence the ceremony."

Lord Ido swung his free hand and there was the wet crack of knuckles hitting flesh. The official fell onto his hands and knees, his cheek split over the bone. He shook his head, spraying blood into the air like a dog shaking off water. Lord Ido glared at the lesser officials who had gathered behind their colleague.

"Lord Meram stepped down in my favor last night. I am the Ascendant, and the council leader. Do any of you stand against me?"

One after the other, the officials cowered into bows.

Lord Ido grunted and jerked his head at the prostrate official.

"Take him away."

Two men hurried across and helped the old man to stand. Lord Ido spun back to face us.

"Get in line," he ordered.

We scrambled into our positions, the row subtly curving as everyone shifted to watch Lord Ido. He placed his hands on Baret's head, thumbs together on his forehead. What was he doing? Uneasy whispering rippled through the ranks of officials. Lord Ido took a deep breath and seemed to draw himself upward, as though dragging energy from the earth.

Then I was slammed back against my heels by the power that burst from him.

It was as though his flesh had become glass. I saw the seven points of power in his body, pulsing in their own colors from spine to crown: red, orange, yellow, green, blue, indigo, and purple. All of them connected by silvery-white streams of *Hua* surging through him from ground to hands and into Baret. In all of this bright rushing glory, my mind's eye was drawn to the green heart-point in his chest. The center of compassion. It was smaller, duller, its flow of *Hua* thin and stuttering.

And then it was all gone.

I slumped forward, sucking in air, feeling the puzzled eyes of Quon and Lanell on me. Lord Ido was doubled over, gasping, his face ashen. He looked up and for a second our gazes met, his shrewd eyes widening as he saw that I had been affected by his power. Then his attention was caught by the arrival of two men at the opening of the ramp.

Quon grabbed my shoulder, his fingernails digging through the silk.

"What did he do to him?" he hissed. We both looked at Baret, who was rocking and moaning, his head buried in the cradle of his arms. "What did you see?"

"I think he marked Baret with his own *Hua*."

Quon let go of me. "Surely that's not allowed. It must be against the rules."

He turned to the officials, but they were all on their knees staring at the floor. His body sagged.

"It's not fair," he said, his voice tiny with defeat. "He's stacking the odds."

Quon was right. If Lord Ido had marked Baret with his own *Hua*, then Baret would have a much greater chance of being chosen by the Rat Dragon. Then Heuris Kane would reap the bonus and the 20 percent tithe, and my master would be ruined. I felt my own hope wither into dry despair. In one bold act, Lord Ido had secured the support of Kane, Baret, and their powerful families, asserted his authority over the council, and cowed us, the other candidates. No wonder my master called him treacherous. The ruthless efficiency of his tactics made me shiver. But at least I was not crying, like Quon.

Lord Ido straightened, his body and breath back to normal. He glanced at Baret.

"Be still," he snapped.

Immediately, Baret stopped rocking, a whimper of pain escaping as he lifted his head.

"Last night, the Dragoneye Council ruled that the ceremony has become too removed from the traditions of our esteemed ancestors," Lord Ido said, and from his tone, it was plain that it was his ruling and the council had just fallen into line. He started to pace along the row. "It was decided that there will be a return to ceremonial combat rather than exhibition."

It took a moment for his words to make sense. Ceremonial combat? Fighting. I would have to fight someone? I felt my body lock into icy panic.

"You can't do that," Quon sobbed, desperation making him rash. "We haven't trained for it."

Lord Ido rounded on him. "Mewling coward," he snarled. "You are not worthy of the Rat Dragon."

Quon dropped into a kowtow, his forehead hitting the floor with a crack. Lord Ido eyed him for a moment, then resumed his pacing.

"According to a very popular historical scroll, the ascending Dragoneye can invoke ceremonial combat if the council agrees." His eyes swept along the row and found me. "An old variation in the Chronicles of Detra."

I looked away from his malicious smile.

He motioned to the two men standing at the ramp. Although they were clad in head-to-toe armor, I recognized the arrogant swagger of the stockier figure.

Ranne.

My innards cramped in familiar fear. Were we going to fight Ranne? But he was a master. Then it all made terrible sense— Baret was Ranne's favorite. Lord Ido was leaving nothing to chance.

"I am told that you have all trained with Swordmasters Ranne and Jin-pa," Lord Ido said as they approached him and bowed. "They will share the honor of sparring with you for the pleasure of the Rat Dragon and our most Heavenly Emperor."

Ranne turned to look at us, a gloved hand on his hip. Instead of the usual lacquered leather he wore during training, his armor was made of metal scales, the helmet edged with a curtain of mail to protect the neck, the polished breastplate engraved with the character for valor.

"This will be similar to the combat training we have done all year," he said. "However, the sequences will not be in or-der of ascendance. They will be random. Do you understand? Swordmaster Jin-pa and I may start with the Rat sequence, or the Ox sequence or the Horse sequence. It will be different for each of you. All of the twelve sequences will be used, but not in the order of ascendance. A good test of reflexes and anticipation."

A low murmur of apprehension rolled along the row. Most of our training had been directed toward a solo exhibition of the sequences in strict order. Not toward combat. Not in ran-dom order.

Jin-pa stepped out from behind Ranne. His breastplate bore the character for duty. I had only ever worked with him once; a fair man who had shown me how to adapt a kick for my lame leg. He took his helmet off, tucking it under his arm. The padding had made indentations on his long face, giving him the look of a kindly death's-head.

"Boys, do not be alarmed. You know all of the sequences. It is now just a matter of trusting your training and letting your movements flow from your *Hua*," he said bracingly. "The rules of ceremonial combat are just the same as training combat—contact with the flat of the sword or the butt of the handle only. And remember, this is about showing your technique and stamina. Concentrate on recognizing the first form of each sequence, then—"

Ranne shifted irritably. "They're as prepared as they're going to be," he interrupted, ignoring Jin-pa's dark look. "Now it is time to meet the challenge and do honor to their masters and ancestors."

"Well said, Swordmaster Ranne," Lord Ido said, waving Jin-pa back. "Will you spar with the odds or the evens?"

Ranne stared down the line as if considering his decision. Through the eye slits of his helmet, I saw his gaze flicker over Baret. How early in our training had Lord Ido planned all this?

"Evens," Ranne said.

Foul acid rose into my throat. Number four—the number of death. Had Ranne drawn it for me, knowing I would be at his mercy?

Lord Ido turned to us. "Those with even numbers will spar with Swordmaster Ranne. The odd numbers will spar with Swordmaster Jin-pa. Is that clear?"

"Yes, Lord Ido," we obediently chanted. I heard Quon's voice break with relief.

The sound of distant drums and trumpets sent the senior officials scurrying to the ramp. Quon and I exchanged knowing glances: the emperor had started the short journey from palace to arena. It would not be long now.

Last year I had stood beside the roadway, one of the crowd watching the long procession that escorted His Imperial Majesty to the ceremony. The marvelous sight was still bright in my mind. I knew that, outside, the wide boulevard would now be filled with ranks of drummers and trumpeters, playing a march composed especially for the day. Behind them would come rows and rows of armored mace wielders, swordsmen, and lancers with silk flags flying from the blades of their weapons. There would be twelve men on matched black horses riding in rows of three and carrying the huge fluttering banners of the dragons, followed by lines and lines of eunuch footmen in the dark blue livery of the inner household, each carrying an incense burner releasing spicy perfume into the air. One hundred lantern carriers would be next, their carved lights swinging on tall gilded sticks. Then the young noblemen currently in favor would stride by in their finery, calling the royal presence with chants of their family's fealty. The crowd would drop to their knees in the swirling dust as the handsome heir, Prince Kygo, rode his horse past. Then the emperor, grave and majestic on a white stallion bridled in gold and pearl, would pass by, surrounded by one hundred imperial guardsmen in tight formation, each armed with a pair of wicked serrated blades held in crossed salute.

It would take at least one half bell for the emperor to enter the arena and ascend the throne set above the darkened mirror of the Lost Dragon. Then another half bell before the ceremony began. One hour before I bowed to the Heavenly Master. Before I faced Ranne's swords.

The Mirror Dragon Third sequence! Did Ranne know I had permission to replace it with the Reverse Horse Dragon Second?

An official wearing the ruby rank ran up to Lord Ido and dropped to one knee, delivering a message.

I had to get to Ranne. Make him understand that I didn't have to do the Mirror Dragon Third.

Lord Ido nodded to the official, the predatory lines of his face tightening in anticipation. "Candidates, go now with your council official. Listen carefully to his instructions," he said. "You will have a short time to prepare before Swordmaster Ranne and Swordmaster Jin-pa call you into position. I wish you all good fortune."

He sent one more searching glance down the row, then strode toward the ramp.

As if given a signal, the twelve officials hurried over to us in a neat line, their bodies bending into bows like windblown wheat as they passed the Dragoneye. Van stopped in front of me and squatted, ducking his head in a quick courtesy.

"Candidate Eon, please come this way," he said. "Do you wish for water now or later?"

I pushed myself upward, every muscle resisting movement. "I must speak to Swordmaster Ranne," I said.

Van stood gracefully, brushing down his long gray robe. "It is my duty to make sure you know the imperial protocol," he said. "And then you will have time to prepare for the ceremony. Do you wish for water now or later?"

"Please, I *must* speak to him," I said, scanning the room. Dillon, Quon, and Baret were waiting to drink at a large water barrel while the rest of the candidates were following their officials to practice areas. Jin-pa was talking earnestly to the ruby official. Ranne was nowhere in sight. "I *must* speak to him now," I repeated. "It affects the ceremony."

"The swordmaster has accompanied Lord Ido to the arena," Van said, shrugging his helplessness. "I doubt there will be any chance to speak to him before the ceremony."

The weight of the last few days made me sway. I pressed the heels of my hands into my eyes. Surely Ranne would know about my change to the sequence.

"My master? Can I speak to my master?"

"He is not allowed to return," Van said.

I groaned.

Van's soft fingers touched my arm. "Could Swordmaster Jin-pa assist you?"

I looked up at his polite sympathy. "Yes. Yes, I could speak to him."

"Wait here."

Van crossed the floor to Jin-pa, waiting as the swordmaster finished his conversation with the senior official. I quickly picked

up my swords and tucked them under my arms, blunt-side up. I did not want Jin-pa to think I had no care for my weapons. Van bowed and relayed my request, his narrow shoulders elegantly lifting to show his mystification. Jin-pa waved me over.

I hurried to them, my steps awkward and stiff.

"What is it, boy?" Jin-pa asked as I bowed to him.

"Swordmaster, I've got permission from the council to change the Mirror Dragon Third sequence for the Reverse Horse Dragon Second," I said breathlessly. "Because of my leg. I'll be sparring with Swordmaster Ranne. Does he know, sir?"

Jin-pa nodded. "Be at ease, Eon. Both Ranne and I know of the dispensation."

I felt some of the tension drain from my body.

"Lord Ido informed us this morning," Jin-pa continued, his words tightening the coil in me again. "Now go and get some water. It will be hot in the arena."

He nodded his dismissal. I followed Van toward the water barrel, my unease increasing with every step. Ranne might know of the dispensation, but would he honor it?

In the next hour I drank water, bowed to an imaginary emperor over and over again under the critical eye of Van, and practiced the forms until my clumsy cold-ridden movements were worked into smoothness. No doubt the minutes passed normally, but it felt as though each was a second, rushing toward the call to the arena.

And then it came.

"Candidates," Ranne bawled from the bottom of the ramp, "get into position."

For a moment everyone stopped still in the room, and then from above the trumpets sounded the arrival of the emperor.

"You remember the order of events?" Van asked hurriedly, herding me toward the ramp. "You will all bow to the Eternal Lord first, then kneel at the base of the mirror of the Lost Dragon and wait until you are announced by the imperial herald."

I nodded.

"And hold that first bow for the count of ten." He pushed me into place in the line behind Ranne. "Don't look up."

"I won't." We exchanged quick nods. "Thank you, Van."

He patted my arm. "Good fortune, Eon." Then he was gone.

Across from me in Jin-pa's line, Dillon smiled awkwardly. Although his betrayal was raw, I returned the smile. We might all be pitched against one another—but the real threat was Lord Ido.

I glanced at Baret. His body seemed strangely lax and his eyes were still glazed; furrows of pain creased his forehead. The red silk around his throat was dark—someone must have doused his face in the water barrel. He looked exhausted. Had Lord Ido miscalculated? Or did he know the effect of his power and had brought Ranne in to coddle Baret through the ceremony?

"Draw into salute," Jin-pa called.

As one, we crossed our swords in front of our chests, the thin blades whirring through the air. An official wearing a red sash over his gray robes emerged from the ramp. He bowed to Ranne and Jin-pa.

"It is time," he said.

Another fanfare sounded from above. Then a clipped shout of command from Ranne. Bodies moving—beside me, in front of me. I followed, unable to think beyond the march, my feet keeping time from the memory of endless drills. Each step closer to the top of the ramp; the air warmer, light brighter, trumpets louder.

I stepped out of cool shadow and squinted against the dazzle of morning sun. We had entered a great circle of white sand. All around the edge, twelve huge mirrors faced inward, each in a heavy gold frame carved with the twelve animal signs and inlaid with jewels and jade. All of the mirrors were dark and dead, except one: the Rat Dragon mirror. It reflected rows and rows of men, the cloth and colors of their robes ranking them—the rich silks of the nobles in the nearby seats, the gold embroideries of the eleven Dragoneyes above their mirrors, the gray garbed officials in clusters, and the bright cottons and duller roughs of the city merchants and workers in the high seats—thousands of men watching us as we marched toward the emperor's throne. The slow beat of drums and the climbing call of trumpets were matched by the rumbling of the crowd. As we passed the Rat Dragon mirror, it caught the sun, flaring into eye-burning light. At its crest was a gold ruby-eyed rat, and sitting above it was Lord Ido, a large bright figure among the gray robes of the ceremony officials. Even from the ground, I felt his power. Or perhaps it was the mirror.

Sweat was sticking my tunic to the small of my back. Ranne called a halt and we stopped before the emperor, who was dressed in royal yellow and enthroned above the darkened mirror of the Lost Dragon. I dropped to my knees, the sand hot through the silk. Van's voice echoed in my head. *Count to ten. Don't look up. Don't look around.*

I lost the count. Panicking, I raised my eyes, looking for a cue to move. My gaze was pulled into the dull mirror in front of me. No reflection, just a dark blank that swallowed the day's brightness. Beside me, Quon tensed, preparing to stand. I followed his lead, pushing myself upright. For a moment, the sun rippled across the mirror's black surface, making it buckle and heave. A strange trick of the light. We marched in our two lines toward it, to wait underneath its dark expanse. A gold dragon undulated across its top, a pearl ball held in its ruby claws. I stared into the inky glass, but nothing else stirred.

At Ranne's command we turned, facing the arena, and dropped once more to our knees, swords held in crossed salute. I narrowed my eyes to soften the glare that bounced off the sand. It felt as though every bit of moisture in my body was being sucked away.

Another fanfare. This time for the imperial herald. They emerged in a neat line, a chorus of eight men matched in voice and height, crouching into bows as they ran to the center of the arena. The crowd stamped and roared. The herald, their short blue tunics like wedges of summer sky, positioned themselves into a royal octagon, smartly turning to face the audience. They raised small bronze gongs over their heads and, as one, sounded a deep resonating note. Immediately, the crowd quieted.

"The cycle of twelve turns again," they chanted in perfect unison. Each voice blended with the others to create one penetrating herald-call. "Pig turns to Rat. Apprentice turns to Dragoneye. Candidate turns to Apprentice. The cycle of twelve turns again."

The crowd whistled and stamped their approval. The men lifted the gongs again and sounded another note. It ricocheted off the mirrors, cutting through the crowd's noise to leave a sudden silence.

"The Rat Dragon seeks a new apprentice. Twelve await to show their worth. By His Imperial Majesty's approval and order of the Dragoneye Council, worth will not be found in exhibition this cycle. Worth will be found in combat!"

For a moment, there was no response. Then the crowd screamed, the hammering of feet on the boards like the fury of the thunder gods. The show had suddenly become a lot more exciting.

I licked my parched lips. Somewhere in the Heuris seats, behind Lord Ido, was my master. I tried to distinguish him in the two rows of dark robed figures set apart from the crowd by their shocked stillness. Then he moved, a familiar squaring of thin shoulders. A defiance of unbeatable odds.

The gong sounded again.

"Candidate Hannon, approach the mirrors," the imperial herald chanted. "Face Swordmaster Jin-pa and show the Rat Dragon your worth."

The crowd clapped and yelled as the eight men bowed

gracefully, then re-formed into a line and ran to the edge of the arena.

Although we were all kneeling at salute, there was a soft shifting of position as Jin-pa and Hannon started their walk to the combat area. It was our chance to watch the competition, gather information, gauge our chances. I pushed my left knee deeper into the sand and followed the momentum until I leaned into a better view. Even as my weight transferred, I realized my hip no longer ached.

In the center of the arena, Jin-pa and Hannon bowed to the Rat Dragon mirror and then one another over their sword hilts—the formal combat courtesy. The crowd subsided into expectant silence. Hannon swung his swords into starting position, his side presented to Jin-pa, weight on the back leg, one sword outstretched, the other drawn back above his head. Jin-pa mirrored the stance, then with a twist of both wrists lowered his swords into two whirring figure eights. The Ox Dragon. Hannon recognized the sequence and stepped into the first form. The easiest of the three. He broke through the defense with a neat swinging back cut, but Jin-pa blocked his blade easily in the crossed hilts of his swords.

Hannon pulled his sword free and retreated, bouncing on the balls of his feet as Jin-pa shifted into the second form of the Ox. The offense. He pressed forward, the rotating blades moving toward Hannon's head. The Ox was all about walls—solid walls of blade that pushed a defender backward and off balance. Hannon needed to block with his right sword and swing his left into the less protected gut area. He managed the block, but his lower cut was too wild, the weight of the sword dragging him onto the wrong foot for the third form; the most difficult. Jin-pa lunged, making the most of Hannon's imbalance, forcing him to stop an overhead blow with a clumsy block, the blade at the wrong angle. He nearly recovered, but Jin-pa countered Hannon's desperate twirl and low cut with a block and head attack that landed the flat of his sword against Hannon's cheekbone. The slap of the blade was like the crack of ice on a frozen river. Hannon shook his head as the crowd groaned, their excited commentaries rising like the hiss from a nest of snakes.

It did not improve from there. Hannon struggled to keep up with Jin-pa, although the swordmaster subtly slowed the pace of each form and pulled his blows. I couldn't help flinching as Jin-pa brought the flat of his blade down on Hannon's body time after time. What was wrong? Hannon was as good as Baret in the approach sequence. He knew each form perfectly and had spent hours refining each move. Was that the problem? Had he learned by rote and now couldn't translate the moves against an opponent?

In the very last form, he managed to hold his technique together. Dropping to the ground on all fours, he kicked backward, disabling Jin-pa's left sword, then twisted around and swung his own right blade across Jin-pa's body, nearly breaking through the swordmaster's hurried defense. A creditable Mirror Dragon Whips Tail. The form that I couldn't do. I glanced up at Ranne. He was rolling his shoulders, warming up for the next candidate. Would he honor my dispensation?

Jin-pa and Hannon bowed to each other, then to Lord Ido, the crowd's stamps of approval and ululating calls following them back across the sand. Hannon bowed shakily to the emperor, then returned to his place in the line. His movements were slow with fatigue and defeat. As he dropped onto his knees, I saw dirty tear tracks running over a red welt on his cheek. The crowd was chanting the herald's call for the next candidate, eager for more entertainment. It was like the baying of blooded dogs.

The imperial herald gonged for silence, then called Callan and Swordmaster Ranne to the center.

"Good fortune," I whispered to Callan, but although I was directly behind him, he didn't seem to hear. He had sunk into some kind of stiff-limbed terror.

With Callan in the center, I had a clear view of the arena and Ranne's unrelenting assault. There was no subtle slowing of pace, no holding back on the stinging slap of the blade. Callan was hit so many times, and so hard, that I feared he would fall and not get up. His Heuris was out of his seat, the restraining hands of his neighbors the only thing keeping him from hurling himself over the Rat Dragon mirror toward his candidate. Lord Ido was relaxed, leaning back in his seat, drinking wine, the officials around him silent and upright in subtle disapproval. It was a relief when Callan finally stumbled back to the line, kneeling with his head down over his swords, his breathing ragged.

Quon was called.

It would not be long now before I was out there.

Quon's opening moves in the Horse Dragon sequence were good, assured. His second form was a faultless defense. I narrowed my eyes, trying to focus on the faces of the darting, twirling figures. Was Jin-pa calling the forms to Quon? It was hard to say; the helmet obscured any detail. The cheers from the crowd acknowledged Quon's deftness as he swung out of the difficult low-defense move of the Monkey Dragon Third and into the form's offensive volley of angled-neck attacks. He was making a good show. The eruption of approval at the end of his sequence made the dark dragon mirrors shiver against the stone barricades. As he and Jin-pa bowed to the emperor, I caught a glimpse of the broad smile on his face. His ancestors must have heard his prayers.

The imperial herald ran back to the center. The deep, combined note of their gongs sounded like a death knell.

"Candidate Eon approach the mirrors," they chanted. "Face Swordmaster Ranne and show the Rat Dragon your worth."

The cheering was ragged, covering a low hum of interest. *Here comes the cripple.* I stood, glad there was no food in my stomach to rise and choke me. I took one tentative step forward—still no pain in my hip. Perhaps the heat of the sands had eased it. I sent a silent prayer to Charra and Kinra, my ancestors, for strength, skill, and endurance. Everything I lacked. A twist of each sword brought them home under my arms, ready. I stared at the patch of churned sand in the center. One step at a time, and I would get there. Ranne moved in beside me, matching my pace, but I did not look up. One step at a time. The arena was quiet—no stamping, no calls. Only the heavy anticipation before the prey was brought down.

Surely Ranne would not ignore the council's dispensation.

"Swordmaster, I have—"

"Silence," he hissed.

For a moment, the arena disappeared into white panic. I stumbled, my focus snapped back by the sudden flare of the moonstones and jade on my hilts. Each gem seemed lighted from within, drawing my eyes into their translucent depths. Something rolled through me.

Power, rising from steel and silver. A lifetime of fighting. An old knowledge.

My mind cleared into pinpoint purpose.

Keep the sun at your back, in his eyes. Distribute your weight evenly. Never cross your feet. Gauge the combat terrain and look for advantage. Keep your grip open to allow your Hua to flow. Close it, block the Hua, to make a hammer-fist.

I looked down at my tightly curled hand. But we had never been taught the hammer-fist.

Ranne stepped into the combat area, turning to face the Rat Dragon mirror. I followed, my gaze caught for a moment in the shock of seeing my whole self in the glass. Lopsided, fine-boned, with the smooth oval face of a child. Did all these men see a girl-boy standing in front of them? A Moon Shadow? Everyone knew that castration melted the bones and muscles of manhood into soft curves. Yes, this creature in the mirror would pass. Still, it was fortunate that most people glanced away from a cripple.

Except when he was fighting a swordmaster.

Beside me, Ranne bowed. I quickly matched his movement, our reflections showing the absurdity of his armored bulk next to my slight body. Above the mirror, Lord Ido sat forward, any pretense of nonchalance gone. I searched the rows behind him and found my master. He was sitting straight, the pale blur of his face tilted toward me.

"Prepare," Ranne said, taking a position with the sun at his back. He twirled his swords out and around his body in a mesmerizing display, then dropped the points into the vertical salute.

Keeping my swords tucked under my arms, I shuffled across the small combat area until the sun was to my right. At least Ranne would not have the glare advantage. Underfoot, the sand was kicked and gouged but tightly packed. The outer edges would be loose and treacherous.

"Swordmaster," I said, watching his eyes narrow behind the helmet slits. "I have dispensation from the council to—"

"I know that, Eon-*jah*," he said curtly. "Get back into position."

I took a jagged breath. "This *is* my position, Swordmaster."

He snorted. "At least I taught you *something*." He shifted to face me. "Let's see if you learned anything else."

I released my swords, pulling them up into salute. We

bowed over our hilts, eyes locked together. Leaning my weight back onto my good leg, I lifted the right sword above my head, stretching the left before me in a straight line aimed at his throat. Ranne mirrored me, his smooth grace fearsome. Both of us poised, watching for a sign: a blink, a glance, an indrawn breath.

It was a blink—a reflex as his outstretched blade swung above his head to twin the other in a wide arc.

The Goat Dragon.

His two swords, angled for slicing, came whirring at my chest. My block was simple: a step of the back leg, a shift of weight, my right sword joining the left in front of me, cutting side slanted down. Ranne's blades hit mine. The impact resonated through my arms, the strain forcing a swarm of bright dots across my vision until his steels slid along my angled edges. I pushed down with his momentum, the pain spreading from bones to muscles. He was not pulling his blows. My left sword lifted, freed from engagement. All I had to do was flip the edge and swing at his throat, but the shock of contact made me slow. I missed the chance—he'd already blocked. I backed away, stabilizing my grip. For a moment, the chant of the crowd rose through my concentration. *Eon.* They were calling for me. I took a deep breath, buoyed by their cheers.

I sidestepped, twirling my swords in front of me for the attacking move of the Goat Dragon Second. Instead, Ranne accelerated toward me, his swords high above his head. It wasn't the Goat Second. He was going into the Horse Third. I braced, raising my swords just in time. The crashing force of steel against steel pushed me back into the soft edge. Ranne's hilts locked into mine. I dug the side of my foot into the sand, stopping my slide. His face was a fingerlength from mine, his rank breath hot on my skin.

"That's not the Goat," I gasped. My back foot was slipping.

"My mistake," he said.

He jerked his body closer, his whole weight on my hilts, making my hands and arms shake with the pressure. Through the pound of my heartbeat, I heard the crowd start to shout down Ranne. I didn't have enough strength to push back. Any moment my arms would give way. He'd slam his elbow into my face.

Rat drops to ground.

It was not a voice. It was a deep body knowledge. Somehow my muscle and sinew and bone knew what to do. I fell backward, pulling my swords with me, turning them in a backhanded sweep that cleared them of Ranne. As I hit the sand, I saw his mouth gape in surprise, a mirror of my own shock. The crowd howled with excitement; the cripple was fighting back.

Snake coils to strike.

I rolled over, then scrabbled onto my knees. Ranne had already recovered and was bearing down on me. His swords were twirling in a tight crossover. The Dog Dragon Third. No more pretense of keeping to the sequences. He was going for the Dog Dragon's punishing hits and withdrawals. I hauled myself onto my feet, swords up, watching for the break.

My first block was clumsy, the blunt of my sword bouncing back too close to my face. The second was at the wrong angle, the jarring hit making my hand convulse against the grip. The deep knowledge was gone as quickly as it had arrived. I gulped for air. His third attack forced me to block with a back-twisted grip. The heavy downstroke hammered my weakened hold, bending my wrist back until it was useless. For a moment Ranne was a dark blur in a gray haze of pain. Then I felt him flick the end of his blade, sending my left sword spinning across the sand. The crowd's gasp filled the arena.

I staggered back, pressing my wrist against my chest. At least it wasn't my right hand. Ranne was closing in, one sword raised, the other with the hilt held ready for the Tiger Dragon Second attack—a series of fast cuffs using the heavy butt as a cudgel. I squinted, trying to focus through the pain. One sword—one block. He'd attack high. I raised my sword, ready to protect my head.

Rabbit kicks out.

The ancient knowledge. Even as my mind fought to stay upright, I was dropping to the ground and swinging my good leg toward his knees. My shin connected. I felt him fold, hit the sand. He looked across at me, his eyes bulging with fury.

Dragon whips tail.

No!

Ranne lunged over the sand with a sword, just missing my foot. I backpedaled from his reach, the drag of my own sword sending up a spray of grit.

Dragon whips tail.

No!

My hip—I can't—

Ranne dug a sword into the ground and pulled himself upright. He lowered his head and charged at me, holding his blades out on either side. He wasn't even using the forms. He was just fighting. I struggled onto my knees, caught between two possibilities: conduit or cripple.

I was a cripple.

Before I could raise my sword, Ranne swung at my head. I jerked backward, feeling the stir of air a moment before his blade vibrated past my face. I was off balance. Nowhere to go. I saw a blur of hand. A flash of metal angled at my head. Then a sickening wave of agony crashed over the light, and I was falling through black air.

CHAPTER FIVE

I OPENED MY EYES. Everything was white glare, pressing more pain into my head. I squeezed my eyes shut again, tears running over my nose and cheek into the rough sand.

"Eon?"

It was a distant voice, too far away. I licked my lips. Dust and salt.

"Eon." A weight on my shoulder, shaking me.

I blinked, letting the piercing light push its way into my eyes again. I was lying under the emperor's mirror, behind the two lines of candidates.

"Master?"

His face came into focus. Frowning.

I had failed him.

"You need to get up, Eon."

I lifted my head and retched, heaving sour water into the sand.

"Surely you don't expect him to make the final bow?"

It was another voice: an elderly official kneeling next to my master. I saw the glint of his pin—diamond rank.

"He recognized me," my master said. "He still has his senses."

"I doubt he will be able to stand," the official said. "It is a difficult situation. You are within your rights to demand Ranne's removal."

"Ranne is just the servant. It is Lord Ido who should be removed," my master said.

"You could make a formal complaint against him." The official was trying to keep his voice measured, but I heard the eagerness in it.

My master gave a sharp laugh. "Sacrifice myself for the good of the council? I don't think so."

"Someone has to curtail Ido's ambition."

"That was your duty, and you've failed. The opportunity to contain him is well past."

The official crossed his arms. "What could we do? He has High Lord Sethon's support."

"I think it is the other way around," my master murmured.

They looked at one another in silence.

"So, you are not withdrawing your boy, then?" the official finally asked. "He will make the bow?"

"He will."

"Then you should get him on his feet. The tenth candidate has already been called. It won't be long now." He rose awkwardly from the banked sand and bowed to my master. "Good fortune, Heuris Brannon."

My master nodded, then turned back to me.

"I am sorry, Master." My voice was a dry croak.

"Here, take some water." He pushed a cup against my lips. I gulped a mouthful, letting it wash down my raw throat.

"I know it will hurt, but you must get up," he said. "You must make the final bow to the Rat Dragon."

"But I didn't finish the sequence. He won't choose me."

My master snorted. "That was no sequence. That was an ambush." He tipped the cup again. I took another sip. "No one knows how a dragon chooses. We will see this through to the end."

He curled his arm around my shoulders and lifted me into a sitting position. I felt his hand smooth back my hair, then rest at the nape of my neck. The arena swirled and rocked. I deepened my breathing until it settled, although my vision separated now and again into blurred doubles. It looked as though two Barets fought two Rannes in the center. I squinted, trying to bring the doubles back to one image.

Baret was doing well. Not surprising—Ranne was using the forms in the ascendance sequence we had all learned. Soon Baret would be a Dragoneye apprentice.

And I would be a runaway.

I moved out of my master's hold, but he kept a hand on my arm.

"Go slow, Eon. You still have a little time before the final bow."

The applause for Baret's performance was laced with shouts of abuse for Ranne. I closed my eyes, gingerly touching my swollen temple. As though from a far distance, I heard the herald call Dillon and Jin-pa. My injury seemed to be shallow, but I slowly traced my *Hua* through the seventh center of power. The damage was like a kink in my energy line, but the flow was not broken. Not dangerous. I opened my eyes, the arena separating into two. I blinked them back together.

And then I saw the dragons.

Crouched on the top of their mirrors, staring down at Dillon and Jin-pa fighting on the sand. The beasts had no solid form or color—just a disturbance in the air that spoke of shape and weight and line. Only their eyes seemed to have substance: a concentration of darkness as though holes had been ripped in the fabric of the world. The crowd was oblivious to their presence. Even the Dragoneyes stared through them. Why couldn't they see their own dragons?

An eruption of cheers and calls announced the end of the sequence. I let the noise and heat wash over me as Dillon bowed to the mirror. The Rat Dragon ducked its shimmering head to study him. For a moment, Dillon seemed to stiffen as he rose from the deep courtesy—was he aware of the huge eyes only an arm's length away? I watched him as he returned to the line, but he just seemed exhausted. The next candidate was called. I closed my eyes, seeking relief from the relentless glare. The noise of the crowd dropped into a distant murmur as a velvety ease settled over the pain.

A hand shook me again, back into the aching light. The arena burst around me into full volume.

"Eon. Stay awake," my master said. "The last candidate is up. It's almost time for the final bow."

I squinted against all the color and noise, scanning the arena. The dragons were gone—at least from my sight. My master pulled me up by my arm.

"Get back in line. I must return to my seat."

It took me the whole of the final candidate's sequence to make my way across the short length of sand to my position, each step making me lurch with dizziness. I dropped to my knees behind Quon just as the herald ran out and formed their octagon. The sound of their gongs cut through the crowd's rumbling excitement.

"The twelve have shown their skill and stamina," they chanted. "Now is the time to see the Rat Dragon. To see the new Dragoneye apprentice."

The crowd stamped and yelled. This was the only time a layman could ever see one of the great beasts—a glimpse in the ascendant mirror as the dragon crossed the sand to make his choice, and then the glorious moments of union when the new apprentice laid his hands on the pearl and the dragon took solid form.

The gong cut off the exultation.

"Witness the final bow! Witness the rise of one boy to the glorious honor of communion with the Rat Dragon!"

The sound of the gong was lost in thunderous applause. The herald ran to the side and formed a line against the wall, waiting to give their final announcement: the name of the apprentice.

Lord Ido emerged from the rampway. As he walked toward the Rat Dragon mirror, the imperial trumpets and drummers began a climbing fanfare. The elderly official who had spoken to my master stepped up in front of us.

"Stand," he said. "Form your line, one to twelve, for the final bow."

I dug the tips of my swords into the sand to pull myself upright. It was an unforgivable breach, but I didn't care. Every limb dragged with heaviness, and my head pounded in counterpoint with the drums. Even so, as I crossed my swords in salute and followed Quon across the sand, a reserve of excited energy made me straighten and step out. Maybe I still had a chance. We lined up in front of the Rat Dragon mirror and in the bright glass I saw the other candidates—faces blanched with fear but heads up, shoulders back, every one of them pushing past their exhaustion.

The fanfare suddenly stopped.

Lord Ido turned to face the mirror. He stood with his legs apart, as though standing against a wind, and raised his arms. In the reflection, I saw his eyes slide along our row and for a shocking moment our gazes locked. His eyes were silvered with *Hua*, the raw energy stealing his expression. I looked away from his blank face.

"One is worthy," he called to the mirror, his voice a curious mix of entreaty and command. "Show us who will serve you."

It was as though the whole audience sat forward and held its breath, every gaze focused on the bright glass.

Light shivered in the air above the carved gold rat. Slowly, a large claw slid into the reflection, pale blue scales glowing above five opal talons. The Rat Dragon was descending from his perch, his translucent body only solid and visible in the mirror as he passed by it. A reflection without an original. It was the first time I'd ever seen one of the spirit beasts in full physical form. My own gasp was echoed around the arena. A powerfully muscled foreleg came into view, the scales darkening into ocean blue as the underside of a broad chest and shoulder followed in the glass. Next, a beard, the white hair thick and tapered like a horse's tail. And for a fleeting moment, beneath the coarse strands, I saw the dragon's pearl—his source of wisdom and power—tucked under his chin and shining with blue iridescence. Then it was hidden by his flared muzzle, the delicate scales and fine horse nostrils accentuating the size of the fang that curved from his upper lip.

The dragon turned to stare across the sand at the emperor, one large dark eye visible in the mirror, his broad brow crowned by two curled horns. I heard nervous murmuring from the crowd as both of his forelegs reached the sand, his sinuous body stretched full length in the reflection. Then it coiled like a snake and dropped behind him, the invisible weight sending up a cloud of sand and dust that fell back over his body, giving us a shimmering outline of him. He shook his head, dislodging more sand, then turned and looked at himself in the glass, the endless depth of his eyes giving him an expression of sadness. Two pale blue membranes extended out from each shoulder and rippled in the sunlight like watered silk, then folded back against his body. The heavy head swung around to face us again, the mirror showing the solid line of his spine and the thick fall of white mane. Although his eyes were no longer reflected, I knew he was studying us, choosing his apprentice.

The sand in front of the mirror stirred as the dragon stepped forward. Beside me, Quon braced himself, his breath quickening. Lanell whispered a hurried prayer. I tried to swallow, but I was so parched the dryness caught in my throat. The swish of a giant snake track appeared in the sand as the dragon moved closer, the graceful sway of his tail mesmerizing in the mirror. Inside me, something was beginning to build like slow bubbles breaking the surface of near boiled water. Was it the dragon's power? I looked down the line of candidates. Some had broken rank and stepped back; Baret was edging away, but Dillon held his place. The heavy indents of the dragon's claws were visible in the sand as he approached. In the mirror, his head was moving back and forth like a dog sniffing the air. He turned to Baret.

Energy was thrumming through my body. I narrowed my eyes, groping for my mind-sight; perhaps if I showed him my power, he would come. The dull thud in my head built into un-bearable pressure. The dragon shimmered into being for me and I felt him pulling energy from my body. His head jerked around, a thick blue tongue licking out, tasting the power. He paced a few steps, then backtracked. I gritted my teeth, trying to hold him in my sight, but the drain was too great. The dragon dis-appeared from my view, the sudden wrench of the connection making me sway.

The crowd's excitement cut through the loud drums and

trumpets. I looked up at the mirror. Had it been enough? The dragon lifted a claw and raked the air then, with a few flicks of his tail, he was upon me. I couldn't see him, only feel his hot breath on my cheek. It smelled of vanilla and orange. Was he choosing me? I tried to merge into my mind-sight again, but my head was too full of pain and pounding power. Sand sprayed into an arc, whipping me across the face. Quon covered his eyes and crouched as the unseen bulk of the beast passed between us. I felt the heavy tail brush my leg, a sliding touch of hard muscle. I looked wildly from the shifting sand to the reflection of the dragon as he reared up behind me, the heat of his body pressing against mine. Was I chosen? I saw Lord Ido start toward me. His eyes were no longer wide and blank; they were narrowed in fury. He must have seen me call the beast.

The dragon suddenly swung around to face the emperor above the dark mirror. He cocked his head to one side, then screamed, the sound like the shriek of a hunting eagle but a hundred times louder. It pushed me down onto my knees. I dropped my swords, pressing my hands against my ears. The scream was in my head, shattering my senses. A surge of energy knocked me sideways. And then the heat at my back was gone.

Struggling to lift my head, I watched the whirl of sand move down the line. He was leaving me. The mirror showed him in front of Baret and Dillon. Screaming again, the beast lunged at Dillon, circling him in a gritty tornado, his huge tail catching Baret in the chest, flicking him to the ground. The closest candidates scattered. Quon grabbed the sleeve of my tunic and pulled me backward. I ripped myself free of his grasp; I had to stay close in case the dragon came back for me.

For a moment, Dillon's slight figure was hidden in the center of the churning sand, then the funnel burst upward like an exploding volcano, falling in a stinging rain on me and the other candidates. Only Dillon was untouched. He stood with his head back, his face a pale O of astonishment. I turned to the mirror. He was staring into the eyes of the dragon, the beast's body curled like a crescent moon over him. The dragon bent closer, his muzzle a fingerlength from Dillon's face. The huge head slowly lifted to expose the shimmering pearl hidden under his chin and beard. Dillon reached up and placed his hands around the sphere. A pale blue flame surged from it, the connection between beast and boy sparking in a rush of silver *Hua* that brought the dragon into shimmering solidity. With a gasp, the crowd shifted their attention from the mirror to the two glowing figures on the sand. The dragon's color was lost in the sheen of energy, but Dillon's red tunic stood out like a splash of blood. The beast closed its eyes and called, the resonating cry holding a lonely question.

Dillon threw back his head, the soft round of his face suddenly lengthening into sharper lines. "Yes, I hear you," he yelled, as if answering the dragon's call. "I am Dillon. I hear you."

The beast shrieked again, a climbing descant of triumph that pierced the crowd's roar.

I was pushed sideways as Lord Ido brushed past me. "Get

back," he ordered, jerking his head to the other candidates clustered beside the mirror. "You're in the way."

He strode across the sand and stopped in front of the dragon and boy locked in their union. I picked up my swords and backed away; each step felt like I was tearing something in me. Lord Ido bowed low to the dragon. Then, bracing his feet in the sand, he pulled Dillon away from the pearl. Silver power crackled through the boy, into the man, snapping the Dragoneye's head back. The beast's howl mingled with Dillon's scream of loss. Then the dragon winked out of sight as Lord Ido caught Dillon's limp body, holding him up to face the audience. I looked back at the mirror. The Rat Dragon was gone.

Lord Ido motioned to the imperial herald.

"Witness the choice," the herald called. "Witness Dillon, the new Rat Dragoneye apprentice."

As one, the crowd came to their feet, chanting, "Dillon."

He stirred and turned his face toward their exultation, his own joy giving him the strength to stand. Lord Ido grabbed his hand and held it up, circling with him in victorious acknowledgment.

In that moment, hate flared through me like a sudden fever, burning everything in its path. The swords in my hands stirred with it, answering the fire. And then, just as fast, the hate froze into a vast, aching emptiness. I looked across at Quon and Lanell and saw the same dark desolation on their faces.

We had failed.

I had failed.

Quon started to sob, the crowd's cheers drowning the sound.

A hand gripped my shoulder.

"Eon, come this way," a voice said close to my ear. It was Van, his thin face soft with sympathy.

The rest of the candidates were being ushered around the edge of the arena by officials. I looked back at Dillon. Why was he chosen? The Rat Dragon had come to me first. Why had the beast turned away? Perhaps it had always been true: no dragon would choose a cripple.

My master had gambled and lost. I looked up into the stands. He was not hard to find—alone and unmoving, the only figure left sitting in the Heuris seats. Part of me wanted to run now, out of the arena and away from his despair, away from his fists and lingering touches. I felt for the hidden coin. It was still there, pulling at the hem. But even if I tried to flee, I would not get far. I could barely push through my exhaustion to stay upright, let alone run.

I slowly followed Van across the sand to where the other failed candidates waited. They were all watching the flurry of activity around Dillon: the herald urging on the crowd, two columns of musicians behind them playing a soaring triumphal. Another official pulled me into the straggling line. Quon lurched into me, his face tearstreaked and white with strain. We moved forward. Ahead, someone stumbled and was shoved back into place. I heard a clipped command and felt Van move into step beside me, watching.

"Let me take your swords," he finally said.

I had forgotten I was holding them, their weight just part of the terrible fatigue. It was an effort to hold the blades up to him, an even greater effort to release the grips.

"We're almost there," Van said.

"Where?" I licked my lips. Were we going for water?

"You must bow to the emperor."

I looked at him, turning over his words for meaning. *Bow. To the Emperor.*

"Then water?"

He nodded. "Not long now."

We stopped. Back under the dark mirror where we had first waited. The emperor was watching the celebrations in the center of the arena; he had no interest in us. A distracted official pushed Hannon forward, motioning for him to bow. Hannon dropped to his knees, his swords held in a wavering salute. For a moment, I didn't think he was going to make it back up, but he finally pushed himself to his feet and was ushered to the other side of the mirror. Callan followed, his bow slow but correct. Quon had to be led to the mirror and eased down to the sand. I saw his bleak face as he was hauled back onto his feet—if a person could die of disappointment, Quon would soon be with his ancestors.

It was my turn. Van handed me my swords.

"Do you need my help?" he asked.

I squeezed the grips and felt a sluggish surge of the ancient energy—enough to get me to the mirror. I shook my head and started to pick my way across the churned sand.

The center of the dark glass had the greenish sheen of a

black pearl. My master had once worn such a gem before he sold it for food. But there were no more gems to sell—only crippled bondservants. I stood and stared into the mirror for a moment, gathering the effort needed to drop to my knees. The dense blackness was strangely soothing. I blinked, trying to clear a stab of brightness from my eyes.

A line of light flared suddenly at the top of the mirror, burning downward like a fuse. It split the glass, peeling back the darkness into a blinding radiance that pushed me off my feet. The swords spun out of my hands; I hit the sand on my back, the impact shuddering through me and locking my breath. Above the mirror, I saw the emperor's guards lean over, shielding their eyes. Had I done something wrong? I finally found air and sucked it in. Behind me, the sounds of the celebration had disintegrated into the clash of faltering instruments and screams.

Crackling energy sheared across my skin. Red flashed through the mirror, too large to have form. The ground shook as sand flew into the air and showered over the arena. Men were scattering—officials, audience, candidates—stumbling and falling in their panic. The reflection in front of me was filled with a landscape of rippling red and orange. I pushed myself up on to my feet, fighting through a heavy press of power.

The brilliant colors rushed past the glass in a river of fire, then suddenly stopped. I finally recognized the shapes: a graceful length of muzzle and the curve of a nostril. Twice the size of the Rat Dragon. Then I saw an eye, as large and round as a cart wheel, staring at me from the glass.

Another dragon.

A dragon I had never seen before.

The image moved again, a dizzying turn of red and yellow that ended in a reflection of two horns arching over a thick mane that shimmered with gold and bronze. The dragon filled the entire reflection, blotting out any sight of the arena. The air thickened with heat; I heard the slide of a huge weight. On either side of me, deep grooves appeared in the sand. Reaching out blindly, I brushed soft ridged scales and snatched back my hand. The rich sweetness of cinnamon was on my tongue a moment before I felt hot breath on my hair. I looked at the mirror and saw myself standing between the beast's forelegs, a tiny red figure almost lost against the bright crimson of the deep chest. The broad muzzle was hanging above my head, the fang only a fingertip away. I spun around.

Curled over me was the real dragon. I could *see* him. The shift of the heavy muscles. The delicate pattern of scalloped scales. The sheen of the gold-tinged pearl held beneath his chin. He ducked his head, bringing his eyes closer, the ancient gaze pulling me into light and dark, sun and moon, *Lin* and *Gan*. He was birth and death. He was *Hua*.

He was the Mirror Dragon. The Lost Dragon.

The great head lifted, offering me the pearl. Offering me his power.

I raised my hands, hesitating as a deep thrum of energy pulsed from the gem. So much raw *Hua*—what would it do to me?

A soft huff of spicy breath touched my face, then the pearl

was pressing hard against my palms. It was warm with his body heat, the surface flaring with a gold-edged flame that flicked my skin in silky stings. I heard a rumbling acknowledgment from the crowd.

They could see him, too. They could see the Mirror Dragon choosing *me*—Eon, the cripple.

Then the deep murmur changed into shouts. I wrenched my gaze from the Mirror Dragon's hold. Men were pointing, cowering in their seats, scrambling away. All of the other dragons had suddenly materialized on the top of their mirrors—eleven massive, solid bodies, their hides gleaming in colors that made the rich silks of the cringing nobles seem dull. The Ox Dragon stretched an amethyst claw toward me, the dark purple of his leg softening into the color of dusk shadows. The Tiger Dragon ducked his emerald head, a bow that showed a thick moss mane flecked with copper. I twisted around to see the others, barely taking in the dawn pinks of the Rabbit Dragon, the bold orange of the Horse Dragon, and the silver of the Goat Dragon.

They were all watching me with their spirit eyes.

The arena was a heaving mass of movement—officials and musicians running for the rampway, men of all ranks scrabbling over seats to the upper levels. In all of the shrill hysteria, one still figure drew my gaze: Lord Ido. His face was stiff with shock, his hands flexing in and out of fists. He tilted back his head, turning to see the circle of dragons. They were all bowing to the Mirror Dragon. Bowing to me. Even the ascendant Rat Dragon. Eleven mighty beasts holding their heads in low obeisance, the huge pearls under their chins reflected in the ring of mirrors like a god's necklace.

Narrowing his eyes, Lord Ido faced the Rat Dragon and braced himself forward, as if hauling a great weight. He slowly drew up his hands, sucking power from the earth. I saw it streaming through him as clearly as I saw the flare of his seven energy centers. He was calling the Rat Dragon. I could hear it, like a deep vibration in my body, demanding the beast's attention. Slowly, reluctantly, the blue dragon rose from his bow. Lord Ido dropped his arms and swung around to stare at me. For a moment, I thought I saw his bold features tighten with fear. But then he smiled—a slow baring of teeth—and I knew it was not fear. It was hunger.

Above me, the Mirror Dragon crooned, and I felt something shift through my being, like a whisper at the edge of my senses. Something important. I laid my ear against the pearl and held my breath, straining to hear. For a moment sound surged closer, pushing up against a dark resistance. I caught a soft lilt with no form, no meaning, and then it faded away like the end of a sigh. I spread my fingers across the hard, velvety surface—a silent plea to let me try again. But it was gone.

The pearl moved under my hands as the dragon lifted his head. He called for me, a piercing shriek that coursed through my body, searching for my core. There was nowhere to hide from the silver rush of energy. It stripped my soul bare, peeling back the shell of Eon. Finding me.

Finding *Eona*.

My true name surged through me, dredged from the very depths of my being. I had to call my name to the world, celebrate the truth of our union. It was the dragon's demand.

No!

They would kill me. Kill my master. I clenched my teeth. The name filled my head, thundering through it, spiking into crescendos of pain. *Eona. Eona. Eona.*

No! It would be my death. I dragged my face off the pearl but my hands would not move, fused by the pulsing power. I screamed, trying to drown out the name in my head, the sound joining the Mirror Dragon's shrill cry. But the name still pounded at me, the weight of a dragon's desire behind it. Too strong. Any moment it would be forced out of me.

"I am Eon," I shouted. "Eon!"

I pushed harder against the pearl, the power shimmering along the surface of my hands and arms. Then I threw my body backward. For a second all I felt was tearing pain, then my hands ripped free and I was falling again. Falling into a blackness that gaped with loss and loneliness.

CHAPTER SIX

I CAME TO MY senses slowly, a dim light penetrating the gray blur of sleep.

I opened my eyes wider. A room. But none of the dimensions were familiar; the ceiling was too high, the walls too far away. Someone was chanting—a low hum of entreaty—and the air was scented. It took a moment to place the sweet smell: the special incense used for the sick. I rolled onto my back and felt soft silk brush my skin.

"Lord Eon?"

I raised my head and saw the silhouette of a woman sitting on a stool. The white blur of her face was topped by a coronet of coiled hair pinned with gold ornaments. A court lady. Standing behind her was a heavyset Shadow Man, dark skinned, his head shaved clean, hands resting on the hilts of two sheathed swords. Then my eye was drawn to a flicker of light in the corner of the room. A paper prayer lantern swinging from the hand of a black-robed Beseecher—the source of the chanting. Beside him was a servant half-hidden in the gloom.

"Lord Eon? Can you speak?" The lady's voice was low and resonant.

I pulled myself up onto an elbow. My head pounded with an echo of the red dragon's power and every part of me felt bruised. I was lying on a bed—a real bed, not just a bedroll. It was as wide as three pallets, with raised sides made of black lacquered wood. A heavy yellow silk sheet covered me. It slipped a little as I moved. I looked down; no red tunic. Just a loose sleeveless night smock that was too big. I hurriedly pulled up the sheet. Had this woman undressed me? Had she seen me?

"Do you need your body servant?" The lady snapped her fingers. The figure in the shadows stepped forward.

Rilla.

My servant?

"You should have some water," the lady said. She waved Rilla over to a long bureau beneath the shuttered window. A reddish glow from a small brazier outlined the familiar shape of a water jug.

This wasn't my master's house. Where was I?

Rilla bowed and passed me a small drinking bowl. It was gold, engraved with a peony. Why was she giving me a noble's cup? Did she want to get me punished? I tried to push it back into her hands, then saw the raw skin of burns and blisters on her fingers.

"What happ—?"

She gave a slight shake of her head and pushed the bowl back to me.

"Thank you." My voice was raspy from disuse. How long had I been senseless? I took a sip, then gulped the cool water, draining the bowl quickly.

"That is enough for now," the court lady chided gently. "The physicians say you must take water slowly or your body will reject it."

Rilla bowed again and took the empty bowl back to the bureau. The court lady signaled to the Beseecher, stopping his low chant, then rose gracefully from her seat. She knelt on one knee and bowed, her long hands folded against one hip.

"Lord Eon," she said, "now that you are refreshed, you must be wondering where you are. This is the Peony Guest Apartment of the Imperial Palace. I am Lady Dela. It is my honor to welcome you to the palace and instruct you on the protocols of the court."

Lord Eon? The palace?

"What"—I cleared my throat—"what am I doing here?"

She straightened and I saw her face in the glow from a covered oil lamp. Rough skin painted with heavy white makeup. Square jaw, cheekbones high and sharp. Dark, deep-set eyes ringed with kohl and set under thin, arched brows. A curved nose spoke of ancestors from the Eastern tribes. Her mouth was generous, an upward curve hinting at humor. It was a strong face, with more hawklike majesty than beauty.

But what drew my eye was a large black pearl hanging from a gold pin threaded horizontally through the skin of her throat. It straddled the round of her windpipe, covering a noticeable knob that jumped when she swallowed.

"Do you remember the ceremony, my lord?" she asked, the pearl trembling as she spoke.

I felt a flash of remembered heat and pain, a sudden image of my hands clawed across the pearl and the dragon curved over me. "I remember the dragon coming to me across the sand."

She nodded. "The Lost Dragon. You are the new Mirror Dragoneye—the first in over five hundred years. His Imperial Majesty has proclaimed the dragon's return as a most auspicious sign."

"Mirror Dragoneye?" I repeated. "But I'm just a candidate."

"Yes, there was some resistance in the Dragoneye Council due to your youth and inexperience, but after much debate they have recognized your position." She paused, the wide mouth quirking up for a second. "You are now Coascendant Dragoneye with Lord Ido."

I stared at her.

"Coascendant Dragoneye? But I'm just a candidate. I can't be a Dragoneye." I pushed back against the pillow, coming up hard against the lacquered headboard.

"My lord, you have been chosen by the Mirror Dragon. There is no incumbent Dragoneye to take you on as an apprentice, therefore you *are* the Dragoneye." Again, the slight smile. "The council used Lord Ido's own precedent of early status to come to a decision."

I looked around the room. "Where is my master?"

"Heuris Brannon is in conference with His Imperial Majesty and the Dragoneye Council," Lady Dela said slowly. "My lord, I know this is a lot to take in, but you must now realize that Heuris Brannon is no longer your master. You are *Lord* Eon. Coascendant Dragoneye. The highest rank in the land except for the imperial family. Do you understand?"

"No," I said, feeling all the air leave my body. "No. I want my master." I felt my throat close, my eyes hazing with red panic.

Lady Dela was beside me in a moment, snatching up my hand. "Lord Eon, take a deep breath. Breathe. Just breathe." Her soft hand cupped my cheek as I struggled to force air past the rigid block in my chest. "You over there," she called. "Help me."

I heard a voice yelp in protest. The pad of running feet. Then Rilla holding something over my nose and mouth. The Beseecher's paper lantern. It smelled of the discarded wax candle. I gulped like a stranded fish and felt air force its way into my lungs.

"He will be here soon," Rilla whispered in my ear. "It will be all right."

I took a deep, shaking breath, and she pulled the paper lantern away.

Lady Dela patted my hand. "That's right, take deep breaths." Her shoulders lifted in a deep inhale, showing me the way. "And out again." She nodded as I exhaled. "You are doing very well, my lord."

She looked around the room. "You, Ryko," she said sharply, flicking her fingers at the Shadow Man, "don't just stand there like a man mountain. Go and get the physician."

"I am sorry, my lady," the Shadow Man said, his voice unexpectedly soft and light, "I cannot leave you unguarded."

She glared at him. "I'm hardly going to be attacked here."

"No, because I am guarding you," he said patiently.

"I'm all right," I said hoarsely.

"Are you sure?" She peered at my face. "I know how it is to rise from humble beginnings. Such sudden elevation can be . . . disorienting." She gave my hand one last pat, then let it rest on the silk cover. "But I'm afraid you will not have much time to adjust to your new position. Now that you have recovered, His Imperial Majesty will expect you to attend this evening's banquet. It will be in your honor. You must bathe and dress. And then I will instruct you on proper court etiquette."

A banquet with the emperor? I felt my breath catch again.

Lady Dela looked over at Rilla. "You seem able," she said. "I will send my girl over to assist you with your master's preparations. She'll help you bathe and dress him for court. His Majesty has given Lord Eon permission to draw what he needs from the imperial stores."

I pulled the cover up farther. Bathed and dressed? I had to find a way to refuse the lady's offer.

Rilla turned to me, wincing as she folded her hands together and bowed.

"My lord, may I speak of your requirements?" she asked solemnly.

My requirements? I stared at her deferential pose, then realized she was waiting for me to give permission.

"Yes, of course," I said hurriedly.

"Your generosity is greatly appreciated, my lady," Rilla said. "However, only I am able to bathe and dress Lord Eon." She leaned forward and whispered loudly, "My master is Moon Shadow. I have been purified and sanctioned to serve him."

Lady Dela's slim body stiffened with shock. "Forgive me, my lord, I was not informed," she said, dropping into a low bow. The nape of her neck was flushed. "I humbly apologize for intruding upon your arrangements. I will have your girl shown the stores and baths, and instruct the imperial staff to enter your rooms only upon your order. When you are ready, send a messenger and I will come to you."

"Thank you."

The Shadow Man was watching me, his expression strangely tender. He must have thought me a brother. I looked away from the undeserved fellowship.

What was I supposed to do now?

Lady Dela was still crouched beside the bed. She lifted her head slightly. "My lord, may I offer you the first lesson?" she asked gently. "You must give permission for those lower in rank to leave your presence."

"Oh." Heat prickled across my face. "Yes, of course. You may go."

She bowed and gracefully stood, the Shadow Man ducking from the waist in a brief courtesy, then taking his position behind her shoulder. Rilla and I watched her leave, dwarfed by the massive guard, the clink of her hair ornaments matching the sway of her walk.

"You may go, too," I said to the Beseecher, trying to sound more lordly. "Thank you," I added. Best not to offend an intermediary of the gods.

He bowed and scuttled out into the passageway, giving Rilla a cold glare as he passed—wax candles were expensive.

"Rilla—" I said.

She held up her hand for silence as she checked the corridor. I heard the fading sounds of retreating steps and murmured conversation. Finally, she closed the door and pressed her back against it, as though stopping it from bursting back open.

We stared at one another for a second.

"*Lord* Eon?" she said, lifting her eyebrows. "This is a deadly path the master has set you on, girl." She sighed. "Has set *us* on."

"Did you always know the truth about me?" I asked, meeting her steady gaze.

"Perhaps," she replied. "But it is easier and safer not to know some things too clearly." She walked over to the bed and smiled wryly. "How are you feeling, my lord?"

"My head aches." I rubbed my temple and felt the lump where Ranne had hit me. "And all of my skin feels like it is bruised. How did I get undressed?"

"Me." She held out her burned hands. "No one else would touch you. Not even the physicians. The Dragoneyes said it was the Mirror Dragon's power sparking from your skin because you were not properly released from the Pearl."

I looked down at my arms and hands. "I don't think I'm sparking anymore. Do you think it might start again?"

Rilla shook her head. "I'm no expert."

Neither was I. Was sparking skin a good or a bad sign? I couldn't even tell if the dragon was still with me. I tried to focus inward, but a new fear was dimming my mind's eye. What if the dragon was gone? I took a deep breath and concentrated again. My mind's eye slowly found the energy lines of my body. There was something different. A change in my *Hua*—it was faster, stronger—and an echo of another presence, like a shadow heartbeat. But it was very faint. I opened my eyes and fell back against the pillows, exhausted. "I think the sparking has finished. I'm sorry you were hurt, Rilla."

She shrugged. "The master used it as an excuse to stop the doctors from poking at you." She touched my shoulder. "It's lucky you're slim hipped and small breasted. How old are you, really?"

"Sixteen." I hugged my arms around my chest to stop myself from grabbing her sore hands. "Rilla, what am I going to do?" I felt panic rise through me.

"You are going to be bathed and dressed by your body servant, and then you are going to go out there and be Lord Eon, the new Mirror Dragoneye."

"How can I be a lord? It was hard enough just being a candidate. I can't do it."

"Yes, you can," Rilla said, and grabbed me by the shoulders. "Because if you can't, then we are going to die. You, me, the master. They won't let us live if they find out what you really are."

What you really are—her words brought a lunch of memory. I pulled away from her grasp. "Rilla, when you undressed me, did you find a pouch?"

"Calm yourself. I have it." She patted the pocket of her gown. "And your gift from Chart."

"How long was I senseless?"

"Two days." She nodded her understanding. "Don't worry, the master told me about the tea. You haven't missed a dose—I got a good amount down your throat, although you never fully roused."

I sighed out my relief. "Thank you."

"I'll make today's dose now." She crossed to the bureau and poked at the coals in the brazier. Next to her, in the corner, was a small rack holding my ceremonial swords. I flexed my fingers, remembering the strange angry knowledge that had come from their steel.

I turned my back on them and swung my legs over the edge of the bed. "Where's Chart?" I asked.

"He is at the master's house."

"But who's looking after him?" The carpet was so thick under my feet that they sunk into it. I wiggled my toes, pushing them through the soft pile. Twice as deep as my master's carpets.

"Irsa." Rilla's voice was flat.

I looked around. "Irsa? But can't Chart come here?"

"The emperor will not allow it. He will not have the bad luck of deformity in the palace."

I stopped making imprints in the carpet. "But I'm here."

Rilla placed a pot of water on top of the brazier. "Yes, but rank and wealth take the stink off such things."

Rank and wealth. I stared down at the jewel colors of the carpet. I now had rank and wealth. Something surged through me, the beginning of a fierce power that had nothing to do with the Mirror Dragon. I was Lord Eon. Not an apprentice—a Dragoneye. I drank out of gold cups and slept on silk sheets. People served me and bowed to me and no one would ever sneer at my limp again or make the ward-evil sign.

"I could order him here," I said.

Rilla turned and smiled. "That's a generous thought, Lord Eon."

I felt the heat rise to my face again. The thought had not come from generosity.

"But I'm afraid even the new Mirror Dragoneye would not be able to overrule the emperor's fear." She stared into the heating water. "It will be all right. The master will not let any serious harm come to Chart."

True, but it was the lesser harms that left a sour taste in my mouth.

Something knocked against the door. I spun around to face it.

"Lord Eon," a voice called from the other side. "The emperor's physician requests entrance."

"Get back in the bed," Rilla whispered. "Don't let him poke

at you." She took the pot off the brazier and hurried to the door. "A moment, please."

I clambered onto the bed and pulled the sheet back over me. Rilla gave me a nod, then opened the heavy door, bowing as a small man strutted into the room. His clothes overshadowed him. Five short tunics of the thinnest silk were set one on top of the other, each a shade of purple—violet to lilac—that created a glorious layered edging at neck and thigh. Under these was a pair of wide-legged trousers in puce with gold embroidery. A maroon physician's cap, close fitting but extravagantly trimmed with pink feathers, completed the magnificence. Among all this rich color, the man's gray face drooped in sour lines, a sparse beard coming to a short frayed point. He was followed by two fat eunuchs in long blue cotton tunics, one carrying a tray with a goblet, the other a box.

"Lord Eon, I am the royal physician," the small man said, his bow a short dip from the waist. "His Imperial Majesty sends you a precious tonic to assist in your recovery." He waved the eunuch with the tray forward. "It was presented as a gift to our Gracious Highness from those foreign devils he allows into our city."

The eunuch dropped to one knee and offered the goblet. His face was puffy, with an unhealthy darkness under the eyes. I could smell a faint sourness about him.

I took the goblet and peered inside. The liquid looked like glossy mud.

"It is called 'cocolat,'" the physician said. "His Majesty takes it every morning."

"I just drink it? Like tea?"

"Yes, my lord. It will be most beneficial after your long fast. For the time being, you must be cautious. We do not want to startle your body. I will have the kitchens prepare some dishes that will enhance your recovery." He leaned over and looked closely at me, his dry lips set in a pucker of thought. "A little bamboo and fish first, I think. Now, drink up."

I raised the goblet. A smell like the aftertaste of Ari's strange coffee filled my nose just before the cocolat slicked my mouth with oily, sweet velvet. I swallowed and tasted a strange bitterness at the back of my tongue. Then my jaw muscles locked. I clenched my teeth, waiting for the ache to pass. The drink was sweeter than honey and strangely soothing. I took a larger sip. This time the bitterness was hardly noticeable in the creaminess that coated my mouth and throat. When I had drained the cup, it felt as though I had eaten a whole meal of sweetings. I belched. Even the return was delicious.

The physician took the empty goblet and nodded approvingly. "I have been informed that your skin is no longer dangerous to the touch. Therefore I shall examine you." He grabbed the edge of the sheet.

"No!" I tightened my hold on the cover. "I don't want to be examined." I ducked away from his hands, but he caught my wrist in a bony grip.

"But you must," he said. "I have to make my report to His Majesty."

"Lord Eon is well," my master said from the doorway. "That is your report, Physician."

"Master!" I wanted to run to him, but the physician was still holding my wrist. I pulled it out of his grasp. "You're here." I couldn't stop the tremble of relief in my voice.

"Of course I am here, Lord Eon," my master said, emphasizing the title with a brief smile. His face was flushed with inner excitement. He walked over to the bed, crowding the physician until the smaller man took a reluctant step back.

"Who are you?" the physician demanded.

My master stared at him for a moment, then turned to me. "I came as soon as I could, my lord," he said. "How do you feel?"

"I feel . . ." I faltered. My master was bowing to me. I pulled the sheet up higher. "I feel well, Heuris Brannon," I finally said, stumbling over his name.

"There you are, Physician," my master said. "Lord Eon is well. He gives you his permission to leave. Don't you, Lord Eon?"

"Yes," I said, hurriedly. "Go. Thank you."

The physician glared at my master. "I shall make my report to the emperor." He stalked from the room, the eunuchs breaking into a shuffling trot behind him.

Rilla started to shut the door, but my master stopped her with a raised hand.

"Make sure all our guests have left the apartment, Rilla. Then go and organize Lord Eon's bath and clothing. There is much to do before we attend the banquet."

She bowed and pulled the door closed behind her.

We were alone.

"How do you really feel?" my master asked softly, sitting on the edge of the bed. "This has not been an easy road for you." He leaned over and examined the lump on my temple, his cool fingers gently pressing my skin. The smell of rice wine was on his breath.

"I am well, Master," I said. "Truly, I am well."

"Good, I am glad to hear it." He drew back, his eyes bright with triumph. "The return of the Mirror Dragon! By the gods, I knew you were special, but I had never imagined such glory." His face seemed younger, as though the fierce joy had stripped away years. "Ido is furious, of course," he continued. "Not only did his dragon choose Dillon over Baret, but now he must share his ascendancy with *my* candidate. I thought he would explode with rage."

"There was a court lady here—Lady Dela—she said I was Coascendant, but how can there be two ascendant dragons?" I asked. "I don't understand."

My master shook his head. "There are so many questions. The council is in uproar. They don't know why the Mirror Dragon has suddenly returned, nor why he has returned out of his own year. The emperor's augurs are casting for the answers, but it cannot be denied that all the other beasts bowed to your dragon during the ceremony. Such unusual behavior must mean he is ascendant too, and that makes you coleader of the council. Ido does not like it, but even he cannot gainsay the emperor and the council majority."

"Do you know why the Mirror Dragon has returned, Master?" I asked. "Why he chose me?"

"No one knows, Eon," he said. "I think it must be your dragon sight. Your raw power brought him back. To be able to see all of the dragons is as rare as a dragon egg itself. And for the time being, it is how the council is explaining your ascension."

Hesitantly, I touched his arm, needing his reassurance. "Will it be all right, Master?"

He looked down at my hand, then finally covered it with his own. "It will be better than all right. You have done so well. We will be more powerful than even I had hoped. And if things go to plan, I will be back on the council and finally able to hobble Ido's ambitions." He smiled. "No more hard times for us, Eon."

I answered his smile, feeling my own exultation finally breaking through my fear. "We can have sweet buns every day," I said, delighted to see him smiling.

"Sweet buns? We can have shark fin every day if we want it." He grabbed my hands and stood up, swinging me off the bed. "I am very proud of you, Eon."

"After Ranne hit me, I thought I had failed you, Master." I returned the squeeze of his fingers. "I thought we had lost."

"Yes, I thought so, too. But like I said, no one knows how a dragon chooses. That's why I sent you out again for the final bow. It was hard, I know, but I had to send you."

"I didn't think I could do it. But I did. "

I felt the smock slip from my shoulder as he pulled me against his body. "Yes, you did," he murmured against my hair. I pressed into him, my body blindly molding itself into his approval. His breath against my ear was like the soft press of lips. "You've done well."

I rested my head on his shoulder as his hands stroked my hair, my neck, the dip of my collarbone. A sharp spark of energy snapped between us, breast to hand, leaving a singed smell.

And then I was standing alone, my arms still holding the moment before.

He stood a few paces back, cradling his hand, his eyes fixed on my bared skin.

"The dragon is still in you," he said. He lifted his fingers to his mouth, sucking away the pain.

I hugged my arms across my chest, the sting of our contact already fading. "I'm sorry, Master."

He shook his head. "You will have no control over your power yet."

"I can't really feel his presence in my mind. Is that normal?"

"It will take time to know his energy."

I nodded.

"I'll get wine," he said, turning away. "We can make an offering to the gods."

"I think there's wine on the bureau." I drew up the smock. "I'll pour some."

"I will," he said, striding across the room.

He was eager to move away from me. I felt for the bed and sat down.

"Of course, your union with the Mirror Dragon is just the beginning," he said. "We have much to plan. I have already laid the foundation in the council, but you must confirm the arrangements."

His muffled footsteps crossed the carpet toward me. I quickly stood up, moving away from the bed. He handed me a goblet, his gaze not quite meeting mine.

"Arrangements? What do you mean, Master?"

"I have urged the opinion that you are too inexperienced to be Coascendant without an advisor. The council has decided that you must nominate your proxy as soon as possible."

"You," I said.

He nodded once. "Me." He lifted his cup. "With thanks to the gods."

"With thanks," I echoed.

We drank. I felt my gut churn uneasily as the sour rice wine met the cocolat.

"What will happen now, Master?"

"Now we play our game to its end. You will study and learn to control your power. I will secure our position in the council. We will be very wealthy and very powerful by the time your tenure as Mirror Dragoneye ends."

"Yes, Master."

"You must stop calling me Master," he said roughly. "You are Lord Eon and when you confirm me, I will be Lord Brannon. That is how it must be." He looked into his wine, the muscles in his jaw tightening. "That is how it must be."

CHAPTER SEVEN

THE BATHING ROOM IN the Peony Guest Apartment was larger than my master's library. I shifted on the carved stool in the scrubbing corner, the wooden seat hard under my bare rump. The walls were tiled in mosaics of the city's three river gods, and at the far end of the room a mirror stretched from floor to ceiling. Steam rose from the large twelve-sided soaking pool sunk into the middle of the mosaic floor, which was constantly renewed and warmed from pipes below. The room smelled of ginger and heat. I smoothed the thin loincloth over my hips, wishing I had one to cover my chest as well.

"Close your eyes," Rilla said.

A warm weight of water broke over my head, streaming down my unbound hair. I coughed and opened my eyes as she held out my arm and rubbed its length with a rough cotton cloth.

"Did you finish the tea?" she asked.

I nodded, still tasting the residue of dirt. The brew was not sitting well with the mix of cocolat, wine, and the braised fish that the physician had sent to ease my fast.

Rilla worked the cloth vigorously down my other arm, hissing with pain as the movement chafed her blistered skin.

"You're hurting your hands," I said, pulling away from her grip. "I don't need to be washed. I had a bath for the ceremony."

Rilla grunted, taking hold of my arm again.

"You're a lord now. Lords bathe every week."

I laughed.

"No, truly," Rilla said with a final wipe. "When I was getting your clothes, Lady Dela's maid told me that her mistress bathes every day." She picked up the second bucket. "That girl has a tongue that flaps like washing hung in a high wind. Close your eyes."

"Why would Lady Dela bathe so much?" I managed to say before the water broke over me again.

Rilla squatted at my feet. "I suppose it's because she's a Contraire." She scrubbed my right leg. "They probably have to purify themselves or something."

"A Contraire?"

Rilla gently touched my bad leg. "May I?"

I nodded, carefully lifting my foot off the ground. Some of the pain in my hip had returned, but not all of it.

Rilla wiped the cloth down my shin. "A Contraire is a man who lives as a woman."

I pushed my wet hair out of my eyes. "Lady Dela is a man?"

"In body, she is. Her maid says she even has a prick." Rilla leaned back on her heels. "But she has a woman's spirit. According to the Eastern tribes, a Contraire has two souls: male and female. She has both Sun and Moon energy. A Contraire in the tribe brings luck."

"So it is accepted."

Rilla snorted. "It is in the Eastern tribes. Here, she is tolerated by the court because it is the emperor's pleasure. But there are some who whisper she is a demon with the Sight. She was even attacked a while back. That's why she has a guard."

"Did they find out who did it?"

"No, they are still searching. Lady Dela was sent by the Eastern lords as a gesture of goodwill to His Majesty. He is embarrassed that their gift has been harmed."

"Does it work the other way around? Can a woman have a man's spirit?"

Rilla sloshed water against my back. "Are you thinking of yourself?" she asked, lowering her voice. "But you don't have a male spirit. This is all playacting, isn't it?"

I shrugged, hunching over as she sluiced the water off me. How could I explain that it was not all playacting? That I felt more of the male spirit within me than the female—a fierceness that whittled me down to a sharpened spear of ambition. And as a boy, I was applauded, not punished, for such raw energy. It was not beaten out of me for my own good, or worn away by women's chores.

"I'm not sure what I am," I said slowly. "Perhaps I just can't remember how to act like a girl."

"Well, that's probably for the best," Rilla said. "Safer for us all." She handed me the cloth. "I expect you'll want to wash your front yourself."

I rubbed it over my breasts and belly, quickly dipping it lower when she turned to drain a bucket.

"Go and soak now," she said. "I'll lay out your clothes and be back to dry you."

She patted my shoulder and hurried out of the room, shutting the door with a sharp click.

I draped the loincloth over the stool and walked over to the pool. A mosaic of the Nine Fish Wealth Circle wavered at the bottom. I bent and dipped my fingers into the water. Very warm, bordering on hot; a good heat to ease the small gnawing pain in my hip. I straightened and started for the shallow steps that led into the water, but my attention was caught by movement in the mirror. Myself. Naked.

So bony and pale. I ran the flat of my hands over my chest and sides, feeling the small softness of breast and corrugation of rib. There was no exaggerated flare of hip like Irsa—I turned sideways—or round behind, but the curves of womanhood were still there. Luckily, the heavy tunics and trousers of court wear would hide them. I traced the scar that puckered my thigh. I was hit by a cart and dragged behind it. That's what my master said, but I couldn't remember any part of the accident. Only the dim shape of a man leaning over me with a tattoo across his face: the driver, perhaps, or a bystander. Just thinking about it sharpened the pain in my hip. I faced the glass again. The scar was not as big as I'd thought. And the twisted set to my leg was not as severe.

I moved closer. My reflection frowned. Something was different about my face since I had seen it in the Rat Dragon mirror. Less softness, more bone. I touched my cheeks, feeling the sharper shape of adulthood. My eyes looked larger, lips fuller. It was a face that was tipped more to the female. I pulled back my wet hair, holding it up on top of my head in a straggly imitation of a Dragoneye loop. A boy wearing a man's clothing and hairstyle. *May the gods let that be what they all saw.*

But it was not just appearance. It was movement, and attitude, and something else that was hard to name. Four years ago when my master bought me, we spent the long journey back to the city turning me into Eon. I studied the boys on the roads and the inns. How they moved decisively and took up space and made competitions of hauling water and chopping wood. I began to act like them, feeling years and years of subdued female movement expanding into glorious freedom. My master drilled me in the men's world of letters and numbers, and I practiced how to sit with my legs apart, my chin up, and my eyes bold.

But most of all I learned how not to be watched.

It was Dolana, at the salt farm, who first told me about the gaze of men; that look of temporary possession that some men gave female flesh. About its dangers and possibilities. "It can be used to survive," Dolana had said softly, showing me the power that lay in reflecting a man's desire. And even at twelve years old, the knowledge of it was already in the way I moved my head, my hands, my shoulders. But Dolana had whispered her secrets to a girl. And I had to become a boy.

When I left the salt farm, I had to stop being alert to the turn of a man's head toward me. Stop glancing up to meet his gaze in fleeting connection. Stop falsely veiling my eyes from his momentary interest. It was hard to train out of my body, but I practiced and learned to cloak myself in the skin and gaze of a boy.

Now that boy had to become a lord.

I let my hair drop down around my face and turned my back on the mirror, carefully taking the first step into the pool. The water closed around my feet, shins, thighs, and then I lowered the rest of my body into its warmth. A sigh eased out of me. It would be hard to act the part of a lord, but this time everyone would expect me to be ignorant and awkward. I would do as I did before—find someone to watch and copy. And my master would help me.

The warmth settled into my thoughts and body, softening my pain and unfocusing my mind. I sat on the low underwater ledge and leaned my head back until my neck rested on the tiled edge of the pool. The room was almost perfectly balanced—no heavy furniture to block the dragon energy, the pool shaped to enhance the circular flow of *Hua*, and the mirror to compensate for the shortened wall. No doubt a Dragoneye had been consulted on its design.

I let the heat rise through me, easing open my mind's eye. The dragons shimmered into being in a circle around the bath. They were almost all the same size, their energy flow unencum-

bered. They seemed to fit into the space they were in—as big
as buildings in the arena, but here only halfway to the ceiling.
And the Mirror Dragon—my dragon—was always twice as big
as the others.

I stood up, trying to see him through the steam. His dark
eyes drew me closer, his head tilted to one side, questioning. I
pushed slowly through the water toward him, but my view did
not clear. It was not steam obscuring my eyes. It was a haze that
hung over the dragon like a sheer curtain. Yet all of the other
dragons were clear in my sight.

Behind me, the sound of a soft knock and the door opening
jolted me out of my mind-sight. I turned, ducking down into
the water.

Rilla bustled in with folded drying sheets draped over her
arms.

"What's wrong?" she asked, pressing the door shut with her
back.

"You startled me." I waded to the steps. "I thought you might
have been someone else."

"No, Lady Dela has made it very clear to the other servants
that your living areas are never to be entered," Rilla said.

She shook out the sheet and held it up.

"You shouldn't be doing that with your sore hands," I said.

"I'm all right. Now come on, we've got to get you dry and
dressed."

I stepped into the dry warmth of the sheet, pulling the
edges around my body.

"Has this been heated?" I asked, stroking the thick cotton.

"Of course," Rilla said, rubbing my back dry through the cloth. "Do you think I'd let the new Lord Dragoneye get a cold arse when he stepped out of the bath? For shame."

We looked at each other and giggled.

After I was dry, Rilla wrapped a clean sheet around me and oiled my hair, deftly braiding it on the crown of my head in a shortened version of the Dragoneye double loop.

"It's the best I can do," she said, stepping back to consider her work.

"How do you know how to do it?" I asked.

She smiled. "I was the master's body servant when he was the Tiger Dragoneye. Quite a few years ago now, but I still remember the hairstyle." She smoothed a stubborn kink near my ear, her smile widening. "Of course these days the master does not need a hairdresser."

I smothered another giggle. Lords did not giggle. "Still, he will be missing you," I said.

Her eyes slid from mine, the light moment gone. "Perhaps. But he saw a chance to protect you here. That is what is important. And Irsa has been waiting for her chance to move higher." She picked up the wet bath sheet and shook it out roughly. "The master will not want for attention."

She opened the door and led the way through the narrow corridor to a nearby dressing chamber. It was a small room, dominated by a large clothespress that had one sliding screen door open, showing stacks of white underwear and folded hose. Next to it, a shabby basket was pushed against the wall; my old belongings from the master's house. Folded across the top were my best tunic and trousers, the faded dark cloth showing the neat patches.

Rilla's gaze followed mine. "It came yesterday. I did not know what you wanted to keep."

I ran to it with a sudden need to touch my old things. "Where are my ancestors' death plaques?" I asked, raking though the basket. "I need to make an altar. I need to honor them." I dug harder. "I need their protection."

Rilla crossed the room and stopped my frantic burrowing with a gentle hand. "They are there, my lord. Safely wrapped at the bottom. I packed them myself. I'll prepare an altar for you." She eased me back. "All right?"

I nodded, turning away from the tumbled basket to face a large mirror on a stand in the opposite corner. Ignoring my pale reflection, I focused on a wooden rack beside it, shaped like the torso of a man and hung with a magnificent three-quarter-length robe. The rich emerald silk had been woven thick with peacocks, butterflies, flowers, and a large waterfall with gold fish jumping through it.

"Am I to wear this?" I asked, shocked.

Rilla nodded.

"But it's a Story Robe."

I had seen them worn by nobles on their way to court celebrations, priceless works of art passed from father to son and often worth a whole estate.

"It was delivered while you were bathing," Rilla said, closing the door. "A gift from the emperor. He chose it for you himself. It's called 'A Summer Waterfall Brings Harmony to the Soul.'" Her voice lowered in awe. "It has even been retailored for you. Can you imagine the work?"

"It's from the emperor?" Gingerly, I touched the edge of a wide silk sleeve. Something deep within me knew that it was both wonderful and dangerous to receive such a gift from the Heavenly Master.

Rilla turned to the clothespress and selected a pair of white undershorts. "Here, put these on," she said, passing them to me. She pulled a rolled strip of cloth out of her pocket. "I've brought extra breast bands with me. I'll store them with my things. To be safe."

I nodded and pulled up the fine linen shorts, tying off the silk drawstring. "Such beautiful cloth for underthings," I murmured, rolling the delicate weave between my fingers.

"You should have seen the silk in storage for the court ladies. I've never seen such embroidery." Rilla moved behind me. "Hold up your arms."

She wrapped the band around my chest firmly, flattening my breasts against the underlying ribs until there were no curves to be seen. I winced as she pulled hard on the last layer and tied the cloth under my arm. Too bad I could not be rid of my womanly shape. It only brought me danger and pain.

"Is it tight enough?" she asked.

I ran my hands over the unforgiving bandage and took a breath, feeling the familiar constriction in my chest. "It's good."

Dressing in court robes was a lengthy affair. By the time Rilla had positioned the sleeveless silk undertunics, fastened the matching emerald green trousers, secured the indoor slippers, and tied the intricate sash that finished the "Harmony" robe, my back and hip were aching from the strain of standing still for so long.

"There, you're ready," she finally said, twitching the hem into place.

"Let me look."

I walked slowly to the mirror, the unaccustomed weight of all the layers dragging at my movements. A solemn boy looked back from the reflection, his fine features and slim body overwhelmed by the magnificence of his clothing.

"With any luck they will see the robe and not me," I said, brushing my hand lightly over the silk.

Rilla tilted her head. "I don't think you need to worry. You have a stubborn chin and a way of moving that is male. And the robe is cunningly cut and woven—see how it makes you look taller and wider at the shoulder?"

It was true. No wonder the Story weavers were so sought after and wooed with expensive gifts.

"The council and court are not looking for a girl," Rilla continued. "They could not even imagine such a deception. Anyway, you are Moon Shadow. You are expected to keep the sweetness of childhood. Which reminds me . . ." She crossed over to the clothespress and slid open the other door. "You will need to carry this."

She pulled out a small red lacquer box and flipped open the

lid, passing it to me. Inside, lying on a soft leather pouch, was a slim silver cone about the length and size of a finger.

"What is it?"

"A horn of tears. The eunuchs use them to pass water." She nodded at the look on my face. "I know. It must be very painful. As a Moon Shadow, you will be expected to have one." She picked up the cone and slid it inside the pouch, pulling the drawstring closed. "Carry it with you always. I think the eunuchs hang them from their sash."

I looked down at the thick, pleated sash around my waist. "Surely not on a Story Robe?"

"I don't know," Rilla said, frowning. "Perhaps Lady Dela can advise you. If you are ready, I'll take you to the reception room and send for her."

Rilla led me out to the formal reception room at the front of the apartment. Most of the outside wall was made of paneled sliding screens that opened up into an inner courtyard of the palace. Only two screens were open, and I glimpsed a jade guardian lion set on a shallow platform that surrounded the rooms. Beyond it was a garden laid out in "Tranquil View" design, with a small bridge and gnarled trees overhanging a pond. Even without using my mind-sight, I could tell that the restful energy of the garden was being cleverly directed toward the apartment.

The reception room was traditional: a straw-mat floor and a low, dark wood table surrounded by flat cushions. There were two matching alcoves in the back wall, each one displaying a painted scroll. A long bureau of matching dark wood stood against the far wall, with a single vase holding an arrangement of orchids. It was a place of quiet dignity. Rilla slid apart the remaining screens, opening up the courtyard view.

"Lady Dela has been summoned, my lord." she said. "Shall I prepare tea?"

Her sudden deference startled me. "Yes. Please."

I walked over to the left alcove, drawn to the vividly colored scroll. It was a painting of a dragon, the swirling tail and elegantly uplifted front claws creating a pleasing symmetry. I peered at the tiny name square and shivered. It was by the great Master Quidan. I crossed to its pair. A tiger, again by the master.

"They are very beautiful, are they not, my lord?"

I turned. Lady Dela was standing on the platform, flanked by her Shadow Man guard. In the daylight, I could see he had the look of a Trang islander about him. Perhaps he was one of the cattle-men. They both bowed, Lady Dela dropping to one knee and folding her hands in the bend of her hip, the pearl-and-gold hem of her cream robe pooling heavily at her feet.

"This, my lord, is the formal court bow of a lady to a lord. In response, the lord nods his head."

I quickly nodded.

"Excellent," she said, rising gracefully.

Although her every move was that of a woman, I could now see the man beneath the careful paint and rich clothing. And yet she was not a man. She was Lady Dela.

"Ryko here, is on duty," she continued. "Therefore, his bow is from the waist and does not require him to lower his gaze. Off duty, of course, he is required to drop to both knees and bow until his forehead is a hand's width from the floor, eyes lowered." She stepped to one side. "Show him, Ryko."

The big man bowed from the waist again. "I beg pardon, my lord," he said softly. "But I am on duty and unable to bow as my lady requests."

Lady Dela clapped. "See! He is a very good guard. Even if I order him, he will not do it."

I saw the hint of a smile twitch Ryko's lips.

"If you order me, lady, I will be in a grave dilemma," he said.

"How so?" she demanded. Her sharp features had softened with amusement.

"Upset a lady or follow my orders? Both are terrible crimes."

"Ha," she said, the black pearl at her throat quivering. "The terrible crime is your attempt at gallantry."

"As you say, my lady."

She turned away from him, her lips pressed together to stifle her own smile. "May I enter, my lord?" she asked.

"Of course."

She stepped out of her slippers and crossed the room, the Shadow Man taking his position at the doorway.

"Lord Eon," she said, returning to business, "all of lower rank are required to bow to you. That is, everyone except the imperial family and the other lords. You only need to acknowledge lower ranks with a brief nod. In a situation where you are of equal rank, say another Dragoneye lord, the younger lord nods to the elder. You will always bow to the emperor or one of his family by dropping to both knees and bowing from the waist at the angle of the crescent moon."

She stopped and looked closely at my robe, her thin eyebrows arching upward. "My goodness. Is that 'A Summer Waterfall Brings Harmony to the Soul'?"

"It was a gift from the emperor," I said.

"Indeed," she said, walking around me, her reddened lips pursed with thought. "Indeed. A most interesting gift." She flicked open a fan that hung from a ribbon around her wrist and waved it gently in front of her face. Above the finely painted edge, I saw shrewd calculation in her eyes. "Now that the Harmony Robe is yours, you should know its history. Perhaps, if we have time, I will tell you at the end of our lesson." The fan snapped shut. "There is one thing, however, we must attend to before we resume." She turned her head away politely, pointing the fan at the pouch hanging from my sash. "Ryko, perhaps you could assist Lord Eon?"

The guard hurried over to me.

"My lord, may I suggest you fold that under the sash?" he said. "The emperor has recently ruled that the court ladies should not look upon such a necessity. Allow me to help you."

He untied the strings and rolled the leather around the horn, quickly working it under the edge of the stiffly pleated sash.

I couldn't help the rise of heat to my face. "I did not know."

He bowed. "My lord, it would be my honor if you felt free to come to me with any questions about . . ." He lowered his voice. "About the way of the Shadow here at court."

I could not meet the kindness in his eyes. "Thank you," I whispered.

Ryko nodded in salute and returned to his position at the door.

Lady Dela swirled around to face me again, her face overly bright. "Now, my lord, what have you learned so far?"

I repeated her instructions back.

"Very good. I am so glad you are quick. The new Rat Dragoneye apprentice is too terrified to retain anything at the moment. Poor child."

"You mean Dillon?" I stepped forward. "You've seen Dillon?"

"Of course, you would have studied together," Lady Dela said smoothly. "I have been instructing him in court protocol. Is he a friend?"

I saw her note my hesitation.

"He is," I finally said. "Can I see him?"

It would be good to see Dillon and clear the air between us; his small betrayal meant nothing now. We had both won the prize. And I wanted to see his face when he saw me in a Story Robe.

"He is at his Dragon Hall, my lord. But you will see him tonight at the banquet. It is as much a welcome to him as it is to you, and he will be officially third guest of honor. In fact, I may be able to arrange the places so that you can speak to one another during the feast. Would that be agreeable?"

"Yes. Very agreeable."

"That is settled, then," she said, and I sensed I had entered a bargain without knowing the price. "Now, let us continue. When you leave the presence of the emperor or one of his family, you must never turn your back. It is an Insult of Death. You must learn the way of backing out of a room. Come, we will practice."

It was a long lesson. We stopped for the tea and mooncakes that Rilla brought in, and Lady Dela made the refreshment part of my instruction. She showed me how to kneel in the Story Robe and take tea in the formal manner of the nobles—which guest drank from his porcelain bowl first, when to eat the tiny festival cakes, and what was said at each stage of the ritual. Although I only ate two of the delicious cinnamon pastries, as prescribed by the ceremony, they added their weight to my unsettled stomach.

Finally, after I had mastered the formal and informal greetings and the backward kowtow out of the emperor's presence, Lady Dela nodded her approval.

"Enough for now, I think," she said. "You have done very well."

I bowed slightly, relieved that the session was over. But I could foresee a very large problem ahead of me.

"Lady, you will think me very stupid," I said, "but I have only ever seen the imperial family and the Dragoneye lords from a distance. I will not know which bow goes with which person."

She shook her head, the gold hair ornaments chiming. "Not stupid at all, my lord. When I first came to the court, I also did not know. It took a long time and many mistakes before I found my footing." She smiled, leaning toward me, and I smelled the sweetness of frangipani. "Don't worry, I will accompany you to the court banquets and gatherings for a while and whisper names in your ear. And also some pertinent information that will help you through the maze of personalities."

There was a small grunt from Ryko at the doorway.

Lady Dela unfurled the fan and hid us behind it. "Ryko thinks my mouth runs as fast as a rickshaw's wheels," she said in a loud whisper that easily carried to the guard.

"No, lady. I think that if Lord Eon is under your instruction in matters of court intrigue, he could not have a better teacher."

She widened her eyes at me. "Now he thinks I am an intriguer."

"I certainly find you intriguing, lady," I said, attempting to match their banter.

Lady Dela nodded her approval. "A deft deflection, my lord." She shut the fan. "I think you will do well at court. Now, would you like to hear the history of your robe? It is something you should probably know before you enter the banquet room tonight."

She took my hand and held it out so that the wide-cut sleeve fell freely.

"This robe was designed and woven by Master Wulan. It was commissioned as a gift for the emperor by the family of Lord Ido when he was chosen as apprentice."

I flinched at the Dragoneye's name. Lady Dela nodded at my reaction, tracing her finger along an emblem woven into the sleeve.

"See here, this is the family device and under it is the character for Ambition, the Rat Dragoneye's area of special influence. The robe tells the story of the bountiful summer, but if you look closely you will see that worked into the waterfall and peacock is a hint of winter—the *Lin* and *Gan* encompassed in—"

"Lady Dela," I said tightly, breaking into her obvious digression. "Why does the emperor give me a gift he received from Lord Ido's family?"

She glanced at Ryko.

"Tell him everything," the guard said flatly. "This is not a time to play games."

"It is the most important time," she snapped.

He glared across the space between them. "No. Even a leaf in the wind settles sometime. You knew this choice was coming."

She opened her fan and closed it, fingering the polished bamboo ribs as she watched Ryko walk the length of the open doorway, surveying the garden.

"Well?" she asked.

He nodded. "We are alone. Tell him."

"All right, all right," she said, holding up her hands. "The robe is the emperor's way of sending a message to Lord Ido and, through him, to High Lord Sethon, his royal brother."

"Lord Ido serves High Lord Sethon," I said, remembering the snatch of conversation between my master and the official at the arena.

"Yes, you are very quick," she said, lowering her voice. "Together they have built a base of power that, in all truth, exceeds the emperor's. It is no secret that Sethon covets the throne, and now, through Ido, he owns the Dragoneye Council as well as the armies. With the emperor ill and Prince Kygo of age but still living within the protection of the harem, Sethon was near making his move. That is, until you came along." She touched my shoulder. "The awakener of the Mirror Dragon. A Coascendant Dragoneye. But more importantly, a potential split in the Dragoneye Council. And the emperor is not wasting any time claiming you and your dragon as his own."

The weight of her words pressed down on me. Without having even seen High Lord Sethon, I had made an enemy of the most powerful man in the land. And the emperor saw me as his way back to supremacy. I was the rabbit caught between two ravenous wolves.

"It is why the emperor is keeping you close," Lady Dela said. "Why you were brought to the palace. Granted, there is no Mirror Dragon Hall at the moment, but you could have gone to one of the other halls. And tonight, when you walk into the banquet room in the Harmony Robe, the emperor will have made his intentions very clear to his brother and to the Dragoneye Council."

I pressed my fingers over my mouth. My master had not reckoned on me becoming the focus of royal attention—I was only supposed to be an apprentice. Ryko crossed the floor and laid his hand on my shoulder, as if keeping me from gathering up the misnamed robe and running from this deadly struggle.

"Courage, my lord," he said gruffly. "There is nowhere to go. You are locked in this game until its endplay."

"Do you know where my master has gone?" I asked urgently. "I need to see my master."

He would know what to do. How to tread softly between these two mighty forces.

"Heuris Brannon," Lady Dela corrected gently, "has returned to his home to dress for the banquet."

A cold realization washed over me. From now on, my master would not always be there to protect and counsel me.

"This is too big. Too big," I said. "What do I do?"

"You follow your destiny," Ryko said. "As we all do. With honor and courage."

Lady Dela rolled her eyes. "What kind of piddling answer is that to give the boy?" She grabbed my arm, her long fingernails digging through the silk. I felt the man's strength in her grip. "Listen to me. You are no longer a penniless candidate. You are a Dragoneye lord. The court is abuzz with the sight of the other dragons bowing to you. You have power that frightens even Lord Ido. So use it."

I could barely sense my dragon, let alone use his power. Lord Ido had nothing to fear from me. But even if he knew that, it would not stop him. I remembered the look on his face as he watched the dragons bow to me. That was what he wanted—all of the dragons bowing to him. And I was in the way.

I pulled my arm from Lady Dela's grasp. She was a man living as a woman—a survivor. She would not align herself with a hopeless cause.

"Who do you think will win this struggle, Lady Dela?" I asked. "Who do you follow?"

She sat back, eyeing me silently. I stayed very still, not even blinking under her scrutiny.

"The emperor," she finally said.

"Why?"

"Because Lord Ido and High Lord Sethon despise what I am."

"And because the emperor is the Heavenly Master," Ryko admonished.

We both looked at him.

"No," Lady Dela said softly. "Because the Heavenly Master now has the most powerful Dragoneye on his side."

CHAPTER EIGHT

"WELCOME, LORD EON," the emperor's whispery voice said above me.

He was seated at the top of a tiered dais, and I could see his foot, swollen and bandaged, resting on a small stool under the banquet table. Beside it, a matching stool had been placed in front of an empty chair; a ghost setting for the empress, dead almost a year.

"The Harmony Robe suits you well," His Majesty said. "You may rise."

I lifted my knee and painfully slid my foot forward, rocking up into the crouching stand that Lady Dela had shown me. I chanced a quick look at the Heavenly Master. His shoulders were hunched, and the sallow, loose skin of his face left the impression that he had recently been a much bigger, more vigorous man. The huge imperial pearl, easily the size of a duck egg, filled the hollow at the base of his throat. Unlike Lady Dela's black pearl strung on a piercing rod, this pearl was in a gold setting and sewn into the emperor's skin. It was a symbol of his wisdom and sovereignty—his descent from the ancient dragons—and would only be removed at his death, to be sewn into the throat of his heir. I could see that the emperor's skin had grown over the gold base, melding man and gem together.

My eyes flicked up to his face and, for a frozen moment, the Heavenly Master's gaze met mine. I looked away as required, but not before I saw his eyes cut to Lord Ido at the table below. His Majesty had also caught the Dragoneye's tension at the sight of my robe.

One of the eunuchs in charge of banquet etiquette appeared at my elbow.

"This way, my lord," he murmured through the rise of whispers behind me. I bowed, preparing to retreat.

"Lord Eon."

The voice was young and forceful.

I looked up and saw the Prince Heir leaning forward in his seat on the lower level of the dais. He had the same determined jaw and broad forehead as his father. His eyes, too, held the same watchful intelligence.

"My esteemed father has suggested you may wish to study statecraft to prepare for your new position as Coascendant Dragoneye," he said. "I am tutored in the mornings by the most excellent Prahn. Would you care to join us tomorrow?"

I gripped the edges of the robe tightly and bowed again.

"It will be an honor, Your Highness."

There was a brief glance between father and son. Lady Dela had predicted a very public maneuver to draw me quickly into the imperial circle. *It will not be a command from the emperor,* she had said. *It will be an invitation from someone known to be his supporter—that way you will be seen to be declaring your colors.*

But even she had not imagined it would be the Prince Heir.

The eunuch touched my shoulder, and we backed up the length of the huge room, in between the two lower tables full of courtiers and administrators. The richly dressed men and their women sat along the gold walls lined with bright oil lamps, and I felt them watch me as we made our slow progress past. Some were just curious, some hostile, some afraid. Halfway along, I saw my master. Until I confirmed him as my proxy the next day, he could not sit with me. He nodded and smiled, but even that did not give me heart.

The eunuch led me along the right wall and up a step toward the high Dragoneye table, beside the imperial dais. The two chairs closest to the royal table were empty; the end one guarded by Ryko, the other alongside Dillon. Lady Dela had kept her promise; I would have a chance to talk to my friend. He sat in stiff-backed terror beside Lord Ido. All of the other apprentices stood behind their Dragoneye lords, ready to serve them. They bowed as I passed, eyes lowered. Their masters were not so polite. I sensed a wave of movement behind me as each Dragoneye turned in his seat to get a better look, and heard their soft words follow me down the row: *too young, a danger, too late.*

Lady Dela seemed to be the only one at ease. She was standing by a large carved screen at the corner of the room. In between the closely worked design, glimpses of dark hair, gold pins, and shades of blue silk marked the positions of three ladies—the imperial concubines currently in favor. Lady Dela was obviously bargaining with one of them, for she made the sweeping hand gesture from forehead to heart that closed a deal. She looked up as the eunuch seated me.

"Lord Eon," she said, hurrying over, the black pearl swinging at her throat. "How pleasant to see you again." She dropped to one knee. "The prince was asking me about you just before seating, and now I see he has asked you to study with him. A most thoughtful invitation." She flicked open her fan and, from behind its cover, showed me round eyes and raised brows. Her court smile was back in place as the fan snapped shut. "And I believe you know Apprentice Dillon," she continued smoothly, rising and nodding to the eunuch to pull out her chair. As she sat, Ryko bowed and moved into his position at her shoulder, his face carefully blank. Beside me, Dillon bent low over his clasped hands.

"Lord Eon." His gaze was fixed on the floor.

"I'm glad we are sitting next to each other," I said. "We have a lot to talk about."

He glanced up, a hesitant smile easing the tight fear on his face. I winked in my old way, and his smile widened.

I looked past him to his master. "Greetings, Lord Ido," I said with a nod, pleased that my voice did not tremble.

"Lord Eon. You are very resplendent tonight," he said smoothly. "I am honored that His Majesty has given you the robe my family presented to him."

I felt Lady Dela shift beside me in warning. We had rehearsed as many of Lord Ido's reactions as we could imagine before she was called to take her place at the table. I forced a smile as false as his own.

"I am doubly honored," I said. "A robe with such a fortunate history can only bring luck to the wearer."

He stared at me for a moment. "As we Dragoneyes know, luck is a fragile force. It can easily turn bad in the wrong hands. Is it not so, Lord Eon?"

Murmuring my agreement, I arranged the robe to hide my shaking hands. Before me was a plate of translucent blue porcelain flanked by silver chopsticks, and a soup spoon cast into the shape of a swan. A perfect frangipani floated in a matching blue fingerbowl. I focused on each piece, finding comfort in their beauty.

"You are doing well," Lady Dela said, touching my arm.

I looked over at the table of ranked courtiers opposite. "Which one is High Lord Sethon?"

"He is not here," Lady Dela said softly. "Gone to quell a border dispute in the East." Her eyes flicked across to Lord Ido. "But he will not be ignorant of tonight's events."

A heavy thump brought sudden silence in the room. The

emperor's personal herald was pounding his staff in the middle of the floor, calling for attention.

"His Imperial Majesty will speak," the man cried.

Immediately, we all bowed over our plates. The Heavenly Master released us with a wave of his hand.

"We are here to honor the changing of the year and, with it, the ascension of the Rat Dragoneye, Lord Ido, and his new apprentice, Dillon." Everyone leaned forward to catch the thin threads of his voice. "But it is also a celebration of a most momentous occasion: the return of the Mirror Dragon and the extraordinary ascension of a young man to Dragoneye status. Lord Eon and his Mirror Dragon are a sign to Us that Our rule is favored by the gods." He lifted a gold bowl. "We give our thanks for such a gift."

I stared at the silver bowl in my hand. The emperor was making me into a sign from the gods. A drowning man groping for a twig. And his dismissal of Lord Ido's ascension was not going to sit well with the Dragoneye.

"With thanks," I said, blending my voice into the tail end of the reverence and wetting my lips with the wine. Beside me, Dillon drained his bowl noisily, his startled eyes appearing over the rim as he realized his mistake.

"More importantly," His Majesty continued in a stronger voice, "the augurs tell me that the Mirror Dragon has come back to us, out of his own year of ascension, for a specific purpose."

I looked up. His Majesty was staring at me.

"It is not a secret that my health is failing. But eighteen years ago, the land was blessed by the birth of my heir, Prince Kygo. The augurs say that the Mirror Dragon, the Dragon Dragon, has returned and chosen Lord Eon to prepare for my son's reign. Lord Eon and the Mirror Dragon are here to build a stronghold of power and good fortune for the Prince Heir."

For a moment there was silence, and then in a ragged wave people rose to their feet and turned to me, bowing and clapping. In shock, I met the Heavenly Master's eyes. They were glazed with the fever of belief. Or desperation.

What could I do? Deny the emperor? It would be immediate death. I stared out into the blur of hands and faces. My master would know what to do. I found him still sitting, his body rigid, his face blanched. He looked up at me, and in his widened eyes I saw the same fevered belief.

Had I been chosen by the Mirror Dragon to stand behind the emperor and the Prince Heir? The emperor and my master believed it. The imperial augurs believed it. Who was I to question them?

An empire resting on my shoulders; it was too much weight to bear.

There was one other person who had not jumped to his feet at His Majesty's announcement. From the corner of my eye, I could see Lord Ido sitting back in his chair, watching me with a grim smile. My elevation to Heavenly Sign had come as no surprise or joy to him.

"His Majesty makes another bold move," Lady Dela

whispered behind the cover of her clapping hands. "Bow to him, quickly, or we'll never eat."

She was right—it was just another move in a game of power. Strangely reassured, I pressed my hands together and lowered my head, away from the expectation in the faces in front of me. The din was suddenly stopped by the thump of the herald's staff. All attention was returned to the emperor.

"Lord Eon will be my guest at the palace until the Mirror Dragon Hall can be rebuilt. And as part of Twelfth Day celebrations, I will be honored to return to him and his dragon those treasures that were saved from the fire that took the hall five hundred years ago. It has been a sacred duty of this dynasty to protect the treasure of the Mirror Dragon. When my father, the Master of Ten Thousand Years, showed me the vault in our library and passed on the duty to me, he offered these words of wisdom." The emperor paused for effect. "'Remember, my son, a dragon is like a tax collector; one piece of gold short, and he will hunt you for eternity.'"

Beside him, Prince Kygo threw back his head and laughed. Belatedly, the room broke into polite giggles, the ladies hiding their mouths behind spread fans.

Treasure? Kept for me?

"Is there really a vault full of gold?" I asked Lady Dela.

Before she could speak, Lord Ido had ordered Dillon out of his seat and was leaning toward me across the generous gap. "His Majesty speaks figuratively, Lord Eon," he said, casting a wry look at the emperor, who was still smiling at his own wit. "The treasure is not gold."

"You've seen it, my Lord?" I asked, hiding my disappointment in the quick question.

"No. But the council holds records of what was saved. It is nearly the only record we have of the Mirror Dragon." He paused, glancing down the table at the other Dragoneyes, all of them lethargic in comparison to his dark energy. His lips quirked upward. "You and your dragon are quite the mystery. As you can see, the council is almost frenzied in its excitement."

I found myself smiling, drawn into his playful mockery.

He moved closer and I saw a flick of silver pass across his eyes. "According to the records, the treasures in the vault include some fine pieces of furniture. . . ."

A wave of nausea suddenly pulled at me. I felt something struggling through layers of resistance, giving me a moment of clear mind-sight. In front of me was a silvery line of power being siphoned from the energy in the room. It flowed into Lord Ido, feeding the yellow point of power in the delta of his ribs. The center of charisma. Above it, the green heart-point seemed even paler and smaller than before.

He was using power to charm me.

My mind-sight receded, leaving a familiar sense of loss. The Mirror Dragon. Gone, again. Lord Ido had stopped talking, his eyes narrowed. Had he felt the dragon, too? I drew back and saw his face harden, but his voice kept its smooth caress.

". . . and a few of the instruments necessary to our art. I believe I saw a jeweled Dragon compass on the list."

I needed to get away from the power that called me to him. To make some space between us. I gave a small bow.

"My thanks, Lord Ido."

"My pleasure, Lord Eon."

He waved Dillon back to the table as the herald called attention to the emperor.

"Let us eat now," the Heavenly Master announced. "At the second sweet course, we will listen to the poets who have prepared their words in honor of the occasion." He held up a piece of carved jade hanging from a red silk ribbon. "And a prize for the artist whose words stir us the most."

"One guess who that will be," Lady Dela muttered. She caught the question in my face and indicated the screen behind us. "Lady Jila has been having a very long winning streak." Behind her, Ryko made a low noise of reproach. Lady Dela sighed irritably. "All right, perhaps I am being unfair. Just because she is the Prince's mother does not mean she is not a good poet."

"She is the prince's mother?" I said. "I had thought the empress was—"

Lady Dela shook her head, placing one finger over her mouth. "That is how it is recorded, but the empress was barren. The firstborn male in the harem is always attributed to the empress if she has no issue of her own. That way, there is no doubt of succession." She beckoned me closer. "You should understand that Lady Jila is a sensible woman. She knows that although she cannot be acknowledged as the prince's mother, it is her issue that will sit on the throne. And after two girl children, she has recently borne another son, so her position in the household is secure." She watched as a sturdy man in a short white tunic knelt by the emperor. "Ah, the imperial food taster has been summoned. The cold course must be finally on its way."

Even as she spoke, two lines of eunuchs carrying covered platters filed into the room and positioned themselves along the front of the tables. The eunuch in front of me placed two dishes on the table, his eyes properly downcast. The herald thumped his staff against the floor, and as one, the servers lifted the silver domes. All along the table were plates full of exquisitely presented food: shredded pork, cabbage tossed with nuts, duck with beans, cold eggs, pickled vegetables, greens dressed in oils, sticky rice rolled in seaweed, cold roasted chicken, smoked flaked fish, and round pea cakes served with ginger.

"So much," I breathed.

Lady Dela studied the pork dish in front of her, then nodded to the server to spoon it onto her plate. "Be sparing, my lord," she cautioned, holding up her hand to stop another spoonful. "There are eleven other courses to come."

Another eunuch stopped in front of me.

"My lord," he said in the soft voice of service. "The royal physician sends you this dish and begs you to eat it first to assist with your digestion."

I looked over at the physician, seated across the room on a lower table. He had changed his outfit and was now dressed in shades of green that did nothing for his pasty skin. I nodded my thanks, and he smiled graciously, urging me to eat with exaggerated gestures. The eunuch placed the plate on the table and removed the cover, displaying crisp green beans and smooth white squares encrusted with sesame seeds.

"What is it?"

"Cold eel, my lord. To boost the blood."

I picked up the heavy silver chopsticks, eager to try the delicacy. It had a strange texture, chewy yet tender, with a nutty taste enhanced by the sesame. Beside me, Dillon was staring at a duck dish, his fingers gripping the edge of the table.

"My lord, can you assist Apprentice Dillon?" Lady Dela asked between mouthfuls.

I signaled to our server, who promptly spooned duck onto his plate.

"Just tell them what you want," I told him, feigning confidence.

He licked his lips nervously. "Look at it all."

I grinned, trying to coax some ease from him. "We are surely blessed, hey?"

His smile did not quite reach the shadowy pain in his eyes. I had seen that look before, on the few occasions he had been beaten by Heuris Bellid.

"How is it?" I asked him softly, nodding toward his new master. Lord Ido had his back to us, talking to the Dragoneye beside him.

The shadows deepened. "As you say, we are surely blessed." He picked up his wine bowl and drained it again.

"I am glad to hear it."

Under the table, I pressed my foot against his leg. He returned the pressure, his eyes blinking rapidly. It seemed we had both stepped into treacherous situations.

"Lord Eon, allow me to recommend the pea cakes," Lady Dela said, claiming my attention.

In between eating the next three courses—an array of soups followed by lobster, then scallops—Lady Dela offered a low-voiced commentary on the Dragoneyes at the table. Lord Tyron, sitting next to Lord Ido, was the Ox Dragoneye and an emperor's man. I leaned back in my seat to look at him; thickset for a Dragoneye, with deep troughs that ran from nose to mouth. He was next in the cycle of ascendancy and so would retire in favor of his apprentice at the end of the year. Next down the line, and in order of ascendancy, was Lord Elgon, the Tiger Dragoneye. "Definitely a follower of Ido," Lady Dela whispered. He was long faced, with a prominent jaw and flat nose that gave him the appearance of a shovel. Lord Elgon would have been apprenticed to my master when he was the Tiger Dragoneye, but I had never heard my master speak of him. Beside Elgon was the Rabbit Dragoneye, Lord Silvo. A pale, handsome man—the drain of his vocation had pared down his face into classic planes and angles. "A fence-sitter," Lady Dela said. "Always trying to make peace between the factions." We had just got to Lord Chion, the Snake Dragoneye, when a young eunuch in the black livery of the harem appeared at Lady Dela's side. He bowed and presented a scroll sealed with wax and hung with jade beads at the end sticks. She pulled the scroll apart and scanned it.

"Does my lady wish to reply?" he asked.

"No." She waved him away and read the scroll again. "Well," she said with a frown, "this will stir things up. I only hope they don't blame the messenger."

I glanced at the flowing characters on the paper but didn't recognize any of them. "What is it?"

"Lady Jila's poem for the competition." She placed the scroll on the table. "Naturally, she can't present it to the court herself, so she has asked me to read it. I translated her book of verse last summer and it was a great success."

"What language is it? Is she from the Eastern tribes?"

"No, no." She leaned closer and whispered, "It's in Woman Script."

"In what?"

Lady Dela smiled at the look on my face. "It's very old. Passed from mother to daughter. I think it started as a way for women to write to each other. To express their feelings. Nothing very learned, of course, but since we are not allowed men's letters, it is a way for us to share our thoughts." She paused, looking down at the scroll. "And our loneliness."

In my mind, I saw a fleeting image of a woman drawing in the sand with a stick, carving out the strokes of a character, her arm around my shoulders. My mother? I let go of the memory and sat back. A Dragoneye lord would not have anything to do with women's writing. Or women's thoughts and fears.

"Tell me about Lord Chion," I said.

Lady Dela picked up the scroll and pushed it into her sleeve, unfazed by my abruptness.

"He is one to watch," she said. "The Snake Dragon is the Keeper of Insight, and Lord Chion is as sharp as they come."

I glanced down the table. All I could see of him was a long hand cradling a wine bowl. If he could see through pretense, then I would do well to avoid him.

"Where do his loyalties lie?"

She tilted her head toward Lord Ido.

The next in the line was Lord Dram, the Horse Dragoneye. Lady Dela opened her fan and waved it comically in front of her face. The Horse Dragon was the Keeper of Passion, she told me, pretending to pant, and Lord Dram was very serious about it. I caught a glimpse of his vivid face as he sat back in his seat laughing; there was more energy in him than the others, although he did not have the vigor of Lord Ido. An emperor's man, Lady Dela added, but not much use since he did not have the respect of the other Dragoneyes.

The next course was being served. Chicken, prepared in all ways, served with large bowls of wild rice. I poked at my serving of chicken feet fried in batter. My stomach was so stretched that my queasiness had turned into pain. Dillon had stopped eating, too, but was still draining his wine bowl every time it was filled by the server.

"Do you know, I have never eaten scallops before?" he said. "Or lobster. I didn't like the lobster. Did you like the lobster? I didn't like it." He was having trouble focusing on my face.

"It's very rich," I said.

Dillon nodded, too many times. "Rich. You're right. Everything is rich." He suddenly giggled. "We're rich."

Lady Dela tapped her fan on my arm. "Look. Over there."

Four musicians had kowtowed into the center of the room, followed by a troupe of twelve men, each dressed as one of the animals in the cycle. The famous Dragon Dancers—I had heard of them, but they never performed outside of the palace. The dancer dressed in the red of the Mirror Dragon bowed before me, his elaborate robe rippling with silver beads worked into the shapes of scaled skin and ending in a long train.

The first notes of the pipe music shivered across the room, stilling the conversation. Then the dancers began to move, their bodies taking on the characteristics of their animal. They danced the cycle, enacting the sacred duty of the Dragoneye to protect and nurture the land and its people. I gasped as they made rain fall with fine silver streamers, changed the flow of rivers with bolts of blue silk, and stilled winds made of sheer muslin. And then, in turn, each dancer twirled and leaped alone, bringing into movement the virtue kept by their dragon animal. When it was the red dancer's turn, he was joined by another in an identical costume, and they twirled and leaped in harmony, a perfect mirror image of each other. They were dancing Truth. My dragon was the Keeper of Truth. The irony made me shift in my chair.

At the end of the performance, the room erupted with shouts and clapping. I stamped my feet along with everyone else, showing our appreciation to the dancers by shaking the floor beneath them. As they bowed out of the room, the servers moved into place, quietly setting down the first sweet course. Pastries awash in cane syrup, candied nuts, sugared plums, honeycombs, fresh berries, tiny cakes, and bean buns.

"Honey!" Dillon yelled, grabbing one of the dripping combs straight from the serving plate. He waved the delicacy at me. "Look, Eon! Honey."

There was a loud crack—bone hitting bone. Dillon's head jerked back.

"You forget yourself, apprentice," Lord Ido hissed, his arm still raised from the sweep of the blow. A thick blue vein was throbbing down the center of his forehead.

Dillon crouched in the chair. "I'm sorry, my lord. I'm sorry. Please, I'm sorry."

"Don't apologize to me. Apologize to Lord Eon."

Dillon scrabbled around to face me, bowing low. "My lord, forgive me."

I stared at his pale nape and small ears. Below his bowed head, blood was dripping onto the floor, mixed with the honey that oozed from the comb still in his hand. I felt Lady Dela nudge me in the back.

"I have taken no offense," I said quickly.

"Get some cloth, clean this up," Lord Ido ordered one of the servers. "And you"—he jabbed a forefinger into Dillon's shoulder—"sit still and do not dishonor me further."

He flexed his hand, easing out the pain in his knuckles. A eunuch hurried up and offered him a damp towel.

"The boy!" he yelled, pushing the towel toward Dillon. "Give it to the boy." He pressed his palm into his forehead and signaled to an etiquette eunuch. "I need air," he said through clenched teeth.

The eunuch bowed and began to clear a way behind the chairs.

Lord Ido stood and nodded to me and Lady Dela, then made the deep obeisance to the emperor. We watched him back away, ignoring the overtures of the other Dragoneyes as he passed.

"That man's fuse is getting shorter and shorter," Lady Dela said thoughtfully.

A very young harem eunuch dropped to his knees beside her, waiting to deliver a message. Lady Dela sighed.

"Let me guess," she said to him. "Lady Jila wants a few words with me before I deliver her masterpiece."

The eunuch nodded, vainly trying to fight off a smile.

"By your leave, Lord Eon," Lady Dela said, gathering the edge of her gown into one hand and preparing to rise.

"Of course."

I turned back to Dillon and touched his shoulder. "Come on," I said. "Clean yourself up."

He pressed the towel against the cut above his eye.

"I forgot," he said, almost to himself.

"All that wine didn't help." I pulled his hand down and peered at the injury. "It's stopped bleeding."

"All this is . . . It's just not as . . ." He stopped, casting a frightened look around for Lord Ido, but the Dragoneye had already left the room.

"Easy?" I suggested. "But it's better than not being chosen, hey?"

He smiled wanly. "When I touched the Rat Dragon's pearl—all that power through me—it was as if I owned the world." He looked up at me, his face clearing into wonder. "You know what it was like."

I returned his smile. "I do."

"And then when I felt his true name rush through me, I nearly burst from the joy."

The air stilled around me. True name? All my muscles locked with a terrible foreboding.

"His true name," I echoed.

"Is that how you felt, too, my lord?" Dillon asked.

I nodded stiffly.

Was that the whisper that had slipped away from me? I remembered pressing my ear and hands against the golden pearl, straining to hear the fading sound. Why did the dragon's name not rush through me, as it had for Dillon? My breath caught in my throat. Was it because I would not call out my hidden name? But it would have meant my death.

I had missed my only chance to learn the red dragon's name.

Dillon wiped blood from his cheek. "It is humbling to know I can now call the Rat Dragon and his power," he said. "Lord Ido has already shown me the courtesies." He looked back at the doorway, relaxing when he saw his master had not returned.

I had no way to call the Mirror Dragon.

No way to call his power.

No way to do the emperor's bidding.

If I could not call the dragon and use his power, I was of no use to the emperor or my master. Or anyone.

"Are you all right, my lord?" Dillon asked.

No one must know. It would mean my death. My master's death. The emperor would kill us both.

"Lord Eon?"

I flinched as Dillon tentatively touched my hand.

"Very humbling," I said, forcing myself to smile.

Beside me, a eunuch pulled out Lady Dela's chair.

"Just a word change," she said, sitting down. "The artist is never satisfied."

For the next few hours, I could not see past my fear or the stark truth that pounded through me; I could not call my dragon. At some point, Lord Ido returned to his seat. More food arrived and I ate until a deep nausea rose into my throat, stopping me from pushing any more into my mouth. The poets read their work and I clapped and smiled, although I could not make sense of the words. Only one verse, spoken by Lady Dela, penetrated:

When Sun and Moon rise together
Heaven holds the Pearl of Night
Bringing darkness to the blinding light
And cool relief to a burning land.

Lord Ido's head snapped up. The polite silence in the room suddenly sharpened, and I felt everyone's attention focus on the two of us. The emperor began to clap, the prince quickly joining his father in the ovation. Hurriedly, the courtiers and other guests added their applause. Lady Jila had won the jade, the young harem eunuch carrying it to her behind the screen.

And then, finally, the banquet was over. We all dropped to our knees as the emperor was carried out of the room in an elaborate sedan chair, followed by the Prince Heir. I stared down at the mosaic floor, trying to find some distraction from the shivering that had taken hold of my body. Slowly, everyone around me stood, their conversation more relaxed now that the imperial presence was gone. I felt Ryko's bulk behind me, then his large hand around my arm, hauling me up.

Lady Dela looked at me closely. "You are not well, my lord?"

I shook my head, afraid to open my mouth in case I vomited.

"I'll arrange for you to be taken back to your apartment."

She motioned to a stocky eunuch and gave him low-voiced instructions. He bowed, then led me across the room, weaving around the groups of chatting guests in such a way that no one halted our progress. I was out in the courtyard before anyone else. The eunuch ushered me quickly along a path that passed between elegant buildings and through courtyard gardens lit by round red lanterns. I breathed deeply as we walked, trying to quell the sickness with the cool night air. I knew I was going to vomit, but not in the Harmony Robe—I had to get back to the apartment.

Finally, the eunuch stopped. "Your rooms, my lord," he said, bowing.

Gasping, I doubled over. I had not recognized the garden

or the apartment in the soft light of the lanterns. A shadow stepped off the low platform, solidifying into Rilla as she hurried toward me.

I waved the eunuch away. "Thank you. Go."

He bowed and disappeared into the gloom. Rilla caught me just as I dropped to my knees.

"I'm going to be sick," I managed. "Get me out of the robe."

Rilla pulled me up into a crouch, half carrying me to the platform.

"The robe," I rasped.

She eased me down onto the step and pulled at the sash, working the ties.

"Hold still," she said. "It's nearly undone."

I fixed my eyes on a lamp, panting. The sash loosened and dropped to the platform. Rilla pulled the robe down off my shoulders. I wrenched my arms out of the sleeves and fell forward, landing heavily on the gravel path. Sharp stones dug through my thin underrobes, sending hot pain shooting through my palms and knees. The first retch brought up spit and snot. The second, only foul gas that made me cough. The third felt as though I was dragging up my stomach. Then, in a choking stream of half-digested meat, soup, rice, and wine, the banquet emptied out of me, over and over again until it felt as though I was disgorging my very bowels.

"By the gods, how much did you eat?" Rilla said, her hand pressed against my forehead, supporting my head.

But I didn't have time to answer. I heaved forward with another retch. And another. Finally, it stopped. I hawked and spat into the carefully cropped grass.

"I'm never going to eat again," I said, wiping my nose. "How do the nobles do it night after night?"

"Tonight was nothing," Rilla said cheerfully. She picked up the Story Robe and arranged the bulky folds over her arms. "Wait until you see the emperor's birthday feast next month. It goes for three days and nights."

I slowly pushed myself up onto my feet. The far screen door slid open and two maids hurried out. One wiped my forehead with a cool damp cloth, the other offered me a cup of minted water. I rinsed my mouth and spat onto the grass. If I did not find my dragon's name soon, I would not live long enough to see the emperor's feast.

CHAPTER NINE

THE NEXT MORNING, I was woken by Rilla pulling back the shutters. Predawn light made the room a landscape of gray shadows, the flicker of red embers in the brazier the only flare of color.

"Feeling better?" she asked.

I rolled onto my back and blinked away the blur of sleep. New shapes in the corner of the room slowly focused into a small altar—floor cushion, offering bowls, incense sticks, death plaques. I had not even noticed it last night; exhaustion had plunged me straight into a dreamless abyss. At least that deep weariness was now gone, but I was still floating in a warm lethargy. I stretched out my arms and legs, pushing past the sharp catch in my hip.

"Much better. Thank you."

And then I remembered—*I didn't have his name.*

I sat up, all lazy comfort gone. Rilla crossed over to the brazier and lifted the water pot off the heat.

"I've got the tea ready," she said, pouring water into a waiting bowl. "Do you think you can manage some food, too?"

My stomach lurched, then settled into a hollow ache. "Maybe a little bit."

I didn't have his name and no one must know. Not even my master or Rilla. Not yet.

Rilla whisked the tea, then carefully carried it to the bedside table.

"Drink that up and I'll be back in a minute," she said, heading to the door.

"Can you make it something plain?" I asked.

"No duck, I promise," she said, smiling. The door closed.

I leaned back against the headboard. Even though the ghost maker's tea was an arm's length away, its dank smell was making my stomach turn. I picked it up and stared into the murky liquid. I had to think of some way to find my dragon's name.

Where does one look for the unknowable? Even if I wanted to risk asking someone, there was no one to ask—who would have the Mirror Dragon's secret name except the Mirror Dragoneye? No, the only one who knew the dragon's name was the dragon. And since I did not have his name, I could not call him in order to ask him his name.

I blew on the tea and drank the bowl in one long gulp, clenching my teeth against the vile taste and heat.

And now, whenever I saw the Mirror Dragon, he was shrouded in mist. I couldn't even feel his presence.

Except for last night.

The thought made me sit up straight. When Lord Ido was trying to charm me, something had pulled me into my mind-sight. It must have been the red dragon—what else could it have been? He was calling me.

Was that possible? I had never heard of such a thing. But then I still knew very little about the ways of the dragons. Perhaps he was just waiting for me to merge into mind-sight. Waiting to give me his name. I set the bowl down and propped myself back against the headboard. Breathing deeply, I tried to relax my body, to narrow my mind's eye and focus on the energy world. But my muscles twitched, my hip ached, and my mind skittered between hope and fear. It was like trying to find rest on a bed of thorns.

The last time I had seen the red dragon was in the warm quiet of the bathing room. Maybe another bath would help me see him again.

Rilla sloshed a bucketful of water over my shoulders.

"They say taking too many baths can weaken the body," she said caustically.

I shifted impatiently on the stool, pleating the loin cloth between my fingers. "I'll go and soak now."

"But I haven't done your arms and legs."

"They're not dirty."

Ignoring the stiffness in my hip, I shuffled across the tiles to the bath and sloshed down the steps, wading quickly through the warm water to the sitting ledge. Rilla crossed her arms, watching me with a frown.

"Is everything all right?"

I found the seat and settled back, leaning my head against the edge, as I had done yesterday.

"You can go now," I said.

She blinked at the dismissal. "Well, I'll be back on the half bell, then," she said, picking up the buckets. "Otherwise you'll be late for the prince." At the door, she looked back at me. "Are you sure you're all right?"

I nodded, closing my eyes until I heard the click of the latch.

With a deep sigh, I lowered myself further into the water until it lapped around my chin. The warmth was working its way into my bones. I glanced around the edge of the bath; no sign of the dragons. The steam was leaving a taste of ginger on my tongue that cut through the bitter residue of the ghost-maker's tea. I stared at the mosaic of Brin, the river god, on the far wall and counted my breaths. On the tenth exhale, I felt my vision blur as my mind's eye reached toward the flow of *Hua* in the room. A slight pulse of energy beat at me, rippling across my skin. Around me, large shadowy forms moved and dark eyes watched. I pushed deeper into the energy. Like the creep of sunlight across shade, the circle of ghostly silhouettes brightened into the solid rainbow bodies of the dragons. All of them, except one.

I pushed away the heavy disappointment and took a deep

breath, inching along the *Hua*, feeling for the Mirror Dragon, my focus on the gap in the circle. The steam shivered and swirled. Gathered form; dark eyes, red muzzle, gold pearl. All swathed in a dense haze.

"I don't have your name," I said. My voice echoed around the room. "I don't have your name."

The huge eyes looked through me.

"Please, what is your name?"

I stood up. Perhaps I needed to touch the pearl again. Stretching out my hands, I waded forward. But each step I took thickened the mist around him until he was almost obscured by a wall of fog. I stopped at its edge. The faint outline of the pearl glowed through the opaque barrier. I reached up for it, but instead of touching a hard surface, my hand passed through air. The dragon was not solid. I thrust both hands through, raking the mist. Nothing.

"What do you want? What do I need to do?" I pleaded.

A whiptail of memory flicked at me—my hands fused to a pulsing pearl and a dragon's desire peeling back layers to a buried name, the name I could not risk shouting. Did he want that name before he would give his own? I glanced around the room. I knew there was no one else there, but I had not spoken the name in four years. My master had forbidden it, and I had trained myself not to say it, not to think it, not to remember it. The name belonged to another person in another life.

I leaned closer.

"Eona," I whispered.

I stared into the mist, holding my breath. The dragon was still shrouded in fog. I let out my breath in despair.

Just as I pulled back, I saw a small gap open in the mist. The thick covering was separating into thin streamers that paled, then disappeared. The colors of the dragon slowly sharpened into clarity: the luster on the gold pearl, the fire of the orange and scarlet scales.

It was working.

"Eona," I whispered again. I reached up for the pearl, shivering with excitement. "Please, what is your name?"

But once more my hand passed through the gold orb. I groped into air over and over again. Although the dragon was bright, he was still not solid. And his eyes did not see me.

My true name wasn't enough.

I sucked in a ragged breath and slapped both hands down into the water, sending a shower over the edge of the bath. Why wasn't it enough?

"What do I have to do?" I yelled.

To my left, a flash of pale blue scales and opal claws reared above me. The Rat Dragon filled my vision, his power fireballing through me. The water in the bath erupted, knocking me off my feet. I went under, struggled for the surface, then felt a force pushing me upward. I broke into the air, gasping, arms and legs flailing as I was propelled out of the water. Then I hit something hard. The wall. Shoulder, thigh, knee. I bounced off the cold tiles, falling backward onto the floor. A moment of quiet numbness, and then my whole side flamed into agony.

"Holy gods," Rilla said, running from the doorway. "What's going on?"

"I don't know," I gasped, curling up against the pain.

And for once I was telling the truth.

The palace guide clapped for attendance at the ornate entrance to the imperial harem. A porter appeared behind the gilded lacework of the gate. I shifted my weight from one leg to the other, trying to find a comfortable position between the old pain in my hip and the new aches from the bathing room. Although Rilla had gently pressed along my bones and decided I was only bruised, it was still costing me to stand and wait while the courtesies of entering the harem were played out.

To take my mind off the failure to connect with my dragon, I concentrated on the two Shadow Men guarding the gateway. Neither eunuch was as large as Ryko, but each had an impressive bulk of muscle across arms and chest. There seemed to be two types of eunuchs in the palace: those who had kept the strength and body of a man, and those whose contours were slowly becoming softer and rounder. What made the difference?

I pulled at the high collar of the day tunic that Rilla had picked out for me. It was a deep burnt orange, the front richly embroidered with pale green bamboo for longevity and courage. A good choice, under the circumstances. Rilla had matched it with a pair of loose gray trousers that ended at the ankle. She had told me to come back and change after the lesson—it was not appropriate to wear a day tunic to the Dragoneye Council.

Before, I had only ever had two tunics: one for work, one slightly less worn for best. Now I seemed to be changing clothes every few hours.

"Here is Lord Eon, come at the invitation of His Highness Prince Kygo," the guide announced.

A clatter of locks and latches sounded, and the gate opened. An old man bowed and motioned me into a dark, narrow corridor. The clash of the gate closing behind me echoed off the stone walls.

The imperial harem was a walled and heavily guarded complex of buildings and gardens set in the center of the palace grounds. It was in the position of Great Abundance, but Lady Dela had told me that this emperor kept only forty concubines and had fathered only twelve children, four of them to Lady Jila. "Apparently, he loves her," Lady Dela had said, raising her eyebrows. It was no wonder; Lady Jila had given him his only two sons.

I was led through the cold corridor into the bright warmth of a courtyard easily the size of my master's Moon Garden. At the far end, a high brick wall with three gates shielded the rest of the harem from view. A row of low buildings on each side, all of them with closed shutters, faced a carefully laid out central garden—narrow paths winding around flower beds, miniature trees hung with bird cages, and a pond that rippled with the orange gleam of carp. Through the whistling of the captive birds, I heard the faint staccato rise of a giggle. It was cut short by a sharp reprimand. I turned to look, and a cluster of women peering through the bars of the central gate stepped back out of sight.

"This way, my lord."

I followed the old eunuch down one of the pathways, breaking into painful jogging steps now and again to keep up with his surprising pace. He led me past the pond to the last building on the right side.

I stepped into a small waiting room. It was dim, the only light coming from the doorway and the small gaps between the carved flowers of the window shutters. A long bench padded with blue cushions was set against the opposite wall, a low table before it displaying a decanter and drinking bowls. A folding silk screen, painted with delicate scenes of long-legged cranes and tall grasses, stretched across the far wall.

The old eunuch motioned me toward the bench. "My lord, may I offer you some refreshment?"

"No, thank you."

He bowed and withdrew.

I had just stepped up to the screen for a closer look, when a soft murmur made me turn. A lady in a long formal tunic of green had paused in the doorway to dismiss her eunuch attendant. She entered alone, sinking into a court bow in front of me, the top of her headdress swinging with jade pendants.

"Lord Eon, I am Lady Jila. Please forgive me for diverting you from your attendance upon His Majesty, the prince. It is only momentary, I assure you."

She looked up, and it was obvious that the Prince Heir

received his handsome features from his mother. Her delicate bones had, in the prince, strengthened into bolder lines, but both of them had large dark eyes and a graceful symmetry to their faces that touched something deep within me. I found myself bowing to her—a breach of protocol—but a quick smile answered my courtesy. It was so full of quiet understanding and intelligence that I could see why an emperor might prefer her company to all others.

"I have come to ask something of you, my lord," she said, her gaze as forthright as her words.

"In what way can I be of help to you, my lady?" I asked, although the last thing I wanted to hear was another request. The expectations of my master and the emperor already weighed too heavily.

She rose and sat on the bench, clasping her hands together tightly in her lap. Reluctantly, I took a seat further along.

"It was the empress's dying wish that Prince Kygo, her only child, study and live within the harem until he was eighteen, away from the dangers and intrigues of the court," Lady Jila said carefully. "But it has not been easy for the prince; he chafes at the scholarly life and yearns to stand beside his father. It is now vital that he do so. You have seen how ill the emperor—" She bit her lip and turned away. When she looked back, her face was once again controlled. "You may wonder why I have cornered you to talk of the prince, but I have watched him grow up, and I am very fond of him."

Our gazes locked.

"Lady Jila," I said, just as carefully, "I am aware of your . . . special interest in Prince Kygo."

"Ahh." She smiled wryly. "Lady Dela?"

I hesitated, then nodded.

"You are fortunate to have won Lady Dela's counsel," Lady Jila said. "Nothing happens in this court without her knowledge." She turned a heavy emerald ring on her slim finger. "So you must know why I am here."

"I can guess."

She took a deep breath. "Lord Eon, I add my voice to the emperor's and ask you to protect our son. I ask you to use your power in his interests. I believe he is in great danger." Tentatively, she touched my arm. "But I also ask you to befriend him. There are not many young men at court who have both the rank and the political allegiance for such a bond. But you are close in rank, and, I've been told, have the same political agenda. He needs a friend, and he could help you as much as you could help him."

"You want me to be his friend?"

"I do," she said.

"But friendship is not something that can be forced. On either side."

She smiled. "Lady Dela told me your thinking was older than your years, and I see it is so." I stiffened, but she did not seem to notice. "I am not asking you to force a friendship, my lord. I am asking you to think about the advantages of being prepared to like my son."

I blinked at her phrasing—Lady Jila sliced up meaning as finely as a master cook cut up shark fin.

"Will you do that?" she asked.

A darkening at the doorway made us both turn. The straight-backed figure of Prince Kygo was silhouetted for a moment, then stepped into the room, a quiet command sending his retinue of eunuchs back out of the door. We both hurriedly dropped to our knees and bowed.

"Will you promise?" Lady Jila said, her voice low and urgent.

"Yes."

The prince's feet stopped before us, clad in soft leather slippers dyed the exact royal blue of his trousers.

"Greetings, Lord Eon, Lady Jila. Please rise, both of you," he said. "Lord Eon, we are waiting for you in the pavilion."

I pushed myself upright, sucking in a breath as my aching muscles unlocked. Lady Jila remained on her knees.

"It is my fault Lord Eon is delayed," she said, bowing lower. "Please forgive me, dear son."

Prince Kygo looked down at her, startled. How long had it been since he had heard his true mother call him son? He glanced across at me, acknowledging the trust of the moment. "Then there is no fault at all," he said softly, "Mother."

He held out his hand and she took it, rising with the grace of a dancer. They smiled at one another, the same sweet hesitancy mirrored in their faces.

"I must, however, take Lord Eon away from you," he said. "Teacher Prahn awaits us."

"Of course." She patted his hand and let go, then nodded to me, her eyes holding my promise. "Farewell, Lord Eon."

"My lady." I nodded politely and followed the prince out of the room.

In the courtyard, he beckoned me to walk beside him. A jerk of his head repositioned his eunuch guards further away, out of hearing range. We walked along the garden path toward the larger middle gate, the birds fluttering in their cages as we passed. I saw him glance at my limp and subtly slow his pace.

"My mother must think highly of you, Lord Eon," he said.

"I am honored, Your Highness."

"Did she, perhaps, ask you to befriend me?"

My misstep answered his question. He smiled at my surprise.

"It was not so hard to divine," he said. "My mother is a woman and so believes the bonds of friendship and love are stronger than the bonds of political alliance." He stopped and turned to face me. "Which do you think is the strongest bond, Lord Eon?"

I looked into his dark eyes, searching for some clue to the answer. Was he like so many others of rank who just wanted to hear his own thoughts echoed, or was he truly interested in my view? All I could see was curiosity and openness. I would have to guard against his charm—his manner could make it easy to fall into the trap of voicing an unguarded opinion.

"Political alliance, Your Highness."

Even as I said it, my thoughts flashed to Dolana and the salt farm. The first night I arrived, she pushed me against the wall and slept in front of me, her body a shield. The next morning she sewed a pocket in my rough tunic for my few belongings and showed me how to hold my body to avoid the whip-master's attention. Later, at the salt pit, when she fell to the ground coughing, I hauled her sack and mine to the carts and kept the line moving. In that one night and day, there had been no time for the higher pursuits of friendship or politics. Our immediate bond had been far more basic.

"Well, my father will be pleased," the prince said.

He started walking again. I matched his pace, pushing through the stiffness that was fast overtaking me. He was frowning. Was my answer wrong, after all?

"I believe love and friendship are stronger," he said abruptly. "Do you think me weak and womanly?"

"No," I said, startled into bluntness.

He gave me a quick, self-conscious smile. "Sometimes I wonder if my thoughts are too much influenced by living here. With the women."

We paused in front of the large middle gate as the porter hurried to lift the latch. Through the gilded bars I saw another courtyard, this one dominated by an elaborate pavilion set in the center of a large pond. A wooden bridge arched over the water to a small veranda, the corners of its gold roof sweeping upward into a carved dragon at each point. Two large folding shutters had been pulled back and showed the figure of a man watching our approach.

The porter swung the gates open, falling to his knees as we passed under the arch of the wall.

"Men also think friendship is a strong bond, Your Highness," I said, feeling the gods' whimsy in my sudden role as authority on manliness. "But it is not something that happens on order, and the trust at its center can take a long time to ripen."

The prince nodded. "That is true." He tilted his head and gave me a long, considering look. "Lord Eon, I will speak plainly. I doubt that you or I have a long time ahead of us if things are left as they are."

It was said in a matter-of-fact tone, but I saw him swallow hard. In the last few days of whirling fear, I had thought the danger and terror were all mine. But now the truth of the situation wrapped itself around me, like a giant web binding me to the destiny of this young prince. Every move I made would send ripples through a dynasty of emperors. A line in one of the Dragoneye texts sprung to mind: *Beware the friendship of a prince.* I was sure it was good advice.

"We may not have friendship yet, your Highness," I said, my heartbeat quickening at the boldness of my next words. "But there is a bond which we can agree upon immediately."

"What is that, Lord Eon?"

An image of Dolana, her thin chest heaving with spasms, flickered through my mind.

"Mutual survival," I said.

We looked at one another; a silent sizing up of a new ally.

"Agreed," he said, and swept his hand from forehead to heart, sealing the bargain.

The Pavilion of Earthly Enlightenment was sparsely furnished compared to the opulence of the other palace buildings. The most interesting decoration was Teacher Prahn: an old eunuch with skin so pale it showed the blue of his veins, and a shaven head topped by a scalp lock that proclaimed his devotion to the scholarly life. Apparently he lived in the pavilion, although I saw no evidence of his tenure. Perhaps he hid his bed roll each morning in the tall bureau, or pushed together the hard cushions we were sitting on and slept under the low table.

". . . and the library covers nearly every subject known to mankind. It would be my honor to show you the holdings after our lesson," Prahn said, sweeping his arms to either side to indicate the buildings that formed the courtyard.

I nodded guiltily, aware that I had drifted into my own thoughts. "Thank you. I would be most interested," I said.

Outside, the intricate weavings of ensemble music drifted from somewhere in the harem complex. "The ladies practicing their instruments," the prince had whispered to me when the haunting melody had started.

"We have all the works of the great philosophers," Prahn continued, "and our maps cover all of the known world."

"Teacher Prahn is the keeper of the library," the prince said. "He knows everything in it."

The teacher bowed his head modestly. "I don't know about that, Your Highness. But it is my honor to care for the collection. It is truly superb—scholars from far and wide come to study our scrolls."

"They come into the harem?" I asked.

"Only to this courtyard," Prahn assured me. "There is a small gate to the east, the Scholars' Gate, that allows entry to the library. And all credentials are strictly checked."

"The library is only open to scholars in the afternoon," the prince said. "The ladies of the harem have their lessons in the morning, after me. Is that not right, Teacher?" His voice was edged with amusement.

Prahn's complexion deepened into a blotchy red. "Correct, Your Highness."

The prince leaned over to me. "My sisters give him a lot of trouble. Always asking questions and debating his answers."

"I did not know that ladies could be educated. Like scholars," I said, my skin prickling with the idea.

The prince nodded vigorously. "My father says he will not have ignorant fools for companions. And my sisters will one day marry into high positions that will require more than music and dancing. Of course, there are some who say educating women can only bring disaster." The prince looked slyly over at Prahn. "But what the emperor commands must be right. Is that not so, Teacher?"

Prahn bowed from the waist. "The Heavenly Master is as wise as he is generous."

"I am glad to hear it," a voice said from the doorway. We all turned to see the emperor seated in a sedan chair carried by two sturdy servants. They were flanked by the royal physician and his pair of eunuchs.

"Father!" the prince said. "You did not say you would come today."

The emperor waved his hand forward, the gold nail cover on his forefinger catching the light. The two servants carried him into the room, setting the chair gently down at the head of the table. The royal physician, this time dressed in gaudy gradations of blue, hovered beside him, ordering the eunuchs to change the position of a small stool for the royal foot.

"Enough," the emperor snapped. His long purple day tunic looked oversized on his shrunken frame, and the imperial pearl, glowing pale and pure at the base of his throat, emphasized the yellow cast of his skin. He looked even sicker than he had at the banquet.

He waved his attendants away, the physician and servants bowing and backing out of the room. The prince dropped to his knees in front of his father. I bowed my forehead to the floor, Prahn prostrating himself beside me.

"Come now, what is the rule of the Pavilion of Earthly Enlightenment?" the emperor chided.

"All who enter are equal in the pursuit of wisdom and knowledge," Prince Kygo said quickly, sitting back on his heels.

"Yes, all are equal in this room. All ideas welcome," the emperor said. "Rise, Lord Eon. And you, too, Teacher Prahn."

I sat up, warily watching the three men around the table. I did not understand this idea of equality. There was rank even amongst slaves; it was the nature of men.

"And what is today's lesson, Teacher Prahn?" the emperor asked.

The scholar glanced sideways at me, his face flushed. "We

are studying the advantages and disadvantages of isolationism, Your Majesty."

"A most worthy topic," the emperor said.

Again, Prahn looked across at me, and I realized that the subject was for my benefit.

The debate began, and although I did not understand all the words or recognize the names of the philosophers, I was able to follow the gist of the arguments. The emperor, jabbing the air with his gold forefinger, mounted a persuasive defense of his policy to open the land to foreigners for trade and political alliance. Prahn took the opposition, and I knew from Lady Dela's instruction that the isolationist beliefs he put forward echoed those of High Lord Sethon. The prince acted as mediator, adding a sharp comment here and there that won him smiles of approval from his father and tutor. Finally, the emperor turned to me, his worn face vibrant from the battle of wits.

"And what do you say, Lord Eon? Does the acceptance of foreigners into our land dilute our magnificent culture?"

What could I add to such a learned discussion? I had no knowledge of foreign policy; no deep understanding of politics. Across from me, the prince nodded encouragingly. I groped for the only thing I had: experience.

"I like the coffee that Ari the Foreigner sells in the market, Your Majesty," I said, knowing my words sounded foolish and naïve. "I do not know about diluting our culture. It is just a drink, and he is just a man who sells it."

The emperor's smile widened. "Yes. Just a man, like any

other." He leaned closer, his gaze holding me still. "And tell me, young philosopher, how can we know a man's heart? How can we know if he means us ill or good?"

There was something behind the question that I did not understand. Some kind of test. What did the emperor want? There was no clue in his politician's face; he'd had a lifetime of hiding his thoughts. The full-hour bell rang through the court-yard, silencing the ensemble music. It was as though the whole palace waited for my answer.

"No one can ever truly know what is in another man's heart," I said. That was the gamble my master and I were taking. I clenched my fists beside my thighs, riding out the long silence as His Majesty studied me.

"Indeed," he finally said. "All men have a hidden nature. I am glad you understand that, Lord Eon."

I licked suddenly dry lips. Had the emperor seen through me? I tensed as he turned to the prince.

"But it is also important to understand that a hidden nature is not always an evil nature," he said to his son. "Is that not correct, Lord Eon?"

I nodded, smiling with relief; there did not seem to be any special knowledge in the emperor's looks or posture. His questions were aimed at other concerns; the instruction of his son and the protection of his throne.

The emperor sighed and sat back in the sedan chair. "A most invigorating debate, Teacher Prahn," he said. "My compliments. But now it is the hour for me to sign the daily edicts."

He clapped and the two servants hurried back into the room, deftly lifting the chair under the unnecessary direction of the physician. I bowed low as the emperor was carried from the room, the physician darting around the chair, murmuring orders to his eunuchs like a buzzing fly.

"Teacher, show us the library's sword collection before the ladies come," the prince said, rising from his own bow.

Prahn smiled. "It is always the swords with you, Your Highness. When will you have such enthusiasm for the philosophy texts?"

The prince shrugged. "You want to see the swords, too, don't you, Lord Eon?"

I nodded, more to please the prince than from true interest. "And I would very much like to see more of your library, Teacher Prahn," I said. "Does it hold Dragoneye texts, too?" Perhaps something in its collections might help my search for the red dragon's name.

"Of course not, my lord," Prahn said, his colorless mouth puckering in shock. "Dragoneye texts are always kept by the Dragon lords in their halls." He stopped, frowning. "Wait, that is not right—we do have one Dragoneye text. A red leather folio bound with black pearls strung on silk. A most beautiful thing. It is a one of the Mirror Dragon treasures saved from the fire." He rubbed between his eyes, as though his head hurt. "I'm sure I saw it among the other things. The restorers will be preparing it for the Twelfth Day celebrations, when His Majesty returns the treasures into your keeping."

"Can I see it? Can you show it to me now?"

"Before Twelfth Day?" Prahn shifted nervously.

"Yes, I need to see it." I tried to control the urgency in my voice.

The prince caught my tension. "Surely there can be no problem with that, Teacher?" he said. "The treasures will soon be Lord Eon's property."

Prahn twisted his hands together. "I am not sure . . . no, no it is not procedure."

I bit my lip and looked across at the prince. I needed to see that text.

The prince's bearing changed suddenly. "Lord Eon will see his property, Teacher Prahn," he said, rising from the floor and standing over the scholar. For the first time, I saw the young ruler within him. "Take us there now."

Prahn froze for a moment, then bowed until his forehead touched the wooden floor. "Yes, Your Highness."

He scrabbled to his feet, hovering in a half bow as the prince walked out of the pavilion. He stayed in that position as I followed the next emperor out of the room of equality and across the wooden bridge.

The low buildings that formed the library were similar to those in the first courtyard, but the shutters were plain and the doors were crossed with thick bands of metal. Prahn, his shoulders still hunched, led us toward the buildings on the left. The prince dropped back slightly to match his pace to mine.

"Do you think this Dragoneye text holds the mysteries of the Mirror Dragon?" he asked softly.

He walked so close that I could smell the spice of the storage herbs on his clothes.

"I'm not sure, Your Highness." It was hard to tell where the dark brown met the black in his eyes, making his expression oddly intense. "It is possible. Although if it does, then it seems strange the text has not been studied before now."

"No, not so strange," he said. "My father told me the vault has been sealed since the dragon was lost."

I nodded, my excitement growing.

"That's the Scholars' Gate, Lord Eon," Prahn said, pointing down a narrow alley between the first two buildings. At the end was a solid metal gate set in the harem's outer wall. One of the large eunuch guards stood at attention, only a slight move of his head showing he had noted our passage.

"There is another gate," the prince whispered. "The Concubines' Gate. An escape route for the ladies of the harem in case of danger. Only the imperial guards know its where-abouts. But I happen to know that women can come in that gate as well as go out." He grinned at me. "We should look for it."

I felt heat rise to my face. The prince stared at me for a moment then his own face flushed.

"I apologize, Lord Eon. Of course, you would have no interest in such things. Forgive my vulgarity."

I nodded, keeping my face carefully averted. Part of me wanted to claim interest, wanted to lean closer and listen, but a Moon Shadow would not continue the conversation. The prince quickened his pace, leaving me to walk by myself.

We stopped at the door in the second building. The window shutters were closed, but yellowish lamplight showed along the edges. Prahn pushed open the door and entered, beckoning us inside. I followed the prince into an overwhelming smell of dust and camphor sweetened by the rich honey of wood wax. A large bureau stood in the center of the room, darkened with polish and glossed by the soft light. On the floor beside it, a young eunuch was kowtowing to the prince, most of his gray tunic covered by a rough smock. A long trestle table was pushed up against the far wall and held an odd collection of silver, jewelry, and porcelain. Another smocked eunuch was prostrated behind an open lacquer chest, stacked with bolts of cloth. I saw red velvet, orange silk, and a rich brown satin, its folds rusty with age.

"The Mirror Dragon treasure," Prahn said, bowing to me.

All of this was mine? I turned in a circle, noting a large brass incense burner and three carved stools under the window.

The prince slid open one of the bureau doors. "This is a handsome piece," he said. "How was it saved?"

"We think it was a new order that had not yet been delivered to the Mirror Dragon Hall, Your Highness," Prahn said.

I touched the oiled wood, leaving a smear on the glowing surface.

"Lord Eon," the prince called from the trestle, "look at this Dragoneye compass. It is magnificent."

It had to be the jeweled compass that Lord Ido mentioned

at the banquet. I headed toward the table, brushing my fingers across the smooth blue head of a porcelain lion as I passed. It was the male of a door guardian pair. I looked for the female, but she did not seem to have survived the fire.

The compass was extraordinary: a gold disc with a large ruby in the center and smaller rubies around the outer edge to mark the cardinal points that formed the first circle. The other twenty-three circles were defined by rings of tiny seed pearls set so closely together that they looked like shimmering paint. I stroked the fine etchings of the animal signs in the second circle. The cardinal points and the animals were the only levels I understood, but soon I would be taught how to use the mysterious characters that ringed each of the other circles. I would learn how to use them to calculate the strongest ley lines, find the pure paths of *Hua*, and focus my power.

If I could find my dragon's name.

"Where is the Dragoneye text?" I asked, inspecting the crowded table.

Prahn nudged his foot into the eunuch kneeling beside the bureau. "Lord Eon wishes to see the folio bound by the black pearls."

The eunuch lifted his head. "Forgive me, Excellent Prahn. I have not seen such a folio."

"What? You must have seen it. Red leather, about the size of my hand, with a string of matched black pearls wrapped around it."

"There are no folios in the collection, most honorable Teacher," the eunuch said, crouching into a smaller target.

"Are you stupid? I saw it myself when I opened the vault," Prahn snapped. "Bring me the manifest from the Dragoneye Council."

The eunuch scrabbled across the floor on his knees, picking up a scroll from a low table. Prahn snatched it out of his hands and pulled it open.

"Well?" the prince said.

Prahn looked up. His wide eyes seemed to hold the only color in his face.

"But I—" He stopped. "My lord, I cannot find any folio listed on the manifest. But I saw one. I am sure of it."

I crossed the room in a few strides and plucked the scroll from Prahn's slack grasp. "There is none listed?"

The prince followed, looking over my shoulder as I read the record.

There was no folio. I let the scroll slither back up into its roll.

The prince's hand flicked out, clipping the old man across the face. It was a light blow, more formality than punishment. Prahn took it without a sound, then dropped to his knees, kowtowing to his young master.

"I am sorry, Your Highness."

"You should be begging Lord Eon's forgiveness for your incompetence," the prince said coldly.

The old scholar immediately gathered himself into a hunched apology. "My lord, please forgive an old man's faulty memory."

The prince turned to me. "Do you want him beaten?"

I stared at his implacable face. I thought I had seen a hint of the young ruler in the pavilion, but that was nothing compared to the young emperor who now stood next to me. I could truly believe he was descended from dragons.

"No," I said quickly. "I am sure he believed there was such a folio."

The prince nodded. "I think you are right. A just decision." He looked down at Prahn. "We shall overlook this failure, Prahn. Your service up to this point has been exemplary. Do not let it happen again." He gripped my shoulder. "Come, let's go and look at the swords." He walked out of the room.

Prahn bowed low to me. "Lord Eon, I apologize again. I was sure there was such a folio."

I studied his upturned face, its puzzlement and hurt pride overlaid with deep unease. Teacher Prahn was a meticulous man—it did not seem likely that he would make such a mistake.

"Tell me, where did you get the manifest?" I asked.

"Lord Ido brought it to me himself," Prahn said.

The crackle of parchment made us both look at my hand. I had crushed the scroll. I loosened my grip, using the moment to hide my fear.

"Lord Ido?" I said, trying for a tone of polite interest, but it came out tense and tight. "Why did he bring it?"

"It was his duty, my lord. As council leader, he opened the vault and checked the contents with me. I am sure the folio was listed. And Lord Ido saw it, too." Prahn frowned. "Although I cannot remember the occasion clearly. Maybe it is true, I am getting too old."

I remembered the flick of silver in Lord Ido's eyes as he tried to charm me. Had he succeeded with Prahn, using his power to confuse the old man?

"It was just a mistake, Teacher," I said, handing back the flattened scroll. "There is no harm done. Let us forget it and join the prince. We should not keep him waiting."

Prahn nodded and bowed, eager to leave his humiliation behind.

I took one last look around the room. There was no proof that there had ever been a folio among the treasures—and who would believe an old scholar's aging memory against the word of the ascendant Dragoneye? But I was willing to gamble my good leg that it did exist, and that Lord Ido had stolen it.

Did it hold my dragon's name? I knew it was only a slim possibility, but it was my only hope.

Somehow, I had to get that folio back.

CHAPTER TEN

I PICKED UP A cup of wine from the tray that the servant held out to me. I would have preferred cold water, but anything wet was welcome. My master shook his head at the offering, tapping his folded silk fan impatiently against his thigh.

It was only midmorning, but the day's bright heat had already thickened the air in the courtyard of the Rat Dragon Hall. Small kumquat trees created a lush green border but didn't cast enough shadow for any refuge from the sun. The other Dragoneye lords stood at the front of the square in clusters of two or three, apprentices at their elbows, their murmured conversations lost in the wide expanse of paving. Although none looked directly at my master and me, it was obvious that all attention was upon us.

"Are you clear on your role today?" my master asked.

He flicked open the fan and waved it, sending a warm breeze

in my direction. I nodded, trying to ignore an itch of sweat under my breast band.

"It seems straightforward enough," I said.

On the short journey to the hall, my master had told me what to expect at the council meeting: he would accept the role of proxy lord, and I would stand aside in order to train. But such a simple transfer of duty did not explain the tension in the faces around us.

I gulped a mouthful of wine. The sourness burned through the knot of panic in my chest. There was nothing to fear—my master knew what he was doing—but I could not shake off my unease. Perhaps it was just being in Lord Ido's domain. I scanned the courtyard again. He had not yet made his entrance.

"This will liberate you from attending council meetings," my master said. "You will eventually need to know how the council operates, but at the moment it is more important for you to focus on developing your Dragoneye skills."

I smoothed an imaginary crease out of the sleeve of my red robe, avoiding his eyes. My first Staminata lesson was later in the day; soon I would be learning how to control the flow of Hua in my body. But how long could I bluff through the classes and training before someone realized I could not call my dragon? I looked around once more, this time for Dillon. Perhaps he had seen the Mirror Dragon folio in Lord Ido's rooms.

My master suddenly drew himself up. Lord Tyron had broken away from his group and was approaching us, trailed by his tall apprentice.

Remembering Lady Dela's lesson, I bowed to the older man. The rich amethyst of his Ox Dragoneye robes brought out the florid tones of his skin and the blue exhaustion under his eyes.

"Greetings, Lord Tyron," I said.

He nodded to me and my master. "Greetings. Allow me to present Apprentice Hollin, in his eleventh year."

Hollin bowed to us, his small dark eyes as shrewd as his master's. Next cycle he would become Ox Dragoneye, so for all intents and purposes, he was my peer. I liked what I saw—he had a level gaze and a long-limbed awkwardness that undercut his air of self-possession.

"It has been a most interesting night," Lord Tyron said. "A real lesson in strategy, hey, Hollin?"

The younger man nodded, a wry smile easing the early worry lines on his face.

"Did our friend try it?" my master asked.

I looked from him to Tyron. Who were they talking about? The three men turned toward one another, blocking me from the conversation.

"He did," Tyron said. "But Dram countered with the older ruling. It stopped Ido in his tracks. Now the decision has been delayed until your position is confirmed."

My master's smile was tight. "No doubt he will try again today. Do we have enough votes?"

Tyron shrugged. "We don't know which way Silvo goes." He bowed and returned to the group he had left, Hollin at his heels like an elongated shadow.

My master shifted to see Lord Silvo more clearly. The handsome Rabbit Dragoneye was standing alone, his pink robes and pale skin a stark contrast to the dark green trees at his back. He noticed my master's scrutiny and nodded.

"He meets my eye," my master murmured. "Perhaps it is a good sign."

"What are you trying to stop Lord Ido from doing?" I asked.

"Lower your voice." He placed his hand on my shoulder in warning. "This is not your concern. I will inform you if you need to know."

I stared down at my feet. How were we to survive this treacherous game if he kept me ignorant of his plans and strategies? Did he forget that we lived or died by each other's actions?

I shrugged off his hand. "No," I said softly, my boldness roiling in my stomach. "How do you know when it is necessary? You are not always with me. I must understand what is happening if I am to play my part properly."

His eyes narrowed, but I forced myself to meet his anger.

"Lord Tyron trusts Hollin with his plans," I added.

We stood for a moment, our wills locked in silent struggle.

Finally, my master sighed. "Yes, you are right."

The victory startled me. He grabbed my sleeve and edged back, setting more space between us and the nearest group of Dragoneyes.

"Ido seeks to bend the council into placing its power at the feet of Sethon and his army," he said, his voice so low I could barely hear it. "We think *Ascendant* Ido aims to withhold the council's power until Sethon can force the Right of Ill Fortune and replace his brother."

I stared at my master, trying to absorb the import of his words. The very first emperor, the Father of a Thousand Sons, proclaimed the Right of Ill Fortune to protect the land from a ruler abandoned by the gods. If an emperor's reign was besieged by too many earth/water disasters, he could be denounced and replaced with a ruler who the gods favored.

"You mean Ido intends to block the Dragoneye control of the monsoon storms and earth angers?" Horror made my voice rise. We were fast approaching the worst season of floods, winds, and earthshakes. It was the sacred duty of the Dragoneyes to protect the land and people from harm.

My master pulled me even further from the others, his eyes cautioning me. "That is exactly what I am saying. And there is a very real fear that he aims to break the Covenant of Service—to actually offer dragon power to Sethon for use in his warmongering."

I gasped. It was forbidden for dragon power to be used in warfare. The dragons were agents of nurture and protection, not destruction. I swallowed, imagining the wild power of all the dragons in the control of one ambitious man. The council and covenant were meant to stop such madness.

My master patted my arm. "I know. But I am working with Tyron and others to stop him. The best way you can help us is to learn how to control your powers as quickly as possible." His head snapped up. "Ah, here is our host."

EON

Like sunflowers turning to the sun, everyone shifted to watch Lord Ido's progress through the courtyard. I fought the impulse but found myself turning toward the force of his presence. He topped all of the other men by more than a head, and as he bent to exchange a quick word or bow, his sheer size gave him an air of authority. The deep blue of his Dragoneye robes was echoed in the oiled gloss of his beard and the tight loop of braids bound at the crown of his head. Behind him, in a matching blue tunic, was the slight figure of Dillon. He was scowling. Lord Ido paused and searched the groups of men until his gaze found mine. I straightened; my body surged with a strange hot energy. Something was drawing me to him. But as he approached, I could see no flick of silver in the amber of his eyes.

"Lord Eon," he said. "Greetings."

I gave a quick bow, raising my head to find him standing over me. I wanted to step back but knew it would be a surrender. Grimly, I held my ground. He nodded graciously, including my master in the brief acknowledgment. Dillon stood at his elbow, eyes down.

"How do you find your first days as Mirror Dragoneye?" Lord Ido asked.

"Busy, my lord," I said. "I have hardly had time to think."

"It is set to become even busier," he said. "I must take a short journey in the next few days, but when I return, we will start your training in the dragon arts."

I could not help it; I stepped back.

"Train with you, my lord?" I turned to my master. "But I thought you would be—"

My master shook his head, the strain around his eyes giving away his own unease. "I no longer have a connection to a dragon, Lord Eon. Since Lord Ido will be teaching his own apprentice the basics, it has been decided that he will take on your initial training as well."

"Of course," I said hollowly. "Thank you, Lord Ido."

My hand was shaking, spilling wine onto the paving stones. How was I going to bluff the Ascendant Dragoneye? I looked around for somewhere to put the cup before I dropped it.

"I look forward to teaching you, Lord Eon," he said.

There was a strange caressing tone to his voice. It thrust me back five years to the salt farm and the smiling face of the whipmaster. My body chilled. I knew that tone; Lord Ido was one of those who took his pleasure in the fear and pain of others.

He pushed Dillon toward me. "Take Lord Eon's wine away."

Dillon grudgingly took the cup, still not lifting his gaze. This was not the friend I knew—he had always jumped to attention, eager to please his master. What had Lord Ido done to him? Perhaps he was just frightened. Then he bowed to us and I saw a discoloration on his neck, a rash of dark red dots. Was he ill?

Lord Ido turned and clapped his hands. "Let us move into the meeting chamber and begin the formalities."

Whether by chance or design, my master stepped between us, and the short walk across the courtyard was completed in silence. A servant slid open the lacquered screen as we approached. We all slipped off our shoes and followed Lord Ido into the room.

The air was immediately cooler, the scent of lemongrass, the green silk wall hangings, and the clean straw matting all adding to a sense of lightness. The bright furnishings made me pause; in my mind, Lord Ido was smooth darkness and threatening shadow. As he led me and my master alongside a long oval table, I counted thirteen chairs, three set at the far end in the place of power, facing the door.

"You and Heuris Brannon will sit at the head of the council table with me until the proxy formalities are complete," Lord Ido said. "Take the center chair."

I sat, my head bowed under the heavy press of curiosity from the Dragoneye lords as they took their places around the table. I chanced a fleeting survey of the room and met the guarded stare of an apprentice standing behind his master, and the belligerent face of Lord Garon, the Dog Dragoneye. As Lord Ido took the seat at my right and my master settled into the chair on my left, I focused back on the glossy surface of the table, trying to avoid the searching eyes of the twenty men before me.

Finally, Lord Ido rose, silencing the few whispered comments. I turned toward him and saw Dillon standing in position behind his master. For a second our eyes met, but there was no connection in his gaze, only blank misery.

"Welcome," Lord Ido said to the assembly. "For the first time in more than five hundred years, we number twelve again. No longer will the Year of the Dragon be without an Ascendant leader. No longer will this council be held back by the absence of the eastern power. Lord Eon's glorious reawakening of the Mirror Dragon has closed our circle. We are once more a pearl of dragons."

Lord Dram, the Horse Dragoneye, smiled at me, then slapped the table with the flat of his hands. The other lords quickly joined him in a loud tattoo of celebration. Heat rushed to my face. I bowed in my seat—once, twice—as the drumming shook the table.

Lord Tyron looked over his shoulder at Hollin, standing behind him. "Be glad, boy. This cycle it would have been your turn in the duty rotation to lead the Dragon Year. A thankless task without the doubled ascendant power."

"Hear, hear," a few of the other lords said.

"Quiet," Lord Ido commanded, reclaiming the room. "Yes, we are back at full strength. And although Lord Eon is untrained and our knowledge of the Mirror Dragon largely lost, there is no doubt that if we are bold, the power of twelve will achieve great things for our land."

"Our first duty should be returning abundance to the eastern plains," Lord Silvo said quickly.

Lord Ido pinned the smaller man with his gaze. "Our first duty, Lord Silvo, is not to the easterners. We now have our full power; our first duty should be directed to the greater glory of the empire."

A murmur rippled around the table. Some nodded their agreement; others shifted uncomfortably.

"With such possibilities ahead," Lord Ido continued, "Heuris Brannon has agreed to act on this council as proxy lord so that our young brother can focus on his training in the dragon arts."

Dram started another thunderous ovation. My master nodded, acknowledging the honor.

Lord Ido motioned me to my feet.

"Lord Eon, do you agree that Heuris Brannon will, from today, be Lord Brannon and represent you on the Dragoneye Council? That his decisions and votes will be taken as your decisions and votes until you are of an age and experience to accept your position among the twelve?"

"I do agree," I said. "And I thank him for his guidance."

I bowed to my master. Under the table, his hand tightened around the folds of his silk fan, the force bending the frail lacquer sticks. He had waited years for this return to wealth and power. I could almost feel the triumph humming through his body as I took my seat next to him.

He did not wait for an invitation from Lord Ido to stand. Although he looked like a frail old man beside the Rat Dragoneye's youthful strength, there was something in his bearing that brought all focus on to him. I saw Lord Ido frown, sensing the shift of attention.

"Heuris Brannon," he said curtly. "Do you agree to act as Lord Eon's representative on the Dragoneye Council? Will you serve as proxy lord until he is of an age and experience to take up his position among the twelve?"

"Yes, I agree to represent Lord Eon on the council," my master said.

Dram thumped the table again, eager to celebrate, but my master held up his hand for silence. Slowly, he turned to face Lord Ido, fan held in both hands like a fighting staff. "And as the coascendant proxy, I also accept Lord Eon's duty of leading this council alongside you, Lord Ido."

Around the room, everyone stilled. The two men stared over my head at one another, like dogs sizing each other up. Then Lord Ido laughed a harsh dismissal.

"You may now be proxy, Brannon," he said, "but you are not Ascendant. Without a dragon's power you cannot claim leadership." He stepped toward my master, but my chair blocked his way. "I will not allow it."

"It is not for you to allow, Ido," my master said sharply. "This is a council. We decide by vote and precedent."

Lord Tyron stood up. "Yes, we must vote on it," he called.

"Vote!" Lord Dram bellowed above the eruption of voices around the table. "Let us vote."

I saw Lord Ido's eyes change. Not with the silver of his power, but with a madness that flared across the amber like dark fire.

"This is my council," he roared through the surging noise. Both of his fists slammed the table, shaking it. "There will be no vote."

"You cannot stop it, Ido," my master said into the sudden silence. "You have already lost."

Lord Ido's lunge was so fast that all I saw was his elbow coming at my face. I flinched, the blow catching me on my chest as he grabbed for my master. He grunted as his heavy body crushed me against the edge of the armrest. I gasped, fighting for air through the suffocating blue silk, sucking in the stink of his rage. I pulled my head free of the cloth and heard a terrible wet rasping. Above me was my master's face, eyes wide as Ido's thumbs pressed deep into his throat.

I clawed at the air, connecting with Ido's scalp in a deep drag of nails. Across the room someone screamed, "Pull him off!" Hands were wrenching back Ido's arms and shoulders. Tyron wrapped his arm around the taller man's throat from behind, brutally pulling with the crook of his elbow. Ido let go of my master. His body lifted, arched, and was hauled back by Tyron and two other men.

I hunched over in the chair, pain stabbing through me with each panting breath. Lord Dram kneeled in front of me. A large rip in the front of his orange robe exposed his bony chest. "Are you all right, boy?"

I nodded, shivering. At the other end of the room, Lord Ido was being held down in a chair by four of the largest apprentices, their combined strength barely restraining his rage. He was shouting, ranting, that this was his council. Behind him, Dillon stood with his back pressed against the wall, watching his master's struggle with a malicious smile.

Dram turned to the man beside him. "Is Brannon all right?"

I looked up for the answer. Lord Silvo, even paler than usual, nodded and patted my shoulder. I turned to double-check and groaned at the sharp pain in the movement. My master was sitting on the floor, rubbing the red finger marks around his throat. An apprentice handed him a bowl of wine with shaking hands. He took a careful sip.

"Under the circumstances," he croaked, swallowing painfully, "I think we will delay the vote until next meeting."

Although my master insisted he was well, by the time we entered the Peony Apartment, the hollows of his face were shadowed with gray exhaustion. He did not resist when Rilla led him to the second sleeping chamber. I stood uncertainly at the doorway and heard his small sigh as he eased himself onto the bed and sagged back against the pillows. He probed the damage to his throat with careful fingers. Something dangerous had been unleashed in that meeting room, and I was no longer certain my master could check it.

He lifted his head off the pillow. "Eon, go to your lesson." He coughed. "There is nothing more important than you attending these classes. We will talk when you return."

"What will happen to Lord Ido?" I asked. "Surely he will not lead the council now."

My master eyed me irritably. "Of course he will remain leader—he is the Ascendant Dragoneye. But his actions will guarantee me the votes for coleadership." He settled into the pillows. "Now, go."

I turned to leave but was a struck by a sudden thought. "Did you mean this to happen? Was it part of your plan with Lord Tyron?"

My master closed his eyes and did not answer.

Unsettled, I made my way to the dressing room, where Rilla was waiting. She hurriedly stripped me of the sweat-damp Dragoneye robes and threw them over the wooden rack.

"The guide is already outside," she said, holding up a cream cotton exercise tunic. "Tell me quickly, what happened in the council?"

I described the meeting and Ido's attack as she helped me into the exercise gear.

"I am afraid for the master's health," she said, shaking her head as she worked the light slippers onto my feet. "I'll try and persuade him to summon the physician. And what about you? Are you all right?"

"I'm fine."

But it was not the truth. As I followed the young palace guide through a series of vaulted passageways and large enclosed courtyards, I felt my bruised ribs press my breathing into tight, painful gasps. Finally, I was forced to stop.

"My lord, is something wrong?" the guide asked. "Do you need assistance?"

"Is it far?"

"No, my lord. The training grounds are just past the Pavilion of Autumnal Justice."

I waved him on. Perhaps I could claim illness and delay the

lesson until another day. The idea was tempting—it would give me more time to find my dragon's name and heal my hurts—but my master's urgency echoed in my head.

Before long I heard the *clack* of wood hitting wood and a cracking roll of applause. The guide looked back at me, nodding encouragement, and we emerged from a dim passageway into sunlight and the glare of white sand.

Ahead of us was a small fenced practice area. Around the edge, brightly clothed courtiers stood huddled under silk parasols and fanned themselves, calling and clapping at the action. Two figures fighting with long staffs flashed past a wide gap in the watching crowd, a twirling maneuver sending up a spray of sand. I shaded my eyes, pretending interest, and walked slowly over to the fence to stop and catch my breath.

It was then that I recognized the taller combatant—Prince Kygo. He wore only cream cotton exercise trousers tied at the ankle. Out of the obscuring robes of his rank, his body had the shape and breadth of a man's. The planes of his chest and stomach were flat and defined, and as he blocked a hit above his head, the stretch showed the width of his shoulders and the sharp cut of muscle in his arms. Sweat had gathered in the small of his back, and I found my gaze drawn down the glistening curve to the narrow flare of his hips. I looked away, aware of the sudden heat that radiated from the sand.

He stepped backward and swung his staff in a teasing arc as his sparring partner feinted and withdrew, seeking a break in his guard. The prince rocked on the balls of his feet, readying himself for the next attack. His opponent—a young nobleman, from the elaborate gold threads woven through his topknot—lunged and jabbed the end of his staff at the prince's head. The royal heir deftly deflected and followed through, spinning around and raising his staff for a blow to the noble's midsection. But the man was already swinging his weapon. Too high—the prince spun straight into a face attack that connected with a sickening *thwack.* Prince Kygo's head snapped back, his staff falling from his hands.

The crowd gasped, their horror holding them unnaturally still. It was forbidden to touch the body of a member of the royal family, even in sparring. The penalty was immediate death. The young noble dropped his staff as though it was hot iron and fell to the sand, his body crouched in a tense kowtow. The prince was doubled over, the heel of his hand pressed into a bloody gash across his cheekbone.

"Your Highness, forgive me," the young noble pleaded into the sudden silence. "It was not intended. I did not—" He stopped as two imperial guards positioned themselves on either side of him, their swords drawn.

The prince straightened and spat out the blood that had run into the corner of his mouth. Already his eye was swelling, and the shadow of a bruise was darkening his skin.

"A heavy blow for one that was not intended, Lord Brett," he said quietly.

"I swear, Your Highness, it was a lucky strike," the young noble said desperately. "You know I do not usually get past your defenses."

Was the prince going to kill him for an accident? I leaned

forward, following the macabre press of the crowd around the barrier.

The two guards were watching their royal master for instruction, their swords aimed at the young noble's head. The prince picked up his staff.

"Get back," he ordered the guards.

Immediately they stepped away. The prince gripped the end of the wooden weapon and swung it with all of his strength across the back of the young lord. The crack of the blow rebounded around the silent courtyard. He threw the staff down and walked toward his trainer at the edge of the sand. Every move was decisive, unyielding, and royal.

"The prince is merciful," a familiar voice said at my shoulder.

I clutched at the fence and turned to see Dillon bowing beside me.

"By the gods, Dillon! You made me jump." I smiled shakily, remembering how we would try and sneak up on each other at training.

"My apologies, Lord Eon," he said formally, but I saw the flicker of an answering smile. "Master Tellon sent me to bring you into the practice hall."

I sucked in a breath. My energy felt all upside down. What was wrong with me?

"Am I that late?"

He nodded. "He doesn't seem too upset, but we should hurry." Some warmth had returned to his voice. I followed him a few paces, then stopped; I had forgotten my guide. I waved the boy over.

"Apprentice Dillon will accompany me. You may go."

"My lord." He bowed to me, then turned to Dillon, "Honored Apprentice."

We both watched him hurry toward the dark arch of the passageway.

"I'm still not used to people bowing to me," I said.

"Me either." Dillon grinned. "My lord."

"Honored Apprentice," I said, matching his pompous tone and crossing my eyes.

Dillon giggled, the familiar sound a balm to my nerves. He pointed to a large hall in the far corner of the square and started toward it. I looked back at the practice sand for another glimpse of the prince. But the crowd had closed the gaps along the fence, blocking my view. I caught up with Dillon and tried to shrug off the taut energy singing through my body.

"You seem . . . better now," I said hesitantly, not wanting to break our fragile harmony.

Dillon's face tightened. "What do you mean?"

I held up my hands. "You seemed ill this morning."

He sighed and massaged his forehead. "It's just this pain in my head. I'm all right. At least I am now that Lord Ido has gone." He looked over his shoulder, then leaned closer. "I think he's insane. Look what he did to your master—I mean, Lord Brannon."

I nodded, but I was focused on something more important. "Where's he gone? For how long?"

"A few days. He's gone to meet High Lord Sethon and ride in with him."

So the high lord was returning to the city. No doubt my master would be interested in that piece of news.

"How come you didn't go, too?" I asked.

Dillon stopped, drawing me nearer with a tug on my sleeve. "He wants me to watch you. He wants me to tell him what you're doing in our lessons."

Did Lord Ido suspect something?

"Why?"

Dillon shrugged. "He just tells me what to do. Not why I'm doing it." He looked out across the square, his narrow shoulders twisting in a tiny shiver. "He has this . . . way of making me do what he says." He paused; the strange, quick anger shadowed his eyes again. "But I am not his slave. He may think I don't have the courage or strength to stand against him, but he's wrong."

I saw my chance in his rebellion. "Tell me, Dillon, have you seen him with a red leather folio bound with black pearls?"

He shook his head. "He doesn't let me go into the library. He keeps it locked, and no one goes near it. Why?"

"I just thought he might have it." We started walking again. If Lord Ido kept the library locked, then it must hold something important. And now he was gone for a few days. . . .

"Dragonpiss." Dillon quickened his pace. "Master Tellon has come out to look for us."

Up ahead, a tall man in a baggy exercise tunic stood at the doorway of the training hall, watching us approach. I tried to hurry but my battered ribs and hip would not let me move any faster. I climbed the few steps onto the low veranda, Master

Tellon's scrutiny making me feel even more awkward than usual.

"You have too much Moon energy," he said, moving aside to allow me passage to the open doorway.

I stiffened, aghast at such quick insight.

"But of course, you are Moon Shadow," he said, nodding to himself.

Dillon's face narrowed with anger. "How dare you speak of Lord Eon's sacrifice."

Tellon stared down at him. "And you have too much Sun," he said calmly.

Dillon stepped back, the shock of his own rudeness draining the heat from him. I swallowed the hard pit of panic in my throat. My master had warned me of Tellon's keen eyes. I would need to press home my Shadow status at every chance and hope it answered his sharp observations.

Tellon bowed to me, the movement loose and fluid. "Forgive me, Lord Eon. I meant no disrespect. Nor to you, Apprentice. I am an old man and tend to speak my mind."

"No offense taken, Master Tellon," I said quickly. "I am indeed Moon Shadow; there is no fault in stating the truth. And it is I who must apologize for my lateness."

I stepped out of my slippers and crossed the raised threshold to stop any further discussion. Inside, the hall was a large expanse of polished parquetry floor marked with old scuffs and indentations. A series of small high windows let in the bright sunlight.

Master Tellon shut the heavy door and waved us over to the middle of the room. "Come, sit," he said. "We will talk first, then start learning the form."

Dillon seated himself on the hard floor. As I settled next to him, I studied his sprawling posture and quickly copied it. I had thought four years of careful self-study had stopped me from moving in the neat, closed way of a girl. Now I was not so sure, and I could not afford to raise any questions in Tellon's mind.

He knelt opposite us, his movements smooth and supple. Tellon had been the Dog Dragoneye in the cycle before my master's, yet despite his age, he moved with more ease than Dillon. He had lost his hair across the crown of his head, but what was left still had as much black as it did silver and was tied back into a thick braid that hung to his waist.

"I do not hold with those teachers who think a student should sit like a lump of rock and just listen," he said. "You may ask questions. In fact, I expect them."

Dillon's gaze slid to mine. None of our other masters had ever welcomed questions.

"You have both been chosen to commune with an energy dragon," he said, smiling his congratulations. "But it will be a long and arduous journey to learn how to control the power you have at your call. And you, Lord Eon . . ."

I tensed as he leaned toward me. Had he already guessed I could not call my dragon?

"Your journey will be even more difficult because you must

travel its paths without an incumbent Dragoneye to accompany you."

I bowed my head to hide my relief. "Yes, Master."

He patted my arm. "Don't worry, you are not alone." He straightened. "You are both here to learn the Staminata, the ancient way to regulate the flow of *Hua*. It will help you withstand the energy drain of working with a dragon." He brought his hands together in a loud clap and rubbed them vigorously. "Now, I know that a lot of rumors fly around about the dragons and their power. So, let's get the donkey's wallop out of the way." He pointed at Dillon. "What do you want to know?"

Dillon blinked at the sudden demand.

"Is it true that a Dragoneye gives up his *Hua* to his dragon?" he finally asked.

Tellon nodded. "Yes. A Dragoneye uses his life force to control the elemental energy of his dragon, and in doing so, gives some of it to the dragon. But the Staminata slows down the loss of *Hua* and promotes its flow." He pointed at me. "Lord Eon?"

I thought of the moment in the bath when the Rat Dragon reared above me and threw me against the wall, and the fireball of energy that had rushed through me.

"Does a dragon always deplete *Hua*?" I asked hesitantly. "Can he not give back energy, too?"

He shook his head. "No. Except at communion, of course."

The answer resonated through me. Did that mean the Rat Dragon had communed with me? Surely that was not possible.

Tellon's finger jabbed the air. "Next question."

Dillon leaned forward. "Master, is it true that *you* can kill someone just by disrupting their *Hua?*"

"I can," Tellon said calmly.

Dillon's eyes widened. "Do we get to learn how to do it, too?"

"No."

Dillon sat back, disappointed. I looked down at the tiny wood tiles on the floor, considering my next question. It was risky and needed to be phrased with care.

"I've heard that it's possible for a Dragoneye to take another dragon's power," I said.

Tellon smiled. "That rumor does the rounds every year. It's not true—one dragon, one Dragoneye." He beckoning us closer, lowering his voice. "But there is a legend about harnessing the power of *all* the dragons. It says that if a Dragoneye kills the other Dragoneyes and their apprentices, then the energy of the twelve dragons will funnel though him, giving him the power of a god . . . just before it rips him apart."

Dillon gasped. "Really?"

Tellon laughed and tapped Dillon on the head. "I wouldn't start plotting the murders of all your colleagues just yet. It is only a story to frighten young apprentices."

Dillon grinned. I could see him lighten under the master's playfulness.

Tellon clapped once again, marshalling our attention. "I will now show you the Staminata," he said. "It is meditation within movement; very slow, very controlled. The twenty-four postures you will learn, together with the control of your breath, will carry the *Hua* around your body along the twelve meridians and through the seven power centers." He ran his hand up from belly to crown, touching each center lightly. "You will eventually learn how to activate each of the centers to carry *Hua* to the physical, emotional, and spiritual levels where you most need it."

He stood up. "Watch."

His body loosened, weight settling into the ground, his long arms held out in front of him. His eyes seemed to lose their focus, yet were still looking at something ahead. Nothing seemed to be happening, and then I realized his hands were gradually rising, the left leading the right. His body shifted, the weight moving from the left foot to the right. Everything as slow as the sun moving across the sky. There was something familiar about it. I squinted, trying to imagine how it would look if each movement was faster. His left arm floated downward, his body turning with the flow, and it was then that I recognized the Rat Dragon Second from the ceremonial sequence. I saw each of the animal forms in Tellon's graceful positions. They were not exactly the same, but the essence of each was present. He finished with the pressing motion of the Pig Dragon Third and stood for a moment, the long angles of his face softened.

"So," he said, his voice deeper. "*Lin* and *Gan* are balanced, the body is energized, yet relaxed. This is called the state of *Huan-Lo*." He smiled and his eyes focused back on us. "Apprentice Dillon, tell me what you saw."

"It was slow," Dillon said, glancing at me for help. "And it was . . ."

He trailed off. Tellon grunted. "And you, Lord Eon? Did you observe anything?"

"I saw some of the animal forms from the ceremonial approach sequence."

Tellon stared at me thoughtfully. "Well, that is interesting. Most of my students don't see that until they are well into their studies." He rubbed his hands together again. "All right. Stand up and we will make a start."

For the next two hours, we learned the parts of the first posture. I'd smugly assumed that since I already knew the approach sequence, it would be easy to slow it down into the Staminata. I was wrong. My movements were too fast; I was holding my breath; the angles of my feet were wrong; one arm was too high, the other too wide; my weight was on the wrong side, or the right side but too heavy. Beside me, Dillon was experiencing similar problems, his newly shortened temper flashing into moments of stamping frustration.

And then, for one glorious moment, I felt the change of *Lin* and *Gan* flow through my body. It was a gentle rocking that moved from my crown to my toes as though my whole body was one deep sigh. All the pain and stiffness was gone. And underneath it all was the faint whispering presence, the shadow heartbeat that I could not quite reach. Within the harmony of my slow movements, I knew I could bring that presence into me. I started to draw it closer, but then I thought of the Rat Dragon's rearing power. If I reached into my *Hua*, would he rise again? As soon as the fear touched my mind, the flow of the form twisted and broke. I was once again stiff, awkward. A cripple.

Despair hollowed me. I had to find my dragon's name soon—I no longer dared to even slip into mind-sight in case the Rat Dragon overwhelmed me. The folio must hold the key to my power. I had to get it back. A tiny barb pierced my certainty; what if the folio held no answers? I pushed the fear down; the folio was my only chance.

Tellon clapped his hands.

"All right, that will do for now. I could see you had it there for a moment, Lord Eon. A good start. Do not be disheartened because it slipped away." He gave me an encouraging smile. "You will probably find that you feel heavy. Try not to make sudden movements." He patted Dillon's shoulder. "A valiant attempt, Apprentice. Now, both of you, go home and sleep. I have made it clear to Lord Brannon and Lord Ido that you are to rest after our classes."

Outside, two guides waited to lead us back to our quarters. The prince's entourage had left, and a lone servant was raking down the practice sand. Dillon and I followed our guides through the large, deserted square in silence. Halfway across, I grabbed his arm and stopped him.

"I want to get into your hall tonight," I whispered.

"What?" He tried to pull away, but I did not let go.

"I want to go into Lord Ido's library and look for that folio. Will you help me?"

"Why?"

Out of the corner of my eye, I saw the guides turning back to us. I raised my hand to stop them.

"The folio is part of the Mirror Dragon treasure."

I watched Dillon's face change as he made the connection. "He stole it?"

"Yes. And I've got to get it back."

Dillon was already shaking his head. "No. No. I can't help you. He'll hurt me if he finds out."

"You don't have to come into the library with me. Just let me into the hall and show me where it is."

"You don't understand." Dillon rocked on his feet, his hands twisting together. "It's not only locked. There's this feeling around it that stops you from even getting to the door. It's like every bad thing you've ever felt."

I let go of his arm. "I thought you said you weren't his slave? But that was just talk, wasn't it? You don't have the courage to go against him. You can't even open a gate without his permission."

"You don't understand what he's like," he whispered.

I had expected him to come at me with quick fury, not this helpless terror.

"Dillon, I need your help. How many times did I save you from Ranne? How many kickings did I take for you?" It was a low strategy, but I had to get that folio.

"Can you save me again?" he asked bitterly.

"What?"

"Ranne got thrown out of the school, and Lord Ido has hired him as a guard."

I stared at him. "That's awful."

Dillon nodded.

I grabbed at a straw. "If I steal the folio back, maybe he'll get into trouble. Lose his job."

Dillon gave a wan smile. "Maybe."

"What do you say?" I tried to keep the desperation out of my voice. "For our friendship?"

He looked down at his feet. "I won't go into the library."

"You don't have to," I said quickly.

"Just the gate?"

"Just let me in and point me in the right direction."

He looked at me, swallowing hard. "I'm not his slave."

I gripped his shoulder. "I know." Under my hand, his body was trembling. "What kind of lock is it?" I asked.

CHAPTER ELEVEN

UNLIKE THE BUILDINGS in the first three sections of the harem, the women's apartments were not set around a square. Instead, they were built along small paved streets, like a miniature town. Most of the houses had two levels, and although every one of them was in good repair, most had shuttered windows and an aura of abandonment. There had been a time when the imperial harem had numbered over five hundred concubines. Now, no more than fifty women and children lived in the compound.

The porter led me through the eerily quiet streets. Apparently Lady Dela's house was not part of the main community near the section gate. It was her choice, the porter had said quickly. He had also told me that she was out making a visit in the palace precinct, but I had waved away his suggestion of leaving a message. I would wait at her residence.

A deep lethargy was making every step an effort. As soon as Dillon and I had agreed that he would let me into the Rat Dragon Hall on the midnight bell, I had directed my guide to take me to the harem. Now I understood why Master Tellon had insisted we sleep after our class. I felt as though there was a space in my head where I was floating, as though I was in a warm, enclosed bath.

We finally stopped outside a small wooden house. It was on one level and stood at the end of a small cul-de-sac, collecting the energy flow from a large communal garden at the top of a narrow laneway. The red door and shutters were open, letting in the cooler afternoon breeze.

"Lady Dela's residence, my lord," the porter said, bowing.

"Announce me."

He clapped and called, "Lord Eon, for Lady Dela."

There was the sound of footsteps, and a figure in a long brown tunic emerged from the gloom: a girl with her hair braided into the neat crown knot of a lady's maid. The light caught three silver tassels hanging from a New Year hairpin thrust through the center of her bun. A costly possession for a servant; probably a gift from Lady Dela. The girl squinted into the light, her nose wrinkling at my exercise garb. Then her eyes focused on my face. Gasping, she dropped to her knees.

"My lord." Her forehead almost touched the ground. "I'm sorry, my lord. Lady Dela is not here."

I crossed my arms over my tunic. "When is she expected to return?" I asked, glad the girl was facedown and could not see the flush of stupidity on my skin; a Dragoneye lord did not call on a court lady in his sparring gear.

"She is not long away, my lord. If you would like to wait inside, I can fetch her for you."

"Yes. I'll wait."

I dismissed the porter and followed the girl into the tiny hallway, the air sweetened by a waft of frangipani—Lady Dela's perfume.

The main room obviously served as both reception and living area. In the corner near the window, two formal chairs were set on either side of a small table, half-hidden by a delicate screen, the blackwood frame covered in thin parchment instead of silk. A low eating table was pushed up against the left wall, with straw seating mats stored beneath. Along the other wall was a day pallet, draped in royal blue velvet and stacked with cotton cushions that ranged from eggshell to midnight. A few darned patches stood out on the velvet like old scars.

The girl led me to the formal chairs. "Would you care for wine while you wait, my lord?" she asked.

"No, thank you." I sat down, feeling the thin wood creak under me.

She bowed and left. Through the open front window I saw her running up the laneway, her hand clamped over the precious hairpin.

The chair did not seem very stable. Afraid it would break, I stood, my interest caught by a collection of small boxes arranged along a shallow shelf above the pallet. Five of them, all different shapes. I knelt on the bed and picked up one made of pale wood inset with black stone in the design of a spider. A symbol of happiness. I hooked my fingernail under the lid and flipped it open. A thin layer of powder lay in the bottom. I sniffed. Chalky roses. It was face powder. I slid it back onto the shelf and pushed myself off the pallet.

The doorway into the next room was closed with a thick curtain of faded indigo damask. It would be an unforgivable breach of courtesy to go through it. I checked the laneway through the window—no one was coming—then moved the curtain aside, stepping into a small dressing room.

The pungent scent of cedar caught me in the back of the throat, forcing a cough. The smell was probably coming from the three large storage chests set against the wall. Opposite them, long, deep shelves were stacked with neat calico-wrapped bundles—Lady Dela's collection of robes: her fortune. A window fitted with waxed paper let in a soft light. Beside it, a long green tunic hung from a rack. I touched the folds, feeling the cloth slide through my fingers like fine sand. Her gown set out for the evening.

I walked over to a plain wooden clothespress and slowly pushed the door across with one finger. Underclothes. Embroidered silk drawers, diamond shaped chemises that tied at waist and neck, even stiff breast bands. It was then I realized I was looking for something that was not female. What was I doing? Looking for a lie, like mine? But Lady Dela was the most truthful of us all. I slid the door shut with a snap, my betrayal framed in the long mirror beside me.

I looked at the wary boy-girl reflected in the glass. This was how I was going to live for the rest of my life. Never able to make an unguarded move. Always watching for suspicion, danger, discovery. The girl I once was, lost in years of pretending to be a boy. Or had my Sun energy just overwhelmed the Moon in me?

On a small table at my elbow was a collection of elaborate hairpins, earrings, bracelets, and a pot of white skin paint. I picked up a long pin with five gold blossoms hanging from a delicate chain. With a twist, I tightened my Dragoneye braids into a knot, like the maid's, and stuck the pin through it. I swung my head to and fro, watching the gold blossoms shimmer against the oiled darkness of my hair. I looked over my shoulder. Did I have time for more? Feverishly, I chose four enameled bracelets, pushing them over my hand and shaking them down my arm, watching my reflection smile as they clinked together. Another four on the other arm, the thick bands accentuating my delicate wrist. Next, a pair of earrings—black pearls hanging like a bunch of grapes from a gold hook. I was not pierced like Lady Dela, so I held them to my earlobes, the bracelets chiming. The fall of pearls made my throat look longer. I tilted my head, watching the smooth line of my white neck. Through my body, energy boomed like another heartbeat. Whispering. Calling.

"Lord Eon?"

I swung around, the energy choked off like a stifled cry. Lady Dela was standing at the doorway, her hand holding back the curtain. Behind her, the maid was on her toes, straining to see over her mistress's shoulder.

Lady Dela rounded on the girl. "Get out. Now!"

She twitched the curtain across, closing off the maid's view. I was still holding the earrings. I thrust them behind me, my eyes fixed on Lady Dela; there was no shock on her face.

"Lady Dela," Ryko's voice was muffled through the curtain. "Please do not barge ahead like that. I need to check your quarters before you enter."

She pulled the curtain closer to the doorframe. "I am all right," she called through the heavy cloth. "I am here with Lord Eon. Leave us be."

She turned back to me, her face drawn.

"I'm sorry," I said. "I just . . ."

I stopped, not knowing what to say.

She shook her head and waved my apology aside. "I am the last person who needs an explanation." She glanced back at the doorway, lowering her voice. "But promise me you will be more careful. I wish you could wear these things and be safe, but there are people around here who will not tolerate this kind of difference, even in a Moon Shadow. And they do not care about rank. They will hurt you. Like they have hurt me."

She pulled down the scalloped neck of her robe. A series of raw gashes, only half-healed, marred the smooth, flat skin over her heart. For a moment all I saw were deep, ugly cuts. Then I saw that it was a character carved into her flesh: *demon*.

She looked down at the mutilation. "See? You must be very careful."

I nodded, caught between horror at the wound and relief that she had not guessed the truth. But she was right. If anyone found out what I really was, they would do more than brand me with their hate. They would kill me. A female Dragoneye was a travesty of everything natural in the world.

I returned the earrings to the table, leaning on it for support. The desire to tell Lady Dela who I was—*what* I was—surged through me. I closed my eyes, riding out the impulse. It was not only my life at stake.

I felt for the pin in my hair and pulled. It was snagged in a braid. Only a tiny pain, but I still cried out.

"Here, let me help," Lady Dela said.

She stepped up behind me and I felt her fingers working through my hair. It brought the memory of another long-ago touch—my mother combing out snags and knots.

"Why do you wear women's clothes? There is no power in being a woman, and you are suffering for your choice," I said. "You could wear men's tunics, and they'd leave you alone."

The pin came free, and she stepped away from me. I heard it clink on the crowded table.

"When I was seven or so, my sister caught me wearing her skirt," Lady Dela said softly. "But even before that, I knew I was different from the other boys in our tribe. Nothing boyish came naturally to me. I hated hunting, fishing, even the ball games. I had to work at it, all the time."

I turned around. Her arms were wrapped tightly around her body.

"Then one day I found the beaded skirt my sister had labored over for months, tucked away in our family's tent," she continued. "When I put it on, I felt complete. I remember thinking that it was just the thing to wear to the mud hole while I pretended to make the special bread our mother baked for Midwinter Feast." She smiled ruefully. "As you can imagine, beautiful beaded skirts and mud do not mix. My sister found me and dragged me back to our mother for a beating. Of course, my sister's righteous indignation was lost in the excitement when my mother and the other women saw me dressed in a skirt."

"What did they do?"

"Instead of a beating, my mother sat me down beside her and showed me how to mill the rice. She always suspected I was a twin soul. She was just waiting for me to come to it myself. A wise woman, my mother. But I did not take on the life of a Contraire until much later. Until I was sure. It is an honored position in my tribe." She gave a small, bitter laugh. "Not so honored here."

She moved in front of the mirror, surveying herself. "I do not wear men's clothing because I am a woman in here," she touched her head, "and here," she touched her heart. "You are wrong when you say there is no power in being a woman. When I think of my mother and the women in my tribe, and even the hidden women in the harem, I know there are many types of power in this world." She turned around to face me. "I found power in accepting the truth of who I am. It may not be a truth that others can accept, but I cannot live any other way. How would it be to live a lie every minute of your life? I don't think I could do it."

I twisted the bracelets around my arm, avoiding her level gaze. I could tell her what it was like, in every fearful detail. But I could not see any power in womanhood. Only suffering.

"Why don't you . . ." I paused, wondering how to phrase it. How would a Moon Shadow phrase it? "Why don't you get rid of the male parts?"

She looked away. "I don't need to be cut to know I am a woman. And the emperor prizes me because I am both Sun and Moon. If I go to the cutters, then I will lose the very thing he values. . . ." She hesitated, then met my gaze. "In truth, I am also afraid of the pain. I am afraid of dying."

I nodded. I had heard that three in ten eunuchs died in terrible agony after the cutting, some lasting for over a week before the inability to piss or the swelling fever led them to their ancestors. Good odds if you were starving in a village and wanted work at the palace for the rest of your life. But I agreed with Lady Dela; they did not seem very good odds to me.

I pushed the bracelets back over my hands and carefully replaced each one on the table.

"I am sorry about all of this." I motioned toward the jewelry. "I did not come to go through your belongings. I came to ask you a favor."

She straightened. "What is it?"

"Do you know someone who can pick a lock?"

She didn't even blink. "Of course."

"You were a thief?" I asked, trying to absorb Ryko's words.

He nodded and paced across the private tearoom at the

back of Lady Dela's house, his bulk making the small space seem even more cramped.

"It wasn't only thieving." He cast a strained look at Lady Dela, who was kneeling across from me. "I did anything if the money was good enough." He looked away. "Anything."

The word fell flatly between us. Lady Dela shifted, biting her lower lip. It seemed she had not heard this before.

"Then how did you get from the islands to the palace?" I asked. A sudden intuition made me gasp. "You're a Trang cattle-man!"

"No!" The denial was explosive.

"Lord Eon!" Lady Dela admonished at the same time. "That is none of your business."

Ryko held up his hand. "It is all right." He let out a long, hissing breath. "No, I was spared the dishonor. I was placed in the palace a year before that happened."

Lady Dela tilted her head, a small frown creasing her painted forehead.

"Placed?" she asked, and her soft tone was suddenly edged. "What do you mean?"

Ryko stepped over to the door and pushed it slightly open, peering through the crack. "Are we definitely alone, my lady?"

She nodded. "I sent my maid to deliver a message."

He shut the door and turned to us, his long islander eyes unblinking.

"Up until a few years ago, my life was thieving, fighting, and drinking. Then one night, I met my match in a dock alley." He stared through us, remembering. "There were two of them. One of them knifed me in the shoulder, the other in my belly. I could see the gray of my own guts." He laid his hand across the flat of his stomach and focused back on me, his smile wry. "It's never a good moment when you see your own innards. I thought it was the end."

Out of the corner of my eye, I saw Lady Dela's fingers brush the cloth over her wound. She, too, must have thought it was the end when that knife had sliced across her heart.

"But it wasn't," I said. To both of them.

Ryko nodded. "My luck was with me that night. A fisherman took me into his house and nursed me back to health. He saved my life." He paused, his face solemn. "Such a thing creates a bond. A debt. So when I found out my fisherman friend was also leading a group resisting Sethon's control of the islands, I joined his cause. And when he needed someone to go into the palace, I saw a chance to repay my debt."

"You're part of the Islander Resistance?" Lady Dela said, her eyes narrowing. She looked down, smoothing her skirt. "You hid it well." Her voice was cold.

Ryko had hid it very well. I thought of Master Tozay and the Trang boy from the docks. There was no doubt both of them were involved. How big was this resistance?

Ryko licked his lips. "Forgive me, my lady. I would have told you if I could. But my orders are to gather information about Sethon, and to get close to the emperor to protect him. Not to recruit."

I had to state the obvious. "But you are guarding Lady Dela,"

I said. "With all respect to you, my lady"—I bowed to her, then turned back to Ryko—"that's not very close to the emperor."

"True. But the wait has been worth it. I am now closer to the emperor than I have ever been."

"How?"

"You, my lord," he said simply. "You are the hope of the resistance."

The hope of the resistance? More people relying on me. Relying on my power. It was too much. Too much. I would be crushed under all these needs.

"No!" I clambered to my feet. I had to get out of there.

"What do you mean, no?" Ryko blocked my way.

"I cannot hold the hopes of your resistance." I looked over at Lady Dela. "Or yours."

"My lord," Ryko said, his bruising grip keeping me still, "you may not like it or want it, but you have it. And unless you intend to join with Sethon and Ido, then you are bound to our struggle. The very fact that you have woken the Mirror Dragon makes you a threat to the High Lord. And you have already shown your allegiance to the emperor."

I pulled my arm out of his hold. This was not my struggle. I had to get away. Hide somewhere. But where? And what about my master and Rilla? What about Prince Kygo? Their lives were bound as tightly to mine as I was to the fortunes of the emperor.

"I do not want it," I said, but it sounded feeble even to me. Everything Ryko had said was true. And inescapable.

"I know you have more courage than that," Ryko said.

I did not feel courageous. But I raised my chin and nodded. What else could I do? Even a cornered rabbit will fight with teeth and claws.

"Good man." He clapped his hand against my shoulder, making me sway.

"If you have finished recruiting," Lady Dela said dryly, "maybe Lord Eon can tell us how he plans to steal back the folio."

I had not told Lady Dela and Ryko the whole truth about the red folio. They knew it was the last Mirror Dragoneye text. They knew it could not stay in Lord Ido's hands. But they did not know it was my only chance of learning my dragon's name. I could not tell them I had no power yet. It might lose me their support. Although it was too dangerous to be the hope of the resistance, it was just as dangerous not to be.

"The plan is straightforward," I said quickly. "Dillon will meet us at the side entrance of the Rat Dragon Hall at the midnight bell. He'll let us in and take us to the library. Ryko will pick the lock, we'll find the folio, and then leave with all haste."

There was silence.

"It's a bit loose on details," Ryko said carefully. He glanced across at Lady Dela but she avoided his gaze, her posture still stiff and unforgiving. "Do we know how many guards will be on duty? Do we know their positions?"

"No," I admitted, "but I'm sure Dillon will be able to tell us."

Ryko crossed his arms. "I think it would be more prudent

if I did this alone, my lord. I've had a lot of experience and, no offense, it would be a lot quicker."

Lady Dela nodded at me across the low tea table. "He's right. You should not endanger yourself, my lord. You are too important."

"But Dillon is already nervous. He won't let you in if you are by yourself," I said, forestalling Ryko's objection. "And he says that there is some force around the library that stops people from entering."

"Dragon power?" Lady Dela asked.

I shrugged. "I don't know. But if it is, I will have a better chance of deflecting it than Ryko."

I said this with as much confidence as I could muster. I had no idea how to deflect dragon energy, but I was not going to wait patiently in my apartments while Ryko might or might not retrieve the only thing that could save my life.

"Lord Eon is right," Lady Dela said, finally looking up at Ryko. "You cannot get around dragon magic on your own."

Ryko rubbed the back of his shaved head. "We need more information. Are you even sure Lord Ido has this folio? Are you sure he keeps it in the library?"

"No. As I said, there is no record of it."

"Well, at least if you do retrieve it, Lord Ido will not be able to say anything," Lady Dela said tartly. "Since he stole it himself."

Ryko shook his head. "It's too dangerous. We should delay a few days and gather information."

"No!" I ground my palms together. "It must be tonight. Lord Ido has ridden out to meet High Lord Sethon. He will be gone from the hall until morning. I swear, if you do not go, I will do it by myself."

"I had heard that Sethon returns," Lady Dela said. "A dangerous time. Beside the victorious general, our emperor will look old and sick."

Ryko sighed. "If Ido is gone, then it is probably the best time to do this," he allowed. "He will probably have taken most of his guards for the journey and left only a basic detail." He paused. "All right then, we will go. I will come to your apartments in good time to meet the midnight bell at the Rat Dragon Hall. Listen for my knock at your window."

"Thank you," I said.

"You will need to find some dark clothes. Can you ride?"

"No." I had not even touched a horse, let alone sat on one.

"Well, we cannot order a chair to take us to and from a theft. And it is too far for you to walk with that—" He stopped, suddenly aware of his discourtesy. "I will carry you on my back," he finished abruptly.

"Well, if being a spy does not work for you," Lady Dela said coolly, "at least you could hire yourself out as a donkey."

"I think I would have more luck as a bullock than a donkey, my lady," he said, bowing deeply.

She did not smile back. "Be careful," she said to me. Her eyes flicked over to Ryko, but he had already turned to open the door.

"Both of you," I heard her whisper.

Rilla opened the front door of the Peony apartment as I approached. Even from the pathway I could see the tight worry in her face. I should have returned earlier.

"How is the master?" I asked as I entered.

She shut the door. "He is refusing to take the sleeping draft prescribed until he has spoken to you. The royal physician is here again."

"Do you think he is worse?"

"I don't know." She shook her head as though chasing away her doubts. "I think he just needs to rest. He has canceled all the evening engagements. He wants to be well enough to accompany you tomorrow."

"Tomorrow?"

"Did you not hear? High Lord Sethon will be riding into the city triumphant, and the emperor has declared a day of celebration. Another feast for you to get through." She smiled sympathetically. "Come. The master is waiting."

Only one lamp was alight in the bedchamber, its glow shielded by a bronze cover. On the wall above the bed head, sticks of the same sweet incense that had burned for me a few days ago were smoldering in a gold holder shaped like two leaping carp. My master was propped up against the pillows, his features reduced to shadowy planes. Beside him, the royal physician was sitting on a small stool studying his patient's fingernails. He was dressed for the evening in a lush crimson coat worn over a silk tunic of soft rose, which complemented his maroon physician's cap. He looked up as Rilla announced me.

"Lord Eon. Come in, come in," he said, releasing my master's hand and dipping into a low bow. "Lord Brannon is not asleep. Merely resting."

My master stirred and opened his eyes, their liquid gleam catching the light. "I am glad you are here." His voice was still rough. He glanced across at the physician. "You may go now."

I thought I saw the physician's face darken at the dismissal, but perhaps it was just a shadow from the flickering lamp as he bowed again. We watched him leave the room.

"Close the door and come here," my master said.

He did not speak until I took the stool next to the bed.

"You have heard that Sethon returns?" he asked softly. The bruising around his throat had deepened into the shape of Lord Ido's grip.

"Rilla told me," I said, but it was an image of Dillon's frightened face in my mind. Would he keep his word and meet me at the gate tonight?

"Ido has left the city," my master said. "There is no doubt that he has gone to meet his master and report on his failure in the council. We have them on the back foot."

"What will happen now?" I asked. He was including me in his plans; he knew we had to rely on one another. The knowledge made me sit straighter and focus.

"They'll try and consolidate their influence in the council," he said. "But I am confident that I will hold the vote." He pushed himself up against the pillows, the determination showing through his fatigue like bones under thin skin. "Tomorrow is a celebration of Sethon's victory in the East. We must counter his show of military strength with a show of our own. We will appear together, dressed in the red of the Mirror Dragoneye. It will be a symbol of our combined force—your ascendant power and my experience."

"Will you be well enough? What does the physician say?"

"Don't worry," he said, smiling. "This is only exhaustion. I have not slept more than four hours since you were chosen. The physician has left me a draft. A good night's sleep will see me whole again."

He tapped my hand, the fleeting touch bringing our gazes together. For a moment something weighted the air between us, and then I looked away from the fullness in his eyes.

"And you?" he said, clearing his damaged throat. "How was your first Staminata lesson?"

"It went well."

For all his protestations, he looked more than tired. I did not want to burden him with my worries about Tellon's keen eyes. Nor could I tell him about the folio. Not yet. Not until I had solved the problem of calling my dragon. And maybe not even then—for the danger would be over and he would never need to know. So many secrets to keep. Each one was like lead in my chest.

"Good," he said. "Tellon is the best person to help you control your power."

I leaned forward, the existence of the folio rising to my

lips. How sweet it would be to share the weight. "Master—"

He shifted irritably. "Eon, I am not your master," he said. "Not anymore. You must remember that." He smiled grimly. "You are your own man."

I sat back. He was right. I was no longer a girl peasant or boy candidate. I was Lord Eon. In this new world of royalty and riches, I was a man. My every word was a command to those beneath me. And a man of such power did not lay his problems on the shoulders of another—even when those problems ate at him like maggots in a mess of rotting meat.

"You should rest," I said. "I'll send Rilla in to you."

I stood up and took my leave of Lord Brannon with the small, formal nod of equals.

CHAPTER TWELVE

THE WAIT FOR RYKO had settled into my muscles like a cramp, forcing me to pace my room to ease the tension. Twice I thought I'd heard his rap on the shutter, only to find the garden outside my window still and shadowy in the warm night air.

I wiped my damp hands down the front of my old work tunic—stealthily retrieved from the shabby basket in the dressing room—and sat on the bed. Although I was strung as tight as a lute, I could feel a deep fatigue lying in wait from the day's relentless pace.

I pushed myself off the bed again and walked over to the beautiful altar that Rilla had made for my ancestors. She had obviously taken Lady Dela at her word and plundered the royal stores. The death plaques were propped on small gilded stands, and behind them, a miniature trifold screen painted with peach blossoms created an elegant backdrop, the design carried through to the offering bowls and incense holders. I knew I should kneel in front of it and pray for protection and, perhaps, some much-needed tranquility. Instead, I felt myself drawn to the sword rack set against the wall.

The polished jade and moonstone in the hilts shone like animal eyes in the lamplight. The swords were mine now, until my tenure as Mirror Dragoneye ended. Two swords with rage woven into their steel. And I had absorbed it during the ceremony, had heard their voice in my head. I reached toward the hilt of the top sword. Slowly, I laid my fingertips on the cold metal.

Like a scream, the rage flared through me.

I jerked my hand away.

Another sound. A soft knock from the window.

In a few strides, I was at the shutters. Ryko was standing to one side, his hand held up to silence my greeting. I saw a glint of a hilt as his sleeve slipped down; he was wearing an arm sheath. No doubt he had a matching knife strapped to his other wrist for a double draw—the weapon choice of a thief, not an imperial guard.

He peered into the gloom, his flattened profile silhouetted against the pale gray of the pebble garden. Seemingly satisfied, he turned and smiled. The sudden curve of white teeth was startling against his dark skin.

"Ready?" he breathed. He'd told me that the hiss of whispers carried more than a low tone.

I looked back at the swords. Silent in their rack. I hoisted myself onto the windowsill, gently lowering myself over the other side to soften my impact on the pebbles.

"Lightly now," he murmured. "These stones are as good as a guard dog."

I carefully followed him toward the servants' path that ran behind the apartments, holding my breath as pebbles crunched and clinked under our weight. We both sighed when we finally stepped onto the rough dirt track.

"We will go out by the Gate of Good Service," Ryko said as we hurried along the path. I ignored the ache already starting in my hip from the speed and uneven surface. "Two friends are on duty tonight. They will pass us with a little encouragement."

The Gate of Good Service was used mainly in the day for the delivery of the vast amounts of food that the imperial kitchens prepared for the royal family and its huge staff. At night, Ryko told me, it was quieter and much sought after by guards wanting an easy watch.

As we approached the gateway, two well-built figures stepped out from their positions, the enthusiastic demand for our names hinting at their boredom.

Ryko identified himself, then bowed toward me. "Here also is Lord Eon."

The smaller of the two leaned closer, the brim of a stiff leather helmet shadowing his eyes. He studied me, then drew back and bowed, obviously satisfied. His partner quickly followed suit.

"I am taking Lord Eon to the Avenue of Blossoms," Ryko said, and I heard the chink of coins in his hand.

A glance passed between the two guards. The Avenue of Blossoms was in the Ward of Pleasure.

"He would not want his passage through this gate to be common knowledge." Ryko opened his hand to show the gleam of silver.

The larger guard licked his lips.

"Our discretion is guaranteed, Ryko. You know that," he said.

Ryko stared at them. "You know what will happen if I hear this in the guard rooms."

They were both big men, but Ryko stood taller and broader. The guards nodded and Ryko tossed them the coins, ushering me through the gate.

"Do they really think you are taking me to the pleasure houses?" I asked as Ryko led me off the main road, onto the emperor's riding track. What use would a Moon Shadow have for the Blossom women?

"Of course they do," he said, and I heard the amusement in his voice. "They know there is more than one way to skin a cat."

I felt heat rush to my face and was glad for the cover of night.

Suddenly, Ryko pulled me behind some bushes. A dung man had rounded a curve in the track and was wheeling his barrow toward us. We both crouched and I peered through the foliage, watching as he stopped in front of us and shoveled up a heap of horse manure. He banged it into the barrow, his vigor sending a foul stench into the air. I clamped my hand over my nose, my eyes watering. Finally, he walked on. I moved to stand, but Ryko pulled me down again, his hand on my arm until we heard the guards jeering as the man pushed his barrow past their gate.

"We will need to cut through the gardens and avoid the paths, my lord," Ryko said softly. "It will be quicker if I carry you."

Before long I was perched on his back, and we were striding through the extravagant band of gardens that separated the Dragon Halls from the palace precinct. The emperor called them his Emerald Ring and allowed only his favorites to walk the paths and enjoy the cool groves. At this time of night, they were deserted, with only the main paths lit with large red festival lanterns strung on ropes between poles. I pressed myself closer against Ryko's solid shoulders as we ran past gilded pavilions and skirted glades and ponds spanned by elegant bridges. Part of me was exhilarated by our speed, another part breathless with fear at what lay ahead. As we rounded a stand of ghostly beech trees, a shadow darted forward. I flinched, sending Ryko into a half crouch that rocked me against his back. The inky shape of a fox slipped into the cover of some bushes.

Ryko let out a breath. "Hara," he murmured, using the island name for the messenger fox god. He straightened, shifting me up.

"A bad omen?" I whispered uneasily.

Under my arms, his shoulders lifted in a shrug. "Hara warns that a message is near, not if it is good or bad."

Hopefully Hara was foretelling the return of the folio. Ryko tightened his grip, and we started running again. There was a strange sense of comfort being held so closely to the body of another. Perhaps it was the faint memory of my father carrying me in the same way. Emboldened by the sense of unity, I pressed myself closer to his ear.

"Thank you for helping me," I said. "You are a good friend."

He turned his head slightly, his cheek brushing mine.

"It is my honor," he said warmly. His voice deepened with urgency. "And we must protect the emperor and his line."

I finally voiced something that had puzzled me. "Why do you support the emperor, Ryko? He gelded the Trang men— *your* people—and forced them into slavery."

Ryko grunted. "The emperor did not order the gelding. The uprising came at the same time as Her Majesty's death. The Heavenly Master placed all military decisions into Sethon's hands. It was Sethon who ordered it." I felt his pace slow. "Quiet now, we approach the road."

He stopped in the cover of a small copse of trees and studied the gentle slope in front of us. We were at the far corner of the Ox Dragoneye burial ground, opposite the Ox Dragon Hall. The carefully placed tombs clustered under an auspicious rise in the land, their curved marble altars like a crooked set of teeth. Beyond was a stretch of the Dragon Circle, the wide paved avenue that lay between the edge of the gardens and the ring of Dragon Halls. It was reserved for the use of the high ranks and, at this time of night, was clear. A lone figure in the neat livery of a servant walked along the rough track beside it.

"This is the best place to cross," Ryko said softly, pointing across the road to the ragged edge of a thick wood. Its dark shadows looked impenetrable. "The Ox Hall keeps a hunting forest that stretches the entire length behind it. We'll go through and come up beside the Rat Hall."

But first we had to make it across the road. We watched the servant disappear from view. All clear. Ryko tapped my leg, a signal to hang on tightly. I pressed myself against him as he launched forward. We both sighed in relief as we gained the cover of the trees.

It seemed to take forever to work our way through the small, dense forest. The tracks were narrow and ill defined in the dim light, and I could feel Ryko's shortened breaths as he wove around trees and pushed through undergrowth. Every now and again a night animal skittered away, a flash of silvered fur becoming shadow. Above, the half moon was rising toward its zenith—the midnight bell would soon ring. And I could do nothing to help our progress except sit against Ryko as lightly as possible.

Finally, the trees began to thin out. Ryko slowed, his shoulders heaving with effort. Ahead of us, across a wide space empty of any cover, was the immense stone bulwark of the Rat Dragon Hall. We stopped in the shadows of the last patch of growth,

Ryko taking in deep breaths as he scanned the top of the thick wall.

"We'll wait," he panted, shifting me more firmly against his back and adjusting the bulky pouch tied at his waist. "Guards may be walking the rampart."

We watched and waited, but no dark helmeted figures appeared.

Ryko turned his head and I saw the corner of a smile. "Time to go." I felt my heartbeat quicken as we crossed the clearing. Could he feel my fear against his back? Keeping in the shadow cast by the wall, we slowly crept toward the front of the hall. Halfway along, we came to a heavy metal gate. I looked up and saw the six gilded spikes that Dillon had described.

"This is it," I breathed in Ryko's ear.

He nodded and released his grip on my legs. I had only just touched the ground when the midnight bell rang. A cracking boom suddenly punched into my ears and whistling fire arced across the far wall, bursting into a flower of falling light. Then I was pushed down into the dirt, Ryko's body across mine, his weight pressing grit into my mouth. Voices—screaming, yelling, commanding—erupted from the hall. I shifted my shoulders and bucked, trying to find some room to draw breath.

The weight lifted. I gasped in air as Ryko rolled to his knees beside me.

"My lord, are you all right?"

We both heard the scrape of a lock opening and looked up. Dillon peered around the edge of the gateway, his eyes round with fear.

"Eon?" He shook his head. "I mean, Lord Eon, is that you?" He saw Ryko loom up beside him. "Holy gods." He ducked inside the gate, but Ryko was faster. He caught Dillon's arm, pulling him back out.

"Be easy. I am Lord Eon's bodyguard," he growled.

Dillon cast a wild look at me.

"It's all right," I said soothingly, nodding at Ryko to let him go. I spat out some grit. "Did you do that? The explosion?"

Dillon nodded. "A couple of Twelfth Day fireworks. We won't have long, though."

Ryko hauled me to my feet. "Your leg, my lord? Is it all right?"

I was stiff and every bit of me felt bruised, but complaining would not change it. And if I did complain, Ryko would probably try to make me stay outside.

"I'm fine," I said. "Let's get going."

Dillon beckoned us through the archway, then carefully closed the gate. We were in a long alley between two buildings.

"How many guards are there?" Ryko demanded.

Dillon flinched at his tone. "Only eight. The rest have gone with Lord Ido." He pointed to the left. "The library is that way, in the formal garden. Built into the hill."

"*Into* the hill?" I asked.

Dillon nodded. "I heard Lord Ido say it is on a ley line. To maximize the power."

For some reason, his words made me shiver.

We walked along the narrow path, Dillon leading, me in

the middle, Ryko guarding the rear. Somewhere in the front carriage yard, a voice was shouting orders. Dillon paused at the mouth of the alley. Over his shoulder, I saw the inner courtyard where I had waited with my master for the council meeting. Large bronze lamps hung at each corner, and in their yellow light, the border of kumquat trees looked eerily like soldiers standing at attention. A servant hurried along the far colonnade and disappeared into a dark passage. Dillon nodded at me, then slipped around the corner.

Bending low behind the cover of the kumquats, I followed him to the back archway, my limping jog frustratingly slow. I had just reached the shadowy interior of the arch when a doorway halfway along the left building opened and a servant girl eased her way through it. Beside me, Dillon sucked in a breath. Ryko, caught between the kumquats and the arch, dropped to the ground. I pressed myself back against the stone wall. The girl paused, pulled a heel of bread out of her skirt pocket, and crossed the yard. Straight for us.

I saw Ryko gather himself into an animal crouch. He drew the knives, the action smooth and soundless. What was he going to do? She was just a servant stealing an extra crust. Leaning forward, he readied the blades, angling them for a throat slash and heart thrust. Quick and quiet. I looked across at Dillon. He had flattened himself against the wall, too. I jerked my head toward the girl. "Stop her!" I mouthed. He gave a tiny shake of his head and closed his eyes. I clenched my fists to stop myself from pushing him out into the yard.

Suddenly, the door behind her slid open, cracking against its stop. A squat figure stood silhouetted in the bright light.

"Gallia. Get back here. You haven't finished these pots."

The girl thrust the bread deep into her skirt and quickly retraced her steps. Dillon sighed as she entered the kitchen and closed the door, muffling the shrill voice of her superior.

Keeping low, Ryko ran the last few lengths into the shadows beside us. I watched him slip the knives back into their sheaths with practiced ease. Our gazes met; a jarring moment of reevaluation.

"Would you rather we were discovered?" he said.

The steel was not only strapped to his arms.

"I'm not going any further," Dillon said, edging back. "I'm not going near the library. Go through this passage; it will take you to the garden. The library is in the Rat Dragon corner."

"Wait!" I grabbed his sleeve.

"No." He wrenched himself free and rounded the archway corner, his receding footsteps a sharp staccato of fear.

"His decoy won't last much longer," Ryko said, heading toward the end of the passageway. "We've got to move fast. The guards will be checking every area."

The sounds from the carriage yard had already quieted. We stood for a moment in the safety of the passage and studied the large space we had to cross. A long paved path curved and climbed across a bridge, beside a pond, and around a small pavilion. Red Twelfth Day lamps hung in blossom trees. A night perfume—jasmine—flavored the air with a soft honey. It should have been a beautiful garden, but the whole effect was ruined by the squat hill at the north-northwest corner. I could already sense the menacing power that hung over it.

"It's clear," Ryko murmured. "Come on."

We cut across the manicured grass, weaving in between the blossom trees. Ryko moved fast, the space between us lengthening as my bad leg jarred against hidden dips in the ground. He became a shadow ahead of me, flickering between the trees, the glow of a festival lamp briefly highlighting the sheen of his skin or a glint of metal. I checked the archway; it was still quiet. Ryko had gone from view. I passed the pavilion, its walls curtained with trailing wisteria. Not far to the library now. I dug my fist into my hip to stop the ache, slowing into a limping walk. The path was in front of me. Just a few more steps.

Something was lying on the paving stones. Something big.

I stopped. It took a moment to make sense of the contorted form. Ryko—his body twisted in agony. He rolled over to face me, the effort forcing out a muffled scream. His forehead and neck were straining with corded veins, his teeth bared.

"Stay back!" His words collapsed into a moan as he writhed across the path, his head hitting the flags with a dull thud. I scrabbled across the paving, thrusting my hand under the back of his skull before it smashed against the stones again. The weight of his head ground my knuckles into the flags.

"They must have come out of the hill," he panted. "Run!"

He was holding his belly, dark blood seeping through his

fingers. Had he been stabbed? I looked wildly around. The hill crouched above us, a curved black metal door set into its side like a screaming mouth. No one could have come out—the door had a huge padlock on it.

"Leave me. Get out," Ryko said. "Now!"

"No," I said, a spark of anger burning across my fear. I couldn't leave him to die. At the edge of my sight, something shimmered. I swung around. For a moment, I saw huge opal talons crisscrossing the hill like a cage and an eye above it, as dark as an abyss.

The Rat Dragon.

Across the garden, the archway flickered with light. Torches. They were still in the inner courtyard, but it wouldn't be long before they checked the garden.

"Ryko, they're coming," I whispered. "We've got to hide."

He nodded, his teeth clenched together. "Trees?" he gasped.

They were too far away. Too evenly spaced for cover. I twisted around, searching for another option. The doorway? Would the Rat Dragon's power force the guards back, too? If we hid in the shadow, maybe they wouldn't come close enough to see us.

"Against the door," I said.

I sat behind him and straddled his body with my legs, hooking my arms under his armpits. "Come on. Help me."

He dug his feet and pushed as I hauled backward. We crept across the paving, his weight grinding my bones into the stone and crushing my chest. Each heave forced a tiny moan from him and pressed my own breath out in rough gasps. Would the guards hear us? The stain on the front of his tunic was getting bigger, wetter, denser. So much blood. I pressed my palm against his stomach, trying to find the source of the bleeding.

The cloth wasn't wet.

I lifted my hand—no blood. No stain.

It wasn't real. *None of it was real.*

"Ryko, you're not bleeding. The Rat Dragon is doing this."

I saw his eyes roll back.

"No!" I jabbed my fingers into the muscle behind his collarbone. If he passed out, I'd have no chance of moving him. "Stay awake. It's not real."

He grunted in pain, his eyes focusing. "Leave me," he breathed. "Run. You mustn't be found." He pushed at my hands.

I hauled us backward again. He scrabbled weakly, trying to help. Another heave and my shoulders hit something solid. The door. I wriggled out from under Ryko, crawling around to roll him into the shadows. If the guards made it up as far as Ryko had, the shadow cast by the hill wouldn't hide us. We would be seen. I pulled myself back against the cold metal of the door. All that effort for nothing.

I looked up at the padlock. We had to get in. But Ryko was in no condition to pick it. I reached up and grabbed the heavy lock, hanging my weight from it. Solid. I shook it. Metal against metal. Immovable.

I looked over my shoulder. Down the path, one of the lights

was now a defined flame, outlining the man who carried it. Fear sobbed in my throat.

There was one last chance. The Rat Dragon. Could I call him? Tellon said it was impossible, but I knew I had some kind of connection. Groping desperately for my *Hua*, I clumsily drew it up through my seven centers of power. It was like picking up fine sand, the *Hua* slipping between the fingers of my control until only a small amount was left, pooled in the cup of my mind. Focusing every part of my being, I hurled it toward the Rat Dragon. A terrible dragging pain made me sway. For a moment, I was hollow. A husk. In my mind, I could see the blue dragon hunched over the hill, its claws intertwined around it. The huge head lifted, the unblinking eyes staring at me. Confusion. Reluctance. He lifted his head and shrieked, a scream of resentment. Then something roared through me, like the searing howl of a fire wind. With a crack, the padlock split, jerking me downward.

I hung there for a moment, gaping at the broken lock above me.

The Rat Dragon had answered.

Ryko groaned. I ripped out the padlock and pushed against the door. Silently, it swung inward. A passageway. I grabbed Ryko's arm and pulled as he scrabbled backward. We slowly moved into the narrow space. As soon as his feet cleared the threshold, I shut the metal door, sealing us into complete blackness.

I leaned against a wall and took a deep breath. Ryko's gasps were lengthening into a natural rhythm. I touched the wall. Stone—the floor, too. Beside me, I felt Ryko stir.

"Did they see us?" His voice sounded normal.

"No, I don't think so." I reached out, my hand banging into the solid muscle of his chest. "Are you all right?"

"Yes." I felt his hand brush mine as he spanned his stomach, searching. "You were right. It wasn't real." He laughed, the relief making the low rumble catch in his chest.

Now that my eyes had adjusted, I could see the solid darkness of Ryko sitting in front of me outlined by the faint light coming from under the metal door.

"You weren't affected?" His voice was tinged with awe.

"Not as much," I said shortly. It wasn't the time to discuss my connection with the Rat Dragon. I pushed myself up into a crouch. "Let's get moving."

"Wait."

I heard the rustle of cloth and the sound of something hollow being set on the floor. Then the scrape of a striker. A spark arced across the darkness. Another flash and then, with a faint *pop*, a small flame burst on the ground, burnishing the planes of Ryko's face. I blinked in the sudden light and saw the small clay pot holding the fire.

"Sap powder," Ryko said with satisfaction. He looked up at me and grinned. "Trick of my old trade." He dug into his waist pouch and produced two candles, thrusting the first into the flame and lighting the wick. Even as he withdrew the second, the sap fire had begun to die away.

"Here." He handed a candle to me.

I held it up, squinting to see down the corridor. Another metal door was only a few lengths away.

"Doesn't look locked," Ryko said, knocking the spent powder onto the floor. With one hand, he deftly wrapped a square of leather around the clay dish and pushed it back into his waist pouch. "I'll go first."

"What if there's more dragon power?"

He hesitated, eyeing the door warily. The line of his jaw tightened. "I'll still go first."

We both stood, our shadows flickering up the rough stone of the wall. Ryko edged forward. I followed, watching him for any ill effects. Nothing. The dragon's protection must have ended outside.

We stopped at the inner door, our candlelight picking out the raised edges of a large design on the metal: twelve spheres linked together in a circle, the two top spheres larger and scored with a swirling shape.

"What is it?" he asked. "Some kind of Dragoneye charm?"

"I don't know. I've never seen it before."

Ryko reached out and pressed the door lever. The latch slid smoothly out of its groove. He glanced back at me.

"Ready?"

I nodded.

With a push, the door swung open. Our candlelight reached across a rich blue carpet and gleamed over shelves stacked with polished wooden scroll boxes. I could make out the legs and edge of a large reading table further inside, its dimensions lost in the shadows. The space seemed to stretch on forever.

It looked like my master's library. Smelled like it, too: dusty parchment and the pungency of ink blocks. But there was something different—a sense of power that rose through my feet and pressed on the base of my skull.

Ryko walked into the room, raising his candle. "It's huge." He turned in a circle. "So many scrolls." He moved further in. "Close the door behind you, lord, and we can light a lamp and have a proper look for your folio."

I stepped inside and pushed the door shut as Ryko held his flame to the wick of a large bronze lamp on a side bench. Immediately, the space brightened, the endless shadows solidifying into the walls and ceiling of a long room. I felt myself drawn toward the wooden reading table that stretched down the center, its sloping surface covered with open scrolls, their corners held down by small brass weights. Along the higher edge of the table, a series of small lamps was fixed in place, the oil safely enclosed behind tiny panes of glass. How easy it would be to study a scroll with such bright light.

"Oh, ho!" Ryko exclaimed. "Now *that* explains a few things."

I looked around. He was standing at the side bench, holding a leather pouch.

"What is it?" I asked.

He poked his finger inside the pouch, then withdrew it covered in gray powder. He pressed it against his tongue. "Sun drug." He weighed the pouch in his hand. "About four months' supply. No wonder Lord Ido is so well muscled for a Dragoneye. And so unpredictable."

"What does it do?"

Ryko tied off the pouch. "It kindles the Sun energy in a man. Builds muscle and increases the fighting spirit. It is meant only for the Shadow Men of the imperial guard. Lord Ido must be bribing someone to get it."

"You take it?"

He nodded. "Every day. It is given to us in our morning meal to keep us from declining into a womanly shape and thoughts. Have you noticed the older Shadow Men who serve as imperial servants?"

I nodded.

"Then you will have noticed their round shapes and high voices."

I eyed the pouch. "You think Lord Ido takes it to stop the weakening that comes from being a Dragoneye?"

Ryko tossed it back onto the work bench. "I am sure of it. And his sudden angers tell me he is taking too much."

"How much are you supposed to take?"

"Only a fingertip a day. Otherwise the Sun energy rises too high and anything can set you off into a mad fury. Or, if you are of a melancholic nature, a darkness that cannot be shaken off." His voice lowered. "There are other effects as well. Dark marks on the skin, like the pox, and all your hair can drop out, even on your privates."

"Dark marks? Like a rash?"

Ryko nodded. "Yes. You've seen it?"

"I think Lord Ido may be giving this drug to Dillon," I said. "He has the rash. And his nature has changed." Did Dillon know he was taking the drug, or was Lord Ido feeding it to him without his knowledge?

"If Ido is not careful, he will kill your friend. Too much can be lethal."

My eyes found the pouch again. If taken carefully, perhaps it would strengthen my Sun energy and help me contact the Mirror Dragon.

"Come, let's look for the folio," Ryko said. "We cannot stay here much longer. We still have to find a way out without raising the guards."

I walked the length of the reading table, catching words here and there from the open scrolls: *myth, forbidden, death.* But no red folio. I rubbed the base of my skull; the pressure had deepened. Was it the Rat Dragon? I held up my candle. At the very end of the room, something reflected my light. A few more strides and I was in front of a wooden case topped with a flat piece of glass the size of an open scroll. How much had such a precious thing cost?

But all wonder at the workmanship was gone when I leaned over and saw two small leather folios about the size of my hand—one red and bound by a string of black pearls, the other black and bound by white pearls.

"It's here!" A surge of exhilaration and relief caught me in the chest.

Ryko was beside me in a moment.

"Is that glass?" He tapped the top. "Beautiful!" Then he saw what was inside. "*Two* folios? What's the other one?"

I studied the case. There were hinges on the back—it would open like a box. "Here, hold my candle," I said.

Gingerly, I hooked my fingers under the lip of the glass and lifted. It opened easily and rested back on the sturdy hinges.

Ryko moved the candles closer. "Look, the black one has the same design on it as the door."

Although half-hidden under the wrap of white pearls, the leather had been tooled with the circle of twelve spheres.

The red folio had no design on the front, but three deep gouges marked the smooth leather as though someone had tried to slice through the tight binding of black pearls. Had Lord Ido been unable to open it?

I reached for the folio.

It suddenly heaved. Before I could snatch back my hand, the string of black pearls had unraveled and snaked up my hand, wrapping itself tightly around my wrist. I yelped, pulling my hand and the folio out of the case. The taste of metal flooded my mouth as a familiar rage scoured my body: the same rage I had felt in my swords.

Ryko dropped the candles and lunged toward me. "I'll pull it off!"

"No," I snarled. The last loop of pearls had bound the folio against my palm. I pulled the text up to my chest, protecting it from Ryko. The rage receded just as quickly as it had risen, leaving a quiet sense of completeness.

"No, it's all right," I said, cradling the folio against my body. "It's all right."

Ryko eyed me uncertainly. "If you say so." He looked down at the black folio. "Will the same thing happen with the other one?"

"I will not touch it!" I snapped, the rage surging again.

Ryko stepped back. "Are you sure you are all right?"

I massaged my forehead, trying to dislodge the anger. "We should go." I wanted to get as far away from the black folio as soon as possible. The feeling was as strong and as sharp as a nail through my hand.

"You don't want to take the black folio?"

"No!" I took a shaking breath, forcing some calm. "No. If Lord Ido owns it, he will be able to mount an official investigation if it is stolen."

I gently pushed at the red folio, directing it up my forearm under my sleeve. There was no resistance; the pearls loosening slightly, then tightening again.

Ryko bent and picked up the snuffed candles. "I'll light them in the lamp," he said.

"No, I'll do it," I said quickly. "You close the case. I don't want to touch it again." Taking the candles, I crossed quickly to the side bench.

The pouch of Sun drug lay next to the lamp. I sneaked a look over my shoulder. Ryko was staring down at the black folio, absorbed. Using my body as cover, I scooped up the pouch and shoved it into the deep pocket of my tunic. Then I quickly lit the candles in the flame of the oil lamp.

Just as I turned, Ryko let out a bellow and jumped back from the case, rubbing his hand. He looked across at me, his face a strange mix of guilt and shock. "I tried to pick up the black one, but the pearls whipped me," he said. He eased the lid down from arm's length.

"We've got to go. Now," I said urgently.

I blew out the lamp. Once more the room became a dark, shadowy otherworld flickering with the light of the two candles. I moved to the door, away from the gap on the bench where the pouch had been. Ryko met me at the end of the reading table and took a candle.

"How are we going to get out?" I asked.

"The guards should have cleared the area by now. If I get hit with the same illusion, then you're going to have to help me get through it," Ryko said, touching his stomach. "Once we are free of that, we'll make our way back to the side gate."

I followed him into the narrow corridor. Turning, I held up my candle and took one last look at Lord Ido's library. Although the case was hidden in the dark shadows, it seemed to throb with soured power. I quickly closed the twelve-sphere door.

Ahead, Ryko extinguished his candle, then opened the outer door a crack.

"It looks clear," he said.

For a moment, intuition held me still. I touched the folio resting beneath my sleeve. "You should hold on to me," I said. "Until we get past the dragon power."

Ryko nodded and took my candle, pinching the flame out.

A rustle of cloth told me he was storing them both back in his waist pouch.

"Ready?" I asked.

His hand grasped my arm. "Ready."

I opened the door, the movement bumping the broken padlock against the metal in a soft clang. The garden was quiet, the shapes of the trees and flower beds edged in silver from the half-moon. I stepped out into the shadow of the hill, feeling the drag of Ryko as he followed. The pearls around my wrist stirred, and for a moment I saw the Rat Dragon's power over the hill, like a thin dome of glass, stretching down the path and ending at a thin stand of blossom trees. I steered us slowly toward them. Ryko met my gaze and nodded; all was well. So far. We passed the spot where he had first fallen. Not too far now. Then I felt Ryko's grip loosen and, before I could protest, he released me. I saw his eyes widen with pain, then he doubled over and dropped heavily to his knees. I lunged for him, digging my fingers into the hard muscle of his arm. The straining tension suddenly left his body. He grabbed my hand.

"Not quite clear yet," I said unnecessarily.

He looked up at me, then bowed his head. "My lord." His voice was soft with awe.

"Ryko, get up." I pulled at his arm. "We are not safe out here."

It was only a few more lengths to the trees. Holding my hand tightly, Ryko pushed himself up onto his feet. I led him off the path into the thin cover.

"It will be all right now," I whispered.

Hesitantly, he pulled his hand from mine. We both paused, but he was clearly in no pain. "I am in your debt, my lord," he murmured, bowing.

I shook my head. "No it's—"

A crunch of leaves made us both spin around. A guard stood behind us, caught midretreat. Although he wore a wide-brimmed helmet, I recognized the blunt, mean features and solid body.

Ranne.

His eyes widened.

He'd recognized me.

Beside me, Ryko tensed with the same realization. It was Ranne's death warrant. In a blur of speed, Ryko drew both knives. As Ranne opened his mouth to raise the alarm, a knife hit him in the throat, sinking up to its hilt. His shout became a wet gurgle as he clutched at the blade. Ryko sprang forward, thrusting its twin up under Ranne's armor, into his abdomen. I heard the puncture of air and the clicking rattle of his death breath as Ryko eased his body on to the ground.

I gaped at them, the living crouched over the dead. I had seen death before—Dolana and others at the salt farm—but they had been worn down by misery and illness into a welcome release. This was a snatching away of life—one moment there was *Hua*, there was will, there was Ranne, and then there was not.

"We have to hide the body," Ryko said, wiping one of the knives on the grass. "In the pavilion."

I shivered at Ryko's words; how quickly a person became just a body. Ranne had bullied me at the school and nearly killed me during the ceremony. Perhaps I should be rejoicing at the death of my enemy. But I couldn't. A man had died and another had killed to protect me.

A few moments ago, I had been fighting just for my own survival. Now there was no standing back from this larger struggle. I was at its center.

"No," I said flatly. I knew where the body had to go. "Carry him to the edge of the dragon power and I'll pull him into it. They'll think it was an accident, and won't be able to retrieve him until Ido returns."

Ryko stared up at me, then pressed his fist to his chest—a soldier's salute. "At your command, my lord."

It did not take long to drag Ranne's body onto the path. I kept my eyes away from his blank stare and swallowed my gorge as my hand brushed against his cooling face. His life warmth was already fading into the chill of the grave. As I stood up from arranging his lax limbs into the position of a fall, I wondered if anyone would observe the nine days of mourning for him.

Ryko hissed at me from the edge of the dragon power. "Come."

We cut across the garden toward the dark archway. The pressure of the pearl binding around my forearm was like a sweet torture—my impatience to open the folio barely held in check by the need to wait until I was in the safe seclusion of my bedchamber.

The inner courtyard was empty when we peered around

the corner of the passage. No servant girl stealing a mouthful. No guards with their torches. No Dillon. He was probably hiding—the Sun drug seemed to be rousing his fear and melancholy more than his fighting spirit.

I crept across the courtyard under the cover of the kumquats and down the alley, Ryko close and silent behind me. As we cleared the side gate, pulling it shut with a soft scrape, I felt eyes upon me. I looked up. Dillon stood on the guard walkway above us. He held up a hesitant hand.

"Thank you," I mouthed.

He nodded and turned away.

CHAPTER THIRTEEN

WHEN RYKO AND I finally reached the pebble garden around my apartments, I was relieved to see only the two corner night-lamps burning, their lights protecting the building from dark spirits—a good sign that no alarm had been raised at my empty bed. We picked our way over the stones to the pale rectangle of my window. The folio was still bound tightly against my forearm, the pearls warm against my skin, as though they held their own *Hua*.

Soon I'd read the word that would release my power. I had always imagined the name of a dragon would be like the shift of a breeze through leaves, or perhaps the sound of water splashing. But how could that be written?

"Shall I stay, lord?" Ryko asked softly.

I shook my head. Except for essential information, we had not spoken at all on the run back to the palace. The past few hours had stripped away some of our illusions about each other and ourselves. Such bare truth was not easily absorbed. And I wanted to be alone when I read the name.

"Thank you, Ryko," I said. "For everything."

He bowed and moved away, only a muffled chink of a pebble marking his careful retreat.

I hoisted myself up over the windowsill and dropped awkwardly onto the thick carpet inside. In a few strides I was beside the covered oil lamp I'd left burning on the bedside table. I pushed up my right sleeve. The cloth snagged on the pearls and folio. Hissing with impatience, I worked the garment over them, my hand shaking with the delay. Finally, the folio was free.

In the lamp's soft glow, the surface of the black pearls swirled with greens and purples like the sheen of oil on water. Underneath them, the red leather had the supple shine of a seal's skin, its smoothness marred by the three deep gouges that raked down the front. Holding my breath, I gently lifted the end pearl. There was a small resistance, as though it was weighted, and then it came away from my forearm. One by one each pearl gave up its position, loosening its hold on the folio. I breathed out as I lifted the last pearl that held the text to me. The folio dropped into my hand. In a clicking slither, the pearls coiled loosely around my wrist.

I stroked the gouges on the leather, feeling the rough edges of someone else's failure. Lord Ido's? I let a small laugh escape; the pearls had unbound the folio for me, but not for the all-powerful Rat Dragoneye. A leather tongue was threaded through a loop, holding the folio closed. With fingers made clumsy from excitement, I tried to unfasten it but could not work the leather through the hole. Perhaps I had laughed too soon. I rubbed the damp tips of my fingers down my tunic and tried again. At last, the tongue came free. I flipped the leather front open, expecting loose pieces of parchment. Instead, there was a thick wad of smooth paper sewn together at the left edge. A book! I had seen another like it in my master's library—a rarity that he had valued highly. I slid my fingers under the tablet of paper and lifted, only to find that the stitching had been sewn through the leather case, too. It was all one piece. I settled the wad back against its leather bed. On the front paper was a drawing of the Mirror Dragon in red ink. It was just a few swirling lines, but somehow it caught the power and majesty of the beast. This was the precious book of the Mirror Dragon secrets. Somewhere inside was his name. Somewhere inside was my power. I took a deep breath and turned the page.

The neat characters did not make sense. I blinked, squinting down at the writing. It still did not make sense. I turned another page. Lines and lines of strange marks. Another page, and another. All unreadable. I flipped over every page, scanning for just one familiar symbol. Just one.

I reached the final page. "No," I breathed. "No."

There was nothing I recognized.

I started at the beginning again, staring down at the paper as if I could draw meaning out of the faded lettering.

Nothing.

Despair howled in my head like a typhoon. Blindly, I felt for the bed behind me and sank down on to it. Why couldn't I read it? A sob burned through my chest in a heaving moan. Then another, grabbing at the last of my breath, leaving me gasping. I couldn't stop them. All the disappointment and fear spilled out of me. What if Rilla heard? Or the master? I doubled over and pushed my knuckles into my mouth, muffling my desolation. Maybe I was not meant to be here. Maybe it had all been a mistake and the Mirror Dragon did not want me, after all. I fell back, curling around the folio, rocking into each ragged whimper.

I had no dragon name, no true power. No hope.

I woke with a gasp, my mouth parched, the skin around my eyes tight with dried tears. A silk sheet covered me. Across the room, the window was shuttered, the edge of each slat bright with daylight. Rilla must have come in while I was asleep. I pushed back the sheet and saw the folio wedged under my chest. Still open. Still unreadable. No miracle had transformed the writing during the night. I pulled the book out and closed it, working the tongue back through the loop. Immediately, the black pearls uncoiled from my wrist in a soft sliding rattle and looped over the leather, pulling it back against the underside of my arm. With a neat flick of the last pearl, they settled. Why were they tying the folio to me? I couldn't even read it.

The dark despair rose up again, closing around my mind like a cold fog.

No! I shook my head, as if I could physically dislodge its hold. I had the folio, and its guardian pearls had unraveled and let me open it. That must mean something. There must be a way to unlock its words. All I had to do was find the key.

I struggled upright. Beside me on the bedside table was a water jug and cup. Rilla had thought of everything. She must have seen the folio and the pearls when she covered me—had she told the master? I poured a drink, gulping it down without pause. Another two cupfuls finally quenched my dryness. All those tears must have wrung the water from my very soul.

The sound of the door opening made me look around. It was Rilla, carrying a tray. I quickly pulled my sleeve down over the folio as she closed the door with her hip. Seeing me sitting up, she bowed and crossed the room.

"They are already gathering at the Gate of Supreme Benevolence for the start of the procession," she said, her eyes flicking to my sleeve and back to my face. She held the tray out toward me. "You've just got time for the tea and some *lo-jee*."

The salty aroma of the breakfast soup made my stomach roll with want. But first, the ghost maker's tea. I picked up the cup and remembered the Sun drug in my pocket. Maybe it would force a connection with the Mirror Dragon. But what would happen if I mixed it with the ghost maker's tea? One drug kindled the Sun, the other suppressed the Moon. Would it tip me too far out of balance? Kill me? Perhaps it was not a good idea to take them both at once.

The ghost maker's tea was tepid, the dirt taste even worse

without the heat. Closing my eyes, I finished it quickly, resisting the urge to gag on the bitterness.

"How is the master today?" I asked, handing back the cup.

"Better," she said. "He is dressing for the festivities." Her eyes flicked to my sleeve again. "You should get out of those peasant clothes as soon as possible," she said blandly. "I will return them to the basket."

I met her gaze, silently asking the question. She shrugged. "What I see stays with me."

"Even from the master?"

Her face tightened, but she nodded. "I am your body servant now."

I leaned forward. "I am doing everything I can to keep us safe." Perhaps I was trying to reassure myself as much as Rilla. "Please believe that."

She picked up the bowl of *lo-jee* and passed it to me. "There is no one else to care for Chart," she said softly. "Please remember that."

My master shifted irritably on the silk cushion beside me and squinted over the heads of our bearers into the dim passageway ahead. It was still blocked by an ornate gilded gate. His movement sent a sour smell into the warm air, and I saw sweat beaded above his cracked lips. His breath, too, was more labored than normal. Although the heavy red canopy of our palanquin trapped the morning heat inside the cabin, it was not hot enough to cause such distress. Rilla might have pronounced the master improved, but I was not convinced he had made any progress.

I leaned out to look at the other Dragoneyes lined up behind us in matching red-and-gold palanquins, and behind them the long formations of men on foot, waiting for the gongs that would open the gate and announce the start of the procession. In the next palanquin, Lord Ido met my gaze. He gave one slow nod. I pulled back, my heart quickening.

I slowly worked my fingers inside the wide sleeve of my Dragoneye robe, checking the placement of the folio against my forearm. After Rilla had dressed me, I tried to unwind the pearls and find a place to hide the book, but there was nowhere secure and the pearls would not loosen their grip. It was both troubling and reassuring. My only option was to carry the folio, and strangely, I felt stronger and more capable with it touching my skin. My fingers brushed the edge of the leather. I had thought to place it higher, but the pearls had settled it under a panel of stiff embroidery that camouflaged their bulk.

I flinched as a servant dropped to his knees beside me, the top of his head just reaching the base of the cabin. He held up a tall porcelain cup. The fresh tang of limes penetrated the fug of heat and sweat.

"With the compliments of Lord Tyron," the servant said. On the other side of the palanquin, another servant was offering my master a matching cup.

"I had forgotten how long it takes for one of these processions to start," my master said, sipping the drink. "Thank the gods for Tyron's foresight." His mouth puckered. "The limes seem to be somewhat bitter this year."

I let the sweet-sour juice rest in my dry mouth before swallowing. I found it tart but not bitter. I looked across at my master, tentatively sipping his drink. Perhaps it was time to ask for his help. I could not tell him everything yet, but if I copied out a few of the folio's strange characters and showed them to him, he might know their origin. I gulped at the remainder of the cool juice, pleased with the plan, and returned the cup to the servant. My master only took a few more mouthfuls before handing it back to the man kneeling beside him.

"Send our thanks to Lord Tyron," my master ordered.

The servant nodded and backed away.

"I think I see the gate officials approaching," my master said. "We will be entering soon." He settled back in the seat, his high collar shifting to reveal the blue crescent of a bruise. "It is interesting that the emperor positions us first, ahead of Ido." There was gentle malice in his voice.

"Did Lord Ido ride in with High Lord Sethon this morning?" I asked.

My master flipped open his fan and started up a warm breeze. "He did—but just through the city gates. A bold declaration of allegiance for those who recognize the signs. But he cannot ride with Sethon in the military procession. He must sit with us below the emperor."

"It is getting closer, isn't it," I said, lowering my voice. "They will make their attempt soon."

My master nodded. "Yes, the game moves into a most interesting phase."

Although I could not see through the velvet curtain at our backs, I fancied I could feel Lord Ido's baleful gaze from the palanquin behind. No doubt he knew the red folio and the Sun drug were gone—he would have returned to his hall to dress for the procession and found the evidence. I pushed away the memory of Ranne's blank eyes. And Lord Ido would have a good idea who had taken them, too. I just hoped Dillon had escaped his attention.

An image of the black folio, lying beside its red partner in the glass case, flashed into my mind. I shivered. What was it about the black book that made me so afraid? Perhaps my master knew something about it.

"Lord Brannon," I said, calling his attention away from the gate. "Have you ever seen a design of twelve spheres connected in a circle?" I traced a circle on my palm. "With the top two spheres bigger."

His fan dropped to his lap. "Where have you seen that?" he demanded, grabbing my wrist. "Where? Tell me."

I pulled back from the alarm in his eyes. "I haven't seen it," I said, frantically searching for a solid lie. "Dillon told me he saw it on the door of Lord Ido's library."

He let me go. "His apprentice saw it on a door?"

I nodded. "What does it mean?"

He looked around us, then leaned closer. "It is the symbol of the String of Pearls." He opened the fan again and waved it slowly in front of us, using its wide spread to mask our conversation.

"The String of Pearls is said to be a weapon so powerful, it can shift continents," he said softly. "It joins the energy of all twelve dragons into one devastating force." He licked his pale lips. "But it is only a legend, a children's ghost story."

"So it is not real?"

He shook his head. "For a long time, I have been collecting old scrolls that mention it, and I have not come across any that confirm it as more than a story. I know that Ido also collects stories of it. Perhaps he has found one that proves it is possible."

A black folio, stamped with the circle and protected by white pearls—there could be no doubt that Lord Ido had found something more than just a story. I could not keep this hidden from my master.

"Dillon also said he saw a black folio with the same design," I said carefully. "Bound with white pearls."

"A folio?" My master sucked in a breath. "Are you sure he said that?"

"I think so."

He rubbed his chin. "I don't like this at all. Tyron and the others must be informed as soon as possible."

"How does this String of Pearls work?"

My master shook his head. "No one really knows. There are so many conflicting legends. One says it is by all twelve Dragoneyes joining together to create the weapon. Another states that two Dragoneyes must join forces for it to form. And then there are others that say there can only be one surviving Dragoneye who inherits all the power."

"Tellon told us about that one yesterday in our class."

He grunted, his mind elsewhere. "It may be nothing; just one of Ido's obsessions. Still, Tyron and the others need to know in case—"

His words were swamped by the deep, resonating note of the imperial gong. He lowered the fan, both of us quickly pulling back from our conversation. Two officials stood at the gilded gate, waiting for the next gong to allow us through the Gate of Supreme Benevolence, into the ceremonial courtyard.

The huge entrance gate to the palace had three vaulted passages set into it. The central corridor, called the Way of Heavenly Conduct, was for the use of the emperor and was wide enough to take eight horses side by side. The right passage—the Arch of Strong Sons—was for the imperial family. And the left, which we were facing, was officially called the Arch of Just and Scholarly Judgment but was commonly known as the Judgment Gate. It was reserved for nobles, generals, high-ranked dignitaries, and the three winning scholars of the annual examinations. All others came and went through the two smaller side gates—the Gates of Humility—that flanked the red-and-gold edifice. I had never been through either of the Humility gates, let alone the Judgment Gate. Nor had I been inside the ceremonial courtyard. And now, here I was, heading a procession into the emperor's presence.

The second gong vibrated through the air. Immediately, the two officials pushed the gate apart. The third gong sent us into the cooler corridor.

"So beautiful," I breathed as my eyes adjusted to the dimmer light.

The walls were gold, stuccoed with dragons coiled around the symbols of the four gracious arts of the scholar: pen, brush, zither, and the crisscrossed square of the Strategy Game. The ceiling was lacquered a rich red and etched with gold landscapes—seas, mountains, plateaus, and an intricate rendering of the palace precinct we were now entering. Above them all, in the vaults of the roof, were gold scenes depicting the eight gods of learning.

We emerged into the bright sunshine again. I blinked, trying to get my bearings in the immense courtyard. Long galleries lined each side. In the center, a huge staircase, built into three marble terraces, led up to an imposing hall with a gold roof that curved toward the heavens. Its walls were painted with the vivid red-and-black designs for good fortune, happiness, and longevity.

Two guards stepped forward and took a position on each side of our palanquin, leading our bearers over the wide expanse of gray paving toward the central staircase. I glanced at my master; even he was stilled by the majesty of the place. About a third of the way across, we stopped behind a thin line on the ground. It was, in fact, a band of gold that had been embedded between the stones and seemed to run from one edge of the courtyard to the other.

"The imperial audience line," my master said. "We must go on foot from here."

The bearers smoothly lowered the palanquin to the ground, the effort showing on the leader's face. I stepped out of the cabin and saw the line of other Dragoneyes and dignitaries waiting their turn to advance. From the next palanquin, Lord Ido was watching me closely with narrowed eyes. I kept my hands clasped tightly together to stop myself from checking the folio again. My master looked across the stone courtyard to the long staircase, grim resignation on his face as he lowered himself slowly into a half crouch. Although the emperor had not yet emerged from the great Red and Black Hall, all who stepped beyond the audience line had to approach in the imperial bow.

It was a long walk to our honored position at the bottom of the steps. My back and hip ached from hunching over, and I could hear the catch in my master's breathing as a silent official led us to our places. A eunuch stepped up behind each of us and held a large parasol over our heads while we stood and waited for the other dignitaries to take their positions, but the protection did nothing for the heat reflecting off the gray paving. My master's face was bleached of color, and his posture looked like it was more from pain than obedience.

"Lord Brannon, you look unwell," I whispered. He did not look up. I touched his shoulder, alarmed. "Master, do you need water?"

He shook his head. "It was just the walk," he rasped. "I will recover soon."

Lord Ido took his place across from us at the bottom of the staircase. The folio felt like a huge block tied to my arm, and I dared not look at him in case he saw its presence in my face. Lord Tyron stopped beside us, his heavy face creasing with concern when he saw his ally's ashen skin and glazed eyes. I measured the time in my master's labored breaths as the officials slowly guided the other Dragoneyes and high-ranked men into position. It was all taking so long.

My master lurched forward, then recovered.

"Old friend, lean on me," Lord Tyron said urgently.

My master nodded, his mouth clenched shut, and clasped Tyron's arm. Over his head, the Ox Dragoneye signaled for me to take my master's other arm. I hooked it under mine and felt his cold skin. This was more than just exhaustion.

"Lord Tyron, did you send us lime juice before the procession?" I asked.

He frowned. "No, why would I . . ." Then comprehension blanched his face. He looked down at my master, shuddering between us, then back at me. "No. I swear I did not."

At the top of the staircase, an official sounded a huge gong. Everyone around us dropped to his knees; the ceremony had started. Tyron met my anxious gaze and nodded—there was nothing we could do but help my master to the ground. His weight sagged between us as we clumsily settled him onto the flags. Another gong. I lowered into the imperial kowtow. Beside me, my master pitched forward into the obeisance, his body convulsing. I grabbed his chilled wrist as though my hold could keep him from slumping over. Would I soon be shivering and panting in the same way? The third gong announced the arrival of the emperor. I held my breath, feeling my master's weight press painfully against my hand as we waited for the order to rise. What was the delay?

Finally the gong sounded again.

I sat back, helping Tyron pull my master upright. His breathing was fast, his eyes fixed and clouded. Above us, at the top of the staircase, the frail figure of the emperor surveyed the courtyard from his sedan chair.

"We must get help," I hissed. I turned to the eunuch behind me. "Get the royal physician."

The man's eyes widened with terror, his forehead hitting the ground. "Forgive me, my lord, it is not allowed. We cannot leave the imperial presence."

Tyron nodded. "He's right. We cannot interrupt an imperial audience." His eyes searched my face. "Are you ill, too?"

"No."

A fanfare from the rank of trumpets behind us blasted across the courtyard, bouncing off the paving and buildings. My master winced and moaned. The clattering of hooves on the stone echoed in the huge space, the thundering noise announcing the arrival of High Lord Sethon and his officers.

"Move closer to him," Tyron ordered as he shifted against my master.

I took some of my master's weight. Patches of sweat under his arms and around his neck had darkened the red silk.

"My chest," he whispered. His hand groped for his collar.

The sound of the hooves had settled into the distinct beat of one horse approaching. I snatched a look. A huge black horse paced toward us, ruthlessly controlled, the rider clad in blue imperial parade armor outlined in red piping: High Lord Sethon. His face was in shadow under an elaborate leather helmet, but the way he carried himself showed the bullish strength that was now diminished in his imperial brother. Behind him, on foot, came three soldiers wearing plain blue skirted armor and carrying banners. I could see their horses behind the audience line, held by aides.

My master stiffened, then doubled over and vomited a foul green bile onto the stones. A murmur of disgust and fear rose around us as men edged away.

I cast around frantically, not sure what I was looking for, only knowing my master needed help. Lord Ido watched us, his face unreadable. A wave of kowtowing moved toward us as High Lord Sethon passed between the ranks of dignitaries.

My master retched again. I braced him against the convulsions, the chill of his body through the thin silk as cold as a winter stream. On his other side, Lord Tyron suddenly dropped into a kowtow. My master sagged against me. I looked up. Above me was the massive black chest of the horse. And above that, the hard gaze of High Lord Sethon.

There was no mistaking his kinship to the emperor; the bold modeling of his forehead and chin and the tilt of his mouth were identical. The high lord's eyes, however, were closer together and set over a broken nose that had healed flat, with a scar that had carved a crescent across his cheek. A warrior's face.

I scrabbled forward, prostrating myself. He had royal rank. He could help my master. The horse sidled to the left but was forced back under his iron grip.

"Your Highness," I pleaded. "Forgive my presumption, but Lord Brannon is ill. He needs the physician."

"You must be Lord Eon," he said. He studied me for a moment. "You are smaller than I expected." His voice was a clipped, cold monotone.

He glanced across at Lord Ido, then turned to the soldier standing at the horse's side. "Shen, find the royal physician and bring him here." The man bowed and backed away.

I kowtowed again, light-headed with relief. "Thank you, Your Highness."

He dismounted, dropping smoothly to the ground in front of us. His every move spoke of decision and command.

"I hope Lord Brannon recovers quickly," he said. "It would be most inauspicious for my brother if a Dragoneye lord died during the Twelfth Day celebrations." He passed the reins to the middle soldier. "Hold him tight, he is skittish."

He looked up at the small figure of the emperor waiting for him outside the hall. Lowering into the shallow bow required of a royal half brother, he began the climb up the staircase.

I returned to my master. His breathing was so slow that I could hardly feel it against my hand. His eyes opened, and I saw the flare of agony in them a moment before his body stiffened and arched against me. His arms thrashed wildly until Lord Tyron grabbed them, wrestling them down. There was nothing I could do but hold him as he writhed and gasped, saliva bubbling from his mouth. He grunted, trying to form words, but his face seemed to be frozen into a mask of pain. He clawed at me until I held each side of his head, using all of my strength to stop the uncontrollable jerking.

"Stop him," he whispered.

"Master—please—" I couldn't break through his pain. He was being wrenched from me, already halfway into the spirit world.

Under my hands, his head snapped back as his body arched in agony. His glazed eyes locked with mine. "Swear you will stop him."

I nodded, watching helplessly as his back arched again. His body thudded against the paving, the last embers of his life force burning in the urgency of his eyes. And then even that pale light was gone.

CHAPTER FOURTEEN

POISON.

I knew it, the emperor knew it, and from the whispers that followed me as I performed the death duties during the nine formal days of mourning, the whole court knew it, too. Lord Tyron called for an investigation, but there was no evidence, or none that led anywhere, and so the official reason for my master's death was the Dragoneye's curse—the crippling drain of *Hua*. I had no doubt who was behind it all, but why had Lord Ido spared me? I could only think of one reason; I was more useful alive and without protection than I was dead.

My master had no family left to prepare his tomb, burn the effigies, and pay the Beseechers to chant him into the spirit world. By default, I became his official mourner. Lady Dela patiently explained the death rituals for a lord, gently guiding me through my responsibilities, while Ryko stood guard, his stoic silence offering a different kind of support.

For the first two days, I had to receive the relentless lines of lesser courtiers and dignitaries offering their small red packets of mourning money. All through their careful speeches of condolence and polite bowls of tea, one question circled interminably in my mind: *How was I going to survive without my master?* He had been as much the creator of Lord Eon as I was.

In between the formal visits, I either prayed at my altar or lay on my huge carved bed staring numbly at the folio and its indecipherable text. My master was gone, and with him my chance to learn the book's secrets. I should have shown it to him. I should have told him about my dragon's name. I should have told him so many things.

Every now and again, Rilla came in with food or the ghost maker's tea, urging me in a soft voice to eat and drink. We had an official taster now, unofficially provided by the emperor, but I was still afraid. Each morning it took all of my courage to drink the tea, and food caught in my throat and made me gag. I left the Sun drug in its pouch, untouched.

Early on the third day—the day of Tomb Preparation—Rilla announced Lady Dela.

"She's waiting in the reception room with an imperial messenger," Rilla said, hurrying over to the bed and stripping the silk cover off me.

I looked up from the folio; I could not even rouse myself to hide it.

"Another gift?"

Since the procession, the Heavenly Master had been too ill

to venture out of his rooms. Nevertheless, he had sent a gift each day of mourning—a great mark of imperial favor. Yesterday, the Day of Herbs and Cloth, a precious pot of unguent and fine linen was delivered for the preparation and wrapping of my master's body.

"I don't think so," Rilla said. She clicked her tongue. "Did you sleep in your tunic?"

I closed the folio and held out my right arm, watching as the black pearls wrapped the book tightly against me. Rilla gasped and stepped back from their slithering clatter—I'd forgotten she had never seen them move before.

"It's all right," I said. "They won't hurt you."

I had once thought the pearls might tell me something about the Mirror Dragon or hold the key to the strange text. But for all their peculiar magic, they were only bindings. I climbed off the bed and stood still as Rilla quickly brushed and twitched my robes into order, avoiding the right sleeve where the folio nestled underneath the thick white cloth.

"After you see Lady Dela, it has been arranged for you to prepare his . . . the tomb." I heard her voice catch but couldn't push a way out of my own dry grief to offer her any solace.

As I entered the shuttered reception room, Lady Dela sank into a low bow. She was not painting her skin, as a mark of respect, and that, along with her severe white robe, emphasized her swarthy coloring and sharp angles. Behind her, Ryko bobbed in a quick duty bow. Even through my listlessness, I could sense a strange excitement in them. An imperial messenger came forward on his knees and offered me a scroll.

"By command of his Imperial Highness." He lowered himself three times into the delivery kowtows of an imperial edict, his forehead touching the straw matting.

I broke the seal and unrolled the message. The Heavenly Master, concerned for my welfare after the death of Lord Brannon, had ordered Lady Dela to become my official chaperone and Ryko to take charge of my personal safety with the command of a small detachment of guards.

I looked up and forced a smile. I was glad to have them with me, but I felt it as one feels a light blow through armor—muffled by thick layers of protection. Even as they spoke about the arrangements, I let myself sink back into the comfort of numbness.

The next morning, Prince Kygo arrived, unannounced and with only two guards shadowing him. He was dressed in plain white mourning clothes with no royal adornment. The gash on his left cheekbone was closing, but the dark bruise was still vivid.

"Lord Eon," he said, and gestured for me to rise. "I do not come as your overlord, but as your friend."

Dully, I stood, waiting for him to speak. He looked back at his guards and jerked his head, sending them out of earshot.

"I would be honored if you would allow me to stand as second mourner for Lord Brannon," he said.

The surprise of his words finally penetrated my apathy. The Second Mourner carried the offerings to the gods and organized the effigies. It was a position of service—duties that were below a prince.

"Your Highness . . ." I stopped, not sure what to say.

He gripped my shoulder. "My father sickens more every day," he said softly. "It is time I stepped out of the harem for good. Remember our agreement, my friend?"

Mutual survival.

I straightened under the weight of his hand. "My master said it would not be long now. They will make their move."

He nodded. "You are the only thing that stands in the way of Ido's control of the council." His grip tightened. "Allow me to stand by your side as an ally at Lord Brannon's passing."

"It would be my honor, Your Highness," I said, and bowed.

We smiled at one another, a grim acknowledgment that it might be too little, too late. The silent understanding was as brief as a heartbeat, but for that one bright moment, I did not feel quite so alone.

Two days later, on the Day of Honoring, the Dragoneyes came, led by Lord Ido. Ryko stood silently behind me as they entered the reception room, his solid presence like another backbone holding me up.

The Dragoneyes all wore white robes and brought thick packets of mourning money as was custom, but I sensed there was also another purpose in the visit. As each man bowed to me, I studied his face. My master's allies were all tense, his enemies shifting with impatience. I met Lord Tyron's eyes as he straightened from his courtesy and they held a warning—but of what? I followed his gaze to a stranger at the back of the group. The man bowed from where he stood, offering murmured condolences. There was something familiar about the way he blinked—in a pattern of three—but I could not place him.

Lord Ido stepped forward from the loose semicircle of white-robed men. He smiled at me—a cold curve of his lips that matched the calculation in his eyes. We both knew he had killed my master.

"My dear Lord Eon, we are all shocked by the passing of Lord Brannon," he said softly. His false sympathy made my gut tighten. "We all grieve with you in the loss of your mentor and offer you, our youngest brother, support during this time of mourning."

For the first time since my master's death, I felt something in my core. Hate. It burned through me like a fireball, laying waste to the numbness and despair. I quickly looked down, in case Ido saw his own death in my eyes.

"With that in mind," Ido continued, "the council has petitioned Heuris Kane to step into the position of proxy lord. He will continue Lord Brannon's work and relieve you of your council duties so that you can study the dragon arts. As Lord Brannon wished."

Heuris Kane—now I recognized the stranger. He was Baret's master and one of Ido's minions. As the prince had predicted, Ido was making his next move to control the council. This was the reason my master was dead. This was the reason my world was hollow. I closed my eyes, hearing my master's last words.

Stop him.

But I was not even a proper Dragoneye. How could I go against this man? He was too powerful. Too ruthless.

Stop him.

The pearls tightened their grip around my arm as though rallying my courage. No one else could stop Ido. I had to try. For the emperor and the prince. And for my master. I curled my hands into fists.

"No."

As soon as I said it, Ryko stepped closer, hovering protectively behind me.

Ido stiffened. "What?"

Tyron's head snapped up. I met his startled gaze, silently pleading for his help. He licked his lips and nodded.

"Of course, I thank Heuris Kane for his concern for my welfare," I said, turning toward the man and bowing, "but I wish to take my position on the council."

Kane blinked rapidly at me, then looked at Ido for guidance.

"This is not a choice, Lord Eon," Ido snarled. "This is what is best for the council."

"You are wrong, Lord Ido," Tyron said. He stepped out of the semicircle. "If Lord Eon does not wish to stand aside, then he has every right to prove himself capable of holding his position."

Prove myself? What did that mean?

"Lord Tyron is correct," Silvo said. "A Dragoneye can only be removed from the council if all other members agree that he is not competent. I, for one, am not convinced that is the case."

"Nor I," Dram said. He smiled encouragingly at me. A few other voices murmured agreement.

Ido rounded on the Horse Dragoneye. "What would you know about competence?" He glared around the semicircle.

"Lord Ido has a valid point," Elgon drawled. The Tiger Dragoneye held up his hand to quiet the rise of voices. "We don't know if Lord Eon will be able to cope with council duties. I propose we have a test to prove whether or not he is capable."

A test? I dug my nails into my palm. If it was a demonstration of power, everything would be lost.

"What did you have in mind?" Tyron asked.

Elgon bowed to Ido. "I defer to our respected leader."

Ido cocked his head to one side. "Tyron, I believe your province has made their annual request to the council to control the King Monsoon rains and protect their crops."

Tyron nodded, the muscles in his jaw tightening.

Ido smiled. "Lord Eon can show us his *competence* by leading that effort. After all, the position he steps into is that of Coascendant and coleader."

"That's too much," Dram protested. "The boy hasn't had any training."

"My point exactly," Ido said smoothly.

Tyron glanced across at me. It was a huge risk for him, as well as for me. If something went wrong, the King Monsoon would flood the area and he would lose a year's income from the devastated crops. He squared his shoulders.

"I have every confidence in Lord Eon," Tyron said.

Ido turned to me, his face avid. He knew I had no chance. "Do you agree to this test?"

All eyes were on me, the tension holding everyone still. I did not even know how to call my dragon, let alone how to control the largest dump of monsoon rains in the season. But there was no choice. I was the only thing standing between a council in the control of Ido and one that still served the emperor and the land.

"Yes," I said, feeling my voice crack on the word.

Ido smiled triumphantly. "Then we will all wait for Lord Tyron's call to travel to his province."

"I gather you will have no objection to me taking over Lord Eon's training before that time," Tyron said stiffly.

Ido shrugged. "None whatsoever."

The monsoon season always started in the Daikiko Province. This year the weather watchers had predicted the King Monsoon would hit the coast in the next week or so. Ido knew I could not cram twelve years of study and practice into less than a week.

"Although," he continued with a soft sigh, "it would not be seemly for Lord Eon to train during the nine days of mourning."

Tyron's face darkened. "I was not even considering it," he said tightly.

He glanced across at me, the dismay on his face mirroring my own. With four days of mourning left, we might not even have a chance to begin the training.

"If you please, my lord," Rilla said, kneeling at the doorway. "Shall I serve the tea?"

I nodded, unable to speak. Ido had maneuvered me neatly into his trap. Now all he had to do was wait for it to spring.

The tinny crash of cymbals and the thump of drums matched the rhythm of my steps as I followed my master's body toward the burial ground. Four stocky men carried him on a litter laden with white orchids, their movements perfectly coordinated. Lady Dela had hired them along with the chanting Beseechers and the other trappings needed to bury an important man. She, of course, was not present; no women were permitted to attend the burial of a former Dragoneye. If I'd had any lightness left in me, I would have laughed at the irony.

The prince walked beside me, matching my uneven strides. He wore the black robes of the second mourner—the *Gan Hua* to my white-robed *Lin Hua*—and carried the silver tray of offerings and ceramic tomb guardians. It must have been heavy, but he did not seem troubled by the burden. An image of him sparring flashed into my mind, the memory of his lean, muscular strength and royal bearing bringing heat to my face. I glanced across at him, afraid he had seen it, but he was concentrating on balancing the tray. Behind us, Ryko and two imperial guards formed a protective line, the jangle of their armor and swords creating another rhythm in the march.

I wiped sweat from my top lip. The morning was already oppressive—the kind of thick humidity that heralded the monsoon. Yesterday, Lord Tyron had sent a formal message to all the Dragoneyes that the weather watchers in his province now predicted the King Monsoon would come in only six days—two days after the official mourning period ended. A spiraling fear rushed through me. Two days of instruction would be almost useless, especially since they would also be spent traveling to the province. Tyron, however, was adamant about keeping to the agreement; he would not even visit me or accept a messenger in case it gave Ido an opportunity to cry foul. Both he and Ido were somewhere behind us, among the other Dragoneyes. I breathed deeply, pressing the panic into a small hard knot at the bottom of my stomach. This was my master's passing day. It would dishonor him if I faltered in my duties.

Ahead, the Tiger Dragoneye tombs shimmered through the heat rising from the paved road. A smoky herb fragrance trailed behind the tiny braziers that the Beseechers carried at the head of the procession. As we approached the double gate, the lead litter bearer called a sharp halt. The procession and music stopped, the sudden silence as stifling and heavy as the humidity.

The entrance to the ground was guarded by two large stone statues. On the left was Shola, the squat death goddess, and on the right, an elegantly coiled Tiger Dragon. I stood, staring at them, suddenly unable to move. When we went through these gates, even my master's body would be gone from me. Behind us the long line of mourners began to murmur restlessly.

"Lord Eon?" the prince whispered. "It is time for us to approach the gate."

I nodded, but I still couldn't move; the world had contracted into a bubble of heat and deafening heartbeat. If I stepped closer, surely my heart would explode. I felt the prince place my hand on his arm. Slowly, he guided me to the statues, his soft whispers of encouragement quieting the thunderous beat in my ears.

I stopped in front of the gate, dragging against his weight. "No! We haven't had time to practice the entreaties," I said. "How can we beseech the gods without the proper entreaties?"

"Lord Eon, look at me." I met the prince's sympathetic gaze. "It's all right. We know them. Remember? Lady Dela taught us. We know them."

I remembered. We had sat for an hour with Lady Dela, saying the words together, our voices blending into one. It had been a warm respite from the cold formality of the duty visits and rituals.

"Are you ready now?" he asked.

I was not. I never would be, but I could not fail my master. Or the prince.

"Yes."

We both took a deep breath and bowed our heads.

"Shola, goddess of dark and death, hear our petition on behalf of Lord Brannon," we chorused, the prince's deeper tones covering the breaks in my voice.

It was my turn now. I took a step closer to the statue and looked up into the frowning face of Shola. "Here comes one into your realm," I said. "Accept these offerings and allow him to journey onward unhindered."

The prince passed me a red packet of symbolic money—a payment to Shola's spirit officials who could either ease or hinder my master's journey. I placed it at the statue's feet, then poured wine into the stone cup cradled in her clawed hand. *Let him pass*, I silently pleaded.

We crossed over to the dragon. It was a faithful likeness; whoever had carved it must have worked closely with a Tiger Dragoneye.

"Tiger Dragon, Keeper of Courage," we said, "hear our petition on behalf of Lord Brannon."

I stepped closer to the statue, its stone fang hanging just above my head. "One who once served you now passes into the land of the spirits," I said. "Accept these offerings and escort him to his ancestors with the honor that he deserves."

I placed a brass chain studded with paste emeralds between the stone talons and poured the last of the wine into a bowl made of green marble. Then I closed my eyes, breathing in the thick, warm air, and felt along my *Hua*, seeking a way past the fog of grief into my mind-sight. All I wanted was a glimpse of the Tiger Dragon—to make sure he knew my master was here and waiting to pass. I opened my eyes, feeling the strange twisting shift of sight, and saw the dragons. All of them, in a ring around the burial ground, each at his compass point. The green Tiger Dragon was more vibrant than the others, his head thrown back, his long throat swelling in a mournful keen. It was not a sound that any human could hear, but I felt the vibration of it like the shivering of the earth.

But my dragon, the Mirror Dragon, was hardly visible. A mere outline, smudged and blurred by a heavy veil of mist. I gasped and shook my head, breaking my link. He was even fainter than before.

The folio pearls tightened against my arm, as if in sympathy.

Lord Elgon stepped out from his position in the procession and approached us. As incumbent Tiger Dragoneye, he was the keeper of the burial ground. He bowed to each statue and then to us, offering me a gentle smile that transformed his shovel face.

"For all of my differences with Lord Brannon," he said softly, "he served as Tiger Dragoneye with great honor. I was most fortunate to be his apprentice."

He bowed again and opened the gates. For some reason—perhaps Elgon's unexpected kindness—all my sorrow suddenly broke out of its tight bindings. My own keen rose into my throat. I forced it back and blinked away the sting of tears. The prince leaned toward me and the mix of herbs, sweat, and smoke on his skin was strangely comforting.

"We are nearly there," he whispered. "You are doing well."

Behind us, the Beseechers began the soft entrance chants. With head down to hide my eyes, I walked beside the prince to our place at the head of the mourners, my lower lip clamped between my teeth until I tasted blood.

Throughout the lengthy chants and effigy burning beside my master's tomb, I fought a grim battle against the grief that threatened to overwhelm me. I had to hold it in. A lord would not fall to his knees and weep like a woman. A lord would not scream his grief and seek the comfort of his royal friend's arms. A lord would stoically watch the death ceremonies and do his duty. And that was what I did. Even when my master's body was pushed into the long tunnel of the tomb and the sealing rock was hammered into place, I kept my desolation behind a stiff mask of control. Throughout the entombment, Lord Ido stood across from me, and I saw that his face was as fixed as my own. But I doubted his mask was disguising grief; more likely, it was triumph.

At last the ceremony ended. I stood mutely as the mourners filed past and bowed to the tomb until finally I stood alone in front of the elegant marble marker. I knew the prince and Ryko waited respectfully a few lengths behind me, waiting for me to say my last good-bye. But all that tight control had worked; I could not find anything to give. No final prayer, no tears, no farewell. My master had left me and I was empty. Yet, as I turned away from his grave, I felt something stir within me.

It took a moment to recognize it.

Anger.

CHAPTER FIFTEEN

EARLY ON THE TWELFTH day of the New Year—my eighth day of mourning—Lady Dela and I sat in the gloom of my shuttered reception room and waited for the palace herald in front of us to rise from his deep bow and deliver his message.

"Lord Eon," the man finally said. "His Highness, Prince Kygo, approaches on behalf of his most glorious father."

He offered me a slip of parchment with the imperial seal. A line of poetry was written under the heavy wax imprint of the royal dragon.

Waves endlessly returning to the shore, bringing renewal
and the ghosts of waves before.

Lady Dela studied the paper. "It's from one of Lady Jila's spring poems," she whispered. "His Highness returns the Mirror Dragon treasures to you. Acknowledge the honor of the visit."

I looked down at the kneeling herald and felt buoyed by

the prospect of seeing the prince. "Thank His Royal Highness for this great condescension. We await his arrival with joy."

The herald bowed out of the room.

"I do not think the emperor would miss this ceremony easily," Lady Dela said. "He must still be too ill to leave his bed." She twitched her shoulders as if rejecting the silent understanding that crouched in the palace—the emperor was in his last days. "Call Rilla to prepare for the prince."

Under my heavy white sleeve, the red folio shifted, the pearls whispering along my skin. Perhaps it sensed the arrival of the other treasures. As I sounded the small gong, a trill of laughter and music from a nearby courtyard made us both turn toward the closed doors. The Twelfth Day feasts and celebrations were starting.

"Happy Twelfth Day," I said to Lady Dela. "May the year bring you fivefold happiness."

"Thank you, Lord Eon. And for you, too."

I nodded. Happiness seemed a long way away.

The Peony household had just assembled in the garden courtyard when one of Ryko's guards called the prince's arrival. I knelt on a small cushion by the path and kowtowed until my forehead skimmed the ground. The boots of the royal guards passed by, and then the soft slippers of the protocol officers. My deep bow was straining my hip. If the prince did not arrive soon, I would not be able to stand without assistance. Finally, the dusty, sandaled feet of the royal litter bearers approached and stopped in front of me.

"Lord Eon," the prince said.

I stiffly pushed myself back onto my heels. The wound to his face was healing well, the bruise fading into dull browns and yellows. He was wearing his official robes—purple silk—and a smaller version of the imperial pearl on a chain around his neck. An emperor in waiting. Behind him, a small pack of courtiers watched us, followed by a double line of servants carrying boxes, brass burners, and heavy chests. A cart pulled by four men, with the bureau and carved stools tied to it, brought up the rear.

"Your Highness, thank you for honoring me with this visit." I smiled, then caught an admonishing glare from a protocol officer. A smile, it seemed, was inappropriate for the occasion.

"It is my honor to return the Mirror Dragon treasures to you," the prince said. "My father sends his gracious greetings."

I kowtowed.

"Down," the prince ordered the bearers. They promptly lowered the litter and a waiting servant handed the prince out. Another knelt and held up a richly embroidered red pouch.

The prince took it, then bowed to me.

"Lord Eon, for generations my royal forbears have kept the Mirror Dragon treasures safe, waiting for the day when the noble dragon would once again grace the circle, and a Mirror Dragoneye rejoin the council. It is my glorious honor to return the treasures that are rightfully yours."

He held out the pouch. I took it with another deep bow. It was heavy, and for a moment I was at a loss for what was inside. Then its circular shape settled in my hand; the Dragon-eye compass. As soon as I recognized it, the folio pearls tightened around my arm, as if they recognized it, too.

As was protocol, the prince entered the Peony Apartment and took a bowl of tea with me and Lady Dela. Our conversation was strictly monitored by the dour-faced officials and limited to polite wishes for the New Year and comments about the monsoon predictions. There was a sadness in the prince's eyes that mirrored my own, but I had no opportunity to offer him the gentle friendship that he had shown me at my master's entombment.

Before the half bell rang, the officers quietly signaled the end of the visit. We all knelt along the pathway again as the prince was ushered back into his litter, and by the time the bell tolled, the royal entourage was making its slow way toward the royal apartments. I watched its progress, hoping he would look back. The litter was almost through the archway before he turned and raised his hand. I raised my own, but then the protocol officer at his side called him to order.

"So, he is taking on his father's duties," Lady Dela said, gracefully standing and dusting down her white gown. "We will be mourning again before long." She shaded her eyes and looked over at the archway. "Mourning for the father and fighting for the son."

"Are you a soothsayer now?" I snapped.

She looked at me, her eyebrows raised. "Some say so, my lord. But my skill is in reading people, not sticks or coins."

Rilla came bustling toward us. "My lord, where do you want the treasures stored?"

The line of servants was still waiting to move the furniture and boxes into the apartment.

"Lady Dela will decide," I said, suddenly wanting to be alone. "Just bring the red pouch the prince gave me to the reception room."

Rilla duly delivered the pouch to me, then softly closed the door on the noisy tramp of servants and Lady Dela's sharp directions. I sat in the cool quiet of the reception room, overwhelmed by excitement.

The compass slid easily out of the pouch and hit my palm with a satisfying weight. I ran my finger over the smooth facets of the round-cut ruby in the center. It was the size of a thrush egg—worth a small fortune. The pearls suddenly rattled down my arm and out of the end of my sleeve, pulling the folio behind them into my lap. Gingerly, I poked at the book. Obviously, there was a connection between folio and compass, but what was it?

I waved the gold disc near the book. Nothing happened. What if the compass was touching it? I pressed metal against leather. Not even a twitch from the pearls. Maybe the compass translated the characters inside the folio. Holding my breath, I flipped open the book and dragged the compass across a page. The writing was still incomprehensible.

Frustrated, I stared at the page, then at the etched figures on the compass. My eyes suddenly focused on one character.

Hadn't I just seen it in the book? I ran my finger across and compared them. Yes, they were the same. I turned the compass around. One of the other characters was on the page, too. I laughed, jubilation pushing me off the low chair into a clumsy Rat Dragon Second, the pearls swinging out like a victory banner.

Then I stopped. Where did the information get me? I still couldn't read the folio. Or the compass. There was no way to break the code.

The characters were on both compass and folio—clearly a special Dragoneye writing. Did that mean another lord would be able to read it and teach me the meanings? But there was only one Dragoneye I trusted now—Lord Tyron—and he refused to see me until the end of my mourning. A wave of disappointment dropped me back onto the chair. He would not even accept my messenger. The first chance I'd have to show him the compass would be in the carriage on our way to Daikiko Province. Would that give me enough time to decipher the folio before the test? It seemed unlikely. My dragon's name felt as far away from me as ever.

I sat back, slowly combing each page of the folio for matches to the compass. There were quite a few, but it was an empty success—I did not understand what I was looking at. The futile study was finally interrupted by Rilla announcing two officials from the Department of Earthly Bequeathals.

I slid the compass back into the pouch and pushed the folio up my sleeve. The pearls slithered up my arm and wrapped the book tightly against my forearm just as the two men entered the room.

Both of them had an air of suppressed irritation, the fatter one's wet lips puckered into a sour pout. No doubt it was the increasingly loud sounds of music and laughter from outside causing their bad temper; their duty was making them miss the Twelfth Day celebrations.

I motioned for them to rise from their low bows.

"Lord Eon, it is the Day of Inheritance," the fat one said, "and we bring to you Proxy Lord Brannon's witnessed bequeathal scroll." He bent double and offered a slim roll of parchment sealed with wax and tied with a silk cord.

I took it, unsure if I was expected to read it in their presence. They both looked at me, the thinner man eyeing me with barely concealed impatience.

"We are at your service if you have any questions, my lord," he said pointedly.

I quickly pulled apart the knot and broke the seal, spreading the scroll open. The bequeathal was short: everything that Lord Brannon had still owned at the time of his death—the house, surrounding estate, and bond servants—was now mine.

I stared at the words, trying to take in their meaning.

I was a land owner. The Moon Garden, my master's library, the kitchen, the courtyard—all mine. It was all mine. I read through it again, my understanding finally catching up with my racing mind. Not only did I own the house and land, I owned all of the remaining bond servants. I owned Rilla and Chart.

And Kuno. Then I couldn't help a low laugh—I owned Irsa.

"When was this drawn up?" I asked.

"The date is on the bottom of the parchment, my lord," the fat one said.

The last Year of the Dog. My master had made me his heir two years ago, before I had even started training for the ceremony. Why had he bequeathed it all to me?

"Do I own the property now?" I asked. "Or must I wait?"

The thin man passed a knowing look across to his colleague. *See*, it seemed to say, *they are all greedy.*

"From this day, you own all that is set out in the scroll, my lord," he said.

I had land. And with land, came another kind of power: money. For a moment, I felt as if all my fear had been lifted. Then I saw the truth—even this great piece of good fortune was not enough. Money would not find my dragon's power.

This day was turning into a series of raised hopes and harsh realities.

I looked down at the bold calligraphy again. The land would be of little use to my survival, but . . . there was the wild promise I had made to keep Rilla and Chart safe whatever happened.

Perhaps now I had the means to honor it.

"Then this property is mine to do with as I wish," I said.

"Yes, my lord. And we often advise beneficiaries to consider their own inevitable journey to the spirit world and draw up a bequeathal as soon as possible." The thin official smiled professionally. "For a small fee."

"That is good counsel," I said, rolling up the parchment. "And I will act on it today. But first there are some things I must consider. Stay here until I return."

"Today?" the thin man said faintly. He looked at the shuttered window. The staccato crack and pop of fireworks sounded from outside, then shouts of pleasure. Twelfth Day was well under way.

I crossed to the door. "That is what I said."

They both bowed; the fat official's cheeks puffing with petulance. No doubt he was imagining all of the free feast food disappearing from his grasp.

Rilla sat opposite me in the heavily curtained litter, her usual calm grace replaced by stiff excitement. She had a basket of food on her lap—leftover delicacies from my table that she had collected for Chart—and her hands clasped the handle so tightly that I could see the shape of her knuckles through the whitened skin. She had not seen her son since we had moved into the palace, and I knew she was worried. I allowed myself a small smile; she would not need to worry about his welfare much longer. The brief moment of pleasure was like a deep breath. It was such a relief to feel something other than relentless grief and fear.

I had ordered the bearer team to arrive just after daybreak, before the Twelfth Day revelers woke and staggered into the streets. I was not supposed to be out in public yet—it was the ninth and last day of mourning—but early tomorrow we would be starting the journey to Daikiko Province. If I had waited for the official end of mourning, there would not have been time to put my plan into place. And something deep in me knew that it had to be done as soon as possible.

"My lord, thank you for letting me visit Chart," Rilla said again. She ducked her head, trying to see out of the gap in the curtains. A sudden smile eased the tense lines on her face. "I think we are nearly home."

I parted the curtain and saw the stone lions that stood guard at the front entrance of my master's estate—*my* estate. The call had gone up announcing my arrival, and the six house staff, led by Irsa, hurried out of the side entrance. They all wore a small piece of red cloth pinned to the left sleeve of their work tunics, the symbol of mourning. By the time the litter stopped, they had lined up along the pathway, demurely waiting to greet their new master. Chart, of course, was not present. No doubt he was waiting for us in the kitchen.

I heard Ryko order the guard detail to their positions around the estate. Then Rilla parted the curtains and stepped down, turning to hand me out of the palanquin. She was taking care to move in her usual dignified manner, but her grip gave away her impatience.

I stepped down, and as soon as my feet touched the ground, all of the staff dropped to their knees and bowed. A surge of fierce exhilaration caught me by surprise. I cleared my throat and walked past them, noting Irsa's nervous fidgeting and Gardener Lon's thick, grimy neck. Then Rilla opened the double front door and bowed, and for the first time in my life I stepped over its threshold and entered my own house.

The foyer was empty except for a well-kept carpet that muffled our footsteps. I breathed in the familiar smell of brazier smoke, broth, washing herbs, and polish. The scent of my home. Of my master. Grief spiked through me, and I stopped at the top of the hallway, lost in pain.

"My lord, may I go to Chart?" Rilla asked.

"Of course."

She started toward the kitchen annex.

"Wait," I said. "I will speak to everyone in the central courtyard in a few minutes. Make sure they are all there. Including Chart."

Surprise furrowed her brow for a moment. Then she nodded and hurried to her son.

I was alone in the hallway. On my left was the door to the formal reception room, one of the areas in the house I was never allowed to enter. I opened the double doors. My master had favored the traditional style for the room, and it had the same low table, hard cushions, and woven mat floor as the formal room in the Peony Apartment. I pulled the doors shut, my attention already on another forbidden room: my master's bedchamber.

It was at the far end of the passageway, opposite the library. I stood before the door for a moment, overwhelmed by a sense of intrusion, then twisted the brass dragon ring handle. The latch lifted with a soft scrape, and the door swung open.

The shutters were open, and the morning light emphasized

the large room's drab austerity. It was almost as starkly furnished as my old storeroom dormitory at the back of the house: a wooden bed, a clothespress, and a brazier. That was all. I knew there had once been rich furnishings—the maids had spoken of a carpet so thick it had to be brushed every day, and a screen painted by a famous artist—but my master had sold them over the last few years.

I walked across the bare floor to the bed. The bleached bed linen was fresh. Probably for me. It was an unsettling thought. A cotton blanket faded to the color of sand had been carefully folded across the end. I looked back at the empty doorway, then leaned down and smelled the cloth. Clean and sunned, but no scent of my master.

Amid all the muted practicality, a bright color caught my eye—a red lacquer box on a small table, initially hidden from sight. The only vivid thing in the room. I skirted around the bed to study the finely made piece. It was trimmed in gold with a jade double-happiness character pressed into the lid. Probably worth a lot of money. Yet my master had not sold it.

Did it mean something to him? I picked it up, the weight giving no clue. Perhaps it was the last of his wealth. I ran my fingertip around the edge and found the small curved leverage. With a flick of my nail, the lid shifted, then came away.

For a moment, the small object inside made no sense. It was too far from its place in the world.

My needle tube.

He must have found it hidden in my old clothespress. Why was it in this box? Kept like a precious jewel?

The answer was as stark as the room.

Because it was mine.

He had loved me. The knowledge of it rose from the same dark place where Eona lived. A ragged breath broke out of me. I had always known it. Always pushed it down into the deepest part of me. What else could I have done? What else could he have done?

I laid my fingertip on the polished bamboo case, stroking the smooth wood. Such a plain, everyday thing, but so treasured; first as a precious gift from a dying woman, and then as a secret keepsake for a dying man.

I sensed someone behind me and turned. Rilla was standing at the doorway.

"The household is assembled, my lord," she said. Then she saw my face. "What is wrong?"

"Nothing." I slid the lid back and snapped it home. "I will be there in a minute. Leave me."

She bowed and withdrew. I placed the box back on the table and pressed the heels of my hands against my eyes, pushing back the sadness. Some things were best left denied.

I took the long passage that led from the main house to the kitchen. It gave me time to harden myself back into Lord Eon and prepare my words for the staff. I had not had a lot of time to make my arrangements, but at least the fundamentals were in place. I touched the thin metal tokens in my pocket; I couldn't wait to see Chart's face when I brought them out.

A few steps away from the courtyard, I heard Irsa announce

my approach. The household was already kneeling on the hard flagstones when I made my entrance. How many times had I listened for Rilla's call, or Irsa's, ready to drop to the ground at my master's arrival. Now I only knelt for royalty.

Even Chart was bowing. Gardener Lon had propped him against his sturdy shoulder and had one hand hovering protectively over the boy's back. Lon had always been a generous man. I saw the strain in Chart's neck as he fought to stay in position, the weaving motion of his head revealing a wide grin. He, at least, was happy to see me. Irsa was stealing quick glances up at me, no doubt worried that her bullying was about to snap back and strike her like a snake. It was tempting to make her pay for all those kicks and slights and petty betrayals, but I had already decided against it. There was a saying that a man's true character was revealed in defeat. I thought it was also revealed in victory.

The yard seemed smaller and shabbier than I remembered, but the same cat was still watching me from its sunning spot near my old door. I cleared my throat and everyone settled back on their heels, waiting for me to speak. The silent deference— suddenly I couldn't remember any of my rehearsed speech. It was all gone.

A movement jerked me out of my panic—Chart, flinging out a hand. He smiled and scrunched one eye into a slow wink. My words returned.

"Lord Brannon, may his spirit dwell in the Garden of Heavenly Delight, has bequeathed this estate and all your service bonds to me," I said, forcing my voice into an even tone.

There was no surprise on anyone's face—news travels fast in the servants' quarters.

"I will be keeping this property and household as it is—except for a few changes."

Irsa shrank back, probably expecting the slave market, but my attention was on Chart. It was not often I got to be the bearer of good fortune.

I held up the two liberation discs—brass pendants stamped with the freedom edict and the imperial seal—hanging from thin leather thongs.

"Firstly, I free Chart and Rilla from their service bonds."

Chart stared up at me, his body stilled by shock. Only his mouth was working, like one of the emperor's giant carp. Beside me, Rilla gasped.

It had not been easy to rush through the bureaucracy to free them, but I had quickly discovered that gold bought efficiency. It had been worth spending most of the mourning money to see the joy in their faces. The best was still to come.

"And I name Freeman Chart as my heir to this estate."

Chart pitched forward, only saved from hitting the flags by Lon's quick reflexes. I covered the short distance between us and dropped to my knees. Rilla squatted beside me a moment later, cupping her son's cheek.

"Are you all right?" I asked. He was lying cradled in Lon's arms.

"He's fine," Rilla said, nodding her thanks to Lon.

Chart's thin hand closed around my wrist. "Free?"

I nodded. "And heir."

"My lord." Rilla grabbed my other hand and kissed it. "Thank you, my lord. It is a wonderful thing you have done."

"Heir?" Chart echoed. "You . . . make me . . . heir?"

"Yes. You'll be head of the household while I'm at the palace. You'll have your own room, and everything."

Tears tracked through the grime on his face. "Head . . . of house?"

I turned to the other staff. "Do you hear? Chart is now heir of my house. His word is my word." I directed the last to Irsa, staring down her horrified disgust. "Do you hear?"

She ducked her head, her mouth a tight line. "Yes, my lord."

I glared at the rest of the staff and they quickly bowed, echoing her obedience.

Chart's grip on my wrist became a stranglehold "How . . . can I be . . . head of house?" he whispered, his face stricken.

Was he afraid? I had been so caught up in my plans that I had not even considered the possibility. "It's all right," I said. "I'll get you a body servant. He can be your arms and legs."

Chart shook his head. "I don't know . . . read or write. . . . Or anything."

Rilla stroked her son's hair. "You can learn," she said firmly. "You've got a good mind." She smiled at me. "Lord Eon has given us a great gift."

Lon suddenly leaned toward me in a shallow bow. "My lord, may I speak?"

"Yes. What is it?"

"May I offer myself as Master Chart's body servant, my

lord? I am strong and I know the letters. I could start his learning."

Lon could read and write? I had no idea. In fact, I didn't know much about him at all. I considered the man in front of me. He had always been friendly to Chart, unfazed by his deformity. And he had ambition—the move from outside to indoor servant would be a big step up in rank and bond pay. He'd be eager to do well. It could be a good solution. I met Chart's gaze, silently asking the question.

Chart slowly nodded.

"Rilla?" I asked.

She looked Lon up and down. "I know you are strong and a good worker. But are you a kind man, Lon? Does another's weakness bring out the best or worst in you?"

Chart rolled his eyes. "Moth . . . er."

Lon smiled down at him. "Your mother is looking after your interests." He bobbed a quick salute to Rilla. "Freewoman," he said, and she flushed at the new title. "I would be bound by my honor as much as by my bond to treat your son with respect."

"Fancy words," she said brusquely, but her mouth had curved upward. She turned to me and nodded. "All right."

"It is settled, then," I said.

The liberation discs were still in my hand. I hurriedly separated them out, untangling the leather thongs. "Here is your freedom, Rilla." As I passed her the token, a sudden realization stopped my hand. Rilla was no longer bound to me. She could leave. Then a darker knowledge whispered its truth: *She was the only person alive who knew my secret.*

"Rilla . . ." I faltered, unable to voice my fear—it would seem as if I distrusted her.

The disc dangled between us. For a brief moment, our gazes met, and I saw the quick understanding in her eyes. She gathered the disc and thong into her cupped palm.

"Honor is not limited to men, my *lord*," she said softly. "I will always be with you."

I nodded, ashamed of my doubt, and held out Chart's disc. "Your freedom, Chart."

He eyed it hungrily. "Put . . . on me?"

I slipped it over his head, arranging the pendant against the patched cloth of his tunic. I would need to organize new clothes for him. He held the disc tightly against his chest as though it might disappear. "Thank . . . you."

"Come, we'll celebrate in the library," I said. "Rilla, will you direct the maids to bring wine? And they should also prepare a room for the new heir."

Below me, Chart giggled.

"Of course," Rilla said. All her grace was back in force, but I had a feeling Irsa and the other maids were about to feel a mother's revenge. With a sharp clap of her hands, she ordered the staff to their duties.

Lon stood effortlessly with Chart in his arms and followed me across the courtyard to the house. I cast a quick look back as we walked through the cool corridor. Lon was listening to his new master's excited commentary. It seemed he had the knack of picking out the words in the strangled sounds. Or perhaps it was just that, unlike Irsa, he was listening for sense rather than nonsense.

I walked into the library unprepared for the ghosts of my master still lingering there: the last scroll he had been studying was stretched across the desk, a pen lay on a half-finished letter, and the smell of the herbs he burned for concentration scented the air.

The familiar ache of grief, kept at bay by the joy of freeing my friends, swelled through me. I shut the door, steadying myself against its solid support, and motioned Lon to the visitor chair. He carefully settled Chart on the seat.

"Thank you, Lon," I said, forcing myself to walk to my master's desk. But I couldn't sit behind it. Not yet. "Find Rilla and she'll tell you what you need to do. Then ask her to join us in the library."

Lon bowed. "Yes, my lord. Thank you." He turned to Chart and bowed again. "Thank you, Master."

Chart's eyes widened at the unaccustomed obeisance.

I waited until Lon had closed the door, then said, "It's strange having people bow to you, hey?"

Chart clapped his hand to his forehead. "Makes . . . my head . . . hurt." He grinned up at me. "You . . . used to . . . it?"

I shook my head. "I haven't got used to anything."

His hand found the liberation disc on his chest. "Hard to . . . be . . . free sometimes?"

I stared at him. Everything had happened so fast that it had never occurred to me that I was free. But of course I was free—I was a lord. Strange then, that I did not feel any sense of freedom.

"Thank you," Chart said seriously, holding up the disc. "Means so much . . . to Mother. And to . . . me." He took a deep breath. "Master told me . . . to tell you . . . something . . . ." He stopped, swallowing convulsively. ". . . when . . . he died."

"Tell me what?" I squatted down awkwardly beside him. Had the master told Chart that he loved me? Did Chart know what I really was? If he did know the truth, he had kept his counsel well.

"He used to . . . come to kitchen . . . at night . . . when he . . . couldn't sleep . . . to talk to me. Needed to . . . talk to someone." He licked his lips, preparing for another long sentence. "He was . . . sorry. Thought . . . it . . . was for the . . . best. But sorry . . . for hurting you . . . so bad. Thought . . . he had . . . killed . . . you."

"Killed me? What do you mean?"

"When he . . . had your . . . hip broken. You nearly . . . died. Don't . . . you remember?"

"Had my hip broken?"

What was Chart talking about? It was an accident. I was hit by a horse and cart—run down in a street soon after my master had taken me from the salt farm.

Something deep and denied held me still. Dim images were slowly sharpening into an awful truth. There had been no horse and cart. No accident. I felt a terrible certainty building inside me. The memory of a bitter taste and heavy limbs, a big man standing over me with a tattoo on his face and a hammer in his hand. And pain. So much pain.

"Why?" I croaked. "Why?" I grabbed Chart's arm. "Did he tell you why?"

Chart drew back in the chair. "No."

But I knew why. He crippled me to hide Eona. He had made me untouchable. To make money. To get power. His betrayal crashed through me like the hammer smashing my bones. He took away my body. My wholeness. I tried to stand, but all my strength was surging into another place. Into rage. My hip throbbed with old agony. I fell to my hands and knees, crawling away from Chart, away from the pain.

"I . . . thought . . . you knew."

"Knew?" I screamed.

Chart's terror registered somewhere in me, but it was too small against my fury. My head hit the edge of a shelf and I pulled myself upright. In front of me were *his* scrolls. His precious scrolls. All lovingly stacked.

I pulled a box out of its slot and threw it at the wall. The crack of splitting wood and slithering parchment shrieked through my blood. The second box hit the desk, sending pens and ink blocks to the floor. One after the other I flung the boxes at the back walls. The clattering crash drove me along the shelves, throwing faster and faster, the noise stoking the rage inside me. Chart cowered in the chair, whimpering. I heard the door snap open.

"Lord Eon!"

I turned, my arm raised to throw.

Rilla was in the doorway holding a tray of wine cups, her eyes wide with shock. "What are you doing?"

Couldn't she see? I was destroying him. I was hurting him. But he was already dead.

I let go of the box in my hand. It hit the floor, smashing open, the parchment uncurling in a hiss of release. Through a blur of tears, I saw Rilla come toward me. And then, for the first time since my master's death, I felt all my sorrow and rage roll into a racking sob.

CHAPTER SIXTEEN

I HUNCHED OVER the small oil lamp beside my bed and dug my finger and thumb into the leather pouch, pinching up a generous dose of the Sun drug. Outside, the sounds of my palace staff preparing for the Daikiko journey carried across the predawn quiet: the clip of horse hooves on stone flags, the creaking of cart wheels, and Ryko's voice ordering his men to check the load straps. It would soon be time to leave.

I dropped the drug into the bowl of ghost maker's tea that Rilla had left with my breakfast. For a moment the powder floated on the top, then broke apart and dissolved into the murky liquid. I tied off the pouch and pushed it into the pocket of my traveling tunic alongside the precious ruby compass.

The Sun drug was my last resort. With only a slim hope of deciphering the folio in time for the test, it was the only other way I could think to forge a quick connection with the Mirror

Dragon. Ryko had said the drug kindled the Sun energy in the Shadow Men, rebuilding their manliness and fighting spirit; surely it would stoke the Sun energy in me, too.

I eyed the steaming tea. Of course, there was no guarantee it would help me contact my dragon. And there was a very big possibility it might turn me into a raging madman like Lord Ido. Or I could descend into sullen despair and crashing head pain like Dillon. Maybe the ghost maker's tea would just cancel its effect. The other alternative—death by poisoning—was like a cold stone of possibility lodged in my gut.

I picked up the bowl and inhaled the bitter steam. An image of my master's dying face, twisted and contorted, shivered through me. Such a terrible way to die.

Yesterday I had cried myself dry in Rilla's arms, but I could not forgive my master's betrayal. Not yet. Even after Rilla had cut through my self-pity with one of her hard truths—that my lame leg helped me hide my sex—I still could not find any forgiveness. Perhaps one day I would, but for now the energy of anger was far better than the lethargy of grief.

I looked down into the cup. The tea had turned very dark, its surface reflecting the shadowy planes of my face. Surely one dose would not kill me; it had not killed Dillon or Ryko. I bowed to the altar in the corner and raised the bowl to my lips. *May my ancestors protect me*, I prayed, and tipped the vessel back, coughing over the last bitter mouthful.

I put the bowl on the tray and sat for a moment, trying to feel the drug in my body. I knew it was too soon, but now that it was finally taken, I wanted to know if it had worked.

A soft knock at the bedchamber door roused me from my inner search. "Enter."

Rilla hurried in with a long traveling coat over her arm. "Ryko says we are ready to go when you are, my lord." She shook out the garment and held it open for me.

"Thank you." I stood and pushed my arms into the wide sleeves. "Is Chart settled in?"

Rilla beamed. "Yes, he is." She gave the stiff neckband of the coat one last smoothing, then dug around in her skirt pocket. "He wanted me to give you this."

I unfolded the small scrap of parchment. There was one character scratched on its surface in wavering black ink: *Sorry*.

I smiled. "Is he writing already?"

"He and Lon worked on it all last night."

"You must tell him that he has nothing to be sorry about. He was just doing as the master asked."

"I'll tell him." She touched my arm. "You have done so much for us. Thank you."

"You have done as much for me." I paced across the room, suddenly overwhelmed by a feeling of dread. "But there is something else I would ask of you, Rilla."

"Of course. Anything."

"If I ever tell you to go, will you take Chart and leave the city as fast as you can? No questions. Just go somewhere safe. Like the islands. Will you do that?"

"But I wouldn't leave—"

I held up my hand. "No. Promise me you'll go. It's important."

She nodded, but her face was troubled. "Do you think it will come to that?"

"I don't know. I hope your free status will protect you. But if it doesn't, then you'll need to move swiftly. And you'll need money." I waved her over to the doorway. "Come with me, quickly."

I led her into the dressing room. My candidate ceremony uniform was stored neatly on a low shelf in the clothespress. I pulled it out and slid my fingers along the hem until they found hard metal.

"Chart gave me this in case I had to run away. Do you remember?"

She nodded. "A Tiger. He showed me when he found it."

I took her hand and closed it over the silk-covered coin. "Now it is yours. It will keep you and Chart for a few months if things go bad."

Rilla took my hand. "But what about you? Won't you need it to get away?"

I didn't answer. Her hold tightened for a moment, and then she turned toward the sewing tools. We both knew that if she and Chart had to run, then it was already too late for me.

The courtyard of the Ox Dragon Hall was a noisy melee of people hauling luggage, hitching oxen to carts, and leading horses. My driver called my name over and over again, gradually clearing a pathway through the crowded square and maneuvering the carriage up to the front entrance of the hall.

A servant approached us and bowed. "Lord Tyron sends his compliments, my lord, and asks for your forbearance. He will be with you soon." The man offered a goblet of wine on a tray, but I waved it away. My taster was in a cart at the rear of the line. I sat back in the opulent carriage and watched an outrider struggle to calm a skittish horse. I knew how the animal felt.

Finally, Lord Tyron emerged from the hall. I made room for him as he climbed into the carriage, his weight rocking the well-sprung cabin.

"So, the prince has lent you his own cart, hey?" he asked jovially, but the tone was at odds with the anxiety on his face. The suspension straps beneath us creaked and swung as he settled beside me. "No one can be in doubt of your allegiance now."

"I don't think anyone has ever been in doubt of my allegiance," I said.

Lord Tyron nodded. "Nor of mine." He rubbed his forehead. "My apologies for sending away all your messengers. We could not risk giving Ido any reason to stop the test."

"Lord Ido doesn't want to stop the test," I said. "He expects me to fail, and he's probably right. Do you really think I can learn how to control the King Monsoon in two days?"

Tyron sighed. "It takes an apprentice the whole twelve years of study to manage his own dragon's power. And the same time to prepare for his year as Ascendant." He patted my shoulder. "But then, you can see all of the twelve dragons. If anyone can do it, you can."

I smiled weakly. He pulled back the opulent silk curtain and watched the rest of his entourage move into position behind us. Now was my chance to show him the compass without any interruption. I pulled it out of my pocket, my excitement so intense I could not even form a prayer.

"Lord Tyron—"

He turned back to me.

I held up the pouch and fumbled with the drawstring. "I wanted to show you this. The prince returned it to me with the other Mirror Dragon treasures."

The ties came loose. The compass dropped into my palm and I felt the pearls around my arm shiver.

"Oh, my, what a beauty," Tyron breathed. He looked at me for permission, then picked up the compass, stroking the ruby center. "Magnificent."

I leaned closer. "Do you recognize the writing, Lord Tyron? Can you read it?"

Squinting, he examined the etched rings around the compass.

"The animal pictures and the cardinal points are the same," he finally said, "but I've never seen this other writing before. It must be very old."

The disappointment was like a blow to my chest. I closed my eyes. Even a Dragoneye could not read the folio. Its secrets were locked away from me forever. There was no way of decoding it.

I still had one chance left—the Sun drug. But what if it didn't work?

"Lord Eon."

I opened my eyes. Tyron was looking over the compass at me. His face was gray.

"Is this the only compass you have?" he whispered. "But of course it is—there would have been no more made after the Mirror Dragon was lost."

I realized why he was appalled. Every compass was specific to its particular dragon, the secret information on it handed down from Dragoneye to apprentice, and set into a new instrument for the trainee. But I could not read my inherited compass, there was no Mirror Dragoneye to teach me its mysteries, and I could not use another Dragoneye's instrument to direct my beast's power. In all of my frenzied attempts to read the folio, such a catastrophe had not even occurred to me.

Tyron wearily pressed his fingers into the hollows of his eyes. "Among those who travel to Daikiko, I can only think of Ido who has an interest in old writings. But we cannot show it to him. If he knows you are unable to read your compass, he will use it as evidence to stop you taking your place on the council."

"He will know at the test," I said shrilly. "He will know when I don't use it."

Tyron passed the compass back to me, briefly closing my hand in a reassuring grip. "Ido will have already made the ascendant calculations for the ley lines. You can use those. And I will teach you the rudiments of focusing your power through the ruby."

"But the calculations will be for the Ascendant Rat Dragon. How can I use them?"

Tyron chewed his top lip. "You're the Coascendant. I'm hoping they'll be same. Or at least close."

"What do you mean, you hope they'll be the same?" I demanded. "Don't you know?"

He shook his head. "No one knows what will happen tomorrow. No one knows what this coascendancy means. We don't know if you have the same doubled powers as Lord Ido, or if the double power is split between you. We just don't know."

I stared at him. "You don't know how to help me pass this test, do you?"

He gripped my shoulder and shook it. "Right now we need to concentrate on teaching you how to control your power. First things first." He leaned out of the carriage and yelled, "Hollin! Get over here."

The lanky apprentice strode up to the side of the carriage. "Yes, my lord." He saw me and bowed. "Greetings, Lord Eon."

"Hollin, I've decided you'll ride with us," Tyron ordered. "Give your apologies to Lady Dela—tell her that Lord Eon has need of you. Then tell Ridley to take your place in the lady's cart."

The young man's face brightened—no back-breaking oxcart journey for him. He hurried away.

"Hollin can remember his early apprentice days more clearly than I can," Tyron said. "He can quickly take you through the basics. Then we can get on to the task of how to direct the King Monsoon."

It was a long day of relentless information, roads lined with bowing peasants, and searing heat. The cabin of the carriage reeked with our sweat, and the silk fans that we waved made no impression on the temperature. It was almost impossible to concentrate on Hollin's earnest voice as he tried to explain the give-and-take between dragon and Dragoneye.

"Do you remember the moment of union, Lord Eon?" he asked, then smiled sheepishly. "Of course you do. Every Dragoneye remembers that moment. Cast your mind back to the feeling of being in two places at once. Of being dragon and man at the same time."

I nodded, trying to hide my panic. I had not felt the sensation of being in two places at once. Only the rush of power from the Mirror Dragon—and then, later, from the Rat Dragon. But I could not explain that to the two men in front of me—it would mean admitting I had never made the full union with my beast. I squeezed the Sun-drug pouch in my pocket. Perhaps my chance of connecting with the Mirror Dragon would be stronger if I took more than one pinch per day.

"The key is in the balance," Hollin continued. "It takes a long time to recognize when you are giving too much *Hua* and not taking enough power." He wiped the sweat from his top lip and looked at his master. "How do we explain the balance?"

It was like that all the way to the first sleep stop; one step forward toward enlightenment and then two steps back, as my lack of experience blocked the way.

As was custom, the Dragoneyes and their servants were lodged in houses deferentially vacated by local landowners. I was so tired that I knew nothing from the moment I entered my borrowed bedchamber to when Rilla woke me the following morning with a cup of the ghost maker's tea. When she left the room to collect my aired clothes, I dumped two large pinches of the Sun drug into the earthenware cup and drank it in one gulp.

The small bedchamber was airless. Rilla had laid out a cotton robe for me, and I wrapped it around myself as I clambered off the raised pallet and headed for the shuttered window. Overnight, Hollin's coaching seemed to have become a jumble of unrelated nonsense; all I could remember was him explaining how to draw power from a ley line and then Lord Tyron urging him to move on to the next subject. And there was another day of hurried instruction to come. I feared very little of their teaching was going to stay with me.

I pushed open the shutters and looked into the compact inner courtyard of the house. The landowner was rich enough to afford a small pleasure garden along the nearby wall, and Lady Dela was walking its short, winding path. Now that the official mourning period was over, she wore a blue traveling gown with a strip of memorial red pinned to her sleeve. She turned as though my gaze had called her and dropped gracefully to one knee, politely averting her eyes from my lack of propriety. I pulled the robe tighter around me and held my hand up in greeting.

"Lady Dela. I hoped you passed the night comfortably."

"I did, thank you." She rose from her bow and I saw that her face was once again carefully painted into femininity. "Would it be possible to speak to you before we continued our journey, my lord? There are some protocol matters to discuss."

"Of course."

"After the breakfast of gratitude?"

I nodded and drew back inside the room. According to tradition, the visiting Lord thanked his host by eating with him and his sons at the formal morning meal.

Compared to what I had experienced in the last few weeks, the fare was simple and sparse: rice porridge with four condiments; raw eggs broken into a hot, fragrant soup; fried soy curd; and finely milled wheat bread. As I dripped sweetener over the pale mush of rice, it occurred to me that I would have once considered this a feast.

The landowner reminded me of a brown dog that used to skulk around the salt farm—always anxious to please. He was so overwhelmed by sharing his table with a Dragoneye lord that he bowed three or four times to every remark I made and was only able to manage one complete statement during the whole meal.

"Your sacred pact to protect us and our land brings us all much comfort, my lord."

His sons—three smaller versions of himself—nodded vigorously, their eyes never leaving me as they silently spooned up their soup. I looked down at my own bowl, my hunger suddenly gone. This was not just about my own survival; the whole land now relied on me to manipulate the earth forces and bring the luck of a good harvest. I fingered the pouch in my pocket. Could I risk another pinch of Sun drug? Three in the space of an hour was probably too much—it would be more sensible to leave it until the evening meal and space out the doses.

Lady Dela approached me immediately after the torturous meal, her eyes tracking every movement around us.

"May we now speak privately, my lord?"

I sighed. A lesson in protocol was the last thing I wanted; my head already felt overstuffed with information. "Can this not wait?" I asked. "Surely we can go through the protocols when we are closer to the village."

She leaned closer until I smelled the frangipani scent of her hair. "It is not about protocols. It is about the test."

"The garden, then," I said shortly. All of my limbs felt as though a clockwork spring was coiled inside them, straining to release. Perhaps a walk would work the tension out of my muscles.

Lady Dela waited until we were at the far end of the garden path before she spoke.

"I have heard some rumors, my lord." She looked around, then led me further from a kitchen maid shaking out bed-clothes. "Lord Ido intends to sabotage your test."

"The way things are going, he won't need to take the trouble," I said grimly. "Did your rumors tell you how?" I balled my hands into fists. Every joint seemed to be stiff and sore, although the usual sharp pain in my hip had dulled into an ache.

She shook her head.

"Then they are not of much use, are they? Don't come to me with vague servants' gossip. Bring me details."

I stalked away from her astonishment. What use were rumors? I needed real information. Real strategies. I swiped past an elegant arch of fronds that hung over the pathway. The branch broke with a satisfying snap.

Back in the carriage with Lord Tyron and Hollin, I could not find any comfortable position—my rump bones felt as though they were pushing through my skin, and the back of my neck itched with a rash. Hollin was dull eyed and yawning from a bad night's sleep, and Lord Tyron was stinking with old man's sweat. I swallowed my nausea and focused on their words.

"As Ascendant, it is your responsibility to clearly give your orders to each Dragoneye so that he can direct his dragon's power and force the monsoon rains away from the crops and into the dam," Lord Tyron said.

"It is a juggling act," Hollin added. "Each dragon has control over a particular direction on the compass, so you must tell his Dragoneye how much power to use at exactly the right time so that the monsoon is shifted." He saw the consternation on my face. "I know it sounds impossible, but the Dragoneyes sit in a circle in their compass position, so it easy to see who is working with each dragon."

"And since you can see all of the dragons too, it should be easier for you," Lord Tyron said encouragingly.

"But how do I know how much power is needed?"

Lord Tyron shot a glance at Hollin.

"Well?" I demanded. "How do I know?"

Tyron rubbed his nose. "It is a matter of practice," he mumbled. "You have to learn how to feel the parameters of your dragon's power."

"A matter of practice? I don't have time to practice." I slammed the heel of my hand into the carved canopy strut. "This is all useless. Useless!" I jabbed the driver's back. "Stop!"

The carriage jerked to a halt, the horses plunging in their harness. I flung myself out of the cabin and marched over to the ditch that separated the noble's road from the dirt peasant track. Vaguely, through my fury, I realized I was hardly limping. Behind the carriage, the rest of the retinue was pulling to a stop, heads craning to see what had happened. I stared out over the low rice fields, unable to settle on a coherent thought amidst the tumble of fear and anger that clamored in my head. At the edge of my vision I saw Ryko swing down from his saddle and lead his horse toward me.

"My lord." He made the quick duty bow. "May I be of assistance?"

"Can you teach me twelve years of Dragoneye knowledge in an afternoon?" I asked bitterly.

"No, lord." His horse blew and bobbed its head over his shoulder.

"Then you cannot be of any assistance. Leave me."

I turned from him, but his hand closed over my shoulder and pulled me around.

"What is that on your neck?"

"Don't touch me," I shrieked. "I'll have you whipped."

The horse shied away, yanking Ryko with it. He tightened his grip on its bridle and soothed it with soft croons. I backed away, my fingers finding a pattern of welts on my neck.

Ryko eyed me sternly. "How much are you taking, lord?"

"I could have you whipped."

"Yes, my lord. How much Sun drug are you taking?"

I looked away from his implacable face.

"Two pinches."

He sucked in a breath. "A grown man can handle only half of that a day. You must stop it, lord. It will kill you."

"I only need it until tomorrow."

"Lord—" He stepped closer.

"Go back to your position, Guard Ryko."

He hesitated, his face a taut war between obedience and concern.

"I said go back to your position." A sudden fury snapped through me. "Or I will have you relieved of duty."

The muscles in his jaw tightened, but he bowed and led his horse around. I pressed my palm against my forehead, trying to relieve the spiked band of pain that was digging into my head. Couldn't Ryko understand that I only needed the drug until I moved the King Monsoon?

I watched him remount his horse and rein it in behind my carriage, all of my anger draining away as quickly as it had risen. He was only doing his duty—trying to guard me from harm. I wanted to call him back and tell him I would stop taking the Sun drug tomorrow, but the curious stares from the retinue held me still.

Lord Tyron leaned out of the carriage. "Lord Eon, we must continue if we are to make the village by dusk."

I lifted my hand to show him I'd heard but turned to look at the rice field again. Surely there was enough Sun drug in me to see the Mirror Dragon. Maybe even enough to finally connect with him.

Narrowing my eyes, I reached for my mind-sight, seeking the pathways of my *Hua*. More pain jabbed into my head as the rice paddies bucked and twisted into the haze of the energy world. But everything was distorted, rushing past in a blur of color—green, orange, blue, purple, pink, gray. A hum, more sensation than sound, grated through my bones. I clamped my hands over my ears and pushed further into the roiling energy, trying to find a flash of red in the streaming colors. But it was all too fast. Too violent. The coursing power circled me—spinning so fast I couldn't focus—until all the colors bled into one swirling, angry blue.

Everything stopped. Then the blue roared through me, stripping me of sight and sound.

For a moment I was suspended in silent, sapphire panic. I fell to my knees, my bones jarring against the paved road. There was nothing but blue: in my eyes, in my ears, in my mouth. My palms shredded as I blindly groped the rough flags for sanity. The blue was tearing me apart. I tasted vanilla, orange—the Rat dragon.

I forced myself back onto my heels, desperately dragging back some inner sight. My silver *Hua* was turning dark, my seven points of power surrendering to the suffocating indigo. There was nowhere to go but deeper. I pushed inward, through thick gray energy that stoked the blue into a bright flare. The Sun drug? I pushed even deeper, flailing at first, then drawn by a faint gold opalescence lodged in my third point of power—a tiny kernel glowing against the dark maelstrom.

Desperately, I grabbed at it. Flung the pale energy into the blue. It punched through the swirling power and I heard a cry, like an injured eagle's, coming from my lips. The roiling mass contracted, split apart, and was gone.

"Lord, what is wrong?"

It was Ryko's voice.

"Lord, speak to me."

I fell on to my side, gasping.

"Get Rilla," he ordered someone. "And Lady Dela."

The darkness brightened into Ryko's face hovering above me. I reached up and grabbed the front of his tunic. "I just need it until tomorrow," I croaked. "Then I'll stop."

The drug was working. I was sure of it. I shifted my head, cradled in Rilla's soft lap, and stared at the passing sky as the carriage swayed along the road. Lady Dela sat opposite us, half-asleep in the oppressive heat. Their undemanding silence was a relief; Lord Tyron had finally conceded I was in no condition to continue the lessons and had retreated to his own carriage, following behind. At least that was one good thing that had come out of my roadside collapse.

I closed my eyes and carefully examined my conclusions about the blue power. There was no question that it had been the Rat Dragon—the vanilla taste of him was still in my body. I was certain that, somehow, the thick gray power of the Sun drug had opened me to his energy, and he had flooded in like water through a sluice, blocking the approach of the Mirror Dragon. There was the terrifying possibility that Lord Ido was using his beast to attack me, but even in the wild panic I had not sensed any controlling force in the Rat Dragon's onslaught. It had been violent, but not an attack.

How, then, had I stopped it? What was the pale kernel of energy deep within me? I suspected it had something to do with my shadow-self, some kind of Moon energy that I had not been able to overcome. Whatever it was, it was strong enough to beat back a dragon. Could it be pushing away the Mirror Dragon, too?

The terrible thought forced my eyes open.

"Do you need water, my lord?" Rilla's concerned face was bent over me.

"No. How long are we from the village?"

Lady Dela yawned, covering her mouth with her open fan. "Lord Tyron said we would be there before dusk, so we should be less than two full bells away."

I nodded and closed my eyes again, returning to the problem of the Rat Dragon. The grazes on my palms stung with a sharp reminder of his overwhelming power.

The Sun drug had opened me to him, so it must follow that it would open me to the Mirror Dragon, too. Both were ascendant, and both were connected to me in some way. The Sun drug was the doorway to my union with them, with the added bonus that it augmented the dragons' power. And surely, if I took enough, it would stifle that remnant of Moon energy left in me.

All I needed was a way to stave off the Rat Dragon so that I could unite with the Mirror Dragon.

The answer was so obvious, I sat bolt upright. I would not need to hold back the Rat Dragon during the test! Lord Ido would be in control of his beast—the blue dragon would not be able to flood me with power and block the way of the Mirror Dragon. All I had to do was to make sure my Sun energy was as high as possible: to open me to my dragon, augment his power, and finally get rid of my Moon energy.

Rilla touched my arm. "My lord?"

"I will take some water after all," I said, reaching for the drug pouch.

We entered the village just as the soft dusk shadows were darkening into night. The roadside had been staked with long torches, and the villagers knelt between them, chanting celebration prayers and bowing as we made our way toward the town center. Red flags hung between houses and shops, and every door had a paper character for good harvest tacked onto it. The smoky fat of roasting pork and the yeasty fragrance of bread flavored the night air, underlaid with the throat-catching sweetness of incense—the taste and smell of Monsoon Festival.

My driver pulled up the horses at the edge of a large square bounded by two-story house-shops. Every window held a red paper lantern, and in their combined light I could make out the central stone compassarium: the circular dais where the Dragoneyes would work their dragon magic.

Lord Ido and the other Dragoneyes were seated at a long banquet table at the far end of the square. There was a vacant seat beside Ido, no doubt for the Coascendant. I suppressed a shiver and stepped out of the carriage. Lady Dela smiled encouragingly at me from her seat as the driver urged the horses forward. Neither she nor Rilla could accompany me—no women were allowed into the square until the Dragoneyes had contained the King Monsoon.

I was met by three elderly men dressed in tan cotton tunics worked with simple embroidery, their ceremonial best. They knelt and bowed.

"Mirror Dragoneye," the man in the center of the delegation said, raising his chin slightly but not daring to meet my eyes. "I am Elder Hiron. It is my immeasurable honor to welcome you and your dragon to our humble village. What joy that the twelfth dragon returns to us. What joy that he chooses a young Dragoneye with such great power. We offer our deepest gratitude for your sacred intervention on our behalf."

I cleared my throat. "Thank you. When is the King Monsoon due?"

The man on the right spoke. "Our weather watchers predict tomorrow afternoon, lord."

Good; that gave me time to take at least another two doses of the Sun drug.

"My lord, please, we invite you to the banquet table for the official welcome."

With Ryko at my shoulder, I was led past the ranks of kneeling village men honoring the arrival of the lords who saved them from starvation every year. A few shadows at the windows shrank away as I approached; women and children snatching a look at the Mirror Dragoneye. One man in the crowd accidentally met my eye, the awe in his face changing into a flicker of fear. I half expected him to make the ward-evil sign, but he dropped into a low bow. I was, after all, the mighty Mirror Dragoneye, the bringer of good fortune. I brushed my hand over the dwindling weight of the drug pouch in my pocket—*let it be so*, I prayed. As if in response, the pearls around my forearm stirred sluggishly. Their grip seemed to have slackened over the past few days.

The elders led me to my seat beside Lord Ido. He sat at ease, his dark, muscular presence palpable at the table full of prematurely aged men.

Dillon stood behind him, still scowling. Now I understood his unpredictable temper and Lord Ido's sudden rages; we all had the same hot spring of Sun drug bubbling beneath the surface of our skin. Did Dillon know he was being dosed? I should have warned him after I found the Sun drug in the library, but my concern had been lost in the sorrow of my master's death. And the anger.

Ryko stepped up behind me, filling the space where my apprentice should have stood. A murmur of greeting rose from the other Dragoneyes. I nodded to Lord Dram, halfway up the table, and Lord Garon across from me, both emperor's men and my supporters.

"Lord Eon, we were beginning to think your roadside troubles had prevented you from attending," Lord Ido said.

His handsome face was all smooth politeness, but his eyes held the night shine of the wolf. How did he know about my collapse? From his dragon? Or just servants' gossip?

"I am here now," I said. "Are you suggesting I would run away from the test?" I heard the heat in my voice and dug my fingernails into my thigh, trying to quell the surge of belligerence.

Ido's expression shifted into sharp attention. "Not at all. I can see that you are all fired up to meet the challenge." His gaze raked over me. "All fired up, indeed."

Lord Tyron sat down in the last vacant chair. "Finally here," he said. "Though I must say, I would rather be in my bed than at a provincial banquet. Let us hope that this year's official welcome is brief."

It was not. The Monsoon Festival was the villagers' most important celebration, and they were determined to honor us with entertainment and food to celebrate the wondrous return of the Mirror Dragoneye. All through the carefully rehearsed speeches, story dances, and platters of local delicacies, I felt Lord Ido's eyes on me. I curled my hand over the rash on my neck and kept my attention on my plate or the performance in front of me—a rabbit pretending the wolf was not pacing beside it.

Finally, the last speech was heard. Lord Tyron sighed with relief as twelve village men, wide-eyed with the honor of their duty, came to lead us to our beds for the night. The men assigned to me and Lord Ido stepped back as Elder Hiron approached us in a running bow.

"Lord Eon. Lord Ido." He bobbed to each of us. "As is custom, the Ascendant Dragoneye is always quartered in our Dragon House, built by our forefathers in gratitude for the Dragoneye service to our village." He motioned to a handsome stone building behind us. "This year, we wish to honor the ascendancy of both the Mirror Dragon and the Rat Dragon, so we have arranged the house into two separate living areas." He smiled proudly at the solution. "I hope it pleases you, my lords."

Share a house with Ido? My horror must have shown, because the elder's smile faltered. Behind me, Ryko edged closer.

"It is an admirable answer to the unusual situation, Elder Hiron," Lord Ido said, and I heard the amusement in his voice. "Do you not agree, Lord Eon?"

Caught in the quagmire of courtesy and the elder's honor, I nodded.

"Then, please, come this way," the old man said happily.

Our three guides led us the short distance to the Dragon

House. The stone frontage was hung with twelve painted banners depicting the Heavenly Animals, with the Rat and Dragon banners larger and centered above the doorway. The village men bowed us inside. I followed Lord Ido through a stone passageway, Ryko close behind.

"You must not stay here, lord," he whispered as we entered a small open courtyard.

In the center was a tiny garden with a carp pond and a sitting bench, set under three carefully tended dwarf trees hung with paper lanterns. To our left and right were doorways, their screens pushed back, showing thick bed pallets. Beyond the garden was another room with closed doors, and a second passageway with a rush mat on the stones that suggested the luxury of an adjoining bathhouse. It was gratitude made solid in stone and wood, built for lords by people who bathed from buckets and slept on straw.

Although Ryko was right about the danger, I could not refuse to stay here without grievously humiliating our hosts.

The elder hurried into the courtyard, his eyes anxiously searching our faces for approval.

I gathered all the courtesy I could find. "It is a most harmonious house," I said. "Thank you."

He beamed. "There is a hot spring bath through there," he said proudly, waving to the passage with the rush matting. His hand swept across to the closed double doors. "And that is a dining area. Your belongings, Lord Eon, have been placed in the left chamber, and yours, Lord Ido, in the right. If you require anything, we have people waiting."

"That is not necessary," Lord Ido said abruptly. "We have our own servants." He smiled, covering the moment of ungraciousness. "You have done well, Elder Hiron. I thank you for your considerations, but now I must rest. To prepare for the exertions of tomorrow." He nodded toward me. "I imagine Lord Eon is also weary."

"Of course, of course," the Elder said, bowing and backing away. "If you need anything . . ."

He disappeared into the passageway.

The three of us stood silently for a moment, suspended in thick tension. Lord Ido moved, as if toward me. Immediately, Ryko lunged forward, the movement a breath away from attack. Although Ido's face was unreadable, his body tightened into the coiled expectancy of a warrior.

"I will be with Lord Eon at all times," Ryko said through his teeth.

Ido looked past him to me, his eyes narrowing. "Call off your guard dog, Lord Eon. Or I will have him flogged for insolence."

The sound of footsteps echoing in the bathhouse corridor made us all turn. Rilla appeared, accompanied by three of Lord Ido's servants.

"Ryko!" My voice cracked on his name.

He stepped back, but his body was still angled for confrontation.

Lord Ido smiled maliciously. "Good dog." He turned to me. "Sleep well, Lord Eon. I look forward to an exhibition of *your* power tomorrow. Let us hope you are more effective than your island mongrel." He snapped his fingers at his servants, pointing them to the right bedchamber.

"I will stay outside your door, my lord," Ryko said grimly as we watched Ido and his entourage enter his room. "And I have already placed men at the window and points of entry."

I nodded.

"And Rilla will sleep at the foot of your bed," he added as she approached. "Won't you?"

Rilla rose from her bow. "Of course." She glanced behind her at the closed screen of Lord Ido's bedchamber. "But he would not be so stupid. . . ."

Ryko shrugged, ushering us to the left chamber. "We take no chances. Tomorrow's test is the key to everything. We will get you there safely, my lord. Then it is up to you."

I nodded again. Fear had blocked my throat, and there was only one thing that could clear the way. I stepped inside the sparsely furnished bedchamber.

"Tea," I whispered, fumbling for the Sun drug pouch.

Rilla followed me inside and slid the screen shut. "Yes, my lord."

The dark security of Ryko's silhouette appeared on the door's waxed parchment panes. I sat on the bed and worked open the pouch drawstrings. Another dose tonight would completely destroy any chance of a restful sleep. I gave a short laugh; with Lord Ido less than ten lengths away, sleep was a faint hope, anyway.

CHAPTER SEVENTEEN

THE LONG HOURS OF wakefulness gritted my eyes as I watched the room brighten into the start of the King Monsoon day. The humidity was already so heavy that it pressed on my skin like another hot, damp body. At the foot of my pallet, Rilla stirred, then lapsed back into sleep.

I eased myself off the bed and poured a cup of water. The tail end of the folio pearls dropped out of my sleeve and swung loose. I tucked it back up, coaxing them around my forearm again. Their grip was slackening more every day.

I carefully pulled out the drug pouch. The generous pinch of herbs sank into the cold water as one lump, then bobbed up to the surface, bursting into dry powder. It should have been dissolved in hot tea, but Rilla had been vigorous in her disapproval last night, and I did not want her to wake and see me taking more of it. No doubt Ryko had told her about its dangers and had asked her to report back to him.

I gulped the gray lumpy mixture down in one bitter mouthful, then crossed over to the door and slid it open. Ryko's face, heavy eyed and drawn, peered in at me.

"Everything all right?" he asked softly.

"Yes." I stepped out. "But it's so hot. I want to sit in the garden."

Ryko scanned the courtyard and nodded. I had just settled down on the elegant bench when a dust-covered messenger, slouching with fatigue, emerged from the passageway, accompanied by one of Ryko's men.

"Sir," the guard said to his captain, "this man says he has a message for Lord Ido."

"He has not yet risen," Ryko said.

The screen door of Ido's room snapped open. The exhausted messenger flinched and swayed on his feet. A servant hurried from the room and bowed to me, then turned to the messenger.

"Lord Ido will receive you in his chamber," he said. "Come."

The messenger bowed to me, then half jogged, half stumbled behind his guide into the room. Another servant immediately emerged, closing the door behind him and standing with arms crossed and eyes alert.

"That messenger has traveled very hard and very fast," Ryko remarked.

"On horseback," his man said. "A good horse."

Ryko nodded. "You've done well. Go back to your post."

The man saluted and headed back through the passageway.

Ryko stood still and silent. No doubt straining, like me, for any sound from Ido's chamber. But I could hear nothing over the morning birds and the distant rumblings of the King Monsoon thunder.

I scanned the ranks of village men kneeling around the edge of the square, chanting their prayers for our success. Where was Ryko? He had left just before midday to find out more about Ido's messenger but had promised he would be back before the test started. I turned my attention to the knot of apprentices, waiting nearby with food and water in case their masters called for sustenance. Dillon was standing a little apart from the others, and Hollin was calming the younger boys, but there was no sign of the big islander.

Lord Tyron looked across at me, his face unusually pale. "Are you ready?"

No, I was not ready, but the weather watchers had sent their runner to the village with the final report: the King Monsoon was heading inland. No more than a half bell away, the man had panted.

I pressed the ruby compass between my palms. The gold disc was cool against my damp skin. Just before the runner had arrived, I'd managed to take another dose of Sun drug with the ghost maker's tea that Rilla had prepared. The drugs had started a thudding ache in my head that was still sending waves of sweaty heat through me.

I forced myself to study the compassarium in front of me.

Last night it had been a low circular stage the width and breadth of a small room, bare of any distinguishing features. Today, it was the Dragoneye center of power. In the bright sunlight, I could now see that the twelve compass points were marked by jade arrows inlaid in the gray stone. A curved bench had been placed over each jade marker, the seat cunningly fitted into its neighbor to form an unbroken circle around the edge of the dais. The flat of each seat was carved with the heavenly animal sacred to that compass point, the wood so beautifully crafted that the rabbit's eyes seemed to glisten, the monkey's hand was only a moment away from grabbing, and the snake caught mid-strike. The wooden dragon that reared across my bench was bright with new varnish—the artisans must have worked hard to finish it in time for the festival.

Earlier, Lord Ido had handed me his ley line calculations with a superior smile; we both knew that, even with them, I had very little chance of success. I mentally overlaid his diagram on the dais and tried to memorize where the deep earth power meridians crisscrossed the huge stone compass. According to Ido, the New Year had changed the energy flows, and the best power could now be drawn from the lines that intersected in the northern sector. Of course, those calculations were for the Rat Dragoneye. Part of me wondered if the lines were really where Ido said they were; maybe he had taken the chance to put another obstacle in my way. Squinting, I took a deep breath and tried to focus on the energy world. Maybe I would be able to see the network of earth power beneath the dais.

"Lord Eon." A voice broke my concentration.

"What?"

Elder Hiron was bowing before me. "My lord, surely it is time to mount the compassarium?"

I nodded, my irritation swamped by fear. The test had finally arrived. The other Dragoneyes were standing a little apart from each other, lost in their own private preparations for the ordeal ahead.

"Shall I open the circle, my lord?" Hiron asked anxiously.

"Yes, we'll start." I searched the crowd again, but there was still no sign of Ryko.

Elder Hiron knelt on the low step that encircled the dais. Carefully he pushed my bench inward, breaking the closed circle of seats, then quickly backed away.

"Lords Dragoneye," I called, but my voice was drowned in the loud prayer chants. I tried again. "Lords Dragoneye, please take your positions."

Finally, I had their attention. Lord Ido, with an ironic bow, stepped up behind me, acknowledging my leadership during the test. The other Dragoneyes silently formed a line after him in order of ascendancy, with Lord Meram, the young Pig Dragoneye who'd ascended last cycle, bringing up the rear. The chanting intensified, and the sound pounded against my ears like the piercing throb of cicadas. I led the Dragoneyes onto the stone dais, careful not to trip on my red silk robe. The pearls around my arm had slackened even more over the past few hours. I touched my sleeve to check the position of the folio.

It had slipped a little, but most of the pearls were still holding it against me.

As was ascendant tradition, I stood in the center of the compassarium. When the other Dragoneyes were standing at their jade markers, Elder Hiron pulled my bench back, locking it against its neighbors and closing the Dragoneye circle. Immediately, the chanting stopped, leaving an eerie quiet. As if on cue, the heat thickened, distorting the air into shimmering waves. Searing heat and silence—the two harbingers of the King Monsoon.

My legs felt stiff as I walked to my seat and turned to face the ring of men who would look to me for leadership through the hours of delicate, exhausting work. One by one, I met their eyes: Lord Silvo nodded, Garon dropped his gaze, and Tyron gave me a strained smile. I saw caution, anger, hope, dislike, anxiety, spite, ambivalence, and lastly, the wolf stare of Lord Ido. He was waiting for me to fail.

I sat down, holding the ruby compass out before me. The other Dragoneyes immediately did the same, the glint of the twelve gold discs flashing in the sunlight. A deep rumble made everyone look to the horizon. A huge bank of black cloud was moving steadily toward us, spitting jagged bursts of lightning that raked the ground.

I licked my lips, silently rehearsing the traditional call to power that Hollin had taught me. Eleven men stared at me, poised over their instruments, waiting for my words. Another cracking boom rolled toward us, sending a flinch of fear through the villagers.

"Dragoneyes," I yelled over the fading thunder. "Call your dragons, draw upon your power, prepare to do your sacred duty for our bountiful land and our glorious emperor."

As one, they chanted, "For our land and emperor."

I had been told that every Dragoneye had his own method of calling his dragon's power. Lord Tyron pressed his compass between his palms, as if in prayer, his mouth moving in a private chant. Silvo, his head back to look at the heavens, held his compass up in the cradle of his hands. I glanced across at Ido, and my body locked in shock. He was pressing a sharpened edge of his compass across his palm, a thin welling of blood rising around the makeshift blade. I watched him grind the blade further into his flesh. Then his eyes half closed, surrendering to an ecstasy I did not understand, his amber gaze flooding with liquid silver.

Repulsed, I broke away from his blank stare. Around the circle, the other Dragoneyes were still easing into trances, slowly connecting with their beasts. Only Lord Ido and I could step into the energy world as quickly as walking through a doorway. Was it because we were both Ascendant? Or was I like him in some other way? The thought made my skin crawl.

I tightened my grip on the ruby compass. Had the Sun drug done its job? That was the real test—whether or not I could finally unite with the Mirror Dragon. For all the stifling heat, I felt a cold wash of hope and dread rush through me. This was my last chance.

I looked down at my compass. Beautiful and useless, but I had to pretend I knew how to work it. I focused on the ruby as

Tyron had shown me and breathed deeply, seeking the pathways of my *Hua*. Slowly, the facets of red stone merged and swirled in my eyes, twisting and folding me into the energy world.

Thunder boomed. Above, the sky was full of dragons—immense beasts crouching over the village, over the roiling black clouds, over the heavens, their huge spirit eyes staring down at me. They towered in a circle, each guarding his compass point. Green, purple, gray, pink, blue, orange. All of them ready to do our bidding. I stood and spun around, eager to see the red Mirror Dragon behind me. Eager to feel his power. Eager to finally be a true Dragoneye.

Gone.

The crushing loss hit me in the chest before my mind made sense of it. There was no dragon. Not even a faint outline of his red body. Only the villagers gaping up at me. Only the dark, thunderous sky.

I staggered back, dropping the compass. It clanged on the stone and rolled away.

My dragon was gone.

I had already failed. The terrible reality dropped me onto my hands and knees. A hesitant murmur around the square rose into the shriller tones of alarm. The villagers knew something was wrong. The other Dragoneyes were still deep in the energy world, their dragons listening, huge heads tilted, answering the call to service.

"Where are you?" I screamed at the gap in the circle. "Come back. What have I done wrong?"

A brutal grip on my arm pulled me to my feet. My eyes focused on blue silk. I looked up into the pitiless face of Lord Ido.

"Quiet." His harsh whisper was hot against my ear. I jerked my head away from the brutal intimacy, but he held me tight against his body. The silver was ebbing from his eyes, leaving gold-flecked triumph. "Get back into your position. I'll take over now."

I wrenched my arm out of his hold. My shock was igniting into fury. At him. At myself. At the Mirror Dragon.

"Let me go!"

I was not quick enough. Ido grabbed my wrist, twisting my arm back into agony, pushing me to my seat. I felt the blood from his wound slick against my skin.

"You have failed, Lord Eon," he called out to the crowd. "Now get out of the way, while I save this province from your youthful pride."

Above him loomed the blue immensity of the Rat Dragon. Lord Ido had broken his communion with the beast to gloat over my failure. I stared up into the blue dragon's dark otherworld eyes. I had called him before. I could call him again. There was still a chance to be a Dragoneye.

I dug into my *Hua*, gathering up the thick gray Sun drug energy in my seven centers of power. I did not have the Mirror Dragon, but I could have the Rat Dragon. With all of my anger and pain, I hurled the energy at the huge blue beast in front of me and grabbed at his power.

Lord Ido gasped as the silver burst back across his eyes. He fell to his knees, dragging me with him.

A moan swept around the village square. My body was pinned to the dais under Lord Ido's weight, but at the same time I rose above it, a huge presence that stared through the earth to the network of power in my domain. I was the blue dragon. I was the keeper of the north-northwest. I was wind and rain and light and dark. I was—

Another presence. My mind flooded with memory. With ambition. With practiced power, insatiable desire, dangerous knowledge. With the essence of Ido. Pain and twisted pleasure. Pride and rage. I fought against the suffocating malevolence, struggling to escape his hold on my body and mind. I thrust the power back at him, but it dragged me down into the mire of his truth.

Let me go.

My scream was silent, but his silvered eyes widened and I knew he heard it in his mind.

His hand closed over my mouth and I gagged on the sweet metal of his blood. I sensed him draw more power, pulling up the earth's life force through the dragon, funneling it through his power centers into me. The color of his eyes deepened from silver to black. He tore into my *Hua*, ripping through to the center of my being. A moment of shocked stillness, a sharp grab of understanding, and then I heard the rasp of his voice in my mind.

You are mine, girl.

Splintered.

All at once I was soaring in the dragon heavens, flailing against Ido's mind, struggling under his weight on the stone dais. There was no center. No self. Just a howling madness fueled by fury, fear, and loss.

Fight.

A voice. Familiar and comforting. It gathered me into myself. Curled me around a flicker of gold truth that he could not touch.

Find it.

Deep within me. A tiny reservoir of power that flowed into my fractured spirit.

Slowly my focus narrowed back into sanity.

But I was not in my body. I was in the heavens, looking down through the blue dragon's ancient eyes. Below me, bright lines slashed the surface of the earth in surging currents. Pulsing points of life force sat, walked, flew, scurried across the grids, drawing and shedding power into the land and air. I tasted the acid snap of raw energy on my tongue.

My focus slipped, plunging me back to the dais. I was standing. When had Ido stopped holding me down? When had he returned to his seat? Above us the circle of dragons waited. I felt the wind fill my eyes and mouth, and the first Monsoon rain shiver across my skin. My arms rose to gather power. But I was not the one moving them.

A huge chasm had opened up between my mind and body.

My eyes moved, forced to the left until I was staring at Ido. He smiled and lifted his hand, gently pushing back. Immediately, my left hand bent backward; sinew, bone, and tendon straining to breaking point. But I felt nothing. Understanding seared through me.

Ido was controlling my body.

He had taken my will.

I screamed, but my mouth did not open and my throat made no sound. Cruel exhilaration caressed me as he released his hold on my wrist. There was no way to shed tears, but in my mind I sobbed with fear and fury.

It will be worse if you struggle. His mind-voice lilted with false sympathy.

My body lurched forward as my legs stiffly walked to the center of the dais. My damaged hip ground in its socket from his long, unfamiliar gait.

"Dragoneyes," I yelled, and they were Ido's words moving my tongue and working my jaw. He could make me do anything, say anything, and I had no way to stop him. "Send your dragons to meet the storm. Circle the center."

He was using me to shift the monsoon. Why? He already had the council. Why was he doing this to me?

Through you I will have the council and much, much more. My mind cringed from the dark pleasure in him and the steel of his ambition.

"Lord Silvo, reduce your power," he ordered through my voice. "Move your beast back. We begin."

Time slipped and stuttered as I was thrust between dais and dragon, a cycle of shifting focus that spun me between the glory of the Rat Dragon and the horror of Ido's control. I raged in silence as he used my body and voice to direct the Dragoneyes. I felt his fierce joy as his power joined with mine, draining me. I watched, helpless and in awe, as the huge circle of beasts slowly contained the energy of the storm and moved it over the dam. Then suddenly, through ancient eyes, I saw the clouds drop their wild weight of water.

I knew the huge beast understood the task was complete, that the familiar tethers from the below world would ease and slip away. I felt the dragon gather itself, ready to be free again.

And then, just before I spun back to the despair of the dais, I saw the messengers.

Six men in the distance, riding toward the village at a hard gallop, wearing the emperor's colors.

I slumped onto the dais, gasping for air. Ido was gone. He was out of my head. I spread my hands on the cold stone, glorying in the movement, reveling in the control of my own body. My left wrist ached from the strain of being bent, but even that pain was welcome. I had my self back.

But for how long?

I whirled around on my knees, fixing on the figure of Ido slouched on his seat. Very slowly, he placed his finger over his lips and smiled. I shuddered. My body was my own—for now— but the press of his power still shadowed me.

Around the dais, the villagers were cheering and prostrating themselves on the ground. The other Dragoneyes, still hunched on the benches, were emerging from their trances. Tyron heaved himself up from his seat and staggered the few short steps to me.

"Such an exhibition of power, Lord Eon. Amazing." His haggard face was vivid with relief and victory. "You have truly earned your place on the council now." He looked challengingly across at Lord Ido.

"I have no argument, Tyron." Ido held up his hand in surrender. "The boy has shown us his worth as both council member and Coascendant." His eyes flicked down to mine; a moment of unwanted collusion.

Tyron turned his attention to me. "And are you all right, Lord Eon?"

I could not look at the kind concern on his face—I was betraying him. I was betraying them all by my silence. "I'm tired," I said.

He nodded and offered me his hand, pulling me to my feet. "And no wonder. Your control of the monsoon was astounding." A small cheer of agreement rose from the Dragoneyes who had clustered around us. I felt a few hands clap me gently on the back.

"But I think we are all feeling the strain," Tyron continued. "The loss of *Hua* was staggering."

Beside him, Lord Silvo nodded. His face was gray and drawn. "Never had so much taken from me before," he whispered.

Tyron patted his shoulder. "We must all rest. Our celebrations can be resumed after we have slept and restored our *Hua*." He bent closer to me. "Acknowledge the thanks of the villagers; then we can all get to our beds."

I faced the crowd. Their roughened faces had relaxed into joy. The solid bank of men separated into a pathway for Elder Hiron.

"Lord Eon," he said, bowing low. "Lords Dragoneye." His bow deepened. "We thank you all humbly for saving our crops and our village once again. You bring us great good fortune."

"Your thanks are accepted, honored elder," I said, mustering a smile. "We must all rest now, but we look forward to the celebrations you have planned this evening."

The elder bowed again and, arms wide, ushered his people away from the dais.

"Clear the way for the Lords Dragoneye. We will show our appreciation in the banquet tonight. Go and prepare."

Tyron waved Hollin over. "Take me to my quarters, boy. I have never felt this bad before. I must truly be getting old."

The other apprentices were being called to help their weakened masters.

Tyron turned back to me. "Is Ryko not here?" he asked. I shook my head, the Islander's absence a spike of dread through my numb exhaustion.

"Then Hollin can assist you, too." Tyron motioned to his apprentice to take my arm.

Lord Ido stepped up beside me, his hand brutally gripping

my shoulder. "No need, Tyron. Lord Eon and I are quartered together. My boy can help us both back to the Dragon House. It is only a few lengths away, after all."

Tyron hesitated, then nodded, his own weariness making the decision. Leaning heavily on Hollin, he shuffled across the dais. I wanted to call out to them, but Ido's hand pinned me into terrified silence.

"Take Lord Eon's other arm," Ido ordered Dillon. "He can hardly walk."

I felt Dillon drape my arm over his shoulders. I slowly turned my head to him, my mouth close to his ear.

"Don't leave me alone," I murmured, tilting my head toward Ido.

Dillon shot a glance at his master, then back at me. His eyes, the whites strangely yellowed, shifted away. There would be no help from him this time.

As we stepped down from the dais, Ido kept me pressed close to his body. I could feel the easy strength in him. He did not seem to be exhausted like the rest of us. Had he stolen power from the other Dragoneyes as well?

Two of Ryko's men appeared in front of us, blocking our way. My heart lifted; he had not left me unprotected. The guards bowed politely to Lord Ido, the senior man stepping forward with professional determination.

"Thank you, Lord Ido," he said, "but our orders are to accompany Lord Eon from the compassarium."

I struggled to free myself, but Ido tightened his grip. The

amber of his eyes smoothed into silver. "Lord Eon says he does not need your assistance," he said softly.

I held my breath. Surely this hard soldier would not be influenced by Ido's dragon charm.

The man frowned, and I saw his dogged gaze waver.

"No, wait . . ." But the rest of my plea was lost in agony as Ido drove his thumb into my shoulder—the same place where my master had dug his will into mine at the ceremony.

Both guards sketched a quick duty bow, then walked away.

Ido laughed softly. "Your power still lingers in me."

He released my shoulder, but I was so dizzy from the pain and fatigue that Ido and Dillon were forced to half drag, half carry me through the Dragon House passageway, into the courtyard. I heard a door screen slide open and raised my head, blearily searching for Rilla. She ran toward me.

"Are you all right, my lord? Where are your guards?" She faced Ido. "What are you doing with him? Let go. I'll look after him."

"Get back, woman," Ido snapped. "We will take him to his room."

She watched as Lord Ido and Dillon lifted me over the raised threshold and eased me back onto the pallet in the dim room. Ido sat next to me, supposedly holding me up, but his fingers dug another warning into my flesh.

"Your master just needs rest," Ido said. "He has the Dragon-eye weariness."

Rilla hesitated and looked to me. "Is that true, my lord?"

"Lord Eon says go. Prepare him food and leave him to rest," Ido said smoothly.

I struggled against him, hoping to stop the dragon charm I knew was coloring his eyes. But Rilla's face relaxed into obedience. She bowed and backed out of the room.

"Go," Ido ordered Dillon. The Dragoneye turned to me, not even waiting for the door to close behind his apprentice.

The sudden release of his grip made me fall back against the pallet. I scrabbled along the bed until my back hit the wall. My limbs still felt heavy from the long hours of his control.

"Get away from me." My voice was small and weak.

"A bit late for that, don't you think?" He smiled, rolling his shoulders and easing them straight. "So you and Brannon thought you could fool the emperor and the Dragoneye Council?" He laughed. "I suppose you were right. You *did* fool everyone. Even me."

He reached across and stroked my ankle. I jerked away from his touch, fear driving new energy into my body.

"But now I know. And that puts you in a very difficult situation, doesn't it?"

I eyed him, watching for any other movement toward me.

"I would say that puts you completely in my power." He laughed softly again. "In more ways than one."

I dug my fingers into the soft pallet. Was he going to enslave me again? I could not endure it.

"How did you do that? How did you control me?"

"Strange to say, I don't know," he said. "My guess is that we were joined through my dragon." He shrugged. "However it was done, it increased my power tenfold. Exhilarating. Too bad the effect is already wearing away, but we will work on that."

The effect was wearing away. Did that mean he no longer had the power to overcome me? I grabbed at the small hope.

"Brannon risked everything for you." He studied me for a moment. "The Moon Shadow disguise was inspired. But are you really deformed? Or was that a masquerade, too?"

I looked away, my master's betrayal still raw.

"So, you are deformed. A pity. Still, I can now see the girl in you, and you are not without your attractions. Was that part of your agreement with Brannon?"

"You're disgusting," I spat, clinging to the strength of my hate. "I know you killed him. You make me sick—"

The blow knocked me sideways onto the pallet, setting up a burning throb across my cheekbone. I saw a light spring into his eyes that sent a chill of knowledge through me. A memory of the whipmaster.

"Do you want to continue?" His voice was soft.

I drew my knees up into a curl of protection.

"How did you commune with my dragon?" he demanded. "And why do you not commune with your own?"

I stared down at the bed. For so long I had kept my true identity hidden, my failure a secret. Now I was stripped of all pretence.

His hand lifted again.

"I don't know," I said hurriedly.

"Really?" I flinched as his fingers brushed the drug rash on my neck. "Are you sure?"

"I didn't unite properly with my dragon in the ceremony. He has slipped away from me." I swallowed against the jab of loss. "But I can call your dragon. I don't know why."

"Neither do I." He cocked his head. "You are quite the mystery. But I think I have the key to you."

"Key? What do you mean?"

"The black folio." He shook his head at my blank face. "No, that won't work. I know you took the red book from my library, along with my supply of the Sun drug."

Instinctively, I pressed the folio closer to my body. I tried to mask the move, but it was too late.

"So that's where you keep it." He grabbed my wrist, pushing up the sleeve of my robe. I felt his fingers trace the pearl rope, feathering my skin. He forced his finger underneath the pearls and pulled at them. They resisted, their loyalty giving me courage. "I see the pearls respond to you—that must mean something." He tightened his hold. "Give it to me."

I fought against his grip, but he grabbed my jawbone and slammed my head back against the wall. "Give it to me or I will hurt you in ways you have never imagined."

My vision blurred with pain. I nodded, and he let go. I pushed at the pearls, easing them down my arm until they dropped to the pallet, the red folio landing heavily on top.

Gingerly, Ido reached for it. The pearls rose like a snake ready to strike. He snatched his hand away.

"Interesting." He looked at me. "Did you try and pick up the black folio?"

"No. I didn't want to."

He grunted agreement. "From what I have read of it, I know why."

I couldn't help myself. "What do you mean?"

He nodded. "You and I are more alike than you think. We are both looking for power, and we both have to *know*."

I raised my chin. He was wrong; I was not like him at all.

"I've been deciphering the black folio," he continued. "It is in a very old script and it's taken a long time to understand even the little I have decoded. It describes a way to combine all the power of the Dragoneyes into one weapon."

"The String of Pearls?" I whispered.

He laughed, a deep sound of delight. "Oh, yes, we *are* alike. No doubt Brannon told you about it. You're quite right: it is describing the String of Pearls. I didn't really understand what I was reading until today. Until I discovered your little masquerade."

He reached over and slid his hand along the silk of my sleeve. "It says that the String of Pearls requires the joining of Sun and Moon. I was sure it meant you, but in your capacity as a Moon Shadow. You can imagine my unease; I am no lover of eunuchs. But now I know that you are female, it makes far more sense. Today was only a taste of our union. Think of what will happen when we are joined not only in power, but in body, too."

I shook my head, sickened.

He curled his hand around my cheek, forcing my head toward him. "Of course, there are other things to put in place before the String of Pearls can be created, but it doesn't stop us getting to know one another . . . and really, you are not unattractive at all."

"I'll bite you," I hissed.

"Please do," he said. "And I will bite back."

"I'll scream. Everyone will come."

He shrugged. "Go ahead if you want to be disemboweled by an outraged emperor and Dragoneye council."

I gritted my teeth.

"A horrible way to die," he murmured. "Especially as the disembowelment takes a full bell. You could, of course, choose death over me," he paused, as though considering the idea, "but I don't think you are the suicidal type. You are too much like me. Where there is life, there is always a chance to win."

He knew he had me cornered. He traced my mouth with his forefinger, a soft caress that moved across my cheekbone until his hand found the looped plaits of my Dragoneye queue. I felt his fingers wind into it, pulling my head back. I turned away from his mouth and the slick press of his oiled beard.

"*Eona,*" he breathed against my skin. "Such a pretty name and hidden so deep."

I struggled against him, against his use of my true name, ripped from the center of my being. My fingernails found flesh. I dug and clawed. But it made no difference. I pressed my lips together, but his mouth was on mine. And then I tasted him—sweet vanilla and orange like his dragon. I gasped, the shock softening my mouth under his kiss.

He pulled back, his face mirroring my own surprise. "Perhaps your inclinations are more like mine than you admit," he said. He cupped my chin. "You could join me willingly. We could take the land together."

I jerked my head away, shocked. "You want to be emperor?"

"There would be no use invoking the String of Pearls just to hand over its power."

"Does High Lord Sethon know your plans?"

He laughed, releasing my hair. "You are quick. But don't think you can deal with Sethon against me. Your female corruption of the hallowed Dragon Halls would stop anyone from listening to you. Especially if I told them you are not even united with the Mirror Dragon. I would be surprised if they even waited for the disembowelment." He dragged his forefinger across my throat. "At least it would be fast."

He was right. As soon as he unmasked me as a girl and a fraud, they would kill me.

He laid his finger across my mouth. "Stay quiet, *Eona*. Do as I say, and you will stay alive. And if you are good, then maybe I will not even hurt you too much. Do you understand?"

I gave a tiny nod.

"Good girl."

He patted my cheek.

I turned my head, unable to shield the fear in my eyes as his hand followed the line of my jaw. I saw his amber eyes flare with intent as his fingertips dropped to the soft hollow at the base of my throat, then traced the edge of my robe to the shoulder fastening.

The sound of running feet outside made him pause.

"Lord Eon," a voice called at the door. Ido pressed his hand against my mouth, his eyes warning me. "Messengers have arrived. From the emperor. They are asking for you, my lord. Please, you must come. All the Dragoneye lords are assembling."

Ido clicked his tongue in irritation. With a smile of regret, he brushed his thumb across my lips and released me. Then he stood and quickly searched my baggage, pulling out a large drying cloth. With a flick, he unfolded it and deftly bundled the folio and squirming pearls into it.

"You may be tempted to get help or even to run," he said softly. "Don't. I will hunt you down, and I will take that maid of yours and her freak son and throw them to my men. I'm sure they would last at least an hour before they died."

He opened the screen and looked at the villager crouched on the ground.

"Next time, do not interrupt your betters." Although his voice was mild, the man stiffened with fear. Ido turned back to me, his eyes lingering over my body. "Congratulations on your success today, Lord Eon," he said. "You have exceeded all expectation." Then he smiled and left the room.

CHAPTER EIGHTEEN

THE VILLAGER AT THE doorway dropped into a bow again. I stared at him, unable to break out of the horror that held me like a vice against the wall.

He slowly lifted his head. "My lord?" he ventured. "Please forgive me, but the messenger said it was most urgent."

I took a deep shaking breath. Ido was gone. At least for now.

"Tell them . . ." My voice wavered. I stopped and took another breath, trying to force strength into my words. "Tell them I will be there soon. Now go."

He backed away, leaving me with a view of the courtyard garden and the grim understanding that Ido's control was complete. I shuddered. Not only did he have my mind and body in his grip, he had cornered me into betraying my friends and allies.

Whatever I decided to do, I would be the agent of their

defeat. If I confessed the truth to the council, I would be killed and the emperor and the prince left without their Ascendant ally or the council's support; Sethon would take the throne. If I obeyed Ido, I would be forced to do his bidding in the council and Sethon would have control of the Dragoneyes. In either case, Ryko and his resistance would have no Dragoneye to rally around, and Lady Dela would be at the mercy of a court who thought her a demon. I could not even run without placing Rilla and Chart in Ido's path.

I had failed everybody. And behind it all was Ido's ultimate ambition: to create the String of Pearls with me and become emperor. Whether or not it was possible, the idea of him with such power made me sick with terror.

There was one other course I could take, but Ido had seen my true nature; it was not in me to choose suicide. Perhaps it was cowardice, but I was not ready to die. Not for my emperor, not for the prince, not even for my friends. And for this shameful lack of courage, I was now slave to Ido's desires.

Perhaps it was this unworthiness that had driven away the Mirror Dragon. I had not even seen a faint outline of the beast on the dais. It was as if he had never existed. And now I had lost the last link to him, the red folio. I touched my bare forearm, missing the reassuring hold of the pearls. Ido had truly stripped me of everything.

Rilla appeared at the doorway. "My lord, Ryko is back."

I stirred, my despair pierced by her words. "Ryko?"

"I am here, lord." Ryko entered the room and bowed. He was covered in mud and stank of stagnant water, but a huge smile lit his face. "Well done, my lord. Your magnificent success has given us all hope."

"Where were you?" I rose from the bed, suddenly furious. "You said you would be back for the test."

"I am sorry, lord." He took a step back from my anger. "I was looking for Ido's messenger, to find out what information he had delivered."

"You should have come back."

"My men had orders to guard you. Did they not do their duty?"

I was unable to meet his frank gaze. "Yes, your men came." I glanced across at Rilla, but her face did not register my lie. Ido's dragon charm had obscured memory, too. "Did you find the messenger?"

"I did, eventually," he said. "Thrown into an old channel with his throat cut."

Rilla grimaced. "But why?"

Ryko scrubbed wearily at the mud caked on his face. "I would guess it was to stop someone like me forcing the message out of him."

"Or perhaps someone else wanted the message and got there before you," I said.

Ryko nodded. "True. But my gut says it was on *his* orders." He jerked his head toward Ido's room.

"Lord Eon!" It was Tyron's voice. "The emperor's own men are here. You must come now." The old Dragoneye, flanked by Hollin, peered in the doorway. "They will not deliver until you are present."

I could delay no longer. I squared my shoulders, trying to find the courage to face Ido again.

"I fear this is bad news," Tyron murmured as we entered the stone passageway. "*Six* messengers to deliver one message—no chances taken."

It seemed as though the whole village had congregated around the stone dais. Now that the King Monsoon had been defeated, the women and children were allowed back into the town center. It should have been full of jubilation and laughter. Instead, everyone stood silently in the late-afternoon sun, watching the six emissaries from the emperor. The men were still mounted on their horses, although the animals were lathered with sweat and fidgeting with the press of people.

A flash of gold and silky green cloth among the drab homespun caught my eye; Lady Dela, escorted by two of Ryko's men, was working her way toward us. The warm greeting in her face drove a barb of guilt into me; I had put my friends into such peril. I motioned to Rilla to go and meet her, then turned to the messengers, every part of me aware of Ido staring at me from the dais. I clenched my hands, forcing back the wild fear that made me want to run from him. Hollin and Ryko moved forward, clearing a path through the tense crowd. As Tyron and I stepped up onto the stone stage, the air thickened with expectation.

"We seek Lord Eon, the Mirror Dragoneye," the leader said, his cultured city voice reaching the furthermost corners of the square.

"I am Lord Eon," I said, unable to bring myself to finish the formal claim of dragon status.

All six men dismounted. The leader thrust his reins into the hands of the man beside him and withdrew a scroll, then dropped to his knees beside the dais and bowed his forehead to the ground three times. Two short swords were crossed over the man's broad back; he was one of the emperor's own personal guard. He held up the scroll, his face solemn.

The parchment was sealed with the wax image of the imperial dragon. Its message was short.

> *Lord Eon, Mirror Dragoneye, Coascendant of the Dragon Council,*
>
> *My honored father is dead. May his spirit walk with our glorious ancestors and bring good fortune to my reign.*
>
> *Return to the city immediately to sit the ghost watch with me. Be advised by Lady Dela, who was given leave by my father to study the rituals and understands your part in the proceedings.*
>
> *Pearl Emperor Kygo-Jin-Ran.*

I looked up at the intent faces around me.

"The emperor has passed into the land of the ancestors," I said.

My focus narrowed to Ido. Although his face was schooled into new regret, I was sure that it was old news to him. The morning message. Had he played a part in the emperor's death? The timing seemed too opportune to be just luck. And how else would his messenger learn of the death and beat the imperial horsemen?

The villagers close to the dais whispered the news until the silence around us broke into a slow moan that shivered through the village square, building into a keen so piercing that it must have reached the otherworld.

"We must all return to the city," Lord Tyron said over the terrible sound.

I nodded numbly. "I am summoned to sit the ghost watch with Prince—" I stopped; Prince Kygo was now the emperor. "With our glorious new overlord."

"You are to sit the imperial ghost watch?" Lord Silvo gasped. "Then the Pearl Emperor makes you second mourner. You are a guardian of the old emperor's spirit." He bowed low. "May your sacred duties ease his way to his noble ancestors."

The keening around us trailed off, marshaled into the gentler rhythms of a prayer chant led by a holy man at the other end of the square.

"It is a wise move on our new emperor's part," Tyron said softly, his low tone drawing Silvo closer. "Especially now that Lord Eon has proven his power and his leadership of the council. This should dissuade Sethon from making a claim."

I stared at Tyron. "What do you mean?"

"Prince Kygo will be Pearl Emperor for twelve days until his father's body is entombed, and then he will be formally anointed as Dragon Emperor," Tyron said. "But the Pearl Days are the most dangerous; any male of royal blood can make his claim for the throne. That is why it is also traditionally the time when the Pearl Emperor kills any younger brothers to stop the internal wars that come with a divided claim."

"The Right of Reitanon," Lord Silvo said, nodding. "But I doubt our new emperor will follow that tradition. He is his father's son."

"Yes, I'm sure he will spare his infant brother—the child poses no threat," Tyron said. "However, Sethon has made no secret of his ambitions, and he has the armies, led by his own younger brothers, backing him."

"I can't stop High Lord Sethon from making a claim!" I grabbed Tyron's sleeve. "You must not rely on me to stop Sethon. I cannot!"

Tyron pulled his arm free from my desperate grasp. "Be easy, Lord Eon. It is not you, personally, who will stop Sethon. He will be stopped by the knowledge that his nephew has your power behind him. You are the Mirror Dragoneye, you are Coascendant, and you now have the council's full support. He would be mad to go against all that. Even with the armies."

I felt a sob thicken my throat. The prince—the new emperor—was building his fortress on the quicksand of my power.

I grabbed at Tyron again. "You don't understand—"

"Lord Eon," Ido's rich voice harnessed my words. "You are greatly honored by our new emperor." I felt his hand close over my bruised shoulder. "He raises you higher and higher. Soon you will not be able to see the humble truth of your beginnings."

With subtle pressure on the older pain, he turned me until I faced Rilla and Lady Dela, standing nearby. Lady Dela's pale makeup was streaked by tears. Did she cry for the death of the old emperor, or for the loss of her protector?

"I will never forget my beginnings," I said through my teeth.

"Nor, I am sure, your responsibilities," he added. I felt his thumb stroke my shoulder before he released me.

"Lord Eon is very aware of his responsibilities," Tyron said firmly. "As we all are at this time." He motioned to Hollin. "Rally everyone," he ordered. "We must leave now to mourn the old emperor and give our support to the new."

The leader of the imperial messengers bowed again. "Lord Eon, to expedite your return to the city, his glorious majesty, the Pearl Emperor, has ordered fresh horses to await you at the villages of Reisan, Ansu, and Diin."

Tyron nodded his approval. "With three horse changes, you should be in the city by morning. We will follow as quickly as possible. If we push, we should be with you by dusk."

The village gong sounded the first of the twelve tolls of mourning. All around us, the villagers dropped into kowtows, their foreheads flat to the stone flags.

"Help me down, lad," Tyron said, "I am so tired, I fear I'll fall."

I grasped his forearm, bracing myself against his weight as he lowered himself to his knees. Then I took my position alongside him and the other Dragoneyes kneeling around the dais.

As the gongs resonated through the square, I recalled the lesson in the library with Teacher Prahn and the prince. Now, with hindsight, it was obvious that the emperor's unscheduled visit had been orchestrated to win my support, but I believed his kindness to a frightened peasant-made-lord had been genuine. And although I was sure it would have meant nothing to one so exalted, I had liked him very much. The emperor's loss lodged in my heart, a small ache compared to the loss of my master, but another sadness that ground its shards into my spirit.

Now the prince—the Pearl Emperor—would be faced with the pain of losing his father, and his own dangerous ascension to the imperial throne. He had made a pact with me for mutual survival, but he had made it with Lord Eon, not a worthless peasant girl in the power of his enemy. I could no more influence his survival than I could my own.

The last toll echoed around the silent square. Beside me, Lord Tyron sighed.

"Go, Lord Eon," he said. "Go and stand your power behind our new emperor. Make Sethon kneel before him."

Lady Dela settled next to me in the carriage, self-consciously smoothing down her heavily embroidered cream gown. In the brief time we'd had to prepare for the journey back to the city, she had fretfully rummaged through her baggage, repeating that her gown was not suitable for mourning. It was not until Rilla grabbed her hands, steered her into a chair, and ordered her maid to find a gown that would honor the emperor that Lady Dela stopped her frantic search.

As well as changing her outfit, the lady had removed her court makeup. Without the distraction of the pale mask, her angular face was muddy and shadowed with grief. She smiled wanly at me, her fingers plucking at the small traveling basket on her lap. Rilla had also hurriedly stripped me of my Dragoneye robe and exchanged it for a somber tunic and trousers for the hard night of traveling. I was relieved to have the red robe off my body—it seemed to hold the stink of vanilla and orange. Unfortunately there had been no time for a bath as well, to scrub away Ido's touch.

The carriage rocked again as Rilla took the small servants' seat facing us. She directed Ryko to place a large basket of food on the floor at her feet. I met her defiant gaze with a frown—we had already had this discussion. I did not want to eat.

"With respect, my lord," she said briskly. "You must take something, otherwise you will not have the strength to honor the old emperor."

Lady Dela nodded. "It is true, Lord Eon. The ghost watch is very demanding."

I knew they were right. I would have to eat and replenish my body, but the thought of swallowing food made my gut jerk with nausea. Perhaps another dose of the Sun drug would renew me. But then again, the drug had failed on every level during the King Monsoon. Maybe it only worked on men. Was that why it had not helped me see my dragon? Or had Ido somehow blocked me from my own beast? I felt the stranglehold of despair close around my throat again.

"Give me something then," I said, trying to focus past the choking emptiness.

Rilla drew out a lacquer box from the basket. She pulled off the lid, bent into a quick bow, then passed it across the small space. Three spiced rice balls, bound with strips of seaweed, lay nestled on a bed of thinly cut cabbage like bird eggs in a nest. A beautiful dish prepared with care. I felt like vomiting.

"My lord, my lord! Please wait!"

It was Elder Hiron, running and waving something. Ryko stopped his approach with a raised hand.

"Lord Eon is about to leave," he said. "What is your business?"

I leaned past Lady Dela. We had already gone through the requisite thanks and farewells with the village leader. What did he want now?

"My lord," he gasped. "He is an honest man, he just didn't know how to approach you, what with the terrible news of our emperor's . . ." The old man bent over, trying to catch his breath.

"What are you talking about?"

"This, my lord." Elder Hiron held up the ruby compass. "Jiecan, our baker, found it near the dais. He is a good man. He came to me with it as soon as he could."

I stared at the gold disc; I had dropped it when I turned to see the Mirror Dragon, and he was gone. The terrible loss twisted through me again.

Elder Hiron paled. "Please, my lord. Do not be angry. It was—"

"I am not angry," I said, drawing back into my seat. "Pass it to Lady Dela." I had not even noticed its absence. Nor did it matter; my dragon had abandoned me. I did not deserve to hold a Dragoneye tool again.

He scurried up to the carriage and held out the compass, sneaking a wide-eyed look at the court Contraire. Lady Dela took it gracefully, smiling at the overwhelmed villager.

"Thank you, Elder Hiron," she said softly.

"Yes, give your baker my thanks, too," I added.

The old man bowed and backed away, still staring at Lady Dela.

Ryko shut the low carriage door and mounted his horse, steadying the animal alongside the cabin. He bent over the saddle to look in at us, waiting for my order.

"Go," I said.

He called the command, and the carriage jerked forward, quickly settling into its well-sprung sway. I looked back at the dwindling figures of Tyron and Silvo—still and silent amongst the noisy preparations of their attendants—but could not return their grave salute.

Lady Dela held out the compass. "You must forgive me, my lord, for neglecting to congratulate you on your glorious victory over Ido," she said. "The sad news of the emperor's death." She stopped and swallowed against her grief, the black pearl bobbing at her throat. "The sad news overwhelmed me. But your courage and power have secured the council. His Majesty was right—you were sent by the gods to bring the prince to the throne. Thank you."

I could not bear the gratitude in her voice. "I was not sent by anyone," I said harshly.

Lady Dela blinked with surprise. "I'm . . . I am sorry, my lord."

Rilla cleared her throat. "Can I offer you some wine, or water, my lord?"

"No, I want nothing."

Hesitantly, Lady Dela held out the compass again. "It was good fortune that this was found and returned," she said, ignoring my rudeness. "I know it is an essential tool for your art. And it is very beautiful." She brushed her finger over the inscribed face.

I did not want to touch it. "Just put it somewhere," I said, waving her hand away.

But she was not listening. All her attention was on the compass. "I know this," she said, tracing an engraved character with her fingertip. "It means *Heaven*. This is an old form of Woman Script." Her finger skipped across to another character. "*Truth*. This one is *truth*." She looked up at me. "Why is a Dragoneye tool written in Woman Script?"

I could not move. A thousand lies were collapsing within me, the roar in my ears drowning out everything except two words: *Woman Script*.

"What does it say?" I whispered.

Lady Dela stared at me.

"What does it say?" I screamed.

She flinched back into the seat. Out of the corner of my eye, I saw the driver look around at us. Rilla was staring at me, her face hollowed with shock.

I forced my voice into a lower tone. "Tell me what it says."

Lady Dela licked her lips, her eyes darting back to the compass. Slowly, she moved her finger around the innermost circle. "It says the Mirror Dragon is"—she paused, her eyes widening—"the Mirror Dragon is the *queen* of the heavens." Her hand covered her mouth. "By the gods, a female dragon."

My dragon was female. The truth of it flooded through me—

a cascade of wonder and hope and horror. She had chosen me, and I had driven her away.

Lady Dela met my stricken gaze. "You didn't know? How could you not know?"

"She's the queen?" Rilla said. "Of course, it makes sense—"

I flung myself across the narrow space, slamming her against the carriage wall. "Do not say it," I screamed, my forearm across her chest. "Do not say it."

The driver turned around again. "My lord, what is it? Shall I stop?"

"Keep driving," I yelled.

Rilla panted beneath me. "I will not say it. I promise. I promise."

"What can't she say, Lord Eon?" Lady Dela pulled at my arm, her man's strength dragging me back into my seat. "What makes sense?"

I snatched at the gold disc, but she jerked it away, the confusion in her face hardening into comprehension. "You're not Moon Shadow, are you?"

I struggled to free my other arm, but her grip tightened. "Are you a girl?" Her fierce eyes held mine, but I could not say it.

"Are you?" she shrieked. It was not anger in her voice. It was terror.

"Yes," I whispered.

She rocked back, dropping my arm as though it was diseased. "Sweet gods, a girl. In the Dragoneye Council. Do you know what they will do when they find out?"

I nodded.

"But you have the Mirror Dragon's power," she said quickly. "She chose you because you are a girl, didn't she? Surely they will see that and . . ."

I could not keep the truth out of my eyes.

Lady Dela paled. "You *do* have her power, don't you?" she asked, her voice rising into desperation. "Tell me you have the dragon's power."

"No."

She closed her eyes and moaned, the terrible sound thinning into a ragged prayer. "Merciful gods of heaven, may our deaths be swift and painless."

"But you moved the King Monsoon," Rilla said.

I looked away from her crumpled face. "Ido moved it. He took my power and made everyone think I was directing the Dragoneyes. He said he would tell the council I was a girl if I didn't do what he said. They will kill me, Rilla." I reached out to her, but she did not move. "He said he'd give you and Chart to his men if I tried to run away or get help."

Lady Dela gave a low strangled cry. "So we don't have the council. We don't have anything." She covered her face with her hands.

Rilla leaned closer. "How could Ido take your power if you don't have any? I saw the red book. There was power there. I saw the pearls move by themselves."

"I don't have the Mirror Dragon's power," I said. "I didn't unite with him—with *her*—properly during the ceremony. But I can call on Lord Ido's dragon. I don't know how. That was the power he took."

Lady Dela lifted her head. "Why didn't you unite properly with your dragon?"

"I don't know. I felt her in the arena—we communed, I swear it. But afterward she started to slip away." I paused, the awful loss closing my throat. "And now she's gone."

Rilla straightened in her seat and brushed down her dress, trying to reclaim some composure. "Maybe she didn't like you pretending to be a boy," she said tartly.

I gaped at her, a tumble of connections falling into line. "The Sun drug."

Her eyes met mine and widened. "The ghost maker's tea."

Lady Dela frowned. "What?"

"Before the ceremony, my master gave me a tea to take every morning. It stopped my—" I could not say it.

"It stops the Moon days," Rilla said quickly. "And the Sun drug is taken by the Shadow Men to keep their maleness."

Lady Dela nodded. "Ryko takes it." She eyed me narrowly. "You mean, you took it?"

"I thought it would help me join with my dragon," I said defensively. "Ido takes it to strengthen his bond with the Rat Dragon." I licked my lips, suddenly recognizing another connection. "I think the ghost maker's tea held back the Mirror Dragon, and she faded from me even faster after I took the Sun drug."

"Could it be the female dragon is called by female energy?" Lady Dela whispered.

Her words caught at my breath, their truth resonating through me. The Mirror Dragon was called by female energy;

and I had done everything to quell it within myself.

"So if you stop taking this tea and drug, you should be able to commune with the Mirror Dragon," she said. "Please, tell me I am right."

I bowed my head. "There is another problem."

Lady Dela and Rilla waited, their bodies tensing.

"I don't have my dragon's name. I can't call her power without her name." The grim irony of what I was about to say warped my mouth into a wry smile. "And the only place I could possibly find her name is in the red folio."

"The one you and Ryko stole from Lord Ido?" Lady Dela asked.

I nodded. "And the one he stole *back* a few hours ago." The echo of his brutal control still lingered in my body. I could not bear to think of it. Instead, I tipped back my head and gritted my teeth, trying to stop the burn of tears. "The folio is written in Woman Script, too. You could have read it to me." I swallowed. "I could have had her name."

Rilla touched my knee. The small gesture made it harder to hold back my grief.

Lady Dela frowned into the distance. "But that means there is still a chance for you to claim her power." The hard-headed courtier in her had reasserted itself. She nodded. "We must get the red folio back."

Hope burst through me. If I had my dragon, Ido would not be able to come near me. "We've got it from him once," I said quickly. "We could do it again."

She held up her hand. "But first, you must warn the new

emperor that he cannot rely on your power. Or the council's support."

"No." I shook my head. "No, he will kill me. We must find the red folio first."

She eyed me coldly. "It is your duty to tell him," she said. "And if you do not, you will die anyway. Ryko will kill you if you betray the emperor again." She looked out of the carriage at the dark figure of the islander riding ahead of us. "As it is, I'll have trouble stopping him from cutting your throat when he learns of your lies." She sighed. "His faith in you was enormous. As was mine."

For a moment, I imagined Ryko's face when he found out the truth. I shuddered; not only from fear, but from the knowledge of how deeply my betrayal would wound him.

Lady Dela sat back. "We must all pray to the gods that the emperor does not have you killed immediately. Let us hope you have time to tell him there's still a chance to claim the Mirror Dragon's power."

"It is a very small chance," I said.

"You should hold on to it as hard as you can," Lady Dela said flatly. "It means your life."

We sat for a moment, each of us silenced by the terrible possibilities that lay before us.

"Well," Lady Dela finally said. "I must tell Ryko." She rose from her seat, swaying with the carriage's motion, and poked the driver's back. "Pull up, man." She looked back to me. "Do not come out. Do not even show your face." She smoothed her hair and I saw her hand was trembling. "This is going to kill him."

The carriage slowed and came to a juddering stop. Immediately, Ryko pulled up his own horse. Lady Dela gave me one last reproachful look, then stepped down from the cabin, hurrying to deflect Ryko's approach.

Rilla started to unpack boxes from the food basket. "You may as well eat something. It will probably be a while before we move on again."

I craned a look over the driver's shoulder. Ryko had dismounted and given his reins to his second in command. As Lady Dela approached, the islander bowed, his head angled questioningly. She motioned him farther along the deserted road, and as they walked away from us, their voices became lost in the clattering calls of roosting birds. Suddenly Ryko stiffened and stepped back from Lady Dela. He turned to the carriage, his fists clenched. Even though I could not see his face clearly in the dusk light, his fury crossed the distance between us. Lady Dela grabbed his arm, and it was not a woman's hold. I watched him turn back to her, the tense lines of his body showing his fight for control.

"I am sorry," I whispered.

"You should have told me," Rilla said. She opened another box—full of silvery poached eel—and placed it on the seat next to me. "Maybe I could have helped."

"How?" I asked. "Do you have the dragon's name written on your forehead?" Instantly, I regretted my sarcasm. At least she was talking to me. "I'm sorry," I said. "You're right. I should have told you."

"More to the point, you should have told the master," Rilla said.

"I thought I could find the name before anyone realized I had no power. Before *he* realized. And then he died."

Rilla sighed. "Well, that's all history now." She stacked the lacquered lids, placing them back into the basket. Then, folding her hands in her lap, she sat for a moment, staring out into the new darkness.

"So," she met my gaze, "is it time, Lord Eon?"

I turned away from her quiet dignity. "I'm not your lord anymore, Rilla."

"Oh, yes, you are," she said, her sharp tone pulling me back to face her. "You have to be Lord Eon for us all. For me, for Chart, for those two out there. And for the new emperor." She lifted her chin. "I ask you again, Lord Eon. Is it time?"

"Yes," I finally said. "Take Chart and get as far away as you can."

Lady Dela finally returned to the carriage—her grim face forestalling our questions—and we resumed our journey. Ryko kept his distance, riding ahead, stiff and straight in the saddle. I watched for a while, but he did not look back. Even when we changed horses, he kept well away.

As the night deepened into the spirit hours, I finally managed to eat while Lady Dela tersely explained the imperial ghost watch. I tried to concentrate on my part in the elaborate rituals and ignore the unspoken dread that hung between us—that I would probably not live long enough to practice them.

Although my mind was past any point of rest, my drained body could hold out no longer; after the third and final horse change, I slept. Occasionally I was jolted awake by a rough piece of road and looked out to see the figure of Ryko, still riding at the front. After the long hours of traveling, he should have been bowed with fatigue, but I could see no change in his tense vigilance. Perhaps he was fueled by his rage. Perhaps hate.

I was glad to return to the oblivion of sleep.

The calls of roadside hawkers finally pulled me out of my exhaustion, and I awoke huddled in the corner of the carriage as we approached the city gates. Lady Dela was sprawled in the opposite corner, the harsh lines of her face softened by slumber. Rilla was already hunting through the basket for refreshment, her hair and gown smoothed into her usual neatness.

"Something to break your fast," she said softly, passing me a small woven dish containing a shelled hard-boiled egg and a few pickled vegetables. At least I would not have to wash it down with the foul mix of Sun drug and ghost maker's tea. I was done with both drugs.

"It is not much of a last meal," I said, attempting a smile.

She ignored the comment, carefully shelling another egg. "When we arrive at the apartments, I will prepare the cleansing bath as Lady Dela instructed." Her voice was low. "No doubt the protocol officers will have sent the proper herbs. Then, while you are washing, I will air the Story Robe. It is a good thought on Lady Dela's part for you to wear it."

"You should just go."

She shook her head. "After you are prepared for the ghost watch."

I was humbled by her dogged loyalty. "Thank you," I whispered. "But after that, *promise me* you will go."

Beside me, Lady Dela stirred. "I did not expect to sleep." She looked out at the line of carts and foot travelers waiting to enter the city on the common dirt road below our paved carriageway. "We have arrived, then."

As we drew up to the city gates, Ryko rode back toward us. I sat up, my fingers tightening around the wicker dish, but he maneuvered his horse alongside Lady Dela's side of the cabin.

"I will leave you now, lady," he said.

She nodded. "Good luck."

"Leave?" I said. "Why are you leaving? We have to get the red folio back."

Ryko finally looked at me, and the hardness in his eyes stilled my breath. "I must warn the resistance to be ready." He pulled on the reins, his horse snorting at the brutal turn. "But don't be concerned for your safety, Lord Eon. I will be back to guard you, as is my duty." His voice was bitter. "I always do my duty."

"And when have I not done my duty?" I muttered. But he was already gone.

CHAPTER NINETEEN

THE SPECIAL BLEND of sweet herbs and frangipani petals floated on the surface of the water and clung to my shoulders in velvety clumps. Rilla had prepared the ritual cleansing bath and left me to wash myself, hurrying back to the dressing room to ready the Story Robe and her escape. I sank farther into the warmth of the soaking pool and inhaled the damp fragrance, massaging my strained wrist. I had already scrubbed my body as hard as I could, but the touch of Ido was still on my skin and in the strain of my hand and hip.

He must never take my body again. I would rather die.

I stopped kneading my hand, shocked by the dark whisper that had pushed itself into my mind.

Was I really ready to die?

I licked my lips, the sweet bath herbs reawakening the vanilla-orange heat of his mouth on mine. *I should run. Escape with Rilla and Chart to the islands.* This struggle for the throne was not my fight. I had been pushed into the center of it by everyone around me: my poor master, the emperor, the prince, Lady Dela, Ryko. Even Rilla and Chart. They all expected me to bring victory. But it was not my fight.

I sighed. That was not true. It *was* my fight now. I lived or died by the Pearl Emperor's hold on the throne. And the lives of too many good people depended on my courage to face the wrath of the young emperor and win his support. Or, if things went badly, the courage to welcome his sword into my body and stop Ido from bringing Sethon to the throne. And from achieving his mad ambition to create the String of Pearls.

The memory of the prince's swift punishment of Teacher Prahn made me shiver. That had been a small mistake by an old man. And there was the young noble who had accidentally hit him on the practice field. I'd heard the prince had broken three of his ribs.

What would he do to me? A girl who had tricked him and betrayed him, who had promised him power and mutual survival, all the while knowing it was a lie. I prayed the small hope I had to offer would be enough to stop his swordhand.

Ido had been right, I could not welcome death. Not while there was still hope.

Yet I did not even know if the Mirror Dragon was still waiting for me. For a moment, the wonder of her pushed back my fear. A female dragon; what an astonishing revelation for the council. It made me wonder how they could have lost all knowledge of her and the female Dragoneyes. It seemed too complete to be an accident of time. But even if it had been deliberate all those generations ago, they could not deny the only female dragon now. And surely, if I made a true union with her, the council would have to accept me, too.

A fine plan, except I could no longer sense her; there had been no sign of her on the Dragoneye dais. Was it just that last double dose of drugs in my body, or was it some terrible failing within me? Perhaps I did not have any hope to offer the new emperor, after all. Maybe the Mirror Dragon was truly gone.

I knew I should reach into my *Hua* to see if she was still there, and at least bring the knowledge of her presence to the emperor. But what if Ido sensed me in the energy world and took me again? I shuddered. He had said it only happened when I communed with the Rat Dragon. I would be a fool to trust his word. What if he could now take me whenever I entered the pathways of *Hua*?

I found myself backed up against the edge of the bath, the tiled wall a solid mooring in the churn of my thoughts. I had to take the chance. So far, all I had offered the prince was lies. But if I wanted to survive, I had to take the new emperor the truth. I had to take him the hope of the Mirror Dragon.

My hands found the beveled holds in the tiled edge. *Please be there*, I prayed. A deep breath eased the block of fear in my chest. Another relaxed the tightness in my heart. I counted out each exhalation to the rhythm of my plea: *Please be there, please be there*. Reflections of the bathing room wavered on the surface of the water; below, the mosaic of the Nine Fish Wealth Circle bent and twisted. I paused, gathering myself for the final push into the energy world, my whole being tensed for the presence of the Mirror Dragon. And for Ido.

The bathing room blurred. I pushed deeper into *Hua*, plunging into the swirling energy, past the gray remnants of the drugs. There was time for one quick look, and then back to safety. I narrowed my mind-sight and listened for the voice of Ido in my mind, for the iron grip of him on my body. There was nothing. Around the edge of the bath, huge densities of energy coalesced. Took form. Muzzles, eyes, horns, pearls. The dragons. I stared at the space in the circle, straining to see a hint of red scale, a glint of gold pearl. But there was still no Mirror Dragon.

"I know what you are," I whispered. "Please, forgive me. Show yourself. Give me some hope."

There was a flash of movement. The large blue head of the Rat Dragon ducked down, level with my face. I felt his energy focus on me. His power licked my wet skin, rippling across it in a wordless question. I tried to step back, but I was already hard against the wall.

"No," I said. "No."

His power kept pushing against me, a wild offering of energy, formless and never ending, ready to be molded into human desire. It was too much. It was a road straight into the heart of me that Ido could walk in a moment.

Like a distant call, I felt my right hand catch on a loose tile, an anchor to the real world. I pushed harder. The muted sting of pierced flesh dragged me away from the dragon's mesmerizing gaze. The pain sharpened and the energy world rushed past me, a maelstrom of colors: blue, pink, purple, silver, green, white. And red. My breath stopped. Had I truly seen red?

But I was already huddled alone in the bath, my hand impaled on the jagged edge of a tile, a steady drip of blood creating scarlet swirls in the water amongst the cream frangipani petals.

I stood before the dressing chamber mirror, rolling my shoulders against the weight of the Story Robe. My cut hand throbbed in its tight binding. I flexed it, trying to work some give into the bandaging.

"Be still," Rilla ordered.

She kneeled and folded the front edges of the heavy silk against my body. In the mirror, I saw the reflection of Lady Dela behind me, freshly bathed and dressed in mourning white, holding the thick Story Robe sash. Our eyes met in the glass.

"Do you remember what I told you?" she asked. "You will not have a chance to speak to the Pearl Emperor until the chorus of Beseechers has left and the Shola priests have sung their ancestry chants."

I nodded.

"When they leave, you will be alone with him for the ghost watch," she continued. "But you must not speak until he speaks to you."

"No." I shook my head. "I will tell him as soon as possible. My words are not going to please him whether I observe the protocols or not. He will either listen to me or he won't." I swallowed the sudden rise of fear. "And we can't afford to waste time."

Rilla looked up. "Do as Lady Dela says. Please. Wait until the emperor speaks. Do everything you can to protect yourself."

I touched her shoulder. "As soon as I am dressed, I want you to go. All right?" Her expression stiffened into stubborn loyalty. "You have to take Chart to safety. You promised."

She held out her hands for the sash.

"It is for the best," Lady Dela said softly as she carefully passed the silk. "This is going to end in bloodshed, whatever way it falls. You and your son are better out of it." Her dark eyes darted anxiously to me, but the prediction only confirmed what I already knew in my heart. Either the emperor quelled his uncle's ambitions with my help, or Sethon took the throne with Ido's power. Whatever happened, there would be blood.

Rilla nodded and absorbed herself in winding the sash around me.

"Are you ready to go, too?" I asked Lady Dela. "There is no guarantee that the emperor will not take his revenge on all who have helped me, whatever their status. If I do not come out of the ghost watch . . ."

"I will wait here for you to bring the red folio," she said firmly.

"And if I don't come? If Sethon and Ido have a clear way?"

"Ryko and I have a plan."

"The islands?"

She inclined her head.

Rilla sat back on her heels. "You are ready, Lord Eon," she said tightly.

I took a deep breath and looked in the mirror. I was, indeed, Lord Eon. The Story Robe had once more created the appearance of manliness in my slim body. To add to the illusion, something had stripped any last softness from my face—the Sun drug, perhaps—and the angularity echoed a new hardness that I felt within me. I lifted my chin; I did not want to give up being Lord Eon. Even with all the danger, all the despair, I had tasted power and respect. It was no wonder Ido craved it.

Rilla straightened a fold that marred the neat line at my calf, her hands suddenly bunching the silk hem. She was crying silently and without fuss. In all the time I had known Rilla, I had never seen her cry.

"It's all right," I said. A stupid, inadequate thing to say, but her tears were ripping away my hard-won composure.

She took my hand, pressing my palm against her cheek. "What you have done for Chart, for me—"

"Tell him . . ." I stopped, my throat blocked with a dry ache. There was too much to say. And nothing to say. "You may go, Rilla," I whispered, letting go of her hand. "Good luck."

She stood and bowed, her gaze meeting mine for a long, bleak moment. "Thank you, Lord Eon."

She backed away. Then she was gone.

Lady Dela sighed. "She is very devoted to you. While you were bathing, she told me how this all came about. The salt farm and Brannon's ambition."

I finally looked away from the doorway. "No doubt you found it an entertaining tale," I said, taking refuge in my flimsy shell of hardness.

"No." She faced the mirror. "I have done many things to survive. Some at least as desperate as yours." She smiled wryly. "I was very harsh in the carriage. It was the shock; you were the only hope—well, you know the burden of hope that is on you. I still think you should have confided in me and Ryko, but I understand why you acted as you did."

"Why do you still help me? I am most probably a lost cause."

She lifted her chin. "Ryko will serve you and the emperor to the end. And so will I."

The peril ahead of us pushed me into blunt advice. "You should tell Ryko that you love him."

A flush deepened the swarthiness of her unpainted skin. "A eunuch and a Contraire. How the gods would laugh," she said bitterly.

"The gods are already laughing," I said. "How else could the future of an empire rest on my shoulders?"

The old emperor's body was laid out in the Pavilion of the Five Ghosts. It was the only building in the palace complex made of precious white marble, its blank façade more imposing for its lack of carving or gilt. My protocol escorts, four of the highest-ranked eunuchs, stopped at the bottom of the nine marble steps of mourning that led to the doorway. Large brass incense burners were set to the left side of every step, the incense sticks filling the air with their heavy, melancholic perfume. Through the open doorway I could hear the soft entreaties of the Beseechers and see the flicker of their swinging lamps. Tomorrow the emperor's body would be moved to the red-and-black Audience Hall in the entrance courtyard for all to mourn. But today, it would lie here under the watchful eyes of the new emperor and his second mourner, set with the task of guarding it from the malevolent attention of bad spirits.

I looked back at Lady Dela. She had accompanied me as far as she was allowed—to the far edge of the Five Ghost Square—and now stood with the other silent courtiers, waiting for me to enter the pavilion. "I'll see you in the apartment," she had said firmly as I was ushered forward by the protocol officers. I had nodded, but we both knew that the laughter of gods did not guarantee their goodwill. Across the expanse of the square, I could not make out Lady Dela's features, but I knew from the angle of her head that she was crying.

The two officers in front of me stepped to the side and bowed.

"Please ascend, my lord," the highest-ranked man said. "His Royal Highness, the Pearl Emperor, awaits you."

I stared up the staircase at the dim arch of the double doorway. As soon as I walked into that pavilion, my life was forfeit. But I had already missed my chance of escape; it had passed me by on the sands of the Dragon Arena as I waited to make my defeated bow to an indifferent emperor. How brief and hidden were the moments of destiny. And now I faced another.

I took the first step, and then the second. Desperation has its own momentum. Now that the decision was made, I was almost impatient to meet the resolution.

But there was no hurrying destiny. I was met at the doorway by more protocol officers and led into the dim hall, past the kneeling ranks of Beseechers, the sound of their whispered entreaties made loud by sheer numbers, the swooshing swing of their lanterns an eerie counterpoint. The wrapped body of the old emperor lay on a stone bier at the end of the chamber. A low table stood beside it, set with offerings of food and wine in gold bowls and goblets.

Kneeling before his father, on a plain woven cushion, was the prince, the Pearl Emperor. He was facing the bier, his head bowed, but I could see that it had already been shaved clean with only the imperial queue, braided with gold and jewels, left at the back. My eyes followed the line of his back to his hips. He wore no sword. No knife.

He had only his hands—although, with all his training, they were lethal enough.

Another cushion lay beside him for the second mourner. Slowly, I knelt on it, the ache in my hip dogging my movements again.

"Good to have you by my side, Lord Eon." The prince's voice was hoarse and hesitant.

My gaze dropped from the tense welcome on his face to the brutal mess of dried blood and bruising at the base of his throat. The Imperial Pearl—its gold claw setting had been sewn roughly into the tender hollow between his collarbones, the wound still seeping into the white cloth of his robe.

I finally looked up and met his pained eyes, my hand going to my own throat in sympathy.

"The royal physician fled last night." He swallowed carefully. "His replacement was nervous." He managed a wry smile. "Very nervous."

"Fled?"

The smile hardened. "He will be found. You and I will have our revenge." He bowed his head again as the Beseechers ended an entreaty progression and struck the gong.

I bowed my head, too, but more to hide my shock at the change in the prince. There was something in his face and voice that made me think of Ido. I pushed back the rising fear and concentrated on the meaning behind the prince's words. He believed the royal physician had been involved in his father's death. And also my master's. Was it true? I went over and over the events leading up to his death and came no closer to a confident answer, but it kept me from dwelling on the moment when I would be alone with this new emperor.

Two hours later, the Beseechers placed their lanterns on the floor in small circles of eternity, kowtowed, and backed out of the pavilion. They were immediately replaced by the twelve Shola priests, there to sing the death chants. As we knelt through three hours of their intricate harmonies, I watched the new emperor's hands slowly bunch into white-knuckled fists. I knew he was bracing himself against the pain; there had been so many times when I had done it myself. He was suffering—and, may the gods forgive me, I found my own hope in his weakened body. Perhaps his exhaustion would give me a chance to plead my case.

The final intonations of the death chants died away into a heavy silence. Beside me, the Pearl Emperor inhaled deeply, drawing in strength to stand. There was no evidence of his pain as he rose, bowed to his dead father, and turned to face the priests. I struggled upright, bowed, then took my place at the side of the bier.

The twelve Shola priests kowtowed and left the room, leaving only the two protocol officers. But they too bowed and backed away, pulling closed the heavy doors until only the mellow light from the Beseechers' lamps lit the chamber.

The ghost watch had begun.

The Pearl Emperor rubbed wearily at his forehead. "Get us some wine, Lord Eon," he rasped, motioning toward a small alcove. "I think I will be able to drink now."

I bowed and edged over to a small table set with two gold bowls and a precious glass jug of wine.

"It is my belief that the royal physician had a hand in Lord Brannon's death," he said, gingerly holding his throat as he spoke. "And perhaps in my father's, although the canker in his leg was already poisoning him. The man will be found and he will pay for our sorrow."

I nodded.

"My messengers reported your success at Daikiko." He walked toward me. "It was well done. You have kept your side of our pact. And I will keep mine."

I picked up the jug, gripping hard to stop the trembling in my hand. The rich fruit scent of the wine swirled up to me as I poured. There was a hung quality in the air, as though time had caught its breath. I picked up the bowls.

"Your Majesty," I said, handing him the wine.

He looked into its depths, then raised his eyes to mine, waiting for me to test it. Slowly, I lifted the bowl and drank, tilting back my head until it was drained. The wine burned as it went down, but it was only the fire of alcohol. The fire of false courage.

His mouth twisted. "Habit," he said, and took a deep drink, wincing as he swallowed. "I do not mistrust you, Lord Eon."

The moment had come.

"I am not Lord Eon," I said.

He stilled. There was no immediate comprehension in his face, but he had heard the tone of betrayal. "What?"

"I am not *Lord Eon*. The Mirror Dragon is female. And so am I."

He tilted his head, his red-rimmed eyes narrowing. "Female? You are a woman?"

I gave one nod, my body tensing for the moment when he understood.

"A woman Dragoneye?"

"Yes."

He stared at me, and I could see his quick political mind forging through the shock.

"The dragon returned because you are a woman." His hand grasped my shoulder. "And you have her power. Is it greater than Ido's?"

I had not expected him to find the heart of the matter so fast.

Before I could mask my face, he saw the truth. His wine bowl hit the floor, his hand as quick as a snake strike under my jaw. In one movement, he had me up against the pavilion wall, the back of my head connecting with the marble, sending sick pain tolling through my body. His face was so close to mine I could feel the heated wine of his breath and smell the sweet decay of the blood-soaked cloth at his neck.

"Do you have power?"

My hands clawed at his fingers. He tightened his grip, his teeth bared for an answer.

"Yes," I gasped.

His eyes searched mine. "You're lying."

Desperately I pulled at his arm. "I have power, but not all of it. There's a book—"

He hauled me off the wall and slammed me back against it, the blow sending jags of black pain across my eyes. I fought for breath. For consciousness.

"Do you know what you have done?" he screamed. "Everything was balanced on you. A woman."

All of his rage was loose and slowly crushing my throat. He was going to kill me. I could see it in his face. I could not stop him. He was my emperor. My lord. My master. His will was mine.

No. Never again. My will was my own.

I let go of his arm. Curled my fingers into my bandaged palm. And with strength made of panic, drove the heel of my hand into the center of the Imperial Pearl. For a moment, I saw the pain crash through his eyes and then he hit the floor, writhing, his broken gasps ominously wet.

I looked at my hand. It was stinging from the blow, smeared with blood. Royal blood.

Holy gods. What had I done?

I fell to my knees and scrabbled across to him. He saw me coming and hit out, his fist wild, his face gray with shock.

"Your Majesty." I grabbed his flailing arms and forced them against his body, then pulled him across my lap. "Lord, forgive me." I saw a sheen of sweat on his skin. "Don't die."

"Not . . . going to . . . die." He took a deep, wavering breath, clenching his jaw with the effort. "I . . . am . . . going . . . to kill . . . you." He tried to lift his head but fell back against me.

I pulled the robe from his throat, wincing as his elbow found my ribs. Clamping his arms down harder, I checked his wound. There was fresh blood around the Imperial Pearl, but only from the edges of the stitching and the bottom of his throat hollow. If I had hit straighter, if the bandage had not cushioned the blow, I would have killed him. I must have struck downward, and the Pearl had hit his chest bone, not his windpipe. The gods had been merciful. To both of us.

"You can't kill me," I said. "You need me."

He struggled upward again, his pallor darkening into fury. He was already recovering his strength. I did not have long to make him understand.

"Listen to me. The Mirror Dragon is the queen dragon," I said desperately. "She chose me and she is ascendant. That is at least double the power of the others." His eyes flickered at that truth. "But I haven't united with her properly. Not yet. I have no way to call her power, but Ido has a book that holds her name. If I can get it, then I will have all her power. At your command."

"How . . . do you know you can call her power?"

"Because I can already call Ido's dragon."

His eyes widened. "You have Ido's . . . power, too?" He cleared his throat. His voice was stronger.

I nodded, keeping my gaze steady. It was half true. I had called the blue dragon at Ido's library. But I could not let the emperor see the other half of the truth—that Ido could steal my body, harness my will, through that connection.

He jerked free of my hands. "Get off me."

I moved out of reach as he slowly hauled himself upright. He looked over at me, his hand at his throat.

"That was a low blow." He swayed on his feet. "You have a woman's sense of honor."

His barb bit deep. "I am trying to keep our pact. Is that not honor?"

He snorted. "'Mutual survival'? You nearly killed me."

"As you did me."

"You're right." He laughed, the sound breaking into a cough. "But then, I am your emperor."

"And I am the only hope you have of keeping your throne."

His lingering smile shifted into harsher lines. "A woman Dragoneye." His eyes scanned my body and I felt heat rush to my face. "My father warned me to watch for men's hidden natures," he said, "but I am sure he had not reckoned on something like you. Why should I believe that you hold my interests? You are obviously a skilled liar."

I bit my lip. "I am here in front of you. I could be halfway to the islands."

He tilted his head in acknowledgment. "True. But I would say your presence is as much in your interest as mine. I have no doubt Lord Ido would hunt down a woman who could poach his power." He paused. "How did you move the King Monsoon? Did you use his power?"

I clutched the silk of the Story Robe. *A skilled liar.* "Yes."

"Then you have made a very dangerous enemy." He motioned for me to stand. "Which is better for me. I trust your fear and self-interest more than I trust your sense of honor, Lord Eon." He caught himself. "But of course you are not Lord Eon. What is your real name?"

I felt my skin flush again. I did not want to be a girl before him. I did not want to become less. "It would be easier if I remained Lord Eon, Your Majesty. I will need the rank it gives until—"

"Until you have your power, or you are dead," he said. "Those are the options I give you, *Lord Eon.*"

I nodded. "They have always been my options, Your Majesty."

He walked over to the table. "You say Ido has a book?"

"It is the Mirror Dragon folio. The only record of the dragon. He stole it from the treasures before they came to me."

"So Prahn was not mistaken." He poured wine into another bowl, his hand shaking. "If Ido has it, he must already know its secrets."

"No. I don't think so." Hesitantly I walked toward him, but he did not stop me. "It is written in Woman Script."

He grunted. "Stands to reason." He raised the bowl to drink, stopping halfway as he saw my surprise. "My mother—my true mother—showed me a few of the characters." He threw back the wine, wincing as he swallowed. "I have always wondered why the Mirror Dragon left the circle. Why *she*"—he met my eyes in fleeting acceptance—"was not in any records. Perhaps your book will tell us."

"Your Majesty, I don't know why she left us. But I do know that your uncle and Ido have plans to challenge your claim. We need to move quickly to retrieve the book." There were no windows in the pavilion to gauge if it was night or day. I quickly estimated the time that had passed. "The Dragoneyes will be back from Daikiko by now. Ido should be in his hall."

"Leave the ghost watch?" He looked over at the bier. "No, you are right. My father would have understood the urgency. We must ride to Ido's hall now and demand the book. He will obey his emperor."

I was not so certain. Nor did I want to face Ido again.

"No, Your Majesty. You must stay safe. I will go, with Ryko." I paused, realizing I did not know if he was back or would even agree to accompany me. "We know where it will be."

"You will obey your emperor, Lord Eon," he said coldly. "I will go to the Rat Dragon Halls and we will finish this business." He started toward the double doors. "Come."

At least we were moving. But toward what?

CHAPTER TWENTY

I STEPPED BACK AS the imperial guard led the horse around to me. The animal's heavy chestnut shoulder was at the same level as my neck, its tossing head a big wedge of unpredictability. Another guard knelt beside it, blithely ignoring the fidgeting hooves, waiting to boost me up into the saddle. The emperor turned his own horse, peering down at me in the torchlight.

"What are you waiting for, Lord Eon?"

"Your Majesty, I don't know how—" I jumped back as the horse blew impatiently.

"I see. You could have told me sooner." From his high vantage point, the emperor looked around at the assembled guards. "I take it your man can ride."

"Yes."

He motioned to Ryko. "Take your master up behind you."

Ryko strode forward, his eyes sliding over mine as he approached the horse. When the emperor and I had emerged prematurely from the Pavilion of Five Ghosts, I had found Ryko waiting in the square. He'd kept his word and returned to guard me, but we had not spoken beyond orders and his manner was still cold. Deftly, he unbuckled and removed the elaborate saddle, then nodded to the guard who was waiting to boost him onto the animal's back. He was mounted in a moment.

The imperial guard had stayed in position for me. Gingerly, I stepped on his offered knee. As I balanced, unsure what to do next, Ryko grabbed my arm and pulled me up, dumping me onto the horse behind him. I caught the flash of teeth as some of the foot guards struggled to hide their smiles.

"Hold me around the waist," Ryko said shortly. "And do not dig your knees too hard into the beast."

I gripped his shoulder with one hand, trying to arrange the heavy silk of my robe into a workable position. After the days of relentless protocol and sadness, the emperor had been eager for some action and would not even delay for the change of clothing urged on him by the flustered protocol officers. Nor had he offered me a sword from his armorer. Already I was less than Lord Eon.

Ryko reached back for my hands and placed them around his middle. I could smell the tang of his sweat and feel the hard muscles of his body tensing to keep us both seated.

"Hold on or you will fall."

I jerked against him as the horse moved. The only way to

manage was to cram myself against Ryko's back. I slid forward and pressed myself closer, knowing the intimacy was as unwanted for him as it was for me.

As we fell in behind the emperor's eight-horse elite escort, I could not bear Ryko's hostility or silent reproach any longer.

"I am sorry," I said. "I am sorry I did not tell you. I am sorry I am not what you wanted."

He turned his head, bright anger in his eyes. "This is not something that can be forgiven with a laugh and a shrug," he said. "We are on a tipping point between enlightenment and the old dark times. You have pushed us back toward that darkness."

I felt my own anger build. "Do you think that was my aim? Do you think that one day I decided to take on a dangerous masquerade"—I looked around, lowering my voice—"a dangerous masquerade to plunge this land into ruin?"

"I don't care about your aim. It is the result that is my concern." He turned away.

"The result is not yet decided," I said. "What do you think I am doing now? I risked my life to tell the emperor the truth, and now I risk it again to get the folio back and claim the Mirror Dragon. I am still here and I am doing everything I can. You know I have power. I saved your life with it, and maybe I can stop Ido and Sethon with it. At least give me that. At least give me the chance to prove my worth."

He was silent, then I felt the rise and fall of a deep sigh.

"Yes," he conceded. "You have power. And you are here. But as to your worth . . ." His shoulder twitched.

"You think that because I am female, I will fail?" I demanded, close to his ear.

"A female dragon," he said, the words hardly more than a vibration. I leaned even closer to catch them. "And a female Dragoneye. Gone for more than five hundred years and then suddenly returned. Lady Dela and the emperor are both ready to jump on the small hope you offer." He turned back to me. His eyes no longer held anger; they were flat with suspicion. "I am no scholar, but I am not so sure. I cannot help wondering—does such a strange union brings us good, or does it bring us evil?"

"You think me evil? Some kind of demon?" I could not keep the hurt out of my voice.

"I don't know what you are. But you are not truthful, and I don't think you are telling us the whole truth even yet." He faced the front again. "Know that I will be watching you, Lord Eon, or whoever you are. And I will not hesitate to protect the interests of the emperor."

I sat back, winded by his words.

We were crossing the expanse of the audience courtyard, approaching the huge Gate of Supreme Benevolence. The side Gates of Humility were already closed to the populace and the night lanterns lit, so only a few lower officials were crossing the large paved area to the galleries on either side. They fell to their knees and kowtowed as their new emperor rode past. It would not take long for the news to spread that the Pearl Emperor had abandoned his duties as a son and ridden out with his guards— and Lord Eon.

The Way of Heavenly Conduct, the massive center gate

reserved for His Majesty, was already being opened. The porters in charge of the Judgment Gate hurried to open the elaborate gilded grilles, while the men keeping the two smaller Gates of Humility were being roused by the cries of the foot soldiers. As the emperor and his elite guard rode through the central vaulted passageway, Ryko steered our horse through the Judgment Gate in deference to my rank. The horse's hooves clattered on the tiled floor, and for a brief moment, I caught the magnificence of the painted dragons on the gold stuccoed walls and the etched red lacquered ceiling. Then we were out again, taking our place among the columns of horsemen and foot guards behind the emperor and his elite.

There was no delay. Even as the last men were marching through the Gates of Humility, we were riding along the avenue that cut through the Emerald Ring gardens and led to the Dragon Circle and the twelve Dragon Halls. I clung to Ryko as the horse quickened into a trot, my rump bones thudding into its back in the wrong rhythm. In the absorbed minute or so as I tried to synchronize my movements with the animal's stride, I missed the tiny event that sent a ripple of unease through the company. All I knew was that Ryko's back suddenly tensed, and ahead, the captain of the guards halted our progress. Around us the men stopped, hands immediately going to their bows, eyes watching every shadow in the lush gardens to our left and right.

"What is it?" I whispered as Ryko reined in the horse.

He nodded to the horizon. A faint glow brightened the night sky. "Fire."

It was close enough to be in the Dragon Circle precinct. "A hall?" The nearest was the Ox Dragon Hall. Were Lord Tyron and Hollin all right?

The captain had already turned his horse to come alongside the emperor. They spoke in voices so low that only the sibilance reached us. Then the captain nodded and motioned us forward. Ryko maneuvered our beast past the elite guard, who were already surrounding the emperor in a protective formation.

"Lord Eon," the Captain said, briefly bowing his head. For a Shadow Man he was very lean, his authority and experience etched deeply in the lines around his eyes and mouth. He turned his attention to Ryko. "You saw?"

Ryko grunted.

"It is in the opposite direction from the Rat Dragon Hall," the captain said. "His Majesty has commanded us to continue."

Ryko stared over at the strange light again. "I don't like it," he said. "It reminds me of the Bano Pass."

The captain nodded, rubbing his chin. They obviously had some shared history. "My own thoughts exactly. But we cannot gainsay the emperor on a phantom from the past. I'll send scouts and we will continue—but at the first sign of something amiss, we will put the safety strategy in place."

"Understood," Ryko said. "But whatever the case, Lord Eon and I will be going on to the Rat Dragon Hall."

The captain nodded and urged his horse along the column of silent men. At his signal, four foot guards broke away from the group and headed into the gardens, avoiding a curved walking path lit with white mourning lanterns.

"What do you think it is?" I asked Ryko as we moved off again.

"Quiet," he ordered. His head was tilted, listening. We rode on, unease building with every step. Finally, the intersection of the Dragon Circle appeared over a slight rise.

Ryko straightened. "Do you hear?"

I struggled to find something above the hooves and footsteps and muffled jangling of our troop. A faint sound, more a disturbance in the air, finally separated from the background noise.

"What is it?" I whispered.

I felt the tension in Ryko's body grow. He bundled the reins into one hand, dropping the other to his sword. We had arrived at the junction, the broad paved Dragon Circle curving to our left and right. Kicking more speed from the horse, Ryko took us around the corner level with the two rear guards of the emperor's escort.

Without the buffer of the gardens on either side, the disturbance suddenly hardened into the faint but unmistakable metal clashes of combat. Ryko pulled the horse around just as one of the scouts broke out of the garden to our right and ran along the edge of the green, his hand held up in a signal.

Ryko squinted into the dim light. "Army," he breathed. He leaned forward as the man came closer, the signal changing into a closed fist. "Attacking."

The captain pulled his horse up beside us, the brutal stop

curling the animal's head to its chest. "Army attacking the Dragon Halls? It can't be."

The scout ran up to us. "Captain, High Lord Sethon's army have taken the Ox Dragon Hall and the Tiger Dragon Hall," he panted. "And I saw one battalion at the north entrance to the inner precinct."

"What about Lord Tyron?" I asked.

The scout shook his head. "Dead, my lord. I saw him beheaded on the roadside. And his apprentice."

"No," I said. "No."

The scout bowed. "I saw it, my lord. The Tiger Dragoneye and his boy, too. But it was not Sethon's men who killed them."

"Who, then?" I demanded.

"They wore no colors."

The captain scanned the dark road behind us. "Sethon must have circled the inner precinct."

"He is not waiting for the formal challenge," Ryko said. "He is going to take the throne by force."

"With Ido's help," I said.

"Then they'll only attack the Dragoneyes loyal to the emperor," the captain said. He looked down at his scout. "Take your best and get to the palace and warn them. And any of the halls that are not breached." The man nodded and ran to his waiting men. The captain dragged his horse around. "I'm getting His Majesty out of here. Do you come with us?"

Ryko shook his head.

The captain gave one quick nod. "Good luck, then. You

know where we will be, Ryko." He kicked his beast forward, calling the command.

For a moment, I saw the pale face of the emperor look back at me, and then his horse was herded along the road by his guards, the group breaking into a gallop.

Something about the scout's report seemed wrong. He'd said Lord Elgon was dead too, but the Tiger Dragoneye was Sethon's man. Why would Ido kill Elgon? My lingering unease mushroomed into horror.

Ido was killing them all. He was building the String of Pearls.

I clutched Ryko's arm. "It is not Sethon killing the Dragoneyes loyal to the emperor," I said. "It is Ido. He is killing *all* the Dragoneyes."

Ryko turned to stare at me. "All of them?" he echoed. "Why would he do that? It would be madness."

It *was* madness. The madness of a man who would be emperor.

"The black folio we saw in his library—it holds the secret to a terrible weapon. Ido thinks that if he kills all the Dragoneyes, he will have that weapon."

Ryko grabbed me by the front of my robe, his sleeve falling back to show the knife strapped to his arm. "Is there anything else I need to know, *Lord* Eon?" he said through his teeth. Our horse sidled nervously across the paving. Ryko tightened the reins and his grip on me, holding both of us in rigid control.

"He thinks I am the key to the weapon," I gasped. "He will

come looking for me. I must have my power to hold him off. That is the truth, I swear."

He released me, his face tight with disgust. "Always half the story. Never the whole." He pulled the horse around. "We will go through the Ox hunting forest."

"What about Lord Tyron," I said. "What about Hollin?"

"You heard the scout," Ryko said. "They are dead. And if you are right, then Ido's assassins will be in every other hall." He gave a short, bitter laugh. "It seems the Rat Dragon Hall is the safest place to be."

He angled his body over the horse's neck, the animal responding with a lurch into more speed. I wrapped my arms around Ryko's waist, praying I would not fall. We would not be on the animal for much longer—the Rat Dragon Hall was the next in the Circle.

A change of gait forced my eyes open. We had dropped to a walk and were heading into the dense cover of the hunting forest. Only a few weeks ago, Ryko was carrying me through the same forest on his back, his friendship and support a steadfast mooring in the treacherous court, the retrieval of the folio a bright hope. Now, here I was again, Ryko more foe than friend, that bright hope worn down by doubt and desperation. We were heading toward the end play, and I was either going to walk away with the Mirror Dragon's power or I was going to die. With Sethon's army marching on the palace and Ido's men murdering the Dragoneyes, the latter seemed more likely. The bleak thought settled in my gut like a midwinter freeze.

The horse pushed through the low outlying scrub into the thick undergrowth and trees. Ryko reined it in behind a dense copse of bushes.

"Off," he whispered.

I edged back and hoisted my bad leg over the side of the beast, sliding down in a tangle of emerald silk robe. I hit the ground and stumbled on the uneven surface, landing on my hands and knees with a soft grunt.

He landed lightly beside me and motioned me to sit. "Wait."

I sat, more from a sudden trembling in my thighs than from obedience. Silently, he led the horse into the bushes. I dug my hand into the joint of my hip, massaging the hot pain. The ride and the sudden lack of Sun drug had made the ache flare into stabbing agony.

It seemed an age before Ryko squatted beside me. He placed his finger across his lips, then pointed to our left and held up two fingers.

"Two men?" I mouthed.

He shook his head. I watched his lips. *Twenty.*

The air around me contracted.

He touched my arm and pointed to our right, planing his hand low along the ground. We were going to crawl to the Dragon Halls? Ahead of twenty soldiers? I doubted my hip would last the distance. I looked at the cold professionalism in Ryko's face. He would carry me if I asked, but I would do this myself. I would prove I was still Lord Eon.

Ryko rose and moved silently into a gap in the undergrowth. I followed him along a sliver of overgrown track that was made more from his imagination than cleared foliage. I was already sweating in the heavy Story Robe, but at least it was mostly dark green and blended into the night colors. Every now and again, Ryko stopped and listened, his face growing grimmer. My ears were not as well trained; all I heard were the calls of animals and the brush of leaves and branches. But by the way he quickened our pace, the soldiers were gaining ground.

Then I heard it; the crack of a breaking branch.

Ryko pulled me down into the dirt and leaves.

I held my breath, squinting into the darkness. I couldn't see anyone. My senses reached out; the smell of our sweat, the hard jab of twigs in my flesh, the sour taste of fear. Beside me, I heard the *snick* of Ryko's arm blades springing from their sheaths. Then his hand was on mine, laying a knife in it, closing my fingers around the handle. I met his eyes. Was it to fight with, or die by? But all I saw was the hunter in his face.

He turned his head to the left, to the right, listening.

A soft guttural call. From our right. It came again.

Suddenly he threw back his head and copied it, a broad smile cutting the sound short.

Around us, shadows in the undergrowth surged and shifted into human shapes.

"For the Pearl Emperor," a voice whispered.

"Solly?"

"Ryko?"

A face appeared in a gap in the undergrowth—pig eyed, big

jawed, with a broken-toothed smile. I lurched back, holding up my knife. Was it some kind of demon?

"Ryko, you scared the piss out of us," the face whispered. "We thought you were army scouts." It was just a man, although the ugliest I had ever seen. I lowered the blade with relief. Ryko's resistance.

"I didn't know if you'd make it," Ryko said.

"Nearly didn't. Not sure how many of the others got through."

"Solly, I have Lord Eon with me," Ryko said quickly.

So, he had not told them the truth about me. Who was only giving half the story now?

Solly's tiny eyes widened. "Lord Eon?" He quickly bobbed into a fervent bow. "My lord, an honor."

I nodded, transfixed by the man's ugliness.

"I counted you as twenty," Ryko said. "Is that right? Are you all armed?"

Solly held up a large metal hook and grinned. "All armed. What do you need?"

"We must get to the Rat Dragon Hall and then back to the palace."

"We'll get you there," Solly said. He turned to me, bobbing his head again. "We'll get you there, Lord Eon."

"Thank you, Solly," I said. "You're from the Island Resistance, aren't you?"

"Yes, my lord. We came when Ryko here called." His smile shifted into a strange shyness. "We all know you're the one who's got the way of beating Sethon. We'll serve you, lord. To the death. For the Pearl Emperor."

"For the Pearl Emperor," I said.

"Let's get going," Ryko said sourly. "Solly, fan out. Once we get to the wall, stay hidden. And send someone back for our horse."

Solly turned to his men and issued soft instructions as Ryko held out his hand to me. I pushed it away and stood, straightening the Story Robe.

"Here," I said, offering him the knife.

He stared down at it. "Have you ever stabbed anyone?"

"No."

"This is the best place." His hand lightly touched the top of my sash, over the delta of charisma. "Aim up and you'll reach the heart. The knife is long enough." He turned away. "Thrust hard and do not be surprised by the resistance of skin and muscle."

A memory leaped forward: Ryko ramming a blade up under Ranne's armor. Was this the knife that had killed Ranne? Pushing away the dark memory, I carefully secured the knife between the thick folds of my sash.

Solly ordered his men into their positions. I followed Ryko as he started the push through the undergrowth, taking some solace in the fact that our backs were now well guarded. The brief stop had rested my hip, but there was nothing I could do to ease the pain caused by Ryko's relentless pace. If someone had offered me a dose of Sun drug, I would have eaten it dry.

I was wheezing by the time we broke out into the sparser

covering opposite the Rat Dragon Hall. Ryko signaled to Solly, and he and his men suddenly seemed to blend back into the denser foliage. I peered into the shadows. There was no sign of them, although I knew they were in there somewhere, watching and waiting for our return. It was a comforting thought.

Ryko scanned the top of the huge wall. "We'll go through the same gate as before." He looked at me more intently. "Are you all right?"

I nodded, taking two deep breaths before managing to say. "It will be locked."

He shrugged. "Locks are no problem. It is the number of guards that worry me."

"Most of them will be"—I forced out the words—"at the other Dragoneye Halls."

Ryko's face held the same haunted question as my own: How many of the Dragoneyes were already dead?

"Come on," he said. "Keep low."

We crossed the dangerously open space between forest and hall, making for the safety of the shadow cast by the wall. I hit the rough stone with my back, gulping for air, but Ryko was already moving toward the gate set farther along the wall. I stayed pressed against the wall. He would need time to pick the lock—time I could use to recover.

Slowly, my heartbeat evened out. Ryko was still crouched in front of the gate lock. I crept along the wall, watching him work with the focus of a craftsman. The small hiatus had crowded my mind with the problems that faced us. Had Lord Ido returned the folio to his library? How were we going to get back to the palace? And was it even going to be possible to reach Lady Dela?

I stopped at Ryko's side. "Nearly there," he whispered.

The mechanism clicked. He smiled, then pulled the two pieces of wire out of the lock and turned the latch, easing the metal gate open. I held my breath as he stepped through the narrow opening. He beckoned me through.

I slipped through the space and followed Ryko up the long alleyway. We pressed ourselves against the stone wall, watching. The courtyard was lit as it had been before, the yellowish light from the bronze lamps casting deep shadows across the kumquat trees. But the sounds of normal hall life were absent. Even the kitchens were dark. I shifted until the arch of the back corridor came into my line of sight. Beyond that was the library. And—I hoped—the folio.

Ryko leaned his head back against the wall. "Either the household has fled or they have moved to a safer location," he said. "It is possible Lord Ido has not been back here."

I looked at him, aghast. "Then the folio will still be with him."

Ryko nodded. I tried to breathe through the swell of desperation. How was I going to get the folio away from Ido without calling on the Rat Dragon?

"We have to check the library," I said. "Just in case."

He eyed me, unconvinced. "Every moment we waste is costing lives."

"We have to check it," I insisted.

Ryko studied the courtyard again. "Come on."

Bending low, I followed Ryko to the row of kumquats, then across to the archway. Nothing moved or made a sound. At the end of the passageway, we stopped and studied the garden in front of us. This time there were no Twelfth Day festival lamps in the blossom trees. There were no lamps at all; the path was lit only by the weak moonlight that silvered paving and pond. The smell of jasmine was strong in the air, and beyond the bridge and pavilion, I could make out the hulking shadow of the library.

"Not all the household has left," Ryko said quietly.

I peered into the garden, finally making out the figures of two guards near the pavilion.

Ryko held out his hand. "Give me the knife."

I pulled it free from my sash and passed it to him.

"Do you remember Solly's call?" he asked, releasing the other blade from its arm sheath. I nodded. "When you hear it, come to the library."

Soundlessly, he ran across the grass, blending into the shadows. I listened for his call, knowing that two men were about to die. So many people were dying for this scramble for power. In my mind, I saw a sick imagining of Lord Tyron's head falling from his shoulders. I shook off the raw images. Better to think of what we had to do: Get the folio. Get the power. Stop Ido.

Or did I really mean *kill Ido?*

Kill him, or be killed.

Kill or be killed.

Then I heard something—a hollow grunt. Not the call.

Some part of me knew what it was, but I didn't want to think about it.

Another sound. This time it was the signal.

I crossed the grass in a limping lope. It was too dim to clearly see the ground, so I jumped real and imagined dips and rocks. I passed the pavilion and joined the pathway, running more easily on the smoother surface. Up ahead, the library loomed with two dark shapes on the ground. Two slumped bodies. I focused on Ryko standing on the path and tried to ignore the silhouettes at the corner of my vision.

"The dragon's illusion is still in place," he said as I reached him. "I'll need your help." He held out his hand.

I hesitated. I did not have the red folio with me, and it was too dangerous to force a connection with the Rat Dragon. There was only one way to find out if I could still protect Ryko. I grabbed his hand and pulled him into the protected area. We both froze, waiting. He blew out a relieved breath, the illusion obviously held at bay.

"You didn't look convinced," he said dryly.

"I don't know how it works," I admitted.

He grunted and pulled me forward. We ran the distance to the metal library door. As before, it was padlocked. This time, however, Ryko was not writhing in pain, unable to pick it. He knelt and, with my hand gripping his shoulder for protection, deftly manipulated a thin piece of metal into the lock. The mechanism released with a satisfying click.

He glanced up at me. "Luckily, *one* of us knows how things

work." Pocketing the piece of metal, he unhooked the padlock and pushed open the door, quickly stepping into the safety of the dark passage.

Ahead was the inner door. The twelve-circle design etched on its surface was barely discernible in the dim light that spread from under its base. Someone had left lamps burning inside. Ever cautious, Ryko stood in front of the door and listened. I heard the *siss* of sliding metal and looked down. His knife was back in his hand. Had he heard something inside? He saw the question on my face and shook his head. Pressing the latch, he sent the door swinging soundlessly open.

Blue carpet, huge reading table, stacks of wooden scroll boxes along the wall, and that same sour resonance of power. Nothing seemed to have changed from our last visit, except this time the oil lamps were lit, giving the room a mellow warmth. Ryko stepped across the threshold.

"It'll be at the back," I said, following him, "I'll get—"

He came from the left, head down, straight into Ryko.

The low tackle sent them crashing into the wall of scrolls. Boxes and parchments spun into the air, smashing down around me. Ryko wrenched his attacker to the floor, landing on top. I saw a flash of a sickly, desperate face—Dillon. Ryko lifted his knife, his other hand holding my friend's throat.

I lunged, catching Ryko's foot. "Stop! It's Dillon!"

Ryko froze, knife still poised for the downthrust.

"I thought you were him," Dillon gasped. "I thought you were him."

"Ido?" Ryko's face was still tense with fight.

Dillon nodded. Ryko let go of his throat and lowered the knife. Suddenly, he grabbed Dillon's jaw, ignoring the boy's terrified flinch, and turned his face to the light. Dillon's skin was yellowed, even the whites of his eyes, and the rash on his neck was twice the size. He struggled under Ryko's hand.

"Let go of me."

"Steady," Ryko said, releasing him. "You've got Sun drug poisoning. Any more and it's going to kill you."

"It doesn't matter." Dillon caught Ryko's wrist in a trembling grip. "He's going to kill me anyway. He's going to kill all the Dragoneyes." His eyes found mine, but there was nothing left of Dillon, only mad hate. "He told me what you are, what he's going to do with you. You've brought disaster on us all." He lurched at me, his hands clawed. Ryko grabbed his shoulder.

"The drug's got hold of him," Ryko said to me. "Get the book. We need to get out of here."

Shocked by Dillon's venom, I stumbled to my feet and threaded past the reading table. Behind me, I heard Ryko reassuring Dillon that we'd get him out, and Dillon's voice, quick and fevered, ranting about Ido's power. The grating energy in the room pressed into the base of my skull. No doubt Dillon was feeling its effects, too.

I ran up to the plain wooden case at the end of the room. Some defeated part of me expected the red folio to be missing. Like my dragon.

But it was there, next to the black folio. I shivered; even the sight of the other book sickened me. I pushed the glass lid back on its hinges and grabbed the red volume. As though suddenly woken from sleep, the black pearls around it stirred, then burrowed into my wide sleeve, binding the folio against my arm in their tight clicking embrace. The surge of victory made me sway. The book was mine, not Ido's.

I stroked the tail of dusky pearls, trying to ignore the darker presence still in the case. But I knew what I had to do. I reached in with my left hand, hesitating over the black leather. The white pearls around it shifted. I remembered Ryko's yelp when he'd reached for the folio—but I couldn't leave it here.

I snatched up the book and held it at arms length, bracing myself for the stinging lash. The pearls reared, curled, then suddenly swarmed up over my silk sleeve, binding the black folio to me.

"Have you got it?" Ryko demanded.

"Yes," I said, my voice cracking. Why hadn't the white pearls attacked me? Gingerly, I poked the rope of gems. They tightened.

"Then let's get out of here," he said. He pulled Dillon to his feet. The boy held himself as if something was very wrong inside.

"I'm all right," Dillon said roughly, pushing Ryko's hands off him.

The islander stepped back. "I take it you can get through the Rat Dragon's illusion?"

Dillon's voice was low and vicious. "Ido may be draining my connection, but I can still call my dragon."

They both turned as I walked stiffly up to them.

"He's draining your power?" I asked. Was that what he had done to me? Was it something he could do to anyone?

Dillon nodded and pointed at the black folio. "He learned it from that." Then he smiled, his teeth bared like an injured animal. "He won't like losing it."

Ryko eyed the folio uneasily. "Well, it's good that we have it now. Perhaps it can be used against him."

He herded us toward the door. Dillon forged ahead, eager to be out of his prison. I followed him, with Ryko bringing up the rear. The pressure in my head slowly eased as I got further along the stone corridor. Just as we stepped outside, I felt Ryko grip my shoulder.

Then something hit me in the chest, crushing the breath out of me. I fell to my hands and knees. I had no air. Through a haze of panic, I saw Ryko writhing in agony, caught in the Rat Dragon's illusions. A sharp pain seared through my arm. I tried to find the breath to scream.

"Let go of it!" My eyes focused; it was Dillon, shouting at me, pulling at the black folio.

Dillon had hit me.

My chest finally opened. I sucked in a deep breath. He swung his leg over my body and straddled my chest, his fingers digging under the white pearls.

"What are you doing?" I gasped, bucking under him. He landed heavily on my hips, sending a spear of pain streaking down my bad leg.

"I need something he wants." He worked his fingers in deeper. "Something to bargain with."

His stupidity forced a rush of angry energy through me. "Bargain?" I yelled. "You idiot!"

I swung my fist at his face. He jerked his head back, my blow skimming his ear. With the strength of madness, he forced my hand down and clamped it under his knee. Out of the corner of my eye, I saw Ryko crawling toward us, his eyes bulging with agony.

"Ido's not going to bargain with you," I spat. "He's going to kill you."

"That's why I need the book." His grip was like a vise. He hauled on the pearls and I felt their hold slip.

"No. You need to come with us."

"You?" he sneered. "A girl? A pretend Dragoneye? I know all about you." He had one coil of pearls off my arm. "You haven't got a chance against him." He closed his eyes and took a deep breath. He was going to call the Rat Dragon.

"No," I screamed. Surely Ido would sense him.

Suddenly, the whole rope released. Dillon fell back, the black folio in his hands. He scrabbled away, hugging the book to his chest, the white pearls whipping like an angry tail.

Near me, Ryko groaned, his face a dull gray. He was fighting the illusion, but it was too strong. Dillon was already on his feet, running. I froze, caught between the two.

I struggled onto my knees and flung myself across Ryko's back. I felt the pain snap out of his body. Across the garden,

Dillon pounded over the bridge and headed toward the archway. I bowed my head. The black folio was gone.

"You should have run after him," Ryko finally said. I rolled off his back, keeping my hand on the flat of his shoulder blade. He looked up at me, his gaze steady. "You should have run after him. But I'm glad you stayed."

CHAPTER TWENTY-ONE

I STROKED THE BLACK pearls hidden under my sleeve, trying to ease their hold as I strained to hear Solly's low voice. The explosions and cries of battle seemed unnervingly close to our position in the forest, although Solly assured us that most of the fighting was at the palace wall. Beside me, Ryko held our horse by its bridle, ignoring the animal's nervous mouthing as he concentrated on Solly's report.

"All the roads up to the palace are held by the army," Solly said softly. His small eyes had almost disappeared under the heavy fold of his frown. "The gardens are crawling with 'em, too. It looks like the guard are holding 'em out of the palace for now, but—"

"Not for long," Ryko finished. He pressed his lips together, considering. "We could go out into the city and come back into the Dragon Circle closer to the apartment precinct." He shook his head. "But who knows what we will find in the city, and we'd lose the advantage of your reconnaissance."

"Through the gardens, then," Solly said, nodding in the direction of the Emerald Ring.

"Did your men see a break in the lines anywhere?"

Solly shrugged. "Not so much a break, more a thinner spread of men at the gate in the West. It was still being held by the imperial guard when you went into the hall. "

Ryko grunted. "Gate of Good Service. That's our entry point, then. Lord Eon and I will ride up as close as we can. But we'll need a diversion."

Solly grinned. "We've got a few ideas in mind."

"I almost pity Sethon's men," Ryko said. He gripped Solly's shoulder. "We have to get Lord Eon into the palace. At all cost."

Solly sent me a reassuring smile. "Don't worry, my lord. We'll get you in there."

A murmur of agreement rose from the men standing nearby.

I nodded, such undeserved loyalty constricting my throat. Some of these men would die—perhaps all. May the gods give me as much courage and honor.

"Let's move," Ryko said. He pushed the horse's head around, leading the animal toward the road.

Solly's hands moved in a series of quick signals, sending his men in various directions around us. I turned and followed Ryko, my dread suddenly overlaid by a frisson of excitement.

Ryko stood next to the horse in the last heavy cover of undergrowth, surveying the gardens. Directly across from us was a path lit by lanterns that hung from ropes strung between poles. My breath caught as the distant figures of soldiers crossed into the light and out again. Then, like shadows, I saw two of Solly's men rise from the ground and run into the dark foliage.

"We'll avoid the pathways as much as possible," Ryko said, "but at some point we are going to hit the road that leads up to the gate, and it will be as well lit as that pathway ahead." He drew his sword from its scabbard, the metal sliding soundlessly past the metal mouth. Greased for silent death. "Do you think you can use this and still keep your seat?" He held it out grip first. The weight caught me off guard. It was twice as heavy as my ceremonial swords.

I readjusted my hands on the hilt. "I have no battle training."

Ryko smiled. "I know. I want you to cut those ropes as we pass, so the lanterns drop. Otherwise, we might as well carry our own torch to give the bowmen a better chance of hitting us."

"Cut them as we pass?" It was hard enough to stay on the beast, let alone swing a full-sized sword at the same time. "Yes, I can do that," I said, but even I heard the doubt in my voice.

"We have a good chance of making it through," Ryko said encouragingly. He held out his hand and I returned the sword, watching him effortlessly resheathe it. "The concentration of soldiers will be at the palace wall and gates," he continued. "There will still be rear guard, but I have worked with Solly and his men before. They have a few tricks that will startle even Sethon's best." He nodded to me. "Ready?"

"Ready."

He stroked the horse's neck and gripped its shoulders, springing up and straddling it with a soft grunt of effort. Settling himself and the horse, he held out his hand. I grabbed it and was hoisted up behind him, the sinews in my shoulder burning with the sudden pull.

I found my seat and my grip around Ryko's waist; then there was a lurch and a moment of fear as we broke cover. Ryko urged the horse onto the lower servants' track, kicking it into a canter.

"Watch ahead," he ordered, his own attention on the gardens to our right. I peered over his shoulder, breathless from the smooth speed of the horse. We were backtracking toward the Ox Dragon Hall.

I eyed the gardens flashing past us. Lots of cover. Solly said the Emerald Ring was crawling with soldiers, but surely it would be better than being out in the open like this? I felt Ryko pull up on the reins as we approached a curve in the road. Parts of the walls and the top of the hall were already visible. We both stiffened as a terrible keening rose in the air, like some demon call from the otherworld.

"What is it?" I gasped.

Ryko yanked the horse across the rough servants' track and plunged us into the bushes, reining the animal into a standstill. I could feel Ryko's breath coming as hard as my own.

I slid to the ground, a terrible intuition driving me forward.

"What are you doing?" Ryko demanded.

But I was already on my hands and knees, crawling through the undergrowth toward the sound. I had to see them. I scrabbled up an incline, my robe catching under my knees and dragging at my throat. In my sleeve, the black pearls tightened protectively around the red folio. A misjudged handhold jabbed a stone into the bandaged gash on my hand. I stifled a yelp. Not that anyone could have heard me over the piercing wail from the roadside.

One last push through a line of bushes and I saw them. Straight ahead, dark shapes on the ground, grotesquely truncated. And people—three servant women—kneeling beside them, wailing for the dead. I flattened myself, my eyes drawn inexorably to the separated heads. One was turned away, surrounded by a glistening dark puddle. The other stared up into the night. It was hard to recognize the features in the weak moonlight—death had dragged down forehead, cheek, jowl into a parody of sadness. But as my mind fitted life back into the mask, I knew it was Hollin. And the heavy body next to it was Tyron's. I recognized the clothing. I clamped my teeth down over my own howl. The last hope that I was wrong—that Ido was not killing the other Dragoneyes—was gone.

"Shut those bitches up," a harsh voice yelled. "Get the corpses off the road."

A soldier came into view. I eased myself back into the

bushes as another five men appeared and kicked away the women, herding them from the bodies.

Every part of me wanted to run screaming to Ryko, but I forced myself to move slowly and silently back over the same ground, every sense reaching behind me for signs that I was being pursued.

Ryko was still on the horse. He glared down at me as I stumbled out of the undergrowth, but whatever he saw in my face tempered his tongue. He pulled me up behind him again. The warmth of his body against mine felt like some kind of talisman against death.

"I'm sorry," I whispered against his back as we rode deeper into the gardens. "I had to see." I pressed my forehead against his shoulder. "They were just left on the roadside."

"Try not to dwell on it," he said gruffly.

Good advice, but the images rose up out of the shadows as we passed: slack features, dark puddles, staring eyes. I was aware of the horse's gait, heard Ryko's breathing, felt his tension as he pulled us away from the path of soldiers, but my eyes were full of dead friends, and my mind caught in a silent chant of guilt.

It was only when Ryko reined us to a sudden stop that I realized we were behind the pavilion near the Gate of Good Service. Up ahead, white mourning lanterns hung along the path like a row of small moons. A resonating thud, mixed with shouts and clanging, told me we were close to the wall. How could we have come so near and not been seen? The answer was on the ground, just beyond the pavilion: two dead army lookouts.

Dark shapes separated from the small building and ran to us—Solly and two of his men. They all bobbed in quick bows.

"They've taken the battering ram to the gate," Solly whispered. "Nearly through. It could be your chance."

Ryko steadied the horse. "Bowmen?"

Solly grimaced. "A full complement, but their attention is on the wall and most of them will be flanking you."

"Are your men ready?"

"You just give the word," Solly said. The two men behind him nodded, one murmuring a quick "for the Pearl Emperor."

Ryko withdrew his sword and handed it to me.

"Bring the lanterns down whatever way you can," he said.

I stiffened my wrist and arm, but it was too heavy, I would have to use both hands. I clamped the other over the grip and held the sword away from the horse's flanks, tensing my thigh and knee holds. The twist to my torso was going to cause problems, but I might just manage it. I inverted the blade and hooked the hilt against my thigh, pressing it into the side of the muscle for stability. Then I grabbed Ryko's shoulder with my free hand. First things first: get to the pathway on the horse and in one piece. Then think about swinging the sword.

"Alert your men," Ryko said. He turned his head and I saw the rise of violence in his eyes. I wondered what he saw in mine. "Here we go."

Solly made the piercing cry of a night hunting bird. Ryko

kicked the horse forward. I touched the red folio for good luck, then leaned into the animal's quickening pace. The effort of staying on and handling the sword made my heartbeat pound in my ears, louder than the boom of the battering ram. Wind made from speed whipped my eyes full of stinging tears.

We gained the path, the dull thud of horse hooves on grass changing into an instant clattering target. On both sides the darkness milled with the forms of men, the path between them a bright strip of death. Up ahead, the gate was bowing under the force of the ram, cries of effort rising above the crack of splitting wood. I shifted and joined my hands around the grip.

"Wait," Ryko yelled.

I caught a blurred glimpse of men running toward us, reaching for arrows. I lifted the sword.

The air pulsed with explosions. To the left. To the right. Was this Solly's bag of tricks?

"Now," Ryko ordered.

I hit the first rope, absurdly pleased with the bouncing demise of its lantern. The follow-through was less successful, the blade swinging close to Ryko's ear.

"Watch it," he roared, jerking away.

I sliced wildly at the next rope. Another lantern dropped from our pathway ahead. A thwanging, skittering sound made me duck. Arrows! From the shadows on either side. I checked for pain: nothing. My focus snapped back to the world rushing by. I was missing lanterns, leaving us exposed. With my back tensed for impact, I swung again. The weight of the sword collected a lantern and sent it into the shadows. Ahead, there was a huge crack of rending wood and shouts of success. The gate was down. I sliced another rope, sending its lantern rolling across the grass. My wrists were weakening, the twist in my backbone sending trembling fire into my thighs.

"I'm going to ride over them. Hold on," Ryko called over his shoulder.

His words didn't make sense. I was too intent on the next rope, on lifting the sword. The horse dipped into an even longer stride, but my body adjusted too late. The sword jerked up, hit the pole, and jarred out of my hands, clanging to the path.

I grabbed Ryko's waist and looked back, the sword already four horse-lengths away. The men who'd run onto the path were lowering their bows. Somewhere up ahead, battle cries rose into the smashing clang of sword meeting sword.

"I dropped it," I screamed in Ryko's ear. "I dropped your sword."

Then I saw the wall of men fighting in the splintered gateway—imperial guards being forced back by Sethon's army. We were heading straight for them, the horse trying to pull to the left, Ryko brutally holding it on course.

The first man we hit cannoned into his opponent. The next man saw us coming and hacked at the horse's neck. Ryko kicked him away, grunting as the blade nicked his leg. Ahead, someone fell, screaming. The horse made for the clear opening, trampling the body. I saw the man's chest cave in under the weight of a hoof. Ryko slashed his knife at a soldier hanging onto his injured leg. I kicked at the man's shoulder, missed, and connected with his helmet. His head jerked back and he lost his hold, falling under the horse. The animal stumbled over him and staggered into an imperial guard, slamming the man against the remains of the gate. Cursing, Ryko yanked the horse to the right, jumping it over two men grappling on the ground.

"Ryko?" The yell was from a heavily built guard up ahead. The man blocked a down cut from a soldier, punching the end of his hilt into the other man's jaw. He turned his attention back to us.

"Get us through," Ryko bellowed over the shouting, clashing mass. The guard nodded, then ducked as a sweep cut nearly took him in the neck. He parried his attacker, locking the man's blade into his own hilt, then threw back his head and gave a long, ululating call that pulsed through the clangor. Something slammed into my back, ramming me into Ryko and knocking the breath out of me. My teeth tore into my lip, the iron tang of blood souring my mouth. I felt myself sliding backward over the rump of the horse; someone was pulling my robe. I swung around, clawing wildly. It was a young soldier, helmet gone, blood smeared across his face. My fingers found an eye socket. I jabbed into soft tissue, hearing a yelp, but his grip on my robe tightened. Ryko clamped his hand down on my thigh, teeth bared with the effort of holding me and the horse. I went for the soldier again, but the horse suddenly ended the battle with a kick that sent the man barreling into the edge of the guard house. Ryko snatched up the reins as the animal skittered forward on its front legs, kicking out at anything around us.

Grimly, we both hung on, my hands locked around Ryko's chest as he fought for control. Finally, the horse stopped bucking, its sides heaving.

"Look," I shouted in Ryko's ear, pointing ahead.

Ryko's friend had cut down his opponent and was now methodically hacking a pathway through the soldiers in front of us. His strange call had gathered the guard around us. We were surrounded by a ring of the emperor's elite, all doggedly holding off the soldiers and forcing a way through the melee. Ryko coaxed the exhausted horse forward one step at a time as the guards inched us toward the edge of the fighting.

"I need a sword," Ryko bellowed.

A tall guard on our right flank drove his blade into the chest of a soldier and pulled the sword free, kicking the dying man away.

"Cover," he yelled, stepping back. The two guards fighting beside him edged together without breaking the rhythm of their blows.

"Here," the guard yelled to Ryko, passing up the bloody sword.

Ryko saluted, quickly testing the balance of the weapon. I watched the tall guard pull out a dagger from a waist sheath and rejoin the fight.

We were almost inside the gateway courtyard. The horse surged forward, sensing safety. With an agility that belied his heavy build, the front guard leaped aside, leaving his two adversaries standing in our path. We plowed through them, knocking one to the ground, Ryko slashing the other away with his sword.

We were through!

Ryko pulled the horse toward the servants' path. I looked back over my shoulder. The guards were forming a line to block pursuers. So few against so many. One of them turned to check our escape. I raised my hand. He gave a quick salute, then turned back to the desperate fighting.

"This animal's not going to last much longer," Ryko said, easing the horse down to a quivering trot on the dark, uneven track. "Are you all right?"

"I'm all right. What about your leg?"

"Just a cut." He reined the horse to a standstill. "Are you able to go on foot from here?"

As an answer, I slid off the beast's back. It sidled away as I landed on the ground and folded at its hooves in a messy heap. "My legs! They've gone all weak."

"It'll pass," Ryko said. "Rest for a minute." He dismounted, keeping the bloodied sword away from the horse's tossing head. I kneaded my thighs as he led the animal off the path and looped the reins over a bush.

"Do you think Lady Dela will be safe," I asked. "With all the soldiers—?"

"Lady Dela can look after herself." He wiped the sword clean on the grass and slid it into his scabbard. A crunching sound up ahead made us both turn. Someone was coming. A lot of someones. Ryko pulled me to my feet. "Time to run."

So began a deadly game of hide-and-seek. Sethon's soldiers had penetrated deep into the palace precinct and were systematically herding all of the occupants into the larger courtyards. As we darted between buildings, I saw groups of shrieking women and cowering eunuchs being bludgeoned to their knees. Too many times, we only just managed to press ourselves into the shadows as soldiers passed by. I was sure they would hear my heartbeat or see the terrified whites of my eyes in the dim light. Once, my cursed hip slowed me down and a young soldier caught my movement. He backtracked to investigate. I would never forget the wet sound of his death under Ryko's knife, or the surprise in his eyes.

When we finally reached the archway to the Peony Apartment, I was sick with the sight of guards hacked to death, servant women struggling under soldiers, and old men kicked into bloody pulps. Even Ryko, who had to be more hardened to such things, was pale, murmuring, "We cannot stop, we cannot stop."

The Peony courtyard was empty, the quiet, manicured garden an abrupt contrast to the screaming, wailing horrors we had just passed. I leaned against the stone arch, pressing my hand against my chest to steady my gasps for air and hold down the sickness rising from my belly.

Beside me, Ryko suddenly stiffened. "No," he breathed.

I followed his gaze. The garden was not empty. There

was a body on the far gravel path—a body in female clothes. Lady Dela? I grabbed the stone archway, the possibility buckling my legs.

Ryko ran across the garden to the dark shape, with no thought for cover. By the time I reached him, he was on his knees, his back heaving. I dropped to my knees, half afraid to look at her dead face.

It was plump, oval, young—not Lady Dela's. Ryko smiled at me, panting in hollow gasps of relief. I couldn't help smiling back; may our callous joy be forgiven.

Ryko gently passed his hand over the maid's face, closing her eyes. Then we both looked up at the silent apartment. The night lamps had been lit, but there was no movement. Was Lady Dela in there?

"I must check," Ryko said roughly. He scanned the garden, then pointed to the grove of ornamental trees near the pond. "You take cover in there. And wait for my signal."

I touched his arm. "No, I'll go, too," I said.

"Don't be foolish. You cannot be risked."

"But what if she's—"

He looked at me sideways. "You think me too soft to do my duty?"

"I didn't mean that."

He sighed. "Forgive me. I know what you meant. It was a kind thought, but you must stay behind."

I did not like it, but I obeyed. The screen panel doors of the formal reception room had been left wide open. Even from my position behind the trees, it was obvious that Sethon's men had ransacked the place. The low table was upended and Master Quidan's beautiful dragon scroll had been torn from its alcove. I watched as Ryko edged his way into the room. He paused for a moment, studying the mess, then disappeared from view. I wrung the edge of the Story Robe into a tight twist, trying to curb the impulse to run in after him. Finally, he reappeared in the doorway and beckoned.

"She's not here," he said as I joined him inside the ruined reception room. "The place is empty. Either she has been taken by Sethon, or she's hiding somewhere, waiting for us."

His face showed the same tense mix of relief and anxiety that was surging through me.

"I don't know Lady Dela as well as you, Ryko," I said. "But it seems to me that if she was able, she would leave us some kind of message."

Affection briefly softened his face. "And even if she was in danger, she would enjoy making it as subtle as possible."

I picked up the torn Quidan masterpiece and laid it carefully on the bureau. "Let us hope it has survived all this damage."

"If I were her, I would place it somewhere you would return to," Ryko said, pacing across the room. "Maybe near something that is dear to you."

"There are only two things in this place that are dear to me," I said. "My ancestors' death plaques. They're in my bedchamber."

I led Ryko through the apartment, noting that none of

the flickering wall lamps had been smashed. Whoever had gone through the place had wanted enough light to do a thorough job. Every room we passed had been ransacked—clothespresses hanging open, linen strewn on the floor, broken cups and bowls, baskets upended, bed rolls opened. There were also two more bodies, but Ryko stopped me from going to them, murmuring that he had already checked.

My bedchamber was more of the same devastation. The bed was stripped, the opulent linen ripped and strewn about. The bureau doors hung open, precious porcelain lying in pieces on the floor. Barely glancing at the ruins, I crossed straight to the altar. It was the only thing untouched—even rampaging soldiers would not risk angering the spirits.

Lady Dela had gambled on that fear and won—a copy of her translation of Lady Jila's *Summer Poems* was next to the offering bowls, undamaged. The scroll was tied with a ribbon strung with a large black pearl—the pearl that usually hung from Lady Dela's throat.

I snatched up the parchment and slid the ribbon off the end.

"I am not fast with my letters," Ryko said, looking over my shoulder. "What does it say?"

"One of the poems has been marked with a crescent moon. The title is 'A Lady Sits in the Shadows of Her Room and Sighs with Love.'"

"She's in the harem. In her house," Ryko said. He took the ribbon and pearl from my hands and carefully folded them into the pouch at his waist.

"How did you get that from the title?"

"She told me that Lady Jila wrote that poem for her." He cleared his throat. "About her."

I nodded. "So we go to the harem."

Ryko's laugh was hollow. "You say that as though it is a trip to the market. The harem has the best fortifications in the palace. And it holds a most precious jewel that Sethon will be keen to get his hands on."

For a moment I did not understand. "You mean the second prince."

"Sethon is a traditionalist," Ryko said dryly. "He will not want either prince alive. But there is a chance that our men got the little prince and the women out of the palace. Lady Dela could be with them."

I studied his grim face. "You don't think they got out, do you?"

Ryko looked around the silent room. "There are no soldiers left here on watch. All the palace occupants have been rounded up into the larger courtyards. I think all available manpower is being directed elsewhere. It's my guess that Sethon is attempting to breach the harem."

I looked around the wrecked chamber, suddenly overwhelmed by the odds against us. "Then how are we going to get into it?" My voice sounded very small.

"With the goodwill of the gods," Ryko said. "And a lot of luck."

I had as much faith in the gods and good fortune as the next person, but we needed more than that. We needed an army. Since that was not available, we at least needed more weapons. And I needed the rage and whispering voice of an ancient Dragoneye. I turned to the rack against the wall, readying myself for the spike of fury that always came with touching the swords. This time I would not ignore their advice.

The brackets were empty.

"They're gone." Stupidly, I waved my hand through the space, as if it would make them suddenly reappear. "Someone's taken my swords." I searched around the rack, then lifted the mounds of linen on the floor. They were definitely gone.

Ryko grunted. "It's not surprising. They would be worth a lot to a soldier."

"But you don't understand. They—" How could I explain that the swords told me how to fight? That without their rage and knowledge, I was only a cripple who knew a few ceremonial forms.

"We'll find you a sword on the way," he said, starting for the door.

I forced myself to step away from the rack—there was nothing I could do. "You've got a plan?"

"I've always got a plan," he said.

"Wait." Although I had lost the brilliant fury of the swords, I could at least have the consolation of my ancestors' death plaques. I snatched up the thin wooden tablets and forced them between the tight folds of my breast band. Perhaps these women, these unknown forebears, would protect me. And if that failed, then maybe whoever found my body would bury me under the emblems of my ancestors.

CHAPTER TWENTY-TWO

I WRINKLED MY NOSE at the smell of decaying plants and peered into the small tunnel.

"Is this it?" I whispered. "Is this the Concubines' Gate?"

I remembered the prince—the Pearl Emperor—whispering to me about it, his bawdy grin turning to embarrassment. Had his guards got him away in time? Was he safe? I touched the plaques at my breast; let him be safe, I prayed. As if in answer, the pearls around my arm lifted and settled.

Ryko crouched in front of the grate and cleared more of the vegetation away.

"It's a hidden emergency bolt hole. What did you expect?"

"It looks like a drain."

"Exactly."

I laid down the heavy sword that Ryko had taken from a dead soldier two courtyards back and helped him pull away the tightly wound vines. He had also taken the dead man's leather armor. "An old ruse, but a good one," he'd said as he tightened the fastenings around his waist and put on the tough leather helmet. A good ruse for him—there was no armor small enough to make me a convincing soldier.

"None of these vines are broken. No one's been through this exit," I whispered.

"They wouldn't have come out here," Ryko said. "The tunnel has another exit farther along the palace walls near the river. The ladies and children would be escorted straight through to the royal barges."

He carefully rolled the grate aside. The metal ground across the stone. We both tensed, listening for signs of curiosity from the small troop of soldiers stationed near the Gate of Officials.

Ryko had been right—Sethon was throwing most of his manpower at the harem. It had taken us over a half bell to carefully circumvent the buildup of soldiers around the women's sanctuary and then another to get to the far west wall. The strain was beginning to tell on my body, and my nerves felt so thinly stretched that screaming madness seemed only another hacked body or shrieking maid away.

"The escort guards should have already lit the lamps along the passage, but just in case . . ." He took the candles from his waist pouch, passing them to me. Then he unbundled a clay dish from a wrap of leather and picked out a striker. His sap powder trick.

"There are five steps down into the tunnel," he said. "Keep close to me."

I picked up my borrowed sword and followed him into the stinking hole.

Five slimy steps. Damp, cold air. Ryko tugged at my sleeve, leading me further into the darkness. We turned corners—at least it seemed like we did. I had lost all sense of direction. Then the rough stone floor suddenly softened under my feet.

"Here," he breathed.

I sensed him squatting down to the floor and heard the scrape of the striker. Light flared. My eyes scrunched shut against the sudden brightness. Ryko tapped my arm.

"Candles. Quick."

I held them out, blinking at the tiny flame in the dish. Ryko quickly lit the wicks, then the sap powder futtered into tiny wisps of smoke. As he passed me one of the candles, its light shimmered across gold and turquoise. The tunnel was no longer a slimy drain. Intricate tilework covered the walls and curved across the ceiling in patterns of gold-edged flowers and fruit. Rich blue carpets were laid along the narrow corridor. It was still cold and damp, but a heavy perfume scented the air.

"It's beautiful," I whispered. I looked down at the thick floor coverings. "How is it the carpets do not rot?"

Ryko gave an amused snort. "I believe they are replaced every month." He studied the rugs. "No one has been through here," he said slowly. "No marks on the carpet. No lamps lit." He collected the clay dish and bundled it into his pouch. "Something has gone wrong with the evacuation."

"Couldn't they have got out another way?"

He chewed on his lower lip. "The Scholars' Gate, maybe."
He stood. "If we are separated, get back to this tunnel and follow it straight through to the river. There is a man waiting with
a boat. He will take you to safety." He saw my reluctance. "Do
you understand? You must not be taken."

I nodded and kept my face under better control.

We walked in silence, our footsteps lost in the thick pile of
the carpets and our candlelight catching the inlaid gold and
blue gloss of the tiles like sunlight across water. Every so often,
Ryko paused and held his small flame against an oil lamp set
into the wall, creating pockets of light behind us.

"For our return journey," he said.

How did he keep such courage and spirit? I raised my eyes
to the vivid ceiling. Above us was an army, headed by a ruthless general intent on claiming the throne and supported by
a madman with the power of an ascendant dragon. Images of
Lord Tyron's body and Hollin's slack face made my throat burn
with a sudden rise of bile. Were all the Dragoneyes and their
apprentices now dead? There was perhaps one who had survived: Dillon. And, of course, me.

Poor Dillon. Could his survival wreck Ido's plans for the
String of Pearls? Did not all those connected to a dragon have
to die before it could be created? I sighed. My problem was, as it
had always been, lack of knowledge. I just did not know enough
about the power of the Dragoneyes. I patted the red folio, reassuring myself. Hopefully, Lady Dela would soon find the most
important piece of knowledge in it. If we found Lady Dela.

Suddenly the earth shivered. A rumbling boom resonated through the tunnel as though the earth itself was moaning in pain. I ducked as dust spun into the air, catching in my throat.

"What in Shola's name was that?" Ryko said, his sword half-drawn.

I coughed, trying to clear the dust. "An earthshake?"

He peered back the way we had come. "Maybe. Come on, I will feel better when we are out of the ground."

We moved on. Finally, Ryko raised his candle and pointed upward. A thick gold band curved across the ceiling and down each wall. It reminded me of the imperial audience line in the ceremonial courtyard.

"This marks the harem wall," he said. "We are almost there."

We passed under the gold boundary without another word. Ryko quickened his pace, and I dug into deep reserves of energy to break into an awkward trot behind him. My sword seemed to weigh as much as a man. Ryko lengthened his stride, and I pushed myself into a run. The muffled sound of our feet and my rasping pants were the only sound. And then Ryko stopped, making me swerve around him to slow down. The carpet had abruptly given way again to rough stone.

I bent double over the sword and sucked in deep, wheezing breaths.

"Maybe it would be best for you to stay here while I find Lady Dela," Ryko said, watching my struggle.

I shook my head. "I will not stay," I managed between gasps.

"I could make you stay."

I straightened, my breathing easier. "I will keep up. Have I not, so far?"

"You have," he conceded. "But I have a feeling that something has gone very wrong above." He cast a worried glance upward. "We'll come up in a service alley on the outer edge. Keep hidden until I make sure it is clear."

He lit a lamp in the wall beside him, then blew out his candle, tucking it back into the pouch under the armor. He took my candle and gave a quick nod.

After we turned two sharp corners, Ryko took my hand and placed it on his shoulder, then blew out my candle, too. I stumbled behind him in the near pitch-black, trying to match my steps to his long strides. We made another turn and I saw dull gray light: a sliced circle high in the darkness. For a few steps, I could not work out what it was, and then the slices made sense. Bars. It was another grate. Beneath it, the planes and shadows of a steep staircase. And then the distant sounds of screams and wails penetrated the silence.

Were we too late?

Ryko lunged forward and climbed the steps using his hands and feet. He crouched at the top, peering through the grate and blocking most of the dim light in the passage. Feeling my way, I found the first step and crawled up beside him.

Beyond the bars, the alley was stacked with large trader chests and burlap-covered bales that blocked the view of the square. There was no way of knowing what lay ahead, but at least we would have some cover when we emerged. Ryko gripped two parallel bars and slowly shifted the grate out of its niche. It hit the stone paving of the alley with a dull clank and thudded against the outside wall. After a few breathless moments, he eased out into the open. I handed the sword through, then followed.

We were in a dead end; the Concubines' Gate was set low into the stone wall of an official-looking building. As Ryko fitted the grate back into place, I crept to the edge of the nearest bale stack and watched the mouth of the alley. The high-pitched screaming was much closer than I'd thought; the stone walls of the passage had muffled the terrible sound. Then something moved between the next two stacks. A man's hand, the dull brown of quilted armor, and a flash of steel. I pulled back. Ryko grabbed my arm and swung me behind him.

He glared down at me. "Where? How many?" he mouthed.

I pointed to the stacks, held up one finger, shrugged; I had only seen one, but perhaps there were more. He pulled out a knife and jerked his head back at the grate, pushing me toward it. Then he edged into the alley.

I waited a beat before creeping back to the corner of the bale. Ryko was crouched a few lengths ahead on the near side of the second stack, his head cocked, listening. I held my breath, straining to hear, too.

Something stirred. Ryko was moving before I even recognized it as steel scraping stone. He slammed his shoulder into the top bale, sending it plummeting between the stacks. It landed with a thud, mingled with a stifled yelp. The cry propelled Ryko over the remaining bales, his knife angled for a deadly downthrust. The stack rocked. Gasps of hard struggle made me step forward. The bales shivered again and then there was the clanging ring of a dropped sword. Was it done? But there was still scuffling. And then a fierce, pained whisper.

"Ryko!"

A sudden tense silence and then I heard a moan. I ran across the small space, my sword raised.

Ryko was kneeling beside the body of a soldier, pressing the heel of his hand hard into the man's shoulder, blood welling between his fingers. The man's chest rose and fell in short rasping pants. Then I saw the swarthy, angular face under the helmet and my breath stopped.

Lady Dela.

Ryko looked up at me, his eyes hollow. The dark stain under his hand was spreading into the quilted armor. "We've got to stop the bleeding."

I dropped to my knees, pushing my sword aside. "Ryko, what have you done?"

"He stabbed me," Lady Dela said, opening clouded eyes. "Idiot."

"You look like one of Sethon's men," Ryko said through his teeth.

"So do you," she said dryly.

"Stay still." He lifted the armor and sliced into it with his knife, cutting through the heavily quilted vest.

Her shoulders jerked, either from pain or the sharp laugh

that resonated through her body. "He's not providing his men with very good armor."

"You stole skirmish," Ryko said, working the knife carefully through the soggy material. "You should have gone for a swordsman, like I did. They get iron and leather." He pulled apart the thick padding to show a nasty wound under the round of her shoulder joint.

"I'll remember that next time," Lady Dela murmured. "Did you see they've broken through? It was Ido, I'm sure of it. I'm sure he used his power. It was like part of the wall just disintegrated. Like an earth anger."

I glanced at Ryko. "That must have been the rumbling we heard."

He nodded. "Check the alley," he said. "Make sure we are still alone."

I crawled to the end of the bales. The alley was empty, but beyond it a group of dark figures crossed the other side of the square; four soldiers dragging two women between them. They seemed to be heading toward the next section of the harem, in the direction of the screaming and wailing. A soft glow brightened the sky. A fire, or the light of many, many torches.

I pulled back. Ryko shot me a questioning look.

"Four soldiers with prisoners, but on the other side of the square. They're heading further into the harem."

"There are so many soldiers," Lady Dela said. "No one would listen to me and I couldn't find Lady Jila." She gripped my arm, her bloodied fingers slipping on the silk. "I saw Sethon. He's got her and the baby in the Garden of Beauty and Grace. We have to do something."

Ryko reached over and pressed my hand against the wet warmth of the Lady Dela's wound, ignoring her pained hiss. "Keep a firm hold."

Lady Dela raised her head. "Did you get the folio?"

"We got it," I said.

"Good. That's good." She shivered. "I took your swords. Didn't want them to get in the wrong hands. They're there." She closed her eyes. "My apologies." Her voice was faint.

My heart lifted as I saw the swords, lying half hidden by the upended bale. I badly needed their fury to burn away my fear. Especially if Lord Ido was nearby. Opposite, Ryko had dug a small vial from his waist pouch and was sprinkling a powder over Lady Dela's wound. It stank like a hot-water spring.

"Lady Dela," I said, rousing her. "Did you see Lord Ido? Is he in the harem, too?"

She gave a tiny nod, wrinkling her nose against the bad-egg stench. "I think so. How can he use his power for war? I thought it was forbidden by the covenant. Surely the council won't allow it."

"I don't think there is a council anymore."

She frowned, losing focus on my words. Ryko squatted beside me and gestured to my robe. "I need bandaging. May I cut some of the silk?"

I nodded.

"Don't hurt the Harmony Robe," Lady Dela protested weakly.

Ryko let out an exasperated breath, but I saw the flicker of a smile. I felt him push the heavy robe aside, and then a firm tug as he ripped the thin undersilks. The amount of warm blood oozing through my fingers seemed to be slowing down.

"Up we go," Ryko said, gently pulling Lady Dela into a sitting position. He nodded for me to stop staunching the wound. I caught her around her waist as he deftly placed a pad of silk over her shoulder and tied it tightly in place. "You'll have to get a physician to look at it soon," he said. "It's still bleeding."

She tested the firmness of the bandage, wincing as she pressed on it. "This will do for now." She held out her good arm. "Help me stand. We need to get to the Garden of Beauty and Grace."

Ryko pulled her to her feet and steadied her as she swayed. Her face drained into a gray pallor.

"We're not going to the garden," Ryko said. "We're going straight back through the Concubines' Gate."

"No." She grabbed his arm, more for support than emphasis. "Sethon has taken Lady Jila and the infant prince. Don't you understand what he's going to do? He's going to kill them and claim the throne. We have to stop him." She turned to me. "Lord Eon, give me the book. We will find your dragon's name and then you must stop him."

In my mind I heard my master's voice, thin with agony as the poison choked his *Hua. Stop him.* Stop Ido. Stop Sethon. It didn't matter which one he'd meant. They both had to be stopped.

My master was not the only one I had promised. I had made a pact with Prince Kygo. Mutual survival. He had said I had no honor. Was it true? Was I a deserter of my own word?

Ryko shook his head. "We go back. It is my duty to get you to safety."

"No," I said. They both stared at me. "I wish it was your duty, Ryko, but it is not. Your duty is to serve me. My duty is to stop Ido and Sethon. For the Pearl Emperor." *And my master*, I added silently. "We do not know if the Pearl Emperor has escaped. For all we know, he is dead and Lady Jila's baby is now our overlord. We must try and save him and his mother."

Ryko had stiffened under my words as though I had cut him with a whip. "As you say, my duty is to serve you. But it is also to protect you. I will not lead you into certain death."

I met his stubborn glare. "You will not be leading me into death. You will be following." I saw the argument in his eyes. "Who else is there, Ryko? You said yourself that I was the hope of the resistance."

"That was when you were Lord Eon, the Mirror Dragoneye."

"I am still the Mirror Dragoneye."

Lady Dela stepped between us. "Enough of this pissing contest. We have no other choice. We must save Lady Jila and the prince."

I nodded. "Give me a knife."

Ryko stood looking at my outstretched hand.

"For Shola's sake, stop fighting the inevitable and give her a knife," Lady Dela said. She leaned against a bale, sucking in pained breaths. "Do it."

He unsheathed a blade and slapped the leather-wrapped grip into my palm. I forced my fingers under the tight ties of my sash and began to saw through the silk.

Lady Dela's head snapped up. "What are you doing?"

"Two soldiers dragging a captured maid to the garden."

The sash fell away. I shrugged my way out of the heavy Story Robe and let it drop to the ground. The moonlight flared across the dark depths of the black pearls and silvered my pale arms. I looked up and saw Ryko staring at my body, now only clad in the three thin undertunics and emerald trousers. Under his gaze, I was suddenly aware of my shape beneath the fine silk and wrapped my arms across my chest. He cleared his throat, quickly moving to station himself at the edge of the bales.

Lady Dela's gaze followed his retreat. "It is a good plan," she said shortly, "but you will have to take off the shoes and the trousers, too. They are wrong."

I removed the scuffed muddy shoes, then crouched down and worked my hand under the tunics, finally finding the trouser tie. I tugged them down and stepped out of them.

"And your hair," Lady Dela said.

I closed my hand over the two Dragoneye braids looped and tied at the top of my head. With her injury, Lady Dela would not be able to loosen them. "Ryko, you'll have to cut it free." I offered him the knife and turned my back.

"This is madness," he growled. His fingers pulled at the base of the loop, bringing tears to my eyes. As he flicked the knife through Rilla's expert bindings, I carefully unwound the pearls from around my forearm and the folio. There was no resistance from the gems, only a slight quivering that could have been my own trembling hands.

"Lady Dela." She crossed the few paces to me, holding her injured arm against her side. I poured the pearls into her good hand and placed the folio on top. "Find her name."

"If it is in there, I will find it," she promised.

"Ryko, you take my swords. I don't want them left behind."

I felt my braids release and fall stiffly against my head.

"There, it is loose," he said gruffly.

I pulled a braid to the front and dug my fingers into it, working the hair free. He walked around and eyed my clumsy return to womanhood. I faced up to the new look in his eye, lifting my chin. Did he now think even less of me?

"If you can throw off your years as a boy, we should pass scrutiny," he said.

He was echoing my own doubts. "I will just be another frightened maid," I said, and gave him a quick, wry smile. "I will not need to act it."

He grunted. "You have the courage of a warrior."

I watched him turn away and gather the clothes from the ground. "No," I said flatly. "I don't."

He paused from stuffing the invaluable robe between two bales. "Are you frightened now?"

I nodded, shame flushing my skin.

"Is it going to stop you?"

"No."

"That is the courage of a warrior." He bent down and picked up my swords, sheathing them in the scabbards on each of his hips.

"It is also the courage of a cornered animal," Lady Dela said caustically. She angled the open folio in the moonlight and squinted at the letters.

"Anything?" I prompted, my fingers busy unweaving the second braid.

Lady Dela clicked her tongue in frustration. "It is very faint," she said. "I need more light." She frowned and shifted the book. "These are the writings of a woman named Kinra. The Last Mirror Dragoneye."

I dropped my hands. "Kinra?"

Lady Dela looked at me. "What? You know the name?"

I dug under the wrap of my breast band and ripped out the two death plaques. "Look." I held up the *Kinra* plaque. "She is my ancestor."

They both studied the worn lacquered memorial. Ryko pursed his lips in a soundless whistle.

"I did not think Dragoneye powers could be inherited," he said.

"Perhaps it is just the Mirror Dragoneye," Lady Dela said slowly. "The female Dragoneye."

I touched the stiff parchment. Kinra had once touched it, too. My ancestor. Pride and awe held me still; I was from a line of Dragoneyes.

An abrupt image flashed into my mind—the first time in Ido's library, when I had reached for the folio and the pearls had wound around my arm. I had felt the same rage in them that I felt in the ceremonial swords. The swords must have once belonged to Kinra, too.

"I've just remembered—"

A huge roar suddenly boomed into the alley, drowning the women's screaming wails. I flinched. Beside me, Lady Dela clutched the burlap bale. Ryko was back at the edge of the stack, knives raised. The terrible pounding cheers separated into the rhythm of a chant: *Sethon, Sethon, Sethon.* It was the sound of victory. And threat.

Ryko suddenly pulled back, his face twisted with self-disgust. "Too slow."

"Oy, who's down there?" a man's voice demanded.

CHAPTER TWENTY-THREE

RYKO GRABBED MY ARM. "Get ready," he murmured.

I shoved the death plaques back into my breast band and sent a quick, fervent prayer to Kinra. *Protect us.*

"Identify yourself," the voice ordered.

Ryko's grip on me tightened. "Swordman Jian," he yelled, beckoning to Lady Dela.

She looked wildly at him, then yelled, "And Groundman Perron." Hastily hiding the folio under her armor, she stepped into place beside me, taking the knife that Ryko held out.

For one silent moment, we met the fear in each other's eyes. Then Ryko pushed me forward, twisting my arm halfway up my back. It was a pitiless hold, and my breath caught as I was forced into a stumbling walk between them. Instinctively, I struggled against the tight restraint, Ryko's strength truly frightening. His face was hard, holding no acknowledgment of me. He jerked my arm higher until my shoulder was a straining curve of pain that hunched me into obedience. As I staggered forward, all I could see were the boots and legs of two soldiers standing at the mouth of the alley.

"What you got there, swordman?" one of the soldiers asked. I heard the leer on his face. The chanting from the next square suddenly stopped.

"Found her hiding in the stacks," Ryko said.

"What are you doing sweeps for? That's not your job."

"I wasn't," Ryko said. "Just found her when I was having a piss. Where do I take her?"

"All of the women are in the garden." The soldier paused. "Give me a look."

Ryko let go of my arm and bunched his hand into my hair. The sudden yank back forced a grunt out of me. Something deep inside crouched, ready to fight. I clamped my hands around his wrist and tried to pull free. My scalp seared with an agony that sent the night sky into a blur of tears.

"Got a bit of fight in her," the soldier said, grabbing my jaw and holding me still. A pair of coldly appraising eyes, half-shadowed under a helmet, swept over my face and down my body. "Not bad," he said. "You know, we don't have to take her in. No one's going to miss a little housemaid."

Ryko jerked me backward. "I found her."

The soldier eyed Ryko's size, then shrugged and tilted his chin at Lady Dela. "What are you doing here?"

"I heard something. Thought I'd check it out." Her voice had lost its lightness and lilt. It was a man's voice, roughened with pain. At the corner of my eye, I saw her hand close over her wound to hide the makeshift bandages.

"You hurt?" the soldier asked.

"It's nothing," Lady Dela said, her eyes cutting to Ryko.

The other soldier, taller and better built, shook his head with disgust. "For Shola's sake, she's not worth fighting over. You'll get better in the pleasure houses." He jerked a thumb to the right, a natural authority in his movements. "There's a bone man set up in that building over there. You should get yourself seen to."

"It's not bad. And I want to see the executions," Lady Dela said quickly.

"Then you'd better hurry. The high lord is whipping himself up into his killing frenzy." His disdain flicked over me, then found Ryko. "*You'd* better make it quick, too."

Ryko grunted agreement and forced me forward, steering me out of the alley. Behind us, one of the soldiers murmured something, the other man laughing derisively. It sent a hot wash of loathing through me.

"Keep going," Ryko urged.

His ruthless hold slackened enough for me to straighten against his body. Lady Dela was not near us. I hoped that she had just dropped back, playing the part of the disgruntled loser.

Under the far portico, two sentries watched our approach.

They were stationed at the main archway to a walled garden. Beyond the arch were the silhouettes of soldiers. Ranks and ranks of them, all transfixed by the voice of one man, the rich cadences of command spiking a memory.

Sethon.

The sentry on the right waved us over.

"Prisoner," Ryko said, forestalling any questions.

I kept my face down, unable to meet any more callous appraisal.

The sentry grunted. "Take her beside the pagoda."

Ryko manhandled me through the archway, into the press of men.

I was not prepared for the sheer number of them: scores and scores of soldiers, the sour stink of their anticipation like the reek of hunting animals. All their attention was fixed on the elegant raised pagoda at the center of the garden square. I could only see the deep curves of its upswept roof over the heads of the men in front of me, but I could hear Sethon's voice booming with victory.

"I am your emperor," he roared. "I am Emperor."

"Emperor," the men roared back, like baying dogs. Hundreds of fists punched the air.

Ryko pulled me closer. "Wait," he said against my ear.

I gave a slight nod. There was nothing we could do until Lady Dela caught up to us. Until she found my dragon's name. I licked fear-parched lips; what if it wasn't in the folio? Or worse— what if she found it and I still couldn't call the dragon?

Four soldiers nearby noticed our arrival with sideway glances. The avidity in their faces made me shrink further into Ryko's hold. It was something I had once seen in the whipmaster when he beat a man to death. Bloodlust. These men wanted to see brutality. They wanted to see death. Any death.

Behind me, I felt Ryko straighten into his full height, his free hand finding the grip of Kinra's sword. Three of the men looked away from the challenge, the fourth meeting Ryko's glare until Sethon's deep, resonating voice pulled his attention back to the pagoda. I swallowed a rise of acid terror. What could we do against hundreds of men eager for blood?

"I am a descendant of the jade dragons. I have the rightful claim," Sethon yelled. "I invoke the tradition of Reitanon."

"Reitanon, Reitanon," the men chanted.

"No," a woman screamed. "No!" Through the shrill terror, I recognized Lady Jila's voice.

I shifted against Ryko, trying to find a sightline. The large square was arranged as a scholar's garden. A series of paved terraces were bounded by sculpted trees, rocks and linked ponds designed to create a flow of tranquil energy. But there was no such peace or harmony today; soldiers trampled the elegant spaces, creating dense, ugly patterns of their own. Finally, a gap opened, and I saw the central pagoda. Inside was a shining god of war: High Lord Sethon in a horned helmet and full armor, the precious metal plates and gold rivets catching the torchlight.

Two soldiers hauled a woman across the floor and pushed her down at Sethon's feet. She was clutching something to her chest. Lady Jila, and her son, the second prince. I lurched forward but was stopped by Ryko's iron grip.

"I know," he said. "I know."

Where was Lady Dela? I twisted around. Where was she? We could do nothing without her and the book.

"By the archway," Ryko whispered.

She was slumped against the wall, one hand pressed into her shoulder, the other wrapped around her stomach—just another wounded soldier eager to see the entertainment. But this soldier's gaze was not on the pagoda. It was on something hidden under the cover of a bent elbow and hunched body.

She must have felt my desperate gaze because she looked up. The despair in her eyes answered my silent question. She bowed her head back to the folio.

"You do not have rightful claim," Lady Jila shrieked. "My sons have the claim!"

A baby started crying. Fierce yells and shrill screams came from below the pagoda, at the foot of the rocks. For a brief moment I saw chained imperial guards struggling with soldiers and a row of kneeling, weeping concubines. Then my sightline was gone.

A breathless tension had settled on the crowd, the faces around us set into savage expectancy. I finally found another sliver of space straight through to the pagoda. Lady Jila was on her knees with her baby locked in her arms. Sethon was standing over them. A casual flick of his fingers sent a soldier grabbing for the child. Another flick started a lone drum into a slow beat. Lady Jila screamed, fighting to hold on to her son. Sethon stepped closer, his gauntleted hand swinging in a vicious blow. Lady Jila's head jerked back, blood running down her face, but she did not let go of her baby. His fist swung again. She hit the ground, the soldier dragging the infant free of her desperate grasp. Against my back, I felt Ryko's heart pounding, every sinew in him tensed against the urge to run to their aid.

"We can't let this happen," I croaked.

"We are too late," he whispered. "Too late."

Lady Dela was still bent over the book. All I could hear was the beat of the drum and the sobbing pleas of Lady Jila. I had to do something. I had to stop Sethon. *Stop him.*

I touched the death plaques at my breast. *Protect me from Ido,* I prayed, then narrowed my eyes and plunged deep into the energy world—an arrow straight into the heart of the Rat Dragon.

Blue energy exploded through me, warping my senses until the crowd and buildings buckled into swirling silver *Hua.* The sensation of Ryko's body against mine dropped away, as though I was floating in water. My mind-sight spun in a dizzy fall, then sharpened.

Hovering above the square was the Rat Dragon, as big as a hall. The only dragon visible. Foreboding swept through me. If all the other dragons were gone, were their Dragoneyes dead?

A set of lethal opal claws raked at the air, and a terrible screech sent pain stabbing through my head. The iridescent blue pearl beneath his muzzle was pulsing. His huge spirit eyes locked with mine, and I knew the endless power of death, and destruction, and *Gan*. Beneath him was the figure of Sethon, his sword aimed at the child dangling helplessly from the soldier's hands.

"No!" I screamed, and opened myself to the dragon's fearsome power. It hit me with the force of a thousand fists—an uncontrollable torrent of blue energy that roared with ancient annihilation.

The drum stopped.

Kill him. Kill Sethon, I ordered, and behind the puny words was the earth's own life force, spiralling into a rush of destruction. Dimly, I heard the child's wail cut short. Too late. Above the pagoda, the dragon threw back its huge horned head and howled with confusion. The terrible keening was joined by a woman's anguished scream. But even that was lost in the multitude of shouts and shrieks from the crowd as a streaming column of blue power burst down from the beast toward the center of the pagoda and the shining figure of Sethon.

Stop!

The order thundered through my head.

Ido.

He was in my mind, the grip of his will closing around mine. For a moment, I saw myself through his eyes, still pressed against Ryko, shaking with the fight for power, only the islander's grim support keeping me upright. Around us, soldiers crouched in uncomprehending terror, watching the deadly shaft of energy. The dragon shrieked, his power splitting and fragmenting. I tasted Ido's sour fury as he struggled to bend me and the dragon to his will, both the beast and I battling the Dragoneye's ruthless command.

Not yet, his voice gasped in my mind.

I felt him channel the blue power away from Sethon, his effort sending shudders of secondhand pain through me. The diverted energy punched into the portico at the far end of the garden, sending marble spinning into the air and raining down on the soldiers underneath. Ido's hold on my mind slipped, the fight to contain his dragon's power ripping at his control.

I dug deeper into my *Hua*, burrowing into the yellow energy of my third point, frantically searching for the strange opalescence that had once saved me from the overwhelming blue. It was there, still tiny, but brighter and glowing gold. I snatched at it, gathering the power, then flung it outward, praying it would find its mark.

The release was abrupt; the energy world snapping away, leaving only the turmoil of the harem garden around me and a bone-deep ache that clenched me like a vise. I slumped in Ryko's arms, his warm solidity my only anchor in the waves of overpowering pain.

He looked down at me, tears running from his eyes. "The prince is dead."

I already knew it, but his confirmation was like a fresh wound. "Lady Jila?" I gasped.

He shook his head. "Dead, too."

"Ido is coming," a voice rasped behind us. "Move!"

Ryko swung around. It was Lady Dela, her eyes tracking

movement in the scrambling crowd. Below the pagoda, the captured imperial guards had broken past their jailers, using their chains as weapons, creating turmoil and blocking Sethon's exit. I followed her gaze to the right of the chaos, my eyes catching on the ordered intent of a small group of men forging past the building. Four guards in a diamond formation around one tall, dark man dressed in the gold and blue robes of the ascendant Dragoneye.

Lord Ido.

The world dipped and spun into a haze of fear.

"Go!" Lady Dela yelled.

She had already pushed her way into the archway as Ryko hauled me toward it. Around us, officers were marshaling their men back into ranks with roared orders and the butts of their swords. The arch was thick with panicked men, some surging out of the garden, others being driven back. A red-faced sergeant stepped in front of us, blocking our escape with outstretched arms.

"Get back!" he yelled over the curses and scuffling.

"Orders to get her out of here," Ryko shouted back, tightening his grip on me. He jerked his head at the pagoda.

The man's eyes narrowed. "Whose orders?" He raised his sword. "What regiment are you from?"

I felt Ryko tense for confrontation, but the sergeant's thin-eyed disbelief suddenly widened into shock as another soldier crashed into him. I heard the sucking gurgle of his breath as Lady Dela, her skin pasty with effort, swung his body around and pushed his weight against the wall. She pressed into him again, the hilt of a bloodied knife in her hand.

"Go," she ground out, propping up the dying man with her uninjured shoulder. "I'm right behind you."

"Make for the grate," Ryko said, then grabbed my hand and pulled me through the archway.

I looked over my shoulder. Ido was well past the pagoda, his men clearing an efficient pathway through the disorganized ranks. Ryko's yank on my arm jerked me into a flat run. We barged past the overwhelmed sentries, joining a straggling exodus of soldiers from the garden. I focused on the dark mouth of the alley across the square. Our escape. My breath snagged in my throat; I forced more strength into my legs and snatched another glance back. Lady Dela had broken out of the archway and was following in a stumbling trot. She faltered and doubled over, coming to the end of her endurance.

I pulled on Ryko's hand. "Lady Dela. She's not going to make it."

For a moment, I didn't think he would stop. Then I felt him slow, pulling me to an abrupt, panting standstill. He let go of me and drew the sword from his left scabbard, shoving it into my hand. As soon as the moonstone hilt touched my skin, a flame of ancient rage seared through me.

"Open the grate and hide," Ryko ordered, then turned around.

A soldier had stopped behind us, his body poised for attack. Ryko pushed me toward the alley, then charged at him.

"Run," Ryko yelled, and elbowed the man in the face.

I ran.

Through me, a rhythm pounded: heartbeat and breath and the drum of another presence. I dodged a swordsman, his face a blur of flattened features and missing teeth, his fingernails raking my arm. Only a few lengths to go. I looked back. The swordsman was following me, his pace outstripping mine. Beyond him, Ryko had reached Lady Dela. I lowered my head and flung myself into the dark entrance of the alley, swinging around to see the soldier draw up a few paces into the passage.

"It's a dead end, girlie," he said, grinning.

I raised my blade.

He cross-drew his two swords, holding them in the ready position. "I don't want to hurt you, so put it down."

I backed up a few steps. Two swords against one. I needed another blade. A few more steps brought me level with the first row of bales. He followed, matching his pace to mine. All I had to do was hold him off until Ryko and Lady Dela arrived. I edged toward the second stack of bales, where Ryko had hidden the dead soldier's sword.

"Come on, now." The soldier smiled encouragingly.

I was at the narrow corridor made by the first and second stacks. I snatched a look. The end was blocked by the bale that Ryko had pushed down. Small pieces of ripped pale silk littered the ground. No sword. Was it behind the bale? If I went down there, I would be well and truly trapped. But the alley was a dead end, and I would have no chance of holding him off and getting the grate open at the same time. I was trapped either way.

I plunged between the two rows, slipping on Lady Dela's blood and scrambling across the stone to the fallen bale. Behind me, I heard the soldier grunt. A fistful of burlap steadied me as I frantically groped between bale and wall. My fingers hit the leather of the grip. I pulled the sword out.

"Got you now," the soldier said, advancing down the narrow space.

I swung around and spun both blades up into starting position, Kinra's sword held above my head, my left hand aiming the point of the other blade at his throat.

"Oh ho," the soldier laughed, immediately angling his weapons. "Who showed you that?"

I watched his eyes, waiting for the sign of attack. It was a small huff of breath, a flicker of his eyelids as he lunged forward. My body was already moving into a block. Kinra's sword took the downthrust of his blade, my body singing with my ancestor's knowledge. With her rage. I swept the other blade around and connected with his hurriedly lowered sword. The impact jarred through my arm, but he was off balance and I pushed forward. I had to get out of the confined space between the bales.

Tiger cuffs and claws.

This time I trusted the instinct that shifted my muscles and sinews into the form, riding the ancient skill that sent both blades working in quick punishing hits that the soldier barely blocked. One tip caught his arm and drew blood. His eyes widened, his breath quickening. Slowly, my volley of blows forced him back into the alley.

"I can beat you," I said levelly. I did not want to hurt this man; I just wanted to get to the grate.

"I don't think so, little girl." His face tightened as he put all his strength behind a vicious blow. I just managed to deflect it, the impact bending my wrist back into sharp agony. He sliced his other blade in a tight arc, the wicked move aimed at my throat. I swung into a block, his blade sliding up into the hilt of Kinra's sword. My muscles tensed, knowing that his next move was a lethal swing at my head.

Rat drops to ground.

I pulled free. My body fell back, landing heavily on the stone paving, all my breath punched out of my lungs. Above me, I saw the soldier's surprise as his sword swung through air, making him stagger. There was no time to think. Gasping, I pushed myself up at him and drove Kinra's sword into his thigh. The tip sliced through flesh and hit bone, opening his leg in a slash that pulsed with blood. He screamed and jerked away, pulling himself off my blade. One sword dropped with a clang as he clutched at the spurting wound. For a second we were both still with shock, then he staggered toward me, fueled by rage and pain, his other sword raised for the killing stroke.

Dragon whips tail.

For a second, I was back fighting Ranne on the ceremony sands. But this time I did not hesitate; I spun over onto my hands and knees and kicked backward, connecting with the soldier's downstroke. His sword hit the stone in a ringing toll as I twisted around and plunged Kinra's sword up into his body, her ancient knowledge guiding the thrust into his vital pathway of *Hua*. I pulled it free, severing his life force in a gush of blood. His agonized cry was lost in the clicking rasp of a last breath. He collapsed on to the ground beside me, the sour release of urine mixing with the coppery stink of fresh blood. The smell of death.

I scrabbled backward up against a crate. The spirit had already gone from his eyes, but their flat stare held me pinned against the rough wood. My swords dropped from my hands. I had done this to him; stopped the flow of precious *Hua*. I groped for reason. He was trying to kill me. I was defending myself. I had survived. Relief surged into fierce exhilaration, then drained into shivering horror. He was so still. Death was so silent. So indifferent. It was only made to matter in the hearts and minds of men.

And women.

I looked away from the sightless stare. This man's death would matter to me forever.

The sound of running steps brought me onto my knees. I grabbed Kinra's sword as Ryko rounded the corner, his arm around Lady Dela's waist, dragging her in a half run.

"Get to the grate," he yelled.

I struggled to my feet.

"Don't kill the girl!" It was Ido's voice.

CHAPTER TWENTY-FOUR

RYKO HAULED LADY DELA past the first stack. Her body was slumped against his tight hold, her face ominously pale.

"Take her," he said. I caught her weight, barely managing to swing her around and rest her against the crate. There was fresh blood seeping through the bandage and ripped armor. Her eyelids flickered.

Ryko eyed the bloodied sword in my hand. "Are you all right?"

"I'm fine," I said.

"Here." He passed me its twin, sending a surge of new energy into my exhausted reserves. "Go. I'll hold them off."

The mouth of the alley was suddenly blocked by men. Four of them in dark, close-fitting armor: Ido's private guard. Two men immediately came forward, swords raised. Behind them,

Ido swept a searching glance along the corridor, his height giving him a clear view. Although his face was in shadow, I knew the moment his eyes found me.

"I want her alive," he ordered, and there was a caress in his voice. "The others you can kill."

Ryko picked up the dead swordsman's weapons. "For Shola's sake, get going," he hissed. "I'm not going to last long."

He ran to meet Ido's front guard. They were already past the first stack and angled themselves for his momentum. The crash of metal against metal reverberated off the stone walls, the force of the guard's blows pushing Ryko back toward us. He was using his body to block the narrow pathway. Beside me, Lady Dela stirred, roused by the clanging danger. Ryko desperately blocked a simultaneous attack by both guards, barely managing to stop their slicing blades. He was not going to hold them off for long.

"Help me," Lady Dela said. She was fumbling in the opening of her armor. "I'll keep looking. . . ."

She withdrew her hand, unable to pull the folio through the tangle of waist bindings. We both knew it was too late, but I tucked my sword under my arm and jerked out the book, pressing it into her hand. The pearls lifted and unwound, clicking into a slide of welcome across my skin. I pushed their weight back onto the folio.

"If things go bad," I said, "get to the grate."

The swords were whispering to me, eager to fight.

Lady Dela's eyes flicked to Ryko. "I'm staying right to the end."

I turned and sized up the battle, my eyes seeing it through Kinra's ancient wisdom.

Ryko had been hit; blood was running from a deep slice in his forearm. Superficial, but it would take its toll. One of his attackers was down, not moving. The other was close to breaking through to me, a young man with overquick moves and a cocky smile. Two more guards were approaching. At the mouth of the alley, Ido was waiting for Ryko to fall. I took a deep breath and yelled, the release of *Hua* propelling me into the fight.

I met the young guard as he broke past Ryko, each of my swords singing in a lethal figure eight. He blocked the lower blade, but mistimed his deflection of the higher slice. It caught the side of his face, snapping his head back and opening his cheek to the bone. I lunged, aiming for the shoulder weakness in the armor, reveling in the borrowed skill and fluid movement. He countered the thrust but the move was soft and clumsy with shock. Even as I swung my other sword, I knew it would hit home. My blade bit into his neck, smashing bone and severing his spinal column. As he started to topple, the ancient part of me was already pulling my weapon free, ready to move on.

I checked on Lady Dela. She was edging behind the stack near the grate, the folio angled to catch the moonlight. Ahead, Ryko was fighting with his back against the bales, two guards raining blows on him. He was blocking most of them and frantically dodging those that he missed, the slicing thrusts ripping dusty holes in the bale behind him.

"Oy!" I shouted, running at the closest of his attackers.

The man spun around. I saw Ryko's eyes cut to me—shock

turning to fury—then my view was blocked by the guard. This one was older, more cautious, shrewd calculation on his lean face.

"You should surrender," he said. "Then perhaps your friends will survive."

I answered with the Monkey Dragon Third: a series of quick cuts aimed at the neck. But this man was no overconfident youngster. He stopped me by sweeping his swords outward, the weight of each connection pushing my swords wide. I felt my grips slip and loosen. He swung his right sword back, lining up a hilt punch to my head. Gritting my teeth, I tightened my right grip and brought my blade down onto his hilt. I heard him curse as the edge just missed his fingers and sliced into the leather binding. He broke away, deftly swinging the sword around. Kinra's knowledge was still bright within me, but my body was tiring. Her rage could not keep me going much longer.

At the corner of my vision, I saw Ido, swords drawn, coming up the alley. Ryko saw him, too, and in a desperate lunge that left him unprotected, slashed a wild stroke at the Dragoneye's head. It missed, and Ryko's back arched as his opponent's sword plunged into his right side.

Then the guard in front of me attacked, and my focus narrowed to deflecting the flicking thrusts that threatened to disarm me. Was Ryko hurt? Dead? I could not take my eyes off my opponent, but the clanging sounds of sword on sword and the heavy pants of pained effort gave me hope.

"Pull out," Ido ordered.

My swinging cut sliced through air as my opponent ducked sideways, making way for his master.

"Try and take the islander alive," Ido ordered, jerking his head back at Ryko. "And then find the freak."

The guard dipped his head and retreated. If Ryko was hurt, he would not last long against such a cunning fighter. I raised my swords, trying to catch extra breath in the momentary lull.

Ido smiled at me and swung his swords up into a mirror of my own. He had discarded the heavy embroidered ascendant coat and his thin linen undershirt showed the broad lines of his shoulders and chest. I had felt his massive strength in the Dragon House at Daikiko. He was quick, too. I flexed my toes, trying to ease the weakness of exhaustion already trembling through my legs.

"You fight very well for a cripple," he said. "Perhaps you have access to more power than you claim."

I met his amber eyes. There was no silver *Hua* threaded through them—he was not using his dragon power—but there was a light in their depths made of madness. How did you fight a madman? I tightened my grip on Kinra's swords: a wordless prayer for the power to stop him.

"You've killed all the other Dragoneyes, haven't you? Even the apprentices," I said, watching for the flicker of tension that would herald his attack. The sounds of Ryko's grim battle echoed against the stone walls, but I could not look away from Ido's eyes.

He edged forward, pushing me back a step. "Sethon has

forced my hand. He thought he could use me to take the throne, then turn around and use the council to kill me." He snorted, his heavy jaw lifting with disdain. "Now there is no council. Only you and me, and more power than Sethon could ever imagine."

"All you've done is left the land without its guardians," I said. "There will be nothing to rule."

"Don't you see? When I have you, I'll be its guardian." His face was alight with his own truth. "It's time for the Dragon Throne to be reunited with the dragon power."

Suddenly his blades were hissing through the air. Kinra's reflexes raised my swords in time to stop the sledgehammer blows, but the impact forced me backward. He swung his weapons around again, the high bludgeoning connections scraping against my hilts and locking into them. My borrowed knowledge told me he was well trained, far more accomplished than a normal Dragoneye. He leaned into the crossed swords, the pressure of his weight straining my muscles. Up close, I could see the rings of exhaustion and drug use under his eyes; my attempt on his dragon had depleted his power. Even so, his strength was overwhelming. And the smile on his face filled me with sick fear. He wanted to hurt me.

The only way I could disengage was to retreat. But if I went further down the alley, he would see Lady Dela. It would be her death.

Horse rears and kicks.

My body knew the form and my mind snatched at the hope. Calling on Kinra's energy, I pushed up against his blades and thrust them outward, sending a vicious kick at his knee that jarred my bad hip. He jumped back and slashed at my foot, just missing it. I staggered a few steps to regain balance and realized I was level with Lady Dela's hiding place. She had slipped down the wall and was crouched on the ground, still hunting through the pages. Her head snapped up. For a second I saw panic in her eyes and then she recognized me, the fear shifting into a moment of desperate, silent communication. She was close to finding something.

I hurriedly looked back at Ido, terrified he would follow my focus. The clashes of Ryko's battle were farther apart. Was his staunch strength finally failing?

"Your skill is far too great for your training," Ido said. "What kind of dragon power is this?"

I ignored the question, watching as he gathered himself for his next attack. I could not risk retreating any further. I swung my swords into the whirring Goat Second and ran at him. The shock of the collision resonated through my whole body. My right sword blocked his chest cut, the strength of his blow too light to be anything more than a feint. The knowledge was not mine, nor was the swinging angle of my left blade that stopped the vicious attack on my legs. Ido pulled back, his smile gone.

"Don't be a fool, girl," he said. "Even with this extra skill, you'll fail. I need you alive, but I don't care what condition you're in."

I suddenly understood his pattern of attack: hacking at hands, slicing at ankles. He didn't want me dead. He wanted me helpless. For a second, the realization made my vision blur with white terror.

"My lord, we have the islander," the older guard called.

Ido kept his eyes on me. "Is he alive?" he asked.

"Yes, my lord."

Ido smiled. "If you surrender now, *Eona*, you can save your friend a great deal of pain."

I tightened my grip on my swords.

Ido raised his eyebrows. "Or do you have enough steel to let him die in agony?"

"No," I whispered.

He started forward. I raised the swords and stepped back. If I gave up he would take my will forever.

Ido's smile widened. "Bring the islander here," he ordered.

The two remaining guards approached us with Ryko's body slumped between them. His head was bowed and a dark spread of blood from under his armor had seeped into the cloth of his trousers. It clung wetly to his thigh. Ido motioned to the guards to drop their burden. Ryko's body folded onto the stone with a slapping thud. His face was turned toward me, his dark skin drained into gray hollows. I chanced a look at the guards—both of them were injured. Ryko had made them work hard for their victory.

Ido kicked Ryko's injured side, forcing a gasping moan out of the islander. He was barely conscious.

Ido looked over at me. "Well?"

I knew Ryko would not want me to surrender. But I also knew Lord Ido; there was no mercy in the man. He would make me watch my friend suffer. And he would enjoy both kinds of pain. I kept my eyes fixed on the Dragoneye, although every part of me longed to glance across at Lady Dela.

"Hold him down."

The older guard settled his knee between Ryko's shoulders and leaned his forearm into the back of his neck. The islander stirred but did not rouse.

"Spread his hand and hold it still," Ido ordered the other guard.

The man squatted beside Ryko and pulled his hand from under his body, pressing it flat on the stone pavings. Ido raised his sword and positioned the tip over Ryko's knuckles. He licked his lips, as though savoring the moment.

"Put your swords down, Eona," he said softly.

May the gods and Ryko forgive me; I did not move.

For a hung moment, Ido stared across at me, an odd smile on his lips, and then he drove the sword tip through Ryko's hand. My friend's scream shuddered through me. He thrashed, trying to pull his speared, spasming hand free, but one guard held his wrist down and the other was on his back, locking him against the stone. A thin line of blood oozed from under his palm.

"More?" Ido asked, but he didn't wait for my answer. He jerked the sword, tearing another scream from the big man. I heard Ryko's teeth connect as he clenched the terrible sound back, his agony forced into rasping pants.

"Get his other hand," Ido ordered.

"No!" I shouted. "No!"

Ryko's pain-glazed eyes found me. "Don't," he breathed.

I dropped Kinra's swords. They hit the stone with an echoing clang.

"Good girl," Ido said.

He motioned to the older guard. "Hold the sword. If she makes a move, rip open his wrist."

The guard released his grip on Ryko's hand and stood, grasping Ido's sword. The grinding shift of the blade sent a shudder through Ryko.

"And you," Ido said to the other guard. "Get the freak. She's behind that last row of bales."

I felt all hope leave me. Ido had won.

Lady Dela's head was still bent over the book, her forefinger tracing a line along a page, her lips moving in silent translation. She, at least, had not given up. The guard pushed himself off Ryko's back and pulled a knife out of a wrist scabbard.

"Don't kill her," Ido added. "Not yet."

The man nodded and advanced. I watched him pass me and warily round the corner of the stack. Lady Dela glanced up at his cautious approach, her face flaring with fear, then she bowed her head, still reading.

And then Ido was coming at me, so fast I didn't have time to move. He grabbed my right arm in a bruising hold and steered me backward toward the end of the alley. I stumbled and felt my feet leave the ground. He half carried, half dragged me to the wall, my shoulder twisting up into agony. With a grunt, he rammed my back against the grimy stone and let go of my arm, only the solid press of his hips keeping me upright. His face was so close that I couldn't focus; all I saw was his mouth framed by the neat line of his oiled black beard and the darkness of his dilated eyes. He was so heavy—solid muscle made of Sun drug and hard training.

I strained, trying to turn from his overwhelming strength, but I felt the warm pressure of his hand curl around my throat. I clawed at his fingers. He gave a slight shake of his head and squeezed. Gasping, I dropped my hands and held very still. He bent his head and pressed his lips against mine, slowly relaxing his hold so that I gulped for air, opening my mouth to him. His tongue licked mine, bringing the taste of vanilla-orange, and then he was drawing his teeth across my lower lip, biting the tender skin into sharp pain. I jerked away, tasting the coppery warmth of blood.

"So now we find out," he said softly against my cheek, each word brushing me like a kiss. "Now we find out what really happens when the last two Dragoneyes become one."

"We're not the last two," I croaked.

He pulled his head back slightly. "You mean Dillon?"

I met his eyes. Thin threads of silver slid through the amber. The caress of his charisma stroked my skin.

"Poor Dillon," he said. "I've bound his *Hua* to mine. He no longer has his own link to the Rat Dragon." He traced his forefinger along my jaw. "And what little power he has will soon be drained." His other hand yanked at the neck of my under-tunics. The thin silk gave way, exposing my shoulder and the tight breast band.

The sound of scuffling snapped his head around, but I could not see past him.

Lady Dela's voice screamed, "She's the Mirror Dragon, she—" Her voice was suddenly muffled, as if someone had slapped his hand over her mouth. What was Dela trying to tell me? I already knew she was the Mirror Dragon.

Ido turned back. "*She?* The dragon is female, too?" He gave a low, wondering laugh. "Of course, I should have guessed; it is the feminine where your power exists. No wonder the black folio speaks of the sun and moon joining."

His hand skimmed over the tight binding at my breast and dropped to my waist, pulling at the thin linen of my undershorts. I flinched, but his other hand tightened around my throat again. The alley closed around me in a haze of gray suffocation. Again he released the pressure, allowing me precious air. His face had hardened into harsh purpose and I knew I could not stop him physically. But he was not going to get all of me.

I lifted my chin. "You cannot make me go into the energy world."

"Do you think I can only force my way into your body?" His eyes were a wash of silver. I felt his power buffet me like a physical blow. "Every time you called my dragon's power, you opened your pathways to him," he whispered against my ear. "And to me."

Sweet vanilla-orange filled my mouth. I felt power pressing into me, searching. Blue power that bent and distorted the alley into roiling colors and shifted Ido's face from flesh and bone to planes of pulsing energy, then back again. He looked up, his fingers forcing my head back; the Rat Dragon was above us, the cloudy blue scales of his underbelly like a summer sky. The beast watched us, the pearl at his throat shimmering with power. His huge spirit eyes reached further into me and found a silvered pathway still darkened with the gray welcome of the Sun drug.

Ido was in my mind. *Now you are truly mine.*

"No," I gasped.

A shrill voice sliced into the blue storm that was rolling over my senses. "She's the *Mirror* Dragon. Do you hear me? Her name is your name! She's the mirror."

Lady Dela. I struggled to focus on her words.

Then, like a turned kaleidoscope, the last few weeks shifted into a new pattern of bitter understanding. At the moment of union, the Mirror Dragon had not tried to rip my true name from me, she had been trying to *give me her name. Our* name. All along—at my master's house, in the bathing room, on the roadside—I had denied her, blocked her, stifled her with drugs. And all along, the tiny gold kernel of my power had been locked within me, waiting.

"Eona," I whispered—and the truth of the name was like a claw ripping through the misunderstanding, shredding the fear and the fading veil of drugs. It reached into the overwhelming blue, forcing a thin sliver of hope.

Ido's fingers dug into my flesh. *What are you doing?*

"Eona," I screamed, the name shaking his hold on my mind. I felt his comprehension and the sharp grab of his anticipation.

You have called her.

A shrieking rise of power rushed into my pathways, rocking me against the wall. Ido's body slammed into mine. He was not going to let go. Not now. The Rat Dragon howled, his heavy blue force driven back by the onslaught of sinuous gold.

Raw, rejoicing energy flooded my seven centers of power; opening, pushing, seeking. And behind it all, a presence exulting in the joy of release and reunion. I looked up and, finally, my mind-sight was clear; I could see the Mirror Dragon. My dragon.

She was rearing on the roof behind me, obscuring the smaller blue dragon, the gold pulsing pearl at her chin bright against the crimson scales on her chest. Her forelegs slammed down onto the roof and two sets of long ruby claws grabbed the edge and sliced into the stone. Fragments of rock showered down, sending up two clouds of dust at either end of the alley. Her fragile wings spread for balance as she ducked her head, the moonlight rippling across her arched neck in fiery reflections. Her warm breath was a summer breeze, spicing my mouth with cinnamon—the taste of power. And joy.

I can see her. I felt Ido's awe shift into stark desire.

Delicately, she lowered her huge muzzle and offered me the pearl nestled under her chin. The luminescent gold orb was the size of a barrel and thrummed with the song of a thousand years, of old wisdom and new life, of balance and chaos.

I reached up and pressed my palms against the hard velvety surface. Gold flames rose and jumped across my skin in flicks of stinging promise.

Ido's hands closed around my wrists. *Bring her to me.*

The scream of his dragon shivered in his mind, sending an echo of pain through me. I laughed and felt an answering exultation through the flaming pearl. The blue power was a mere shadow under the glorious incandescence of our connection. The Red Dragon's fathomless eyes met mine, and her question—deeper than words—rode the rush of my *Hua*.

Would I give her Eon?

What did she mean by "Eon"? Then the answer rose through me; she was asking for the masculine power within me, the male energy I had fostered from my core. The only self I had come to trust.

My mind floundered. Didn't she want Eona—my female energy? Wasn't that the point of it all? Why did she want Eon? I hesitated, as I had in the arena, a chasm of doubt ripping through the gold euphoria. I had fought so hard to bring my male energy forward and subdue the female within me. If I let Eon go now, what would replace him? I had made Eona too small. Too weak. What if the dragon took Eon and there was nothing left?

I dragged my gaze from the shimmering flames of possibility to Ido's silver eyes. His hands were locked so tightly around my wrists that I could feel my sinews grinding under his hold. He was waiting for my power. Waiting to take everything. What if he was too strong for the Mirror Dragon? He had overpowered me every time we had met in the energy world. Won every time we had clashed through the might of the blue dragon. Would it be different through the Red Dragon?

It had to be different. She was my dragon, my power.

I thrust my hands against the gold pearl. *Let me be enough,* I prayed. *Let us be enough.*

"I am Eona!" I roared. "I am the Mirror Dragoneye!"

And then it happened—a tearing release of old needs, stunted power, and narrow pathways built from fear and skewed belief. The gold nugget of power within me exploded into radiant strength.

The Red Dragon shrieked, a piercing celebration that resonated in every part of my mind and body. But within the joy was the soft, keening presence of other voices. A bereft chorus that wove its way into our union. Was it the other dragons? The faint song of mourning was suddenly cut short.

My mind-sight split; I was the Mirror Dragon, my huge head whipping around to face the fury of the blue dragon on my back. His huge jaws closed around the arch of my neck. His opal claws sliced down my flanks, opening up bright, searing wounds of golden light.

But I was also in the alley, fighting Ido as he slammed my hands back into the wall and locked my wrists against the cold stone with his forearm. He forced his leg between mine, his other hand tearing silk and linen. Above, the Mirror Dragon rolled, and I was a desperate twist of red and orange muscle that sent a rumbling shock of power through the air. Paving and dirt flew up as my effort plowed a seam of devastation along the alley. I heard Lady Dela scream and watched from above as the guards ran for cover, leaving the tiny figure of Ryko crouched under the rain of stones.

Give her to me. Ido's hunger was like a fist punching through my mind.

"No!" I screamed.

The Red Dragon shrieked my defiance, meeting the Blue Dragon in a thunderous clash of heavy chests and raking claws. The world burst into pure energy as the dragon and I fused into one shimmering being. In front of us, the flesh and blood of Ido melted into a streaming network of *Hua.* The silvery pathways were dulled by a coating of Sun drug, but his life force pumped frantically through the swirling catchments of his points of power. His hold on us faltered, the Blue Dragon rearing back in confusion. We watched Ido's fear flick and jump in the flow through his transparent body, collecting in the bright red point at the base of his spine. Above it, on the central meridian that held the seven points, the orange sacral and the yellow delta flared with his power—his charisma and the burn of his desire.

Then we saw the dull green point in his chest. The heart point, the center of compassion and unity. Gray and shriveled, the flow through it choked into a thin, stuttering thread. A sickness. Easy to heal. We channeled our power into it, watching the grayness drain from the green point and slowly build into a huge rise of dark emotion. It crashed over us; a thick roiling mass of thwarted desire, wounded innocence, harsh rejection. So much hopelessness and anger. The Blue Dragon howled. Our hand touched Ido's chest and the connection of *Hua* shivered between us. Gold and silver power blending, building into a burst of compassion that snapped his green point wide open, releasing the mass of leaden pain.

Ido screamed and staggered back, ripping my other hand off the pearl. The brutal rending from my dragon twisted me out of the energy world and back into the alley.

She was gone.

It felt as if my spirit was wrenched from my body. I slumped back against the wall, groping for some sense of our union. It was there—a warm, gold echo of her presence that cushioned the shock of our separation.

Ido dropped to his knees, his energy body molding back into the solid planes of flesh and heavy muscle. Waves of shivering spasmed through his bowed form. He lifted his head, his eyes muddy with shock.

"What have you done to me?" he gasped. "I have never seen such power."

With trembling hands, I pulled the edges of my shredded tunics across my exposed body. I was not sure what I'd done. What we had done.

"Your heart point is open," I said.

He took a deep, sobbing breath. "You have made me feel it all," he said. "All at once. Everything I've ever done." He rocked forward, doubling over with inner pain, his arms wrapped across his chest.

The clink of stone hitting stone made me look up. Something was moving. It took a moment for the dusty, ragged mound to make sense; Ryko, dragging himself through the razed alley toward us, his mutilated hand held to his chest. Panting, he edged past the sprawled body of one of the guards, his eyes fixed on Ido.

"Kill him," he said hoarsely. "Kill him. While you've got the chance."

Lady Dela emerged from behind a pile of tumbled bales and struggled upright, one of my swords in a wavering grip. Her face was caked with dirt and streaks of blood. She lifted the weapon, the effort making her sway. "I'll do it."

"No!" The words burst out from somewhere deep in me. Somewhere newly forged. "We can't."

"Why not?" Ryko demanded.

I bit my lip, knowing my reasons would mean nothing to a man who had just been tortured. I hardly understood them myself. Part of me still felt the touch of Ido's hands on me and wanted him to suffer and die, but a bigger part—a golden part— wanted to stop his pain. In forcing compassion onto Ido, I had somehow opened my own heart to him.

The Dragoneye slowly pushed himself back onto his heels. The arrogant tilt to his head was gone. "Because if you kill me, you kill Dillon," he said quietly.

Ryko looked across at me. "Is that true?"

"I don't know," I said. "Perhaps. He has bound Dillon's *Hua* to his—" A sudden fear clipped my words short. Had I somehow bound Ido's *Hua* to mine?

The sound of sliding pebbles pulled my attention past Ryko. The older guard was stumbling out of the alley, his limping haste sending a clear message.

"He's going to get help." I stepped away from the wall. "We have to go."

"There's unfinished business here," Ryko said. He pushed himself to his knees, hooking the dead guard's sword toward him in a drag of dust.

"No!" I met the vengeful hardness in the islander's eyes. "I have her power, Ryko. I called the Mirror Dragon." The wonder of it edged my voice; I had united with my dragon. I forced myself away from dwelling in the joy. "We can still help the Pearl Emperor and the resistance. But not if we get taken by Sethon. We go. Now!"

"You have her power?" His fierceness turned on me. "Is that the truth?" He looked over at Lady Dela, searching for confirmation. "Did you find the name?"

She nodded, a smile forming through the dirt and blood.

Ryko's face brightened for a moment, then settled back into grim pain. "You're right. We go." Wearily, he dug the sword tip into a crevice and used it as a balance to stand.

Ido was doubled over again, enduring another wave of shaking. Seeing his powerful body in the grip of such weakness shocked me. But deep below my pity stirred a dark exhilaration. My power had brought Lord Ido to his knees.

Clutching together the remnants of the tunics, I started toward the grate. Even as I took the first step, I knew something fundamental had changed; my bad hip was flexing into a new stretch of muscle and sinew. No pain. No awkward gait. I stopped, disoriented, then stepped forward again; a longer stride that should have buckled into a limp. But it was straight and true. I yanked back the edge of the tunic and touched the pale skin over my hip. It was smooth. No scar. I was whole again. A laugh broke out of me; my dragon had healed me, too.

"What is it?" Lady Dela asked. "Are you injured?"

"No," I said. "My hip is healed!" I ran my hand down the smooth line of my thigh again.

"Healed? By your dragon power?"

I nodded, meeting her wonder. I was free. No longer a cripple. No longer untouchable. I was strong and powerful. I ran a few steps then lunged, finding my balance with a quick confidence that made my heart sing. Distant shouts cut through my elation. The guard had raised the alarm. There was no time to revel in my new body. Not yet. I squatted in front of the grate, smiling at the easy movement, and quickly dug away the dirt and broken stones that had piled up against the metal cover. As I wrapped my fingers around the bars, it occurred to me that I was also feeling invigorated. Did the new energy come from my bond with her, too? Our true union. I smiled—even just thinking about the red dragon started a rise of jubilation, a yearning to call her name. Our name. I wrenched the grate out of its niche and eased it to the ground.

"This is for my hand," Ryko said.

It was the tone, more than the words, that spun me around. The islander was standing in front of Ido, the heavy sword hilt aimed at the Dragoneye's bowed head.

"I understand," Ido said. He closed his eyes.

With a savage jerk, Ryko slammed the hilt into Ido's face, the force of his own blow making him stagger. Ido collapsed to the ground in agony, his hands pressed to his forehead. He made no sound, just rocked into the pain as blood ran between his knuckles.

I stood, appalled. "Ryko! Stop!"

The islander let out a deep breath. "Now we can go." He dropped the sword.

Lady Dela crossed to me, a pile of emerald silk draped over her uninjured arm.

"Leave it," she said, blocking me with her body. "He's trying to follow your orders. Trying not to kill him."

I caught the warning in her voice and nodded.

"Do you still have the red folio?" I asked.

She patted the armor over her chest. "It's safe." Her eyes flicked over my nakedness, and she held out the Story Robe. "Here. Put this on."

Gratefully, I slid my arms into the wide sleeves. I brushed my hand over the plaques pushed into the breast band—they were still secure, too—then tied the inner binding. The robe was loose, but at least it covered me. I glanced at Ido. He was slowly pulling himself up into a sitting position. The old Ido would never have sat still for a beating. How long would this change last? I did not trust it.

Ryko limped up to us. "I have one of your swords. The other is over there," he said, indicating a nearby crate. He leaned a hand on the wall and sucked in air through clenched teeth. Was he going to make it to the river?

"You go first," I said to Lady Dela. "Help Ryko through."

I expected a protest, but Ryko just nodded. As Lady Dela eased her way into the hole, I ran and picked up my second sword. The familiar jolt of rage added its own strength to the renewal in my body. I returned to the grate just as Ryko awkwardly crawled through the small opening. For a moment, I saw Lady Dela's strained face as she steered him down the first step, then I set a foot into the opening and pulled the grate up toward the wall. It was not worth wasting the time to fit it back in place. I dropped it.

"I am sorry," Ido said across the few lengths between us. "It is not enough, but I am sorry."

He was watching me out of one eye, the other already swollen shut, and his breathing was ragged—every inhalation edged with pain.

I drew the Story Robe tighter across my body. "I know you are." I had felt it in the meld of *Hua*.

"My ambitions have made us the last two Dragoneyes. Sethon won't rest until he has our power harnessed to his war machine." The harsh arrogance in his face had been stripped away.

"There's Dillon, too," I said stubbornly.

He wiped the blood from his mouth. "We both know I have ruined him." He shook his head, the movement making him wince. "Sethon knows about the String of Pearls. He knows about the black folio. Do you have it? Did you take both folios?"

I shook my head, thinking of Dillon wrenching the black folio from my arm. But I was not going to share that with Ido.

Shouts of command beyond the alley made me duck into the hole. I turned on the small top step and looked out. Ido had lunged for the sword abandoned by Ryko. He dragged the hilt on to his lap, the effort making him pant.

He looked across at me with some of his old authority. "Find the black folio. It has ways to bind dragon power and force its use. Make sure Sethon never gets it, or we will be his slaves."

Was Ido trying to trick me? "How could Sethon bind us?" I demanded. "He is not a Dragoneye."

"No, but he is royal. He has the dragon blood. Anyone with the blood can bind us with the power of the black folio."

"I thought the dragon blood was a story."

Ido lifted his shoulder in a tiny shrug. "I thought *you* were a story." He raised the sword hilt, the point barely lifting from the ground. "Go, I'll keep them away from the grate as long as I can."

"You can hardly hold the sword."

"You forced this new generosity on me, so don't waste it," he said harshly. "Get out of here."

He was right. I should go—let him make his grand gesture of atonement—and get myself and my friends to safety. I owed him nothing. But even as I backed further into the hole, something stopped me. I could not leave him to face Sethon. My power had ripped his strength away; I had made him vulnerable. I doubted he even had enough stamina left to connect with his dragon.

I leaned out of the hole again.

"You could come with us." Even as I said the words, I knew they were a mistake. I did not want him near me; I could already feel the rage that was forcing its way through my compassion. A sharp, deadly female rage that was not forgiving or pitying or merciful.

He angled his battered face to see me more clearly. "No." A sudden, lopsided smile made him look younger. "I think my chances of survival are better with Sethon than with your islander friend."

I did not smile back; the image of Sethon aiming the sword at the infant prince, Lady Jila's anguished screams, and the child's sudden silence were too huge in my mind. The high lord was not only ruthless, he was vicious.

"Sethon will know you killed all the other Dragoneyes by now," I said. "He'll make you pay."

Ido's smile tightened into a thin line. "I know. But he has to take me first."

Could he hold off Sethon? Perhaps. After all, he did have an ascendant dragon. Still, a Dragoneye had to be conscious to use his magic, and Ido was barely strong enough to stand.

"He won't kill me," he added. "Not until he has you."

We both heard the jangle of armor and weaponry.

"Go," he said. "Or else he will have both of us."

I ducked my head back into the grate hole and felt for the second step with my foot.

"Find the black folio," he called. "Find it before Sethon does."

I scrabbled down the steep staircase, Kinra's sword clinking as I found handholds in the darkness. The black folio was with Dillon. Or it had been, a few hours ago.

Keeping my eyes on the faint glow emanating from the passageway, I brushed my palm along the wall and followed it around the two corners. The lamp-lit corridor stretched before me in all its blue and gold grandeur. Up ahead, Lady Dela was struggling to keep Ryko upright. I ran along the soft carpet, the thud of my new, even footfalls swinging both of them around into tense readiness. Lady Dela stepped in front of Ryko, Kinra's sword raised.

"It's you," Lady Dela said. She lowered the blade.

"Ido is holding them off," I said. "He won't last long. Come on."

Ryko gave me a hard look. "When did he become our ally?"

I bent under his arm and pulled it around my shoulder. "I would not call him an ally," I said.

I did not know what to call him.

Although I took some of Ryko's weight and carried both swords, our progress was heartstoppingly slow. The three of us lurched along the carpet, our heavy breathing obscuring any possible sound from behind. I constantly looked back, expecting to see Sethon's men pounding toward us, but there was no one. Ido was keeping his word.

Finally, we reached the entrance that Ryko and I had used, the glow of the wall lamps abruptly ending. I peered beyond the soft light of the last lamp into the darkness beyond.

"River," Ryko said, feebly gesturing further along the corridor. "Waiting for us."

Lady Dela leaned against the bright tiled wall, the vivid colors accentuating her pallor. "Will they still be there?"

Ryko cast a scornful look. "Tozay will wait."

"Tozay is waiting for us?" I asked, the name prompting an image of a broad, tanned face and the sea smell of a long-lost home. "Do you mean Master Tozay?"

"He is our leader," Ryko said as I took the lamp from its niche.

I grabbed Lady Dela's good hand and pulled her up, then urged Ryko forward again.

"I have met Master Tozay," I said. "Before the ceremony." I eyed Ryko. "That wasn't a chance meeting, was it?"

Through his pained exhaustion, Ryko smiled. "Tozay made it his business to meet every candidate," he said. "You were all potential allies for the resistance."

So much had happened since Master Tozay and I had bowed side by side as Lady Jila passed by in her litter. Now the poor lady was dead, her baby slaughtered, and her other son, the Pearl Emperor, fleeing for his life. I sent another prayer of hope to the gods. *Please, keep him safe.*

We labored onward, the weak lamplight only ever showing the next few steps along the corridor. The rich blue pathway seemed endless. Ryko's shallow inhalations were breaking wetly in his chest, and Lady Dela's hand rested heavily on my other shoulder. Even my renewed energy was beginning to flag. Then, the carpet suddenly ended. I held up the lamp, the sight of the rough stone floor and the curve of a corner filling me with giddy relief.

It was the same design as the other entrances; we climbed the steep stairs and pushed out the grate. I guided Ryko and Lady Dela through the small hole, then ducked out behind them into a clump of concealing bushes. We were by the river, outside the Dragon Circle. Dark clouds obscured the moon, or perhaps it was the smoke from the battlefield. The air smelled of fire and fear. To our right was a small jetty moored with the royal barges, waiting for the concubines that would never come. Ryko nodded at a small spit of land on the left, almost hidden by a copse of elegant water trees. We hobbled toward it. Ryko wet his parched lips and made the low bird signal he had used to call Solly. A figure emerged from behind the thick trailing branches.

"Tozay?" Ryko whispered.

The stocky man hurried up to us, catching Ryko's limp form as he staggered forward. "There, I've got you."

With astounding ease, he turned the islander toward a small rowboat waiting in the water, manned by another shadowy figure. "Come," he whispered. "We must move swiftly or lose the tide."

I pulled Lady Dela's arm across my shoulders and took her tired weight against my side as we slipped and skidded down the shallow embankment.

As Master Tozay delivered Ryko into the hands of his assistant, the moon finally broke from the clouds and gave me a better view of the man I had met by the road a lifetime ago. The last few weeks had carved even deeper lines into the master fisherman's face. He steadied Lady Dela as she stumbled to him, and half lifted her into the small craft. Then he turned to me and gently took Kinra's swords from my tense hold, passing them to his man. I smoothed back my hair and met his silent scrutiny.

"Greetings, Master Tozay," I said.

He bobbed his head in a bow. "Lord Eon." I caught the flash of a grim smile as he held out his hand to help me into the boat, his foot holding the vessel still. "So, a dragon had the sense to choose you after all, my lord."

"She did," I said.

His eyes widened. "She?"

"Yes," I took his hand and stepped into the boat. "But I am not Lord Eon. Not anymore. I am Eona, the Mirror Dragoneye." I looked up at the black smoke that hung over the palace and Dragon Halls, then turned my attention back to the startled man beside me. "And I want to join your resistance."

Author's Note

The Empire of the Celestial Dragons is not a real country or culture. It is a fantasy world that was at first inspired by the history and cultures of China and Japan, but rapidly became a land of imagination with no claim to historical or cultural authenticity. Nevertheless, I did research many aspects of ancient and modern cultures, which I used as a springboard to create the empire and the dragons. If you are interested in the research road I traveled, I have detailed some of my favorite findings and listed some of the books I used on my Web site at **www.alisongoodman.com.au**.

Acknowledgments

I would like to thank the following people:

Ron, my wonderful husband.

Karen McKenzie, my best friend and writing soul sister.

Charmaine and Doug Goodman, my ever supportive parents.

My excellent agents Fran Bryson, Jill Grinberg, Antony Harwood, and their associates.

The Viking team: Sharyn November, editor extraordinaire and all-round rock goddess, Regina Hayes, and all those who helped ready *Eon* for the world.

Sammy Yuen, Jr., for the sensational cover illustration.

Simon Higgins for teaching me how to handle a Chinese sword, checking my battle scenes, and his unstinting support and friendship.

My writing group, who generously read and commented: Karen, Judy, Carrie, Jane, and Paul.

Pam Horsey for her friendship and staunch support, not to mention her excellent taste in jewelry.

Mark Barry and Caz Brown for their Web site expertise.

And, of course, Xanderpup and Spikeyboy.

THE STRUGGLE FOR THE
EMPIRE OF THE CELESTIAL DRAGONS
WILL CONCLUDE IN

EONA

THE LAST
DRAGONEYE

TURN THE PAGE....

CHAPTER ONE

THE DRAGONS WERE CRYING.

I stared across the choppy, gray sea and concentrated on the soft sound within me. For three daybreaks, ever since we had fled the conquered palace, I had stood on this same rock and felt the keening of the ten bereft dragons. Usually it was only a faint wail beneath the golden song of my own Mirror Dragon. This morning it was stronger. Harsher.

Perhaps the ten spirit beasts had rallied from their grief and returned to the Circle of Twelve. I took a deep breath and eased into the unnerving sensation of mind-sight. The sea before me blurred into surging silver as my focus moved beyond the earthly plane, into the pulsing colors of the parallel energy world. Above me, only two of the twelve dragons were in their celestial domains: Lord Ido's blue Rat Dragon in the north-northwest, the beast's massive body arched in pain, and my own red dragon in the east. The Mirror Dragon. The queen. The other ten dragons had still not returned from wherever spirit beasts fled to grieve.

The Mirror Dragon turned her huge head toward me, the gold pearl under her chin glowing against her crimson scales. Tentatively, I formed our shared name in my mind—*Eona*—and called her power. Her answer was immediate: a rush of golden energy that cascaded through my body. I rode the rising joy, reveling in the union. My sight split between earth and heaven: around me were rocks and sea and sky, and at the same time, through her great dragon eyes, the beach surged below in timeless rhythms of growth and decay. Silvery pinpoints of *Hua*—the energy of life—were scurrying, swimming, burrowing across a swirling rainbow landscape. Deep within me, a sweet greeting unfurled—the wordless touch of her dragon spirit against mine—leaving the warm spice of cinnamon on my tongue.

Suddenly, the rich taste soured. We both sensed a wall of wild energy at the same time, a rushing, shrieking force that was coming straight for us. Never before had we felt such driven pain. Crushing pressure punched through our golden bond and loosened my earthly grip. I staggered across uneven rock that seemed to fall away from me. The Mirror Dragon screamed, rearing to meet the boiling wave of need. I could feel no ground, no wind, no earthly plane. There was only the whirling, savage clash of energies.

"Eona!"

A voice, distant and alarmed.

The crashing sorrow tore at my hold on earth and heaven. I was spinning, the bonds of mind and body stretched and splitting. I had to get out or I would be destroyed.

"Eona! Are you all right?"

It was Dela's voice—an anchor from the physical world. I grabbed at it and wrenched myself free of the roaring power. The world snapped back into sand and sea and sunlight. I doubled over, gagging on a bitter vinegar that was cut with grief— the taste of the ten bereft dragons.

They were back. Attacking us. Even as I thought it, a deeper part of me knew I was wrong—they would not attack their queen. Yet I had felt their *Hua* pressing upon us. Another kind of terror seized me. Perhaps this was the start of the String of Pearls, the weapon that brought together the power of all twelve dragons—a weapon born from the death of every Dragoneye except one.

But that was just a story, and I was not the last Dragoneye standing. The Rat Dragon was still in the celestial circle, and that meant at least one Rat Dragoneye was still alive, whether it be Lord Ido, or his apprentice, Dillon. I shivered—somehow I knew Lord Ido was not dead, although I could not explain my certainty. It was as if the man was watching me, waiting for his chance to seize my power again. He believed another story about the String of Pearls—that the union of his power and body with mine would create the weapon. He had nearly succeeded in forcing that union, too. Sometimes I could still feel his iron grip around my wrists.

"Are you all right?" Dela called again.

She was at the top of the steep path, and although she was unable to see or sense the dragons, she knew something was wrong. I held up my trembling hand, hoping she could not see the afterwash of fear. "I'm fine."

Yet I had left my dragon to face that bitter wave of need. There was little I could do to help, but I could not leave her alone. Gathering courage with my next breath, I focused my mind-sight and plunged back into the energy world.

The crashing, rolling chaos was gone; the celestial plane was once more a smooth ebb and flow of jewel colors. The Mirror Dragon looked calmly at me, her attention brushing across my spirit. I longed to feel her warmth again, but I let her presence pass by. If our communion had somehow called the grieving dragons from their exile, I could not risk their return. I could barely direct my own dragon's power, let alone manage the force of ten spirit-beasts reeling from the brutal slaughter of their Dragoneyes. And if these sorrowing creatures were now lying in wait for our every union, I had to find a way to fend off their desolation or I would never learn the dragon arts that controlled the elements and nurtured the land.

In his place in the north-northwest, the blue dragon was still curled in agony. Yesterday I had tried to call his power, as I had in the palace, but this time he did not respond. No doubt the beast's pain was caused by Lord Ido. As was all our pain.

With a sigh, I once again released my hold on the energy plane. The pulsing colors shifted back into the solid shapes and constant light of the beach, clearing to reveal Dela's approaching figure. Even dressed as a fisherman, and with her arm in a sling, she walked like a court lady, a graceful sway at odds with the rough tunic and trousers. Since she was a Contraire—a man who chose to live as a woman—her return to manly clothes and habits had seemed like an easy disguise. Not so. But then, who was I to talk? After four years of pretending to be a boy, I found my return to womanhood just as awkward. I eyed Dela's small hurried steps and elegant bearing as she crossed the sand; she was more woman than I would ever be.

I picked my way across the rocks to meet her, finding my footing with a smooth ease that made my heart sing. My union with the Mirror Dragon had healed my lame hip. I could walk and run without pain or limp. There had not been much time or occasion to celebrate the wondrous gift: one dawn sprint along the beach, each slapping step a shout of exaltation; and tiny moments like this—swift, guilty pleasures among all the fear and grief.

Dela closed the short space between us, her poise breaking into a stumbling run. I caught her outstretched hand.

"Is he worse?" I asked.

The answer was in Dela's dull, red-rimmed eyes. Our friend Ryko was dying.

"Master Tozay says his bowels have leaked into his body and poisoned him."

I knew Ryko's injuries were terrible, but I had never believed he would succumb to them. He was always so strong. As one of the Shadow Men, the elite eunuch guards who protected the royal family, he usually fortified his strength and male energy by a daily dose of Sun Drug. Perhaps three days without it had weakened his body beyond healing. Before the coup, I had also taken a few doses of the Sun Drug in the mistaken belief it would help me unite with my dragon. In fact, it had done the opposite, by quelling my female energy. It had also helped suppress my moon days; as soon as I stopped taking it three days ago, I bled. The loss of such a strong drug would surely take a heavy toll on Ryko's injured body. I looked out at a heavy bank of clouds on the horizon—no doubt caused by the dragons' turmoil—and shivered as the warm dawn breeze sharpened into a cold wind. There would be more rain soon, more floods, more devastating earthshakes. And because Lord Ido had murdered the other Dragoneyes, it would all be unchecked by dragon power.

"Tozay insists we leave Ryko and move on," Dela added softly, "before Sethon's men arrive."

Her throat convulsed against a sob. She had removed the large black pearl that had hung from a gold pin threaded through the skin over her windpipe—the symbol of her status as a Contraire. The piercing was too obvious to wear, but I knew it would have pained Dela to lose such an emblem of her true twin soul identity. Although that pain would be nothing compared to her anguish if we were forced to abandon Ryko.

"We can't leave him," I said.

The big islander had fought so hard to stop Lord Ido from seizing my dragon power. Even after he was so badly wounded, he had led us out of the captured palace to the safety of the resistance. No, we could not leave Ryko. But we could not move him, either.

Dela wrapped her arms around her thin body, cradling her despair. Without the formal court makeup, her angular features tipped more to the masculine, although her dark eyes held a woman's pain—a woman forced to choose between love and duty. I had never loved with such devotion. From what I had seen, it brought only suffering.

"We have to go," she finally said. "You can't stay here, it's too dangerous. And we must find the Pearl Emperor. Without your power, he will not defeat Sethon."

My power—inherited through the female bloodline, the only hereditary Dragoneye power in the circle of twelve. So much was expected of it, and yet I still had no training. No control. I stroked the small red folio bound against my arm by its living rope of black pearls. The gems stirred at my touch, clicking softly into a tighter embrace. At least I had the journal of my Dragoneye ancestress, Kinra, to study. Every night, Dela tried to decipher some of its Woman Script, the secret written language of women. So far, progress had been slow—not only was the journal written in an ancient form of the script, but most of it was also in code. I hoped Dela would soon find the key and read about Kinra's union with the Mirror Dragon. I needed a Dragoneye's guidance and experience, even if it was only through an ancient journal. I also needed some counsel; if I put my power in the service of Kygo to help him take back his rightful throne, then wasn't I breaking the Covenant of Service? The ancient agreement prohibited the use of dragon power for war.

Putting aside my misgivings, I said, "Did you see the imperial edict? Sethon is already calling himself Dragon Emperor, even though there are still nine days of Rightful Claim left."

Dela nodded. "He has declared that both the old emperor's sons are dead." I heard the rise of doubt in her voice. "What if it is true?"

"It's not," I said quickly.

We had both seen High Lord Sethon murder his infant nephew as well as the child's mother. But his other nephew, eighteen years old and true heir to the throne, had escaped. I had watched him ride away to safety with his Imperial Guard.

Dela chewed on her lip. "How can you be so sure the Pearl Emperor is still alive?"

I *wasn't* sure, but the possibility that Sethon had found and killed Kygo was too terrible to contemplate. "We would have heard otherwise. Tozay's spy network is extensive."

"Even so," Dela said, "they have not found his whereabouts. And Ryko . . ." She turned her head as if it was the wind that brought tears to her eyes.

Only Ryko knew where his fellow Imperial Guards had hidden the Pearl Emperor. Ever cautious, he had not shared the information. Now the blood fever had taken his mind.

"We could ask him again," I said. "He may recognize us. I have heard that there is often a brief lucid time before . . ."

"Before death?" she ground out.

I met her grief with my own. "Yes."

For a moment she stared at me, savage at my denial of hope, then bowed her head.

"We should go to him," she said. "Tozay says it will not be long now."

With one last look at the heavy clouds, I gathered up the front of my cumbersome skirt and climbed the path behind Dela, snatching a few moments of muted joy as I stretched into each strong, surefooted step.

The sturdy, weather-bleached fisher house had been our sanctuary for the past few days, its isolation and high vantage giving a clear view of any approach by sea or land. I paused to catch my breath at the top of the path and focused on the distant village. Small fishing boats were already heading out to sea, every one of them crewed by resistance with eyes sharp for Sethon's warships.

"Prepare yourself," Dela said as we reached the house. "His deterioration has been swift."

Last night I had sat with Ryko until midnight, and I had thought the islander was holding his own. But everyone knew that the predawn ghost hours were the most dangerous for the sick—the cold, gray loneliness eased the way of demons eager to drain an unguarded life force. Dela had taken the early watch, but it seemed that even her loving vigilance had been unable to ward off the dark ones.

She hung back as I pushed aside the red luck flags that

protected the doorway and entered the room. The village Beseecher still knelt in the far corner, but he was no longer chanting prayers for the ill. He was calling to Shola, Goddess of Death, and had covered his robes with a rough white cloak to honor the Otherworld Queen. A paper lantern swung on a red cord between his clasped hands, sending light seesawing across the drawn faces around Ryko's pallet: Master Tozay; his eldest daughter, Vida; and faithful, ugly Solly. I coughed, my throat catching with the thick clove incense that overlaid the stench of vomit and loose bowels.

In the eerie, swinging lamplight, I strained to see the figure lying on the low straw mattress. *Not yet*, I prayed, *not yet*. I had to say good-bye.

I heard Ryko's panting before I saw the over-quick rise and fall of his chest. He was stripped down to just a loincloth, his dark skin bleached to a gray waxiness, his once muscular frame wasted and frail.

The tight linen bandaging had been removed, exposing the festering wounds. His hand, resting on his chest, was black and bloated: the result of Ido's torture. More shocking was the long gash that sliced him from armpit to waist. Swollen sections of flesh had torn free from the rough stitching, showing pale bone and vivid red tissue.

The herbalist shuffled through the inner doorway. He carried a large bowl that trailed an astringent steam, his deep voice murmuring prayers over the slopping liquid. He had sat with me for some of my vigil last night, a kind, perpetually exhausted man who knew his skill was not up to his patient's injuries. But he had tried. And he was still trying, although it was clear that Ryko was walking the golden path to his ancestors.

Behind me, I heard Dela's breath catch into a sob. The sound brought Master Tozay's head up. He motioned us closer.

"Lady Dragoneye," he said softly, ushering me into his place by the pallet.

We had agreed not to use my title for safety's sake, but I let it pass without comment. The breach was Tozay's way of honoring Ryko's dutiful life.

Vida swiftly followed her father's example and shifted aside for Dela. The girl was not much older than my own sixteen years, but she carried herself with quiet dignity, an inheritance from her father. From her mother came her ready smile and a practical nature that did not recoil from oozing wounds or soiled bedclothes.

Dela knelt and covered Ryko's uninjured hand with her own. He did not stir. Nor did he move when the herbalist gently picked up his other, mutilated hand and lowered it into the bowl of hot water. The steam smelled of garlic and rosemary—good blood cleaners—although the whole arm looked beyond help.

I signaled to the Beseecher to stop his calls to Shola. There was no need to bring Ryko to the attention of the death goddess. She would arrive soon enough.

"Has he roused again? Has he spoken?" I asked.

"Nothing intelligible," Tozay said. He glanced at Dela. "I am sorry, but it is time you both left. My spies have Sethon heading this way. We will continue to care for Ryko and look for the Pearl Emperor, but you must go east and seek safety with Lady Dela's tribe. We will rendezvous with you once we have found His Highness."

Tozay was right. Although the thought of leaving Ryko was a hundredweight of stone in my spirit, we could delay no longer. The east was our best chance. It was also my dragon's domain, her stronghold of power. Perhaps my presence in her energy heartland would strengthen our bond and help me control this wild magic. It might also help the Mirror Dragon hold off the ten bereft dragons if they returned.

Dela shot a hard look at the resistance leader. "Surely this discussion can wait until—"

"I am afraid it cannot, lady." Tozay's voice was gentle but unyielding. "This must be your good-bye, and it must be swift."

She bowed her head, struggling against his blunt practicality. "My people will hide us beyond Sethon's reach," she finally said, "but the problem will be getting to them."

Tozay nodded. "Solly and Vida will travel with you."

Behind Dela, I saw Vida square her shoulders. At least one of us was ready for the challenge.

"They know how to contact the other resistance groups," Tozay added, "and they can act the part of your servants. You'll be just another merchant husband and wife on a pilgrimage to the mountains."

Dela's focus was back on Ryko. She lifted his inert fingers to her cheek, the swinging lamplight catching the shine of grief in her eyes.

"That may be," I said looking away from the tender moment, "but our descriptions are on the lips of every news-walker, and tacked to every tree trunk."

"So far you are still described as *Lord* Eon," Tozay said. His eyes flicked over my straight, strong body. "And crippled. The description for Lady Dela cautions everyone to look for a man or a woman, making it just as useless."

I was still described as Lord Eon? I was sure Ido would have told Sethon I was a girl, either under duress or as a bargaining tool. It did not make sense for him to protect me. Perhaps the Mirror Dragon and I had truly changed Ido's nature when we healed his stunted heart-point and forced compassion into his spirit. After all, that first union with my dragon had also mended my hip, and I was still healed. I pressed my hand against the waist pouch where I kept the family death plaques of my ancestors Kinra and Charra: a wordless prayer for the change to be permanent. Not only Lord Ido's change, but my own wondrous healing. I could not bear to lose my freedom again.

"Sethon will not only be looking for you, Lady Dragoneye," Master Tozay murmured, a touch to my sleeve drawing me a few steps away. "He will be seeking anyone close to you that he can use as a hostage. Give me the names of those who you think are in danger. We will do our best to find them."

"Rilla, my maid, and her son Chart," I said quickly. "They fled before the palace was taken." I thought of Chart; his badly twisted body would always attract attention, if only to drive others away before his ill fortune tainted them. I felt a small leap in my spirit: never again would I be spat on as a cripple or driven away. "Rilla would seek somewhere isolated."

Tozay nodded. "We will start in the mid-provinces."

"And Dillon—Ido's apprentice—but you are already searching for him. Be careful with Dillon; he is not in his right mind, and Sethon will be hunting him for the black folio, too."

I remembered the madness in Dillon's eyes when he had wrenched the black folio from me. He'd known the book was vital to Ido's plans for power and thought he could use it to trade with his Dragoneye master for his life. Instead, he had brought Sethon and the entire army upon himself. Poor Dillon. He did not truly understand what was in the small book he carried. He knew it held the secret to the String of Pearls. But its pages held another secret, one that terrified even Lord Ido: the way for royal blood to bind any Dragoneye's will and power.

"Is that all who may be at risk, my lady?" Tozay asked.

"Perhaps . . ." I paused, hesitant to add the next names. "I have not seen my family since I was very young. I hardly remember them. Perhaps Sethon would not—"

Tozay shook his head. "Sethon will try everything. So tell me, if they were found and held, could Sethon coerce you with their lives?"

Dread curdled my stomach. I nodded, and tried to dredge up more than the few dim images I had of my family. "I remember my mother's name was Lillia, and my brother was called Peri, but I think it was a pet name. I can only remember my father as Papa." I looked up at Tozay. "I know it is not much. But we lived by the coast—I remember fishing gear and a beach—and when my master first found me, I was laboring in the Enalo Salt Farm."

Tozay grunted. "That's west. I'll send word."

Beside us, the herbalist lifted Ryko's dripping hand from the bowl and laid it back on the pallet. He leaned over and stroked Ryko's cheek, then pressed his fingertips under the islander's jaw.

"A sharp increase of heat," he said into the silence. "The death fever. Ryko will join his ancestors very soon. It is time to wish him a safe journey."

He bowed, then backed away.

My throat ached with sorrow. Across the pallet, Solly's face was rigid with grief. He raised a fist to his chest in a warrior's salute. Tozay sighed and began a soft prayer for the dying.

"Do something," Dela said.

It was part plea, part accusation. I thought she was talking to the herbalist, but when I looked up she was staring at me.

"Do something," she repeated.

"What can I do? There is nothing I can do."

"You healed yourself. You healed Ido. Now heal Ryko."

I glanced around the ring of tense faces, feeling the press of their hope. "But that was at the moment of union. I don't know if I can do it again."

"Try." Dela's hands clenched into fists. "Just try. Please. He's going to die."

She held my gaze, as though looking away would release me from her desperation.

Could I save Ryko? I had assumed that Ido and I were

healed by the extra power of first union between dragon and Dragoneye. Perhaps that was not true. Perhaps the Mirror Dragon and I could always heal. But I could not yet direct my dragon's power. If we joined and tried to heal Ryko, we could fail. Or we could be ripped apart by the sorrow of the ten bereft dragons.

"Eona!" Dela's anguish snapped me out of my turmoil. "Do something. Please!"

Each of Ryko's labored breaths held a rattling catch.

"I can't," I whispered.

Who was I to play with life and death like a god? I had no knowledge. No training. I was barely a Dragoneye.

Even so, I was Ryko's only chance.

"He is dying because of you," Dela said. "You owe him your life and your power. *Don't fail him again.*"

Turn the page for the first chapter of Alison Goodman's debut novel, featuring a heroine every bit as strong as Eona!

My Mother and Other Aliens

I saw the assassin before she saw me. She was eating noodles at one of the hawker bars, watching the university gates. I knew she was a killer because old Lenny Porchino had pointed her out to me at the Buzz Bar two nights ago.

"Hey, take a look at that skinny kid with the frizzy hair," he'd said, nodding his head towards the doors behind me.

We were sitting in Lenny's private booth, hidden from general view. I shifted in my seat until I could see her. Skinny, frizzy, and mean.

"What about her?" I said, banging my harmonica against the flat of my hand. I had just finished jamming with the band and my harp was full of slag.

"That's Tori Suka. She's a culler for the hyphen families. If she's in town, someone's gonna die."

Tori Suka didn't fit my idea of someone who would work for the big-money families. Too rough. She was wearing the same kind of student gear as I was: black long-wear jeans, matching jacket. Standard stuff you can get from any machine.

One of Lenny's waiters came up to the table. He was all nerves.

"Mr. Porchino, there's a guy in the crapper done too much smack. Looks like he's croaking it."

Lenny shook his head.

"Don't know why they still go for that antique screte," he said. He looked over at me. "Joss, don't ever do any of that old-fashioned powder. Does you in and wrecks your looks." He turned to the waiter. "Get Cross and Lee to dump him outside St. Vinnies."

The waiter weaved through the crowd towards two bouncers lounging against the wall. Lenny watched until he saw Cross and Lee move towards the toilets.

"Suka's not the best gun around, but she gets the job done," he said. "I wonder who the mark is? And who's hiring?" He was pulling at the ends of his mustache. Lenny always made it his business to know who was putting out a contract.

I looked at the kid again. She was leaning against the bar, throwing nut meats into her mouth. She chewed with her mouth open. How did she become an assassin? Did Careers tell her she was suited to murder?

Lenny's son, Porchi, strutted over from the bar and slid next to me in the booth. He pressed his thigh against mine. I moved away from him. Porchi's been trying to snork me since we met after I pulled his dad out of the river a year ago. Old Lenny had "fallen in" the Yarra with a bit of help from some DeathHeads on a grand-final rampage. I happened to be cruising the area and grabbed Lenny out of the river before he was mulched by the cleaning system.

Later Porchi told me that half the DeathHeads were wiped out when their hangout was bio-bombed. Very ugly. Lenny believes in paying his debts: I saved his life, so now he looks out for me. I've even got a permanent bedroom upstairs at the Buzz Bar. I think Lenny's got some fantasy about me and Porchi breeding little Porchinos and living happily ever after. Like I said, Porchi would be happy to get stuck into the breeding part of that scheme.

Lenny is the closest thing I've had to family this past year. I haven't actually seen my mother for about eighteen months. She's always in production or in a meeting. I end up talking to Lewis, her secretary, via CommNet. Reverse charges, of course.

"I'm sorry, Joss, Ingrid is unavailable right now," he always says with his ferret smile.

"Well, tell her I called. She does remember who I am, doesn't she?"

"I'm sure she has a vague memory. I'll pass on the message."

Then he signs off before I bash my head through the screen.

Let's fact it, Ingrid Aaronson is not going to win the Mother of the Year award. Not that she needs it. She's won nearly every other award that a news presenter and VR star can win. She's even won the Thinking Man's Lust-Beast award, which is funny when you know she didn't even snork anyone to make me. I'm a comp-kid. Straight from the petri dish to you. Lust factor: nil. Ease factor: ten.

Sometimes I wonder if the petri dishes got mixed up and I should be living in the mall-highrises with Mamasan and Papasan. You see, my mother is all gold hair, big blue eyes, maximum curves, and honey skin (rejuvenated twice now, but who's counting?). I'm all black straight hair, brown cat's eyes, and pale, pale skin.

Once I asked Ingrid how many people were used to make me. A comp-kid like me can have up to ten gene donors. The bioengineers just split different genes and stick them together using viruses. It's like being glued together by the common cold. Ingrid swore she only used one male donor. Name unknown, of course. If that's the case, Ingrid's Nordic heritage has been bashed into submission by my father's genes. She's positive I also inherited my attitude problem from him. She says being chucked out of twelve schools must be genetic. Sometimes I imagine he knows I'm his daughter and is keeping tabs on me, waiting for the right moment to show himself. Yeah, sure.

I swung my pack onto my shoulder and walked past the noodle bar towards the university gates. The assassin eye-balled me as I passed her. She was smiling. I was tempted to stop and ask her about career opportunities, but Tonio Bel Hussar-Rigdon suddenly grabbed me on the shoulder. He was in dress uniform.

"You're late," he said. "Camden-Stone's so mad he's ready to expel you on the spot."

Professor Camden-Stone was always threatening to expel me. You'd have thought the Acting Director of the

Centre for Neo-Historical Studies would have better things to do than pick on a lowly student. Wrong again. Old Stony Face was building a career out of making my life miserable. Tonio thinks Camden-Stone has the hots for me. If he has, I'd hate him to really love me. He'd probably put a laser through my head. Even Lenny has dropped a word of warning about the dear professor. He told me Camden-Stone beat the screte out of a girl a couple of years ago and had to pay a lot of money to keep it quiet. You've got to wonder how a creep like Camden-Stone wound up in charge of the world's only time-travel training center.

Tonio was shifting from foot to foot, eager to get back to the ceremony. According to the campus bookies, he was going to be my time-jumping partner.

Every year, the top fifty first-year students at the university can apply to study at the Centre. If you're interested, you have to take extra classes with Camden-Stone and go through tons of tests. There's only twelve first-year places at the Centre, so it's ultra competitive. I just scraped in: number eleven. Tonio Bel Hussar-Rigdon was number eight.

Tonio wasn't bad for a hyphen kid, but he was so nervy it made me want to scream. At least he wasn't a wankman like all the other hyphens. Then again, it wouldn't have mattered if he was Mr. Nice Guy of the universe. The last thing I wanted was a partner. Especially a partner who lived, studied, and worked with me. Talk about cramp your style. There was no way I was going to survive six years living in the same quarters as Tonio. Or anyone, for that matter.

"Come on," Tonio urged. "You've got to get changed and down to the Donut. Partnering is about to start."

I looked through the gates at the Donut. The huge circular hall was buzzing with vid-crews. There was even a small group of protesters standing behind a banner. Something was up. The ceremony to partner time-jumping students didn't normally rate channel time or demonstrators.

"I thought partnering was supposed to be tomorrow," I said.

"No one could find you to tell you what's happened. How come you don't carry a screen?" He leaned closer, shifting into gossip mode. "Listen to this. They've moved the ceremony for diplomatic reasons. A flaphead is coming into our time-jump class."

Tonio stepped back, a smug grin all over his pointy little face. This was big news and he knew it. The university had finally accepted one of the Chorian aliens as a student. Not only had they accepted one, but they had shoved it in the middle of our time-jumping class.

"But, that makes thirteen in our group," I said. "It won't have a partner."

"Robbie's been dropped," Tonio said softly. "He was number twelve on the list. I don't think he's been sober since Stony told him."

Poor Robbie. He must be burning. I was lucky they weren't letting two Chorians into the course. I would have been skidding on my cheeks, too.

"Come on," Tonio said, pulling me towards the gates.

I let him pull me because I was in memory overdrive. Ever since I first saw the Chorians on the vid-news, I've been obsessed with them. I was ten and expected to see some kind of giant insect. Talk about chronic disappointment. Two arms, two legs, and a head with two eyes, just like us. Then again not many humans have two noses, two mouths, and two huge double-jointed ears that flap around.

The Chorians are really into this Noah deal: everything in twos. They even have two sexes in one, like slugs. When the anti-alien lobby got wind of that, they started calling the Chorians "sluggos." The government PR people knocked themselves out trying to stop that one. The campaign posters were a scream; a big slug with a red cross through it. Really subtle. I suppose it worked. Now everyone calls them flapheads.

When I first heard the Chorians were hermaphrodites, I thought they could snork themselves. You know, the ultimate wank. That sounded too good to be true, so I did some fancy detective work on the Net. I found out that self-snorking was out. Instead, two adults fertilize each other then each of them produces one child to form a birth pair. So every Chorian is a kind of twin. I've always thought it would be great to have a twin. Instant best friend.

A few years ago Ingrid made a documentary about the Chorians. She called it "Our New Friends from the Dog Star," which is a bad name for a bad documentary. The Chorians aren't even from Sirius A, the Dog Star. They're from a planet that has Sirius A as its sun and Sirius B as its white dwarf partner. Like everything else that has been written or made on the Chorians, Ingrid's doco was pretty short on information. At least it showed the original recording of the first contact. It's the funniest history vid I've ever seen.

Six or so years ago, the first delegation of Chorians appeared in Mall 26, just before it was joined to the Mall Network. The Chorians thought 26 was a center of government and the concert stage was parliament. A traditional Disney pantomime was playing, and it scared the hell out of them. Let's face it, an enormous mouse jumping around to tinny music isn't really the height of human culture. Of course, the panto audience went into panic mode and cleared out in about ten seconds. The only one left was poor old Mickey. So the Chorians were left standing alone in front of a stage with a big mouse cowering in the corner.

It took the government people exactly five and a half minutes to arrive, shunt Mickey off into the arms of a therapist, and set up their probe equipment. Meanwhile the Chorians were trying to say hi, mind to mind. They quickly worked out we're not telepathic, so they scanned the brain of one of the feds to learn our lingo. Now Chorians speak by harmonizing words using their two mouths. Imagine being confronted by a group of aliens who all dipped imaginary hats then sang, "Howdy pilgrims, sure is nice to meet you."

The fed was a John Wayne fan.

Later the PR people made "howdy y'all" the most irritating phrase in the world. Whoever thought of setting it to lullaby music for the "Don't Be Afraid" campaign should've been shot.

About a year ago I bought an underground code from one of Porchi's contacts. It's supposed to only access RAVE-REVIVAL boards for free, but with a bit of jiggling, it also got into the government's news-boards. I found out why the Chorians were here. They've got some kind of time/space warp gizmo that lets them jump around the universe without a ship. Now they want to swap that technology for our time travel know-how. They need to learn how to manipulate time accurately. We want to learn how to get off Earth without expensive ships and space stations. So far none of these negotiations have appeared on the public vid-news channels. The PR people have been quiet, too. Although today, as Tonio pulled me past "official" vid-crews, it was obvious the government's policy of silence was about to change.

"This'll do," Tonio said, stopping in front of a reactor access hut. I opened the door. The faint thrumming of the reactor's cooling system buzzed through my feet. Tonio let go of my arm.

"I'd say you've got about thirty seconds to get changed and get back to the Donut. I'll see you there." He ran towards the crowd.

Tonio was right. I had to change into my dress uniform. Too bad it was still hanging in Lenny's office at the Buzz Bar. Turning out for a ceremony in jeans and a T-shirt, even if they were regulation, was not going to go down well. I was heading towards expulsion number thirteen, but this time I wasn't happy about it. And Ingrid would really crack the kuso. She'd spent a lot of money buying me a place in the university. She'd even bought mega shares in the Centre. The half-finished admin building is already being called the Aaronson Administration Complex.

I dumped my pack on the floor of the hut. All I could do was clean up a bit and hope Camden-Stone was in a good mood. I pulled on a new T-shirt and used the chrome handrail as an emergency mirror. What had I forgotten? My harp! I slipped it into my jeans pocket for luck and shoved my pack under some piping. Joss Aaronson was ready to meet her fate.